Praise for *St. Burl's Obituary*

"Transcending both the usual boundaries of the genre and the standard flaws of first novels, Akst's comic debut begins as a thriller about a journalist who witnesses a mob killing, then slowly evolves into an exploration of identity as experienced by a delightful protagonist who will invite comparisons to John Kennedy Toole's Ignatius Reilly. . . . Akst handles the labyrinthian plot twists deftly, employing a style that is at once literate and funny as he explores contemporary links among food, sex, identity and death. But the true star here is Burl, whose appetites, charm, intellect and Houdini-like ability to get himself in and out of tight situations will win readers' minds and hearts."

—*Publishers Weekly* (starred review)

"A peculiar and wonderful first novel, full of surprises and small excitements, just the kind of thing to put the pleasure back in reading."

—Frederick Barthelme, author of *Painted Desert: A Novel*

"Inside every fat man is a thin man wildly signaling to be let out. In Daniel Akst's novel, the thin man makes his escape, but he has to die and be born again to bring it off. The story of his getaway, a comedy and a mystery at once, is a four-star feast."

—Jack Miles, author of *God: A Biography*

"A comedy as dark and dense and rich as a Viennese torte, *St. Burl's Obituary* is a narrative—and gastronomic—juggernaut, and Daniel Akst should be crowned our new poet laureate of all the delicious and soul-fattening sins of excess and desire."

—Bob Shacochis, author of *Domesticity: A Gastronomic Interpretation of Love*

"A delightful black comedy with the most unlikely and endearing of heroes."

—*Buzz* (three-star review)

"Akst's prose keeps its savor to the very end. It's witty, exact and lyrical stuff, and it virtually ensures that by the time you're done, you'll be hungry . . . for seconds."—*New York Newsday*

"*St. Burl's Obituary* is an extraordinarily contemporary version of the familiar novelistic quest for self-definition: appetite as temptation, waist-line as character, weight as destiny. . . . The breathtaking twists of plot and character, the sharp, witty language Akst gives to Burl and other major characters, and the mouth-watering menus all combine to make this a highly entertaining novel. . . . Whether the reader simply enjoys the comedy or follows Daniel Akst deeper into the meaning of fatness, this is a very satisfying novel; Burl Bennett is worth knowing, even if his precise nature remains humanly elusive to the end."

—*Bloomsbury Review*

"Akst treats corpulence, what might be seen as an un-politically correct subject matter, with wit and empathy." —*Gallery*

"An outrageous, superb novel. . . . The adage says that truth is stranger than fiction, but no truth is stranger than Akst's fiction. . . . Akst never lets the plot get away from him. He makes the unbelievable unexpectedly believable." —*Philadelphia Inquirer*

"*St. Burl's Obituary* is a map of the contemporary world, a black comedy that carries Burl, fearfully fleeing the Mafia, into the belly of the American beast. . . . With its delicately handled echoes of Dante, and its unblinking look at contemporary America, *St. Burl's Obituary* is ingenious and thought-provoking. But the book is in no way difficult reading. Bizarre and ambitious the plot may be, but Akst tells his tale in no-nonsense, journalistic prose that keeps the story moving at a swift clip. It goes down as easily as cotton candy, one of the few foods that Burl Bennett does not down in this epic of consumption."

—*Washington Post Book World*

"Complex and rewarding . . . *St. Burl's Obituary* does not read like a first novel. Not only does Akst tackle some thorny problems of identity in our postmodern age of social construction, he addresses some classic American themes as well. . . . Burl especially is a genuine character . . . magnificently obese." —*Los Angeles Reader*

"Burl Bennett . . . explores every nuance of his own identity and what it means to be fat in contemporary America . . . an amusing story."
—*Library Journal*

"The plot of *St. Burl's Obituary* is peculiar, labyrinthine, and funny. As we watch Burl wind his way in and out of bizarre and unusual situations, it's easy to see that Akst is a genuine storyteller who is able to entwine all the aspects of a thriller, a love story, a comedy, and an allegory into one brilliant first novel. *St. Burl's Obituary* is a rollicking, deftly orchestrated success, and well worth the read." —Robert Greer, KUVO Denver (radio review)

"Akst's sharp wit and his Ignatius Reilly-esque protagonist will captivate readers from the opening pages—as will the cast of characters he encounters in his picaresque adventure. . . . The odyssey of Burl's 'death' and eventual resurrection is classic comedy, full of shifting identities and offbeat situations, and rude mocking of death. And on almost every page Akst regales us with lavish descriptions of Burl's gourmet meals—which transcend the ordinary, both in the sheer quantity he consumes, and in the sensual fervor with which he eats." —*Missouri Review*

"It is not so much the plot of *St. Burl's Obituary* that pulls a reader along in Akst's book. It is the writing. A combination of just-the-facts-ma'am clarity and deadpan hilarity, Akst is as insidious as trying to eat one potato chip. . . . The ending is a surprise. Burl is not who he thought he was, nor is he 'Abraham Alter,' his disguised other self. But he is a highly original creation, and Akst shows himself to be a terrific wordsmith."
—*Denver Post*

"In *St. Burl's Obituary*, Daniel Akst has crafted a remarkable novel that gives life to Cyril Connolly's adage that 'imprisoned in every fat man, a thin one is wildly signaling to be let out.' . . . Rather than simply portray Burl's world realistically, Akst's stunning allegory of self-transformation goes one step further: We decipher the hidden meanings, the concealed patterns, of our own lives by watching Burl dramatically change his. . . . For readers, it's a journey worth taking." —*Los Angeles Times*

HARVEST AMERICAN
Writing

St.

BURL'S
OBITUARY

BURL'S
OBITUARY

DANIEL AKST

A Harvest Book
Harcourt Brace & Company
San Diego   New York   London

Requests for permission to make copies
of any part of the work should be mailed to:
MacMurray & Beck, Inc., 1649 Downing Street, Denver, Colorado 80218.

This Harvest edition published by arrangement with MacMurray & Beck, Inc.

Publishers note: This is a work of fiction. Names, characters, places, and
incidents either are the product of the author's imagination or are used
fictitiously. Any resemblance to actual events, locales, or persons, living or
dead, is entirely coincidental.

Library of Congress Cataloging-in-Publication Data
Akst, Daniel.
    St. Burl's obituary/Daniel Akst.—1st Harvest ed.
        p.   cm.—(A harvest book)
    ISBN 0-15-600514-X
    1. City and town life—New York (State)—New York—Fiction.
    2. Journalists—New York (State)—Fiction. I. Title.
[PS3551.K25S25 1996b]
813'.54—dc20   96-43962

Designed by Susan Wasinger
Text set in Weiss by Pro Production
Project management by D&D Editorial Services

Printed in the United States of America

First Harvest edition 1996

A C E F D B

St

BURL'S OBITUARY

PART One

Mr. Worldly Wiseman is an alien,

and Mr. Legality a cheat.

—*The Pilgrim's Progress*

THIS WAS BEFORE BURL had written his own obituary. It was a humid night, cooler than the day had been, but the darkened streets were damp in an unclean way that suggested the day's perspiration, and Burl trod gingerly, in his heavy, steady style, the hundred yards from his parking space to Gardenia's, where they would have his customary mooring comfortably prepared. He would have the fried squid in hot sauce, a Caesar salad, clams in that gray salty broth so good you used bread to sop up the liquor, and finally the veal saltimbocca, slender elegances of flesh blanched in wine and butter, draped in mozzarella and crowned with swirls of salty red prosciutto, spoken with just two syllables, the last and silent vowel dropping from the rest like Sicily from the Italian mainland. The whole would be set over fir-green spinach shocked by boiling water and garnished with exquisite gratuitousness: hard egg and, against the brine, a vinegary heart of artichoke. Burl's bushy eyebrows rode high, his face alight with expectation. It had been a good day, a hard but satisfying day in which his skills had shone, and so instead of the usual

Chianti he would have a big Barolo, which would set his tonsils tingling toward the end.

All this tasted so good in his mind that he didn't think about what he looked like on the street, and at this hour, after midnight, there were no others to remind him with their startled stares. Most times he imagined himself, without actually looking, of course, gliding like a battle cruiser or on windy days a stately sailing vessel, a great red pennant flying spotless from his neck, a seeming acre of cotton whiteness billowing across his chest and belly, his blue eyes purposeful if a little furtive, his jacket perennially unwrinkled, perennially unbuttoned.

Burl could taste the summer ending—he ascribed all sensations to taste—in the coolness of the breeze across his sweaty back, or the swirling of the newsprint along the sidewalk like some urban tumbleweed. But the sour smell of putrefaction lived on, the toxic-looking puddles a nasty olive green at the odd curbside depression. The end of summer was always a relief for such a large man, even if autumn was just a brief respite before the onset of treacherous winter and its slippery streets. He shivered a little as he came to the restaurant's familiar entryway, but the heft he expected was missing from the dark wooden door, flogged with chains to look antique, which flung weightlessly open as he grabbed for it.

He stood face to face with a small, intense man whose expression was so astonished that he might have just killed somebody. Burl blushed in embarrassment; he was used to this. You'd think no one had ever seen a fat man before.

"Sorry," he said sheepishly, and then repeated "sorry," with a little laugh, as if in larger apology for himself.

The man just stared until suddenly Burl was alone, the residue of the other's hatred dripping from his face like spit. Definitely the Barolo, he thought, pushing the inner door open.

It was the intense stillness that struck him first. The tableau made him think of a surrealist painting: the twilit restaurant empty, the white tablecloths giant toadstools sprouting from the blood-red carpet on the floor, all spotless except for an outburst of humanity to the right of center, where two men in business suits sat like discarded mannequins slumped around a half-eaten meal. A third man lay face down on the floor not far from an overturned chair. At his feet but to the right, Burl noticed a flesh-colored rubber mask; it lay like somebody's face staring up from the floor. Off to the left was Burl's place, the corner booth all ready for him, the table laid with silver and crystal, yet spookily unoccupied, vacant now like some shrine to an unknown eater.

Drinking in this grotesque still life, stunned by its silence and the unreal men suspended in positions of such egregious discomfort, Burl felt the damp hair stand up on the back of his neck as his own movements ceased. He knew himself to be among the dead now, and it was hard to figure out what to do. Heart pounding, unwilling to leave the way he had come and hating his unhidable bulk more than ever, Burl lumbered out toward the kitchen. Where was everybody who was normally at Gardenia's at this hour? What had become of the staff? On his way, just in the corner of one eye, he saw a dark spot on the floor that he knew with uncharacteristic pessimism to be a gun. Impulsively, with a soiled handkerchief, he picked it up and took it with him.

When he passed through the swinging door into the familiar cooking area, the room seemed empty, but there wasn't the same stillness, and he could hear the labored breathing of the terrified as his own thudding footfalls mocked his efforts at delicacy. Behind a bank of counters, in the large area at the center of the kitchen, he saw that the floor was covered with people lying face down: kitchen help in white, waiters in black, a couple of hapless diners in street clothes, and his Uncle Lou, the manager, looking thoughtful as he rested his chin on his hands.

"Burlie, thank God it's you!" Lou said, jumping to his feet. "I thought they were back."

The two of them hurried toward the office, where Lou called the police. Then Burl called his paper, which normally didn't care about a few murders one way or another in a place like New York, especially at that hour, unless the victims were somebody important. Burl assured the kid on the desk that in this case the paper would care. Shrewd Louie Naumann didn't mind; in New York, something like this gave a place cachet.

"I need a drink," he said. "Have some brandy with me, hanh? I got some Calvados back here, I don't put it at the bar. Some good stuff."

The liquor swirled like melted amber in their snifters as Burl munched little fish-shaped crackers from a glass bowl. His uncle fidgeted with a wart above where his hairline might have been.

"Relax," Burl said, his mood fast improving with drink. "It's over. They knew who they wanted. By this time tomorrow it'll be like it never happened."

"As far as I'm concerned, it's that way now."

Burl said nothing.

"And as far as you're concerned too, if you know what's good for you," Lou added, swallowing a large mouthful. "You din' see anything, know what I mean? This was private business."

"Private business. Then you knew it was coming?"

"No! My God, Burlie, what the hell does your old man say about me behind my back? No, I didn't know it was coming. But I know what it was, and so do you. Private. Not some skunk knockin' off an old lady for the social security. This was different. You don't mix in this."

"Hey, I didn't ask them to do this in our restaurant. Did we forget to pay somebody this month? I thought we weren't supposed to have these troubles."

"Believe me, we pay, we always pay. I think this was a little bigger than our people."

"We ought to make this a Chinese restaurant," Burl said.

"They pay too. In this town everybody pays."

"Three men died in our dining room, I came within inches of being a fourth. Somebody better pay."

"Burlie, I don't know what you think you're talking about, but rest assured, somebody will pay. That's one thing you don't have to worry about. Believe you me."

Lou sighed, drank, and rubbed his balding scalp with a large hand, a claw out of proportion to his small body. He seemed to regret being so emphatic. Burl always thought of him as his mother's sportier brother, always with a bit of mystery to him. He was built like a football, with no connecting parts: no neck, no waist, short limbs. Burl was silent, holding in his mouth the fermented apples of Normandy, their fumes atop his hunger an intoxicating form of knowledge, enough to make him dizzy.

"You didn't see anything anyway," Lou said. "When did you come in? If you'd seen something, you wouldn't be sitting here now. You kiddin' me?"

Burl swallowed, and the brandy bit him on the throat. Fruit of a poisoned tree, as the lawyers like to say. It was great until you swallowed it.

"So let me understand this," Burl said. "There were two guys in Laurel and Hardy masks, right? One of them herded everybody into the kitchen—"

"And then we all got down, and that was the last I saw or wanted to see."

"But you said he went out, right? He didn't stay and watch anybody."

"He didn't have to stay and watch. He said he'd be back in a minute and kill anyone who wasn't in the same spot. Then he went back into the dining room with his partner, we heard six *pffft* kind of noises, and the next footsteps we hear I thought were gonna be my last, except instead of those hoods it was my hungry nephew over here."

Lou reached over and poured his hungry nephew some more brandy, for which Burl saluted him with his glass. Lou waved dismissively, unhappily.

"Those men pleaded," he said. "Not desperate, they didn't break down and cry. But they knew what was coming. They pleaded. 'Why?' one of them kept saying. 'Joey sent you, right? What does he wanna do this for?' Very sad. Two of them came in here now and then. I knew them. Gentlemen."

Lou waved again, angrily. Burl, retreating as always before fervor, put the snifter up to his nose. Calvados. Where did the name come from? Before France. Calvary? *Calvaria*: the Latin land of skulls. He inhaled deeply. It was like sniffing glue. Things didn't look nearly so dire through its morbid fragrance. He had the hot liquid in his mouth when he heard the knocking at the door, and he swallowed when his uncle said, "Come in."

The police part made Burl feel like he was in a movie. He told them everything, and at the sadly faded beaux arts palace that was still their precinct station, downsized cruisers parked haphazardly in every direction, he pored over vinyl binders filled like Satan's photo album with yeggs of every stripe, their stupid, vicious, sullen faces staring out in silent protest from mug shots taken by a photographer who might have made the Queen Mother look felonious. There was such umbrage in the eyes of these men, as if they were affronted by this latest and most unwarranted humiliation. Was it hurt that he saw? Was it shame?

It was not an easy job. Burl wondered if he could recognize the killer from one of these unnatural images, enshrined in greasy plastic. He thought back, trying to recapture the moment. In his mind he saw the man's eyes—blue, weren't they?—and for some reason his hairline, its black hairs rising like soldiers straight from

8

white skin of surprising delicacy. The two men had had a good look at one another, but Burl wondered if he would know the killer even in person. Likelier the man would know him.

And then what? The thought had crossed his mind in the car that he was still alive only because the gunman had left his weapon in the restaurant, without prints or serial number. (The man, apparently, had worn gloves.) Burl thought about all the things he had done which kept him that night from arriving at Gardenia's 30 seconds sooner: how careful he was about parking, his brief conversation in the hall with the photo chief, even his shoelace. Tying his shoes was an ordeal, but abandoning lace-ups for slip-ons would have seemed such a surrender, like giving up one's feet. He had to tie them sitting down, one thick leg uncomfortably crossed at the ankle over an opposing knee, the upper and lower portions of his extremities like fresh sausage links, their skin thin and soft. Now he could fairly say that his life had hung by a thread. His weight had saved him.

Exaggeration—the man hadn't killed anyone else in the restaurant. Besides, Burl wouldn't have been in Gardenia's if not for his weight—that is, if not for whatever it was that drove him to eat in this way. Certainly he wouldn't have been there at that hour. His weight had always been the central mystery of Burl's life. Thus, it struck him as fitting that he should stumble into the most dramatic scene of his life in a restaurant, driven by hunger. Where did this insatiability come from? His parents weren't fat. His grandparents weren't fat. None of them ate as he did, but that was just another way of stating the same question. Burl's intake of food was no more voluntary than his intake of air.

If his appetites did not appear to be hereditary, his presence at Gardenia's probably was. Burl owned the place, or most of it anyway, thanks to a surprising provision in the will of an old family friend whose life Burl's father had saved in Korea and who later died fat and rich on Long Island. Burl's family had been involved with the place for years. His mother had worked there as a waitress after the war, which was where she had met Burl's father, and Burl's Uncle Lou had been the manager since anyone could remember—so long, in fact, that it seemed to most people his.

Actually, it remained largely Burl's, although Lou owned a substantial interest, purchased from his nephew while Burl was in college. The business was not enormously profitable, and Burl left matters largely to his uncle, confining himself to monitoring the cuisine by taking a good portion of his dividends in trade. His mother had made the staff promise not to serve him three entrees, but they never listened. Later, in order to finance an expansion, he had sold another stake to his old friend Frederic LaChaise, the well-known transatlantic chef, who liked to keep his interest secret because of cuisine unbecoming an avatar. Red sauces, fiaschi. How would it look?

A killing—three killings!—in his very own restaurant. Burl remembered Uncle Lou's stash of Calvados and began to think that perhaps he needed to pay more attention to the place. He'd known vaguely for years that Gardenia's was a gathering spot for the wrong kind of people, but always he had put them out of his mind. They were inconvenient. It did not leave a good impression, after all, for a newspaper reporter to own even a part of such a place, and from an ethical standpoint, even if mobsters did like Gardenia's, they had to eat somewhere. Is it Burger King's fault that some maniac feasts on Whoppers before killing all his neighbors? It was only a restaurant.

In the police station, his stomach grumbling, Burl castigated himself for the moral lassitude that had led him to this pass. And what if he did pick out the killer? Burl tried to picture the trial, the testimony, the man's stare again, perhaps a jittery look over one's shoulder on a quiet evening. But it would be fun. Burl would feel a hero and do it without hesitation. Besides, didn't one have to tell the truth?

But he didn't recognize the man, somewhat to his relief, and then went through the odd ritual of coaching an artist in the creation of a police sketch of the suspect. Like all police sketches, the creature who emerged in this one looked boxy and constipated, the artist indebted to Herblock in his conception of the human face. Burl tried as hard as he could, but somehow whatever came out didn't resemble a human being, although the face on the page, with its high forehead, sensitive eyes, and perhaps overemphasized five-o'clock shadow, met the verbal description of the man Burl had seen. The drawing captured none of the intensity, though, replacing it with a melodramatic scowl, and none of the strange blueness of the man—his black hair the color of midnight, his cheeks faintly blue from the hairs he would shave the next day, his suit the richest immaculate navy.

Burl had been in the police station half the night. When it was over, he still hadn't eaten, and by now there was no prospect of the fine meal he'd imagined or anything even resembling it. He wondered if he was even still hungry. He had been a police reporter for a while in his lightly padded youth, and the scene at Gardenia's was disconcerting even by the crispy-critter standards of his own experience. He had never been alone in the same room with a dead person before; it was almost enough to renew one's faith in the soul. How else could there be people and no life simultaneously? The stillness! Like being a voyeur. Still, he'd been all set for a serious meal. And it wasn't as if there had been blood and guts all over the floor. These killings were neat and professional, and Burl had to acknowledge that his appetite was largely unaffected. He ran through the local possibilities in his mind: the kitchen at Terrell's would be closed by now, Ho Sai Gai was closed for sure, he was never really welcome at the Chateau, and fast food was hateful to him, if for no other reason than the uniformity and skimpiness of the seating, which seemed such an apt metaphor for the whole experience. He'd been stuck once in one of those neocolonial swivel chairs that are attached to the plastic tables at McDonald's. He could cook—Burl liked to cook—but there was nothing in the house on the scale of what he'd promised himself, and anyway, it was exhausting to consider at this hour. His lower back, often sore by this time of day, radiated protest at the very thought. He waited behind a narcotized-sounding pregnant woman who spoke with excruciating slowness about the arrest of someone named Jimmy, and when she was finally finished with the phone he deposited a quarter and called Sally, whom he loved.

"HEY, BURLIE, HERE YOU GO," Sally said in cheerful greeting, sliding his giant wooden spatula from the oven. "Just the way you like it."

Burl smiled across the counter in delight. Sal's pizza was like a living thing, bubbling with passion, quivering with tenderness. Burl regarded him as an alchemist, or a medieval craftsman, un-lettered but trained in long apprenticeship and scornful of pre-tenders. Like the guildsmen of old, he was protective of his mar-ket. "Everybody make-a the pizza today," he complained. "Greeks, Arabs. A Chinese guy from Panama over on Court Street. Can you believe? Do I make babaganouzh? 'Anh? Chicken chow mein? I don' stuff no grape leaves!" Sally worked his art at a little place around the corner from Burl's apartment, and he had the usual ready when his biggest customer arrived: a large pie with extra cheese and sauce, crisp and hot. Burl was a purist when it came to pizza.

"Sally, you saved my life."

"What are you, working late or something? What's tomorrow's headline?"

"'Three Dead in Gangland Slaying.'"

"No kiddin'! Where?"

"Gardenia's, on Smith Street. My uncle's place. I almost walked in on it."

"Ma-*don*'," Sally said, breaking his rhythm as he dusted the pie with garlic powder, salt, pepper, and oregano. This was how Burl liked it, knowing from long experience that garlic powder is better on pizza than real garlic. Sally looked at him seriously.

"You lucky, 'anh?"

"Uh, yes and no."

Sal shot his chin at him questioningly.

"Well, I'm alive. But I saw the guy."

"Hey, who knows what you saw?" Sal seemed to seal up the box a little too vigorously. "You be careful, Mr. B. I like to read you in'a newspaper. Adon' wanna read about you, know what I mean?"

Burl was always happy to get home. He lived in a World War I–vintage building of maroon-colored brick, its towering yellowing lobby and fake fireplace the more impressive since thieves kept it absolutely bare. His apartment faced out onto an airshaft that might charitably qualify as a courtyard only in a dictionary of real estate euphemisms. But the rooms were spacious and cheap, with nice wood floors, and with the blinds always drawn it felt like a secret hiding place. It was furnished with heavy old pieces crafted of dark wood, some thick area rugs, and a great many books, which lined the walls and cascaded onto the floors, tabletops, and upholstery. The sofas and chairs weren't old, but they sagged under their nightly burden, and Burl's imprint in that sense was everywhere. A large lime-green wing chair rose like Neptune's throne from a sea of newsprint, which Burl cleared away whenever it threatened to engulf his place, and this was lit by a tarnished brass floor lamp that was always left on. The old-fashioned doors were of oiled wood, and the walls thick lath and plaster that accepted nails indifferently but helped seal out noises, so that the place always seemed to Burl a refuge, a sanctuary, and himself a rare bird who couldn't survive for long outside this unique environment, where safety and special foods were available. Pizza, for example. Living so close to Sal's meant the pie was always hot when he got it home, but just the same, he lit the oven so the rest might stay warm while he worked on the first few slices. The table was all set, as usual. There were napkins, a few interesting magazines, a well-worn deck of cards, and a remote control for the television, which, turned off, was practically the only reflective surface in the apartment. The mirrored door of the medicine cabinet had been ejected years ago to make mornings possible; Burl by now was well used to shaving without seeing himself. He got a bottle of Chianti out of the refrigerator and then opened the box. What he beheld inside was beautiful, but the red sauce and the spreading grease stain on the cardboard reminded him of the three dead men. One of them had been eating what looked to be eggplant parmigiana, which must have grown cold and distasteful as the police dusted and photographed and finally allowed the bodies to be carted away. It was annoying to be so hungry and see it going to waste. Imagine how the homeless must feel, amid such plenty. Why hadn't Lou had someone fix him something? Burl kicked himself for not asking. On the darkened screen he saw only drab shapes lit by the glow of a lamp in one corner. You could barely make them out—it was almost like a funhouse mirror—but Burl knew who and what he was seeing. He poured himself some wine and aimed the remote control at the set. "Divert me, knave!" he boomed in what he imagined to be the voice of a worry-worn king commanding his fool. And so at last he ate.

It was not a bad life, and if it was not necessarily a good one, well, how many could even pretend to such a standard? The pizza, which Burl ate with relish, was so good it made him smile, and elbows flapping, he eagerly ground more pepper. He was luckier than most of the men who had ever lived, he knew. Everyone had one or two little sorrows, at the very least. Burl happened to be heavy. Very heavy. He had tried diets, pills, organized weight-loss programs, and half a dozen therapists, including one for just a single session.

"What seems to be the problem?" the psychiatrist had asked from behind his big leathery desk.

"You said on the phone you could help me with my eating. I eat too much." Burl hesitated to state the obvious. "I'm overweight."

"I can help you, if you want to be helped."

"Can I ask a question? What do you run, about 290? 295?"

The psychiatrist shook his head condescendingly. "I can deal with it," he said.

"But you're about my size, right? You're almost as heavy as I am."

"I can deal with it," he insisted.

Burl did not think so, although later he wasn't so sure. He had given up dieting now and ate whatever he pleased, considering himself infinitely the happier for it. Perhaps that's what the fat psychiatrist had meant. What was so terrible, really? Oh, there was the public disapproval, of course, but Burl could put up with that. I live for art, he thought with gentle self-mockery, and I re-create the world not just every time I swallow a bite of food (and here he bit with care into the crust, taking pains to avoid burning the roof of his mouth) but every time I set word to page, or electron to magnetic storage medium, or whatever. In print, Burl's name was attached not to his corporeal mass but to his intellectual oeuvre, and more people judged him that way than by his appearance. He looked up at the shelf holding his own heterogeneous works. This was a risky business; he could look over this stuff and come away with a nasty sense of futility. I'll never be Tolstoy, he would start to think, consoling himself that this had been the case from the first fateful meeting of sperm and egg and thus, if a sin, was original. Or he would decide that he was at least a good writer, but that his kind of writing didn't matter. When Burl had reported on business, earlier in his career, he had met entrepreneurs who founded firms that put hundreds of people to work. Later, reporting on medicine, he met researchers whose work saved lives.

What were his scribblings by comparison? It doesn't matter what one writes, Burl would think at such times. But tonight for some reason his shelf was a pleasure. There were the two reserved-looking novels, the slim and obscure volume of poetry, the play that looked almost like a pamphlet, and the large type and loud colors covering the commercial works that he also wrote, each really a piece of *writing* even if the buyers and critics didn't see them that way. There was true crime, how-to, celebrity autobiography by the world's heaviest ghost, and a collection of obituaries, an assignment that had begun as a sort of exile and become a labor of love. It started because nobody knew what else to do with him. His standards were so exacting (or his self-importance so inflated) that he couldn't be edited. He criticized everything else in the paper—justifiably, most people agreed, but still—and was in general such a colossal nuisance that none of the desks wanted him around. So he was sent off into a corner, like some journalistic dunce, to contemplate his sins and do penance cleaning corpses. He bore this mortification with injured dignity and stopped talking to people for a while. The idea was to send Burl down into the underworld, but the obit beat became for him like Simeon's tower, a way to look down over the world untouched by it. He made his own schedule and began to work nights, leaving his days free for "real" writing. For a while he left his phone machine on all the time; soon the only way to reach him was by electronic mail.

This act made him feel better and would seem less fraudulent to his colleagues than the truth, which was that he genuinely relished his new duties. No more chasing around after dumb stories, no more late-night calls or taking work home or 18-hour days. No more editors, or living people of any kind, practically. Most of his work was done with books, clippings, and other documentary materials. He made phone calls and people were glad to speak to him. A call from Burl while the subject was still living could be like a visit from the angel of death, but at least it implied something larger than oneself—in Burl's case, often twice as large. Sometimes Burl was forced to call people during their time of grief, but they were usually willing to talk even then. He had learned over the years that most people, except the rich and famous, are pleased to have someone take account of their grief. It gives a life the illusion of meaning.

He soon became an advocate for the dead, working their hobbies and foibles into his accounts as if to restore flesh to the fleeting spirit or capture its full colors in typographic amber. He argued with editors about an old woman's passion for Siamese cats, a retired executive's impressive collection of tulip bulbs, and the Anglophilia that took one deceased, while he was alive, to the Lake District of England every year for more than two decades. His whole life had been a futile dream of retirement there. Of another, Burl wrote, "As a young man he married his great love, and family members said his life always seemed to them remarkably free of regret, perhaps as a result." Modest good deeds and enduring private passions, wherever practicable, were suddenly recorded for posterity in the newspaper's death coverage. But it was also Burl's job to decide who should be immortalized in *The Tribune's* obituary section and who excluded. He tried to err on the side of generosity in this respect, just as he imagined St. Peter might do in his post at the pearly gates, balancing empathy for individuals with the need to avoid running down the neighborhood.

Writing obituaries also helped his other writing. It didn't drain him the way other kinds of work did; it gave him ideas, yielded insight into character. He was even convinced that the obit beat would help him finish at last his longest and most frustrating project, "The Passion of Joseph Smith," an epic in terza rima about the founder of Mormonism, who died in a hail of bullets. No hagiography, Burl's work aimed to explore the role of the prophet in the modern world, particularly a prophet as enigmatic and ambitious as Smith. Burl figured there ought to be a movie as well. If only he could get the time to retrace the gradual migration Smith and his followers had made in the nineteenth century from New York State to the little town in Illinois near where Smith was killed. Nauvoo, it was. Burl hoped that by experiencing the landscape firsthand he might close the yawning psychological gap between himself and his subject. But the opportunity to make such a journey never seemed to arise, and Burl had begun to wonder if perhaps he was afraid of something in it. Retracing Smith's route wouldn't alter the embarrassing scantness of his own experience with women, after all. Was it crazy for a man who had never had sex to try and capture, in an epic poem, someone who'd had dozens of wives?

The work was giving him a good deal of trouble. He could never get the meter right; prosody for Burl was a dense wood dark as Dante's. Other unpublished works crowded another shelf, where the finished ones were lined up in anonymous manuscripts differentiated only by their plastic binding or here and there a rubber band. Burl was prolific. There were always two or three works in progress, so that his desk was covered by white manuscript pages, yellow legal sheets, and hundreds of coded but probably indecipherable index cards covered with notes he would likely never find useful or even interesting again. These materials tended to gather dust and the occasional cobweb. His agent was under the impression that Burl was writing a sexy novel about Joseph Smith, a compromise, since his idea had been for Burl to write *The* Real *Lives of the Saints: the Scandalous Inside Story,* which he was sure would get the author on *Oprah.* Burl knew that his agent was right, and that he would be driven to despair if he learned that one of his most productive writers was pouring his energies into an epic poem (after spending weeks desultorily reading up on saints; he'd even discovered, in an odd crossing of ecclesiastical wires, that some of Smith's wives were later canonized as Catholics). Scanning his published works, Burl noticed as he always did that the commercial books leaped out at him, their garish jackets like the plaids and polyesters of pushy salesmen bent on closing a deal. That was all right. They are all God's children, Burl thought. But not one bore his photo.

This was a matter of propriety. Fat wasn't really all that bad, he assured himself as he bit into the pizza, which left his fingers floury, as if covered in talc. Noisily, oil dripped down onto the cardboard and sank in. The renunciation of sex was often painful, but Burl tried with some success not to remind himself how much so. It was not, strictly speaking, much of a renunciation, since this pleasure was one Burl had never tasted in the first place and probably, he felt sure, couldn't get even if he wanted it, which he often did (how had those early Mormons done it, with all those wives?). But he preferred the willfulness that renunciation implied, the priestly discipline, and he found that after a point, sex was something one wanted less the less one had. God is merciful in His own inscrutable way. He damps the fires that needn't burn, He heals our sorrows, He gives us this delicate crust and spiny vintage so that even a fat man could feel his life touched by grace. Chewing, Burl almost believed.

IT WAS A SLOW night. The inventor of the flip-top can had died earlier in the day, and Burl deftly captured for all time the significance of the man's great insight, which had come to him when forced to open a six-pack on the bumper of an old Chevy during a picnic in the Adirondacks 35 years before.

Since then, not a single funeral home had called, so Burl was chipping away at the backlog. Not seriously. To do a proper advance obituary for Yehudi Menuhin or Jimmy Carter or Saul Bellow was hard work, which he relished once he got going, and for which he would be mightily glad should one of them suddenly die. But he wasn't in the mood tonight. Such concentration was beyond him without the pistol of a deadline at his temple. *The pistol of a deadline.* It must have been the morning's editions that put such thoughts in his mind. There'd been a little item about a gangland slaying in Brooklyn, all they could get in at that late hour, and there would surely be a major follow-up today. Hanks had already talked to him about it; he was all excited. Big story. A capo, his son, and an unidentified third man wiped out in some kind of internecine feud. It seemed to imply, to underworld watchers, that a new generation was seizing power in the Mandoli crime family. Besides, the tabloids would go wild; they'd missed it the first time around. It affected a man's concentration. Burl sighed and reached for a snack, unwrapping a sandwich of Black Forest ham, green leaf lettuce, ripe tomato, and thin-sliced cucumber, slathered with aioli and coarse ground pepper on a length of crusty French bread. Through a straw, he sipped merlot from a little grape juice bottle with a wraparound styrofoam label. He closed his eyes. The wine helped him imagine himself in California, living in gracious sunshine and sensual hills in a place where even the eyesores seemed to have a weird sort of grace, or humor. Instead he sat in his grubby corner of the vast and littered newsroom, its fluorescent lights and phosphorous screens casting a cold predawn glow across the proceedings at any time of night or day.

Burl's desk was in the netherworld between the Metro department and the copydesk for the weekly suburban inserts known as Neighbors. Advertisers did not want to display their products amid Metro's dismaying accounts of local politics, grisly sex crimes, and eccentric homeowners, with the result that the section had the most staff but the least space. Neighbors, by contrast, had acres of space because ads were cheap and the sections were zoned, as the name implied, by neighborhood. But since there was nothing to write about, the Neighbors sections adopted for themselves a gazetteer function, harking back to the role of newspapers long ago. They listed every court case, police item, and property transfer, every Little League score, garage sale, church supper, and Rotary meeting. Parking stories were a Neighbors staple.

Neighbors editors worked furiously to shovel all this material into print, and so Burl was surprised to see a theological discussion—of the kind that occurs on copydesks everywhere—break out in Neighbors. But there was Elroy, the copychief, poring over the stylebook. Elroy was a potbellied, greasy-haired, nearsighted paragon. He didn't say much, and when he walked he limped so badly he looked as if he needed a hip replacement. His hobby was drinking. Elroy had learned the paper's style—its practice when it comes to commas, spelling, and so forth—the way itinerant scholars once devoted themselves to the Talmud, as a living text that both embodies faith and calls forth questioning, and to which it was appropriate to devote one's life.

"Fluffernutter's not in here," he said patiently to some supplicant, laying down his copy of the stylebook. "I knew it wasn't, but it always pays to check. I checked in the system too."

Neighbors had begun publishing school-lunch menus.

"I say we hyphenate," the appellant suggested, "and use double quotes."

"Can't we just say 'peanut butter and jelly?'" someone else asked. "You know, 'PBJ' on second reference."

Elroy stared at his screen for a moment before handing down judgment.

"No. Run it closed up, without the antlers. I'll send a note to Regina."

Regina was the Queen of Style. Elroy would see to it that this question was resolved for future emergencies. Meanwhile, he had established a precedent.

"Uppercase? Right now it's lowercase in the copy."

Elroy shook his head grimly.

"Absolutely upper. It's a proper name."

Between editions Burl ducked out early and drove north on Madison Avenue, past the fancy shops and tall buildings and down the hill into Harlem, where he had business.

He parked warily, in a highly visible but illegal space, made sure his press pass was in the window, put up his "car has no radio" sign, and headed for Rebecca's, which was not far from the place where he usually bought shoes. The neighborhood was grim, but the restaurant had a smoky kind of class, and he felt at home even if he was the only white in the vicinity. At least there were other fat people. Their presence was a relief for Burl, who did not like trendy places. The slender clientele, the carefully disinterested waiters, the small tables and cramped seating all repulsed him, much as he knew he might enjoy their food. He savored reviews of these restaurants sometimes, marveling at what was done with obscure fowl and puff pastry, radicchio and raw fish. He even tried to send out for it. Why were there no laws to protect the rights of the fat? How could gluttony, in a land of plenty, register as much of a crime? Burl sometimes imagined himself a black man during Jim Crow, bristling at the leavings of life's feast.

Shields was already there when he arrived, nursing an illegal drink (there was no liquor license), and Burl could see that the shiny spot on the table across from him was a black-and-white glossy photograph.

"That him?" Shields said in greeting.

"What do you mean, 'that him?' No hello, no how ya doing, just pick him out? I expect a drink and maybe something to eat at least."

"Hey, man, this isn't our first date. I've had you."

"You guys are all alike—"

"Watch it, fat boy—"

"I meant cops, but never mind. That's the guy."

Shields nodded and smiled broadly, extending a hand that felt cool and dry in Burl's.

"Sit down, you son of a bitch," Shields almost laughed.

It had been a long time, nearly seven years, since they had seen each other last. They had been close when Burl covered the story of the man known simply as the Stalker, and then wrote a book about the case. They had spent many days and nights together, exchanged home phone numbers, used each other in all the ways they could without harming one another, and had come to share a certain trust on that basis. At one point they had something like a friendship. The birth of Shields's son and the end of their common work interest had allowed them to drift apart, but there was also Gardenia's. Shields didn't want to go around with someone who owned that kind of restaurant; he said it looked bad for a cop, and he never would set foot in the place. They had argued about this.

"So how're you doing these days, Burlie?" Shields asked. "Where you keeping yourself? Seems like forever since we talked."

"Last time was about that podiatrist missing in Douglaston. He ever turn up?"

"He's in Long Island Sound somewhere, feeding the fishes. Or someplace else we'll never find him."

"Mixed up in a fast crowd for a podiatrist."

"Look who's talking. Imagine you walking in on three dead men. And almost being one yourself."

"Nah, the guy didn't have a harpoon."

Shields laughed. He was a slight man for a police officer, with a receding hairline and the sensitive features of a poet or an internist. He wore a white shirt and a tie with brown and tan stripes that faded into one another and varied in thickness, a subtlety years out of fashion. He had a small cyst or wart on one eyelid that made him look skeptical and a little sleepy eyed, like a friendly lizard in repose. He seemed relaxed.

"So who is he?" Burl asked.

"Listen, this is off the record, understand? I don't wanna see anything in the paper tomorrow except what's out already."

"Okay, so who is he?"

"Johnny Implamenti, but you didn't ask the right question."

Burl considered for a moment.

"Why did he do it?"

"You're warm."

"I'm always warm."

"He did it for money and loyalty and all that stuff," Shields said dismissively. "The real question, for a scholar such as yourself, is *for whom* did he do it?"

Burl could never sort out who versus whom. He felt himself being mocked.

"Okay, for whom?"

Shields's hard-sided briefcase opened with a clack-clack, and he removed another photo, placing it before Burl with a certain satisfaction.

"Giuseppe Paolo Gemignani. Joey Gem around the old neighborhood."

Burl smiled at the way Shields snapped out these trochees, as if concluding a musical phrase. New Yorkers have some kind of ethnic thermostat; Shields was feeling a little blacker, perhaps, with his drink and the evening's surroundings. Regretting his own prosaically mongrel ancestry, Burl picked up the photo and examined it. It was a good picture, a candid shot, like one of an actor, balding, about 35, whom someone has told, "Okay, now look sinister."

"Joey Gem," Burl repeated aimlessly.

"Nice Italian fella," Shields said. "Lives in a real nice neighborhood, sends his kids to parochial school. Votes Republican."

"Joey Gem. Great name."

"Not a great guy, Burl. Know what I mean?"

All those stresses in a row, and it works for him. Nothing I write scans. Maybe they do have rhythm, Burl thought guiltily. Derek Walcott. Langston Hughes. Like Coltrane, music in oppression.

"He does have that lean and hungry look, which I so abhor."
Shields took the picture back and regarded it with fondness.

"A bad guy, as we say in the trade. But this whole business was
a departure for him. Really not at all characteristic."

"Has he never done anything like this? What is he, the
Quaker don?"

"I couldn't even believe he did this one, but the folks in Organized Crime Investigations picked this up. They said Implamenti on behalf of Gemignani, they had some kind of informant.
See, Joey's one of these new mobsters, more a finesse kind of guy,
a man born into a family business from a different era. Tries to
leave the violence to some of the newer immigrant mobs, the
Colombians, the Chinese, you name it. Joey's never done a hit
personally. Nonononono. He concentrates on just giving people
what they want, unfortunately for them. He's of the 'you-can-
steal-more-with-a-briefcase' school. Thinks he's going places. But
no, he's no pacifist. Not evidently."

But by now Burl's attention was taken up by the menu. He had
not often eaten soul food and was struck by how simultaneously
seductive and lethal most of the choices sounded. Pigs' feet in
vinegar, lime, and peppercorns, chitterlings in onions and broth,
stewed oxtails, salt-fish cakes, catfish, frogs' legs, barbecued
turkey wings, Southern fried chicken, fried brains and garlic
scrambled with eggs, roast pigeon and cornmeal mush in pan
drippings, fish-head stew and rice, and an array of vegetables—
collard greens, black-eyed peas, candied yams, spinach, okra, and
so forth, much of it, Burl suspected with delight, cooked in bacon
grease or some other fat circumscribed by polite society.

Strangest of all was that their waiter was black. Burl realized
that he had not been served by a black person since his last nut-
ted cheese sandwich at Horn and Hardart. The restaurant world
that he knew was entirely white.

Generous portions soon arrived. Shields had his usual pork chops, breaded and cooked pinkish white inside, with candied yams and rice. Burl, who overcame his customary resistance to tasting other people's food (would they think him a glutton?), couldn't remember when he had had such moist and flavorful pork.

For his own meal he was constrained as usual by fastidiousness, or an overdeveloped sense of propriety. Burl loved barbecue, for example, and fried chicken, but was too self-conscious to eat it in public, imagining himself in the eyes of onlookers as a living Thomas Nast cartoon, or Henry VIII brandishing a drumstick. He settled on smothered rabbit, cooked crisp in an iron skillet but salty and moist on the inside, heaped with sautéed onions and served over grits, with coconut sweet potatoes and greasy, smoky-tasting stringbeans. During their feast the two men talked about opera—Burl's diversion but Shields's passion—and reminisced about the days when Burl covered the police beat. They ate with gusto, Shields's hearty appetite a relief, since it made Burl less embarrassed.

"So what are you working on now?" Shields asked him.

"Outside of obits? An epic poem, about Joseph Smith. The first Mormon."

"Latter-Day Saints, huh? I remember the to-do before they finally decided they could have black priests. All of a sudden they had a revelation, said it was okay. How's it coming?"

"Slow. What kind of an epic would it be if it didn't take years?"

"Nobody reads poetry anymore; you ought to do it as an opera. Guy says God talked to him, gave him some gold plates only he could translate, nobody believes him, he marries a bunch of wives and dies a martyr's death, his religion lives even though nobody's sure he wasn't a crackpot or a fraud."

"Good idea, but I don't know enough music."

"Find yourself a composer, man. You stick to the libretto; your story's got everything. Think of Vaughan Williams doing *Pilgrim's Progress*. Or *Nixon in China*."

Afterward Burl could not resist a menu offering called Third World Coffee. Their waiter, lights reflecting in his pomaded hair, brought cups with cinnamon, cloves, orange and lemon peel, brown sugar, and brandy. He casually lit this mixture with a kitchen match and then doused the flames with hot java. With a deep breath, the two men ordered dessert.

"You don't have to do this, you know," Shields said at last.

"Right, I'm being polite. I really hate peach cobbler with rum raisin ice cream. Look at me, will you Godfrey? Am I forcing myself? This is my just dessert."

"About Implamenti."

"What do you mean?"

The pie came, heaped with ice cream, and Burl went at it.

"I like you, Burl," Shields said, distracted a little by the sight of his friend using a fork to hew great chunks of food and lift them into his gaping maw. "You don't have to do this. These guys kill each other all the time. The dead ones are no better than the killers."

"Funny," said Burl, swallowing a mouthful and smacking his cold lips. "That's what they say around the desk about shootings right here in Harlem. 'Happens all the time.'"

"They're right. It does."

Burl shook his head, wattles jiggling, mouth full of sweetness.

"Makth no differenth," he said through the peaches and chilly cream.

"That's what you say now, but let's see what you think later on. Don't get me wrong, man. I've been after this guy for years. He's a scumbag, and he'd look better as a feather in my cap. But you don't know where this might lead. The suggestion that Joey

Gemignani might actually be a killer is gonna mean a lot of heat, toward what end I don't know. So you don't have to do this."

"I do, I do," Burl said, scraping his dish with the side of his fork. "No man is an island and all that."

Shields regarded Burl's empty plate. He'd barely begun his own dessert.

"You keep eating like that, you'll be a continent."

Burl waved dismissively. "I'll live to be 100," he said, and regretted it instantly, for it was then he remembered about Shields's little boy. He blushed at this misstep and thought he caught the detective's eyes flicker. Joking references to mortality were to be avoided, even if Shields was in the homicide department. Murder somehow wasn't the same. It was so rarely senseless, they both knew.

"Taken care of," Shields said when Burl tried to pay for their meal.

"C'mon, Godfrey, I can pay my own way," said Burl, looking for a waiter.

"Taken care of," said Shields. "You ain't the only one who's highly welcome in certain restaurants in this town."

Back at the office Burl read the clips on Joey Gem. There were plenty, but they mostly involved charity balls, society functions, movie and theater openings. Two were of more direct interest. One cited Gemignani's name in passing; it was a larger story, six years ago, about the Mandoli crime family and how the young had drifted away from the traditional rackets. It mentioned Gemignani in what sounded like a sanitized passage about his trading company. The other story, about two years old, described the disappearance of an aging Mafia don whose removal from the scene was believed to have helped Gemignani consolidate his increasing power within the family. It also contained more personal information. He was 33 at the time, which would make him about the same age as Burl, and was supposed to be one of a new breed of Mafiosi who were more sophisticated, more publicity conscious, and perhaps more ruthless than their fathers had been. Joey attended Colgate and later got an MBA. There was even one of those slightly grainy photos of him getting out of a car and buttoning his cashmere coat. It was obviously taken from a distance and enlarged. But instead of an attached brick rowhouse in Brooklyn, there was an august-looking Upper East Side apartment building. According to the article, the co-op board had tried to keep him out, but Gemignani threatened to sue, claiming they were prejudiced against Italian Americans because there were none in the building. His wife was a pediatrician, and he was active in a number of high-toned charities. Who were they to exclude such a family?

What a character. As a reporter, Burl had never been terribly interested in the mob, and regrettably, neither was the paper, despite the organization's influence on the life of the community. Maybe this sort of killing *was* private. The dead men were all gangsters—there was no intimidation of innocents going on here—and he who lives by the sword, etc. Burl tried to feel comforted.

A little while later he looked up to find Hanks sitting on the edge of his desk, an arch expression on his face.

"So what's this I hear about one Giuseppe Gemignani and the Gardenia's slayings?"

Hanks had allowed his command of journalistic cliché to corrupt his speech. He would tell of beefing up the insulation in his attic, or having crossed swords with some editor who was always wreaking havoc with his copy. He was disgruntled, irate. Funds in his language were forever being earmarked. Hanks believed that we all have heartstrings, and that his highest calling was to tug on them.

"I hate when you use words like 'slayings,'" Burl said. "There must be some mistake. Gemignani was an Italian composer. He lived in Corelli's shadow, as well as Vivaldi's, Haydn's, all of them. A minor figure. He was an Italian guy who carried a violin case, but he used it, as far as we know, to carry a violin."

"C'mon," Hanks wheedled, as if cajoling a small child. He was proud of himself. "The checkout list in the library says you've got the clips."

"I wish I could help. You need 'em? Here, you probably do. Make sure you take them back; they're in my name."

"So I'm not wrong, right?"

"If I could help you I would. But I've been sworn to secrecy."

"I get it," Hanks said, winking broadly.

IN THE NEXT DAY'S PAPER, Hanks had got someone at the police department to confirm that authorities were examining "a possible connection" to Joey Gem, followed by twelve paragraphs of background taken from the clips. Carelessly, Hanks had called the restaurant Gardena's, without the i. Burl felt like all those people who complain, when they know something personally of the matter in print, that the reporter has always got it wrong. As agreed earlier, there was no mention of an eyewitness.

Burl read Hanks's account over his morning coffee, which usually sufficed for breakfast. As a concession to his doctor, he no longer started the day at his favorite coffee shop with scrambled eggs and corned beef hash, or at a friendly little place where they made lovely eggs Benedict with homemade hollandaise, or spicy huevos rancheros, as much as he loved such foods. It was a point of pride by now for Burl not to consume solids before noon. He consoled himself with the thought that by such small sacrifices one might live to eat again some other day.

He began the day with a weigh-in, stepping onto one of those sliding-weight scales of the kind used by doctors. Burl had found 300 pounds to be some kind of natural plateau, and this nice round number was easy for him to maintain, just so he didn't feel things were getting out of hand. He generally concurred in the pronouncement of Thomas B. Reed, America's portliest Speaker of the House, who held that "No gentleman ever weighs more than 300 pounds." Feeling himself a gentleman was important to Burl. This morning, on the scale, his eyebrows jumped. The thing wouldn't balance until he dislodged the big weight from its notch at 300, moved it down to 250, and then slid the smaller weight all the way over to the right, almost but not quite to the end. Two ninety-seven! He smiled. What grand eating lay ahead. Reading the paper, he wondered momentarily what Shields would think of the story. The phone soon put an end to any speculations.

"What was that in the paper today? Are you nuts? You gave me your word, for Chrissake. What kind of an untrustworthy asshole am I dealing with here?"

"Hey, hey, I didn't have anything to do with that! That was Hanks; some idiot on your side gave him the story. And watch your mouth, will you? There's no need—"

"Watch your own ass, and never mind my mouth. Thanks to the power of the press, your friend has dropped out of sight."

"Hanks?"

"Implamenti! Remember him? Your best customer at Gardenia's."

Burl felt guilty, but what could he do? He hadn't been the source of what Hanks reported and in fact had kept scrupulously out of it. Shields calmed down after a little more venting, insisting that Implamenti would turn up later in the investigation. "It's not your fault," he said at last.

But the whole conversation left Burl feeling low on his day off. When he went out for the competing papers it was humid and gray but a little windy. Summer's charms were exhausted even for the neighborhood children, who were back in school by now. There was nothing interesting in any of the dailies, and at this point in his career Burl could do more than skim only if he forced himself. He was in no mood. Instead he drove over to his bank machine, drew $200, and set out to buy dinner.

He drove everywhere, of course. Buses were too small and train seats too cramped. One of his most humiliating episodes had occurred when he became trapped in a subway turnstile at the height of the evening rush. What exactly is the legitimate use of a turnstile, he wondered? This one gripped him implacably for two hours while commuters rushed past on every side, staring and clucking that one of the few usable entries was blocked. As if he wanted to stand there! Like a boulder in the middle of a stream, the human flow rushing past in a kind of unity. After that he decided to travel only in Checker cabs, until the thought struck him that he might just as well buy one of the big cars himself. From then on he went everywhere in his customized Checker, complete with extra-small steering wheel to allow for his stomach. He liked the car, it felt armored, and there was so much floor space it was like a portable living room. It felt very much his, too: a statue of St. Dagobert, the patron of barbecue, watched benignly from the dashboard as he steered, and Burl settled himself comfortably into a driver's seat that had formed itself around his body as if designed for him. The car was getting old, though, and the company had gone out of business, so parts had begun to be a problem. Maintenance was imperative, as he was reminded by the jumpy images he spied in his right side mirror, which hung loose from the car's battered body and rattled with its useless shock absorbers.

He drove toward Bay Ridge, his spirits rising as he approached his favorite bakeries and pork stores, and when he parked he went marketing with a vengeance, accumulating in his battered back-seat a comestible bounty that made his car look like a produce truck. The vegetables he bought, sampling as he went, still tasted of the earth, and the meat was so tender it seemed almost alive. He bought for several different dishes, anticipating a series of meals all at once even before having had the first. He bought for dinners at his desk, because making sense of people's lives made him hungry. He bought for the refrigerator and the cupboards, because his nature abhorred a vacuum. And he bought for the road, so he could nosh between samples at shops to which a stop by Burl was like a visit from royalty.

At home, surrounded by his afternoon's plunder, he began. Burl first halved an enormous eggplant, drizzled green olive oil over the top, and pushed it roughly into a hot oven. Then he quickly sliced an onion, a carrot, and a green pepper, searing the lot in a hunk of butter with three fat garlic cloves, which had shed their peel beneath his crashing blows against the side of a knife blade. Checking on the eggplant—time to turn it face down—he set a saucepan full of water to boil atop the stove, lit another burner under some milk and wine, and then diced a couple of large ripe tomatoes and tossed them in with the onions. In the milk, meanwhile, he briefly seethed a pound of fresh-ground veal. The water boiling, he added salt and olive oil and inserted a little linguine. He squeezed tomato paste into the vegetable mixture, added the meat, and splashed in Chianti from his glass. He stirred everything and, checking the eggplant again, rubbed his hands before the oven's warmth. Sipping his wine, he tried to think what was missing. He sprinkled oregano and ground hot peppers into the mixture, sprayed it with salt, and worked the pepper mill until his arms got tired. Cheese! Quickly, from the icebox, he retrieved a hunk of pecorino Romano, which he grated vigorously but, for Burl, sparingly, into the pan. He checked on the eggplant again, poked it with a fork, and decided it was done. With a potholder, he removed the sizzling purple and olive fruit and set it down beside the range. Shutting off the linguine, which he must drain momentarily, he stole a gulp of wine and went to work with a tablespoon, scooping out the steaming flesh of eggplant and depositing it in the saucy mixture on the stove. When the purple shells were empty, he chopped and mixed the skillet ingredients with a spatula until they were blended, meanwhile noting with satisfaction that the shells were drenched in olive oil and furiously hot. He quickly drained the pasta and grabbed the eggplant shells by the stem to get them onto an oblong plate of the sort diners favor. With a big spoon, he filled them with his mixture of veal, onions, tomatoes, peppers, cheese, etc., and practically hurtled toward the refrigerator for his block of white Vermont cheddar, which he grated in big slivers across the two purple and red canoes that would compose his dinner. He slid the plate under the hot broiler and in a matter of seconds withdrew it, the cheese a molten glory. At the sink, he grabbed a burning handful of pasta and tossed it with a yell between and, well, atop the two purple boats. He covered this with a last, sparing spoonful of the mixed meat and eggplant, shocking next to the faintly yellow cheddar, and felt the glorious heft of the thing in his hands as he moved toward the table. Burl ate it alone, but as if making love, without reading or watching television or listening to the radio. When the food was really good, he liked to concentrate, and afterward, recalling his intense pleasure in the meal, he lit what was for him a rare cigarette. This eggplant recollected in tranquillity brought him a smile. In consuming, he thought, I am consumed. Yet consumed, I remain undiminished; on the contrary, I exceed my former self, am greater now than ever, like someone who finally has found a way to eat his cake and have it too. Which put him in mind of dessert. He'd brought home several, from three different bakeries, including an extraordinary white cake supersaturated with rum. But Burl was no hog. He would sip his wine and wait a few minutes. His apartment was warm and cozy, completely quiet. There was no hurry. Feeling happily monkish, he might even make some cappuccino.

The phone interrupted his reverie, and in answer to its ringing he struggled upright and hastily traversed the room, his stocking feet pounding against the floorboards as the walls grunted in sympathy.

"Hello?"

There was no response.

"Hello? Hello!"

Burl hung up. It would be mistaken to call what he had heard silence. It wasn't breathing, or rustling, or a noise that anyone could identify. Rather it was the manifestation, somehow, of a person, almost the aura of one, emanating from the receiver. What a funny place the world is, Burl thought. Like a fickle lover it rejects, yet turn your back to it, and you can't be left alone. An unfortunate thought crossed his mind just then, which prompted him to look superstitiously—ceremonially—over his shoulder.

That night he slept poorly, even without the cappuccino, and the only dream he remembered from his fitful slumber was scary. It was about a slender man Burl knew to be himself. He was much thinner, yet people reacted to him with greater shock than ever, until suddenly Burl realized why: his head was encased by an earthenware helmet, with features painted on and little jug ears sculpted from the same pale pink material. Burl saw himself having slender conversations with people who tried to disguise their horror. He spoke to a woman, longing to ask her for a date. Inside his helmet—like a spaceman's, or a diver's—his face burned with shame. It was hot inside this crock, dank in his nostrils and heavy atop his shoulders. Voices sounded hollow, faint, but what choice was there? Now Burl was in a restaurant—but how to eat in public?—and felt like darts the pitying glances of the other diners. His companion was sympathetic yet unfamiliar. He had a face but no identity. Eyes lowered, he seemed to eat quietly, almost abstemiously, as if in slow motion. But Burl's food was untouched, his painted smile unchanged, and he realized that during this meal he wasn't eating anything at all.

Burl did not sleep well for much of the next week. His nights at work were taken up by dowager philanthropists, retired chemical executives, sad young set designers with AIDS, writers of children's books with innumerable survivors. He got one wrong and the paper, eager to project exactitude at such negligible cost, ran a correction. Burl rarely made errors, and this reminder of his own fallibility left him anxious and guilt ridden. In no mood for memento mori, he sent a computer message to his friend Norma on the foreign desk, asking if she would come to dinner as usual on the one night off they had in common. He fidgeted and read the wires until she answered "yes but at my house" in the telegraphic and uncapitalized computerese she preferred. Like that cockroach who used to hop around on the typewriter keys. Mehitabel? Burl tried to remember that not everyone had as much down time as an obituary writer and then sulkily consumed a sandwich of smoked turkey breast with avocado and sprouts on whole wheat. From an apple juice bottle, he drank chardonnay, relishing the oaky vanilla flavor at first but then absently blowing bubbles through the straw. What if, using positive reinforcement for the right keys and mild electric shock for the wrong ones, you could teach the roach to type "food" when hungry? Progressing to water and so forth, could you teach the creature language? Could you type "food" onto the screen and test for secretions that might show that the roach anticipated a meal? Could this be done with a higher animal? Or what do we mean by language? Norma messaged, "what do you want to eat," and Burl, roachlike, tapped back with a finger, "food."

NORMA AND BURL HAD been friends for years, yet dinner at her house was always a ticklish matter. There was crystal and chintz, there were colors and themes, there were proportions. Burl was uncomfortable, an interloper in this measured world, a caveman in a Regency drawing room. He had to be careful where he sat or trod, lest he crush the cat.

"i feel like cooking," she'd said in electrons.

They drank red wine while waiting for their meal, which, since Norma was cooking, was sure to be elaborate. Food preparation for Burl was quick and savage; he relied on instinct and high heat. He served fish and steaks half raw; he favored clear, vivid flavors; he loved all peppers. He would do anything for salt. Just being in the kitchen put him in a trance of automatic motion. Norma, by contrast, prepared dishes of dizzying complexity that required searing, boiling, and baking at the very least, demanding intermediation from the chef for shaping or arranging between processes, so that Norma was always struggling with spatulas and forceps, graters and mashers, double boilers and basting brushes.

Frequently she burned herself. Grapes were often involved, or exotic fungi. A raft of special ingredients was inevitably procured. There was always a cookbook, and it was always followed precisely. Norma knew by now to have most of this done before Burl's arrival, because while following a recipe she could bear no interruption. This was perhaps for the best. Watching her find her place with a finger, sift the flour, crush the peppercorns, fret over the oven temperature, and sigh with worry; watching a little of her dark hair fall in her face, a bead of sweat on her brow—all this was for Burl an act of silent worship that neither of them would want to encourage if they allowed it to surface. Norma was tall and dark and somewhat pear shaped, but with a delicate fullness that was never ungainly. Her high, narrow face had sharp cheekbones and mobile, expressive lips, which parted to show spanking white teeth that emerged in the slightest hint of overbite when she held her mouth open, as she listened about to laugh or exclaim. She would pay very close attention to one thing at a time, which at the moment was their meal, and her concentration made Burl's breath come short. He had loved this woman for seven years, from the moment they met, and to be a fly on the wall of her life, to see her lip twitch as she read, to feel her solitude in the silence of her apartment, all these things made him heartsick with tenderness.

They ate clinking heavy silver against fine china, a sound that Burl, the child of Melmac and stainless steel, found cold but irresistible. The food was soft and lukewarm, but satisfying, and they drank a lot of good wine because Burl as usual provided it. There would be dessert; he rarely wanted this but accepted in order not to seem embarrassed about his weight. It was for the same reason that Norma, by some complex logic, unfailingly offered it to him.

"So are you still happy writing obits?" Norma was always consciously making conversation.

"Love it," Burl said, taking some wine and swirling it in his mouth. He swallowed with a gulp. "Best move I ever made."

"Don't you miss writing real stories sometimes, though?" Norma caught herself. "I mean, about living people."

"Not at all. There's too much corruption in the rest of the paper. It's all commerce, really. Selling papers, selling ads, unconscionable editing. And you have to deal with so many assholes. There's honesty in death. Peace, even, I mean for me. And responsibility. Remember, I decide who goes in and who doesn't. What power! Death is no fairer than life, I guess."

It was Burl's mistake now. Norma had lost her parents and her twin brother in the past couple of years and had assumed an air of bearing up.

"Is there any news on the killings?" she asked bravely, with a look that parodied concern. Oh, he loved her, loved her need to surpass her own real worry with a more visible fake concern, loved her drive to adopt this role, the way she played it, the tenderness that motivated it, her sticking with the morbid despite her own discomfort, her perhaps secret need that she could only indulge in this way. Burl had long ago beatified her so that whatever Norma did glowed in the light of this crackpot sainthood.

"Nothing at all," he said with a sigh, whose cause he imagined she couldn't dream. "The main suspect is missing, which is just as well, since I'm the only one who saw his face and lived to tell the tale."

"The only brush with death I've ever had was my car accident," Norma said, rolling her head around as if to remember the whiplash.

"Let's not hang any crepe around this thing yet. I prefer not to think of it as a brush with death."

"Oh, right, sorry. Are you finished there? Can I get you some more?"

Burl always dreaded this question, since it left him torn between displaying approval for the food by demanding more and proclaiming his dietary virtue by declining seconds. He chose self-deprecation.

"Thanks, it was great, but I've got my figure to worry about."

Norma gave a pained smile and swept out with the dishes.

Burl's evil thoughts set in later, on the sofa. They drank port and talked about movies, the cat draped characteristically over Burl's lap, his claws casually and without warning digging through Burl's trousers into the ample but sensitive flesh of his crotch.

"Is he bothering you?" Norma asked. "Scat, Alexander."

"No no," Burl insisted lamely, but Norma dumped her pet on the floor, saving her guest from what he regarded as certain emasculation. She knew that he found cats macabre; the way Alexander's muscles and sinews moved beneath his pelt made Burl's own thin skin crawl, and Alexander's open mouth suggested nothing so much as some horror-movie insect.

As usual, Burl had brought a videotape to watch after dinner, but he and Norma were having fun talking and drinking, and he couldn't help noticing the voluptuous spread of her haunches within the dark silk of her dress. Her chestnut hair usually flopped around her face, except when she washed and brushed it and parted it on the side, all of which she had done tonight, so that she looked elegant and beautiful. Burl had previously expressed the opinion that in matters of hair, asymmetry was essential, and the thought flickered across his mind that she had done this tonight specifically for him. Maybe it was the wine, or maybe he was ready to believe the offered mythology about his "brush with death." As delicately as he could, he kissed her.

At the very least, his lips came as a surprise. Burl himself was startled at the noise they made. Norma, taken completely aback, had reached to set down her wine glass on the coffee table and managed only its edge, so that the glass fell to the carpet. Burl's wine meanwhile splashed on the off-white sofa, as well as on his hand and his shirtcuff, as she pulled away. The red wine everywhere was like spilled blood, and from a doorway Alexander was a stealthy and astonished witness. Although a threat to the color scheme, the spill was a welcome distraction, and Norma leaped to her feet with enthusiasm to tackle the problem. They spent the next half hour energetically working on the stains.

"I saw some stuff on late-night television that seemed to take up wine stains like magic," Burl offered.

"It's all right, it's nothing. I can get it up."

"Look, I'm sorry about this—"

"No—"

"Really, I'll pay for the cleaning, replace the rug, whatever."

"It's nothing, really."

"Maybe I better go."

"No! No, don't. Stay with me while I do this."

They both drank some more and spent a good long time on the floor stain, sitting side by side on the carpet's random geometry—might the stain look purposeful?—as they worked to eradicate this stubborn blot on their friendship. Norma attacked it first with seltzer, which Burl swigged straight from the bottle in parody of his voraciousness, and then with liquid carpet cleaner the color of blue hair, which Burl also started to swig (lips tightly shut, hoping it wasn't caustic but maybe wanting to burn them just a little) until Norma halted this theatrical purgation, his embarrassed liquid hara-kiri.

"Stop, Burl," she said, putting one hand on his arm and reaching for more wine with the other so she wouldn't have to look. His lips burned. He took the little brush and set to work intently, eyes riveted to the stain.

"It was nice that you kissed me. Burl?"

He looked up momentarily but kept at the stain.

"I haven't been kissed in a long while. It was a surprise."

He looked at her now, because it was too embarrassing not to.

"I'm very attached to you, Burl. You remind me of my brother. Such a gentle guy."

He had died slowly, of AIDS, tended by a lover who was himself dead a year later. Norma said at the time she felt she'd lost him twice. Caring for her dying twin was strangely like standing by as you passed away yourself, she found, or even like watching a rare species die off, go from endangered almost to extinct. It was like being the last passenger pigeon in the world, living out its life in the Cincinnati Zoo. She and her brother had shared a childhood tongue known only to themselves, as well as some strange empathy of thought—the only cause Norma ever found to believe that there is more to the world than what can be seen or touched. She spoke to Burl now, but in doing so she often felt she might have been addressing her brother, who was the next best thing to herself.

"I guess I just don't think of you in a sexual way. I don't think of anybody that way, really. It's kind of sad. But you know, if I did think of anybody that way, it would be you."

To Burl there was something deliberate about this speech, premeditated even, that made it excruciating.

"Does that help?" She touched him again.

"I should go," he answered, struggling to get up.

"Burl. I want you to make cassoulet for me this winter." She pressed him down, turned, and took his face in hand so softly he felt faint. "I don't want to lose you."

On the way out he was humiliated by having to turn sideways to pass through the narrow doorways—he entered rooms this way as well, crablike, sheepish—and drove home in a funk. How could he have done such a thing? What a terrible mistake, thinking even for a minute that he should be other than by himself. But can't a fat man love? He did not often indulge himself with the desire to be thin, but he plunged now into this feeling with abandon, sighing and mumbling, "O! That this too, too solid flesh would melt."

The next day Burl was off, and at work the day after that he logged on to find a brief cummingsesque message like a found poem in his queue. "i love you burl if you would just lose 100 lbs i would fuck your brains out if not i love you anyway for your cassoulet." She'd let the computer sign it, "Ruifelen N."

Mesmerized for a moment, he quickly cleared the message from his screen. For a minute he just stared at the montage of postcards, notes, cartoons, clippings, timecard, and other paraphernalia stuck with push-pins onto his partition, not seeing any of them. He reached into his bottom desk drawer and withdrew a brown paper bag, which he stowed under his arm as he headed for the door. Gaining speed, he lumbered up two flights of stairs to where the foreign desk was situated, threaded his way through the desks, chairs, and partitions, and headed straight for Norma on the rim, the large curve of copyeditors that handled stories from the paper's far-flung correspondents and wire services. Burl rarely came up here, and a couple of people said cheerful hellos as he passed. Alerted by these, Norma saw him, but except for a little smirk stared at her screen as if she hadn't. Burl didn't care. He walked right up to her and deposited his parcel in her lap.

"Enjoy," he said.

Then he left. Unsure how to behave, Norma tried at first to ignore it. She put the bag on the floor and acted absorbed by the account of Somalian famine on her screen, but she couldn't resist the mystery and finally, as casually as she could, looked inside. There was an apple, a banana, several apricot hamentashen, a bottle of purple liquid she guessed to be Chianti ("Gattinara," Burl corrected later), and an epic sandwich of dry salami, cappacola, prosciutto, provolone, sweet red and hot green peppers, oil, vinegar, and red leaf lettuce on Italian bread. Wrapped, it looked like a weapon. "o burl," she messaged, and after the first edition carved the sandwich up and handed pieces around the rim. It fed four.

Chewing, Norma thought about Burl with an odd thrill. What if he succeeded? She tried to conjure him thin. She imagined him on one of those anthropology charts that are supposed to show the ascent of man from ape in profile, except she saw a progress from fat to thin, until at the end the Burl she knew was transformed into a kind of upright and deep-chested Everyman, unclothed. Homo sapiens. Peering into her screen, Norma fished around in the queue of stories waiting to be copyedited and came up with one about the troubles of India's Congress Party in the upcoming elections. She hadn't really thought very carefully about her offer; it was intended more in the way of consolation. Did she love Burl? Her feelings were as complicated as any serious philanthropy. She felt he needed her, in so many ways, and what a great thing it would be if he could at last lose all that weight. It made her happy to know she could use her body to motivate Burl, who was all the brother she had left, and the whole thing was in keeping with the genteel martyrdom she always had in mind for herself, in keeping with her sense of herself as a gift.

He set out with an iron will. It was almost more than he could dream, to have Norma with her hair the color of raisins and her touch on his arm like velvety cabernet on the tongue. He had lost weight before, though never 100 pounds, and had done so by strict vegetarianism. No fats, no wine, no sweets, and leave the Checker parked. He lived on spinach, potatoes, carrots, fruit juice, oatmeal, vitamin pills, and diversion. He began losing quickly, almost precipitously, and his diet or his success made him giddy. He felt feverish sometimes. Armed with a guidebook like a tourist, he tramped through the city, reveling in its vastness and filth. He was tireless and without fear. Children might taunt him, but dedicated in his purpose, he shook off their insults, and no adult stranger within easy reach would do more than look. Burl had never been mugged and was a favorite among moving friends. He had the strength of a dray horse and had once showed off by lifting a sofa like a laundry basket, carrying it propped against his hip with one arm. Now, though, it was not his weight but his purpose that made him feel invulnerable, like a knight armored with the affections of his lady love. He saw himself on a quest and viewed his wanderings as expeditionary: complete the task and win the fair maiden. Burl's relations with the opposite sex were so rare and so ancient that he saw them through a chivalric haze, the women airbrushed into princesses or twisted into dragons breathing fire. He liked Norma partly because she acted the role of maiden so effectively, for he yearned to be someone's knight. He wished he didn't smell so when he sweat.

Even filtered by euphoria, the city he observed on his marathon wanderings was no Camelot. Bodies lay in the streets and the very buildings oppressed the scurrying masses with their great indifferent weight. The simplest gestures of humanity were missing. What could a knight accomplish in such a place? Often Burl walked from his apartment in Brooklyn across the Brooklyn Bridge and up through Manhattan. There was vitality downtown; everyone seemed to have a story, and the streets bubbled with tales whose endings weren't known. The city grew more static as he moved north. In the East 20s, a neighborhood of solitary walkers, people looked affluent but lonely. Up further, in the afternoon, there were rich children everywhere, happy, pretty, well dressed and well spoken. He would see them coming from schools named for dead Anglo Saxons, European saints, the occasional

P.S. in which the parents took a fanatical interest. These children were a sign; their presence implied the start of his work day, and he would walk as fast as he could downtown. The West Side was dirtier, quirkier, peopled by exhibitionists, freethinkers, vampires, beret-wearers, Democrats, a woollier lot likelier to travel in groups, or at least in pairs. People in Brooklyn, where Burl lived, seemed happier. Carroll Gardens was delighted, Boro Park filled with zeal. He saw a jogger with the fringes of his prayer shawl hanging out of his sweats, or on a basketball court, kids so little they heaved the ball hoopward off a shoulder, like a second head. Sometimes Burl walked the other way, toward Brighton, where the white people looked foreign, like Eastern Europeans huddled in kerchiefs and coats against the slightest breeze, hunkered down and hanging on. They all seemed old. When he circled back through Flatbush, the blacks were younger, quicker of step, perhaps glad at last to have arrived in some of the city's leafier quarters. Walking on Church Avenue was like a quick visit to the Caribbean, and on the crowded sidewalks Burl would sometimes buy mangoes, papaya, and guava when he was in the mood to carry them home, until one day he noticed someone as out of place as he himself must seem. Another white man, not an elderly holdover, no youthful homesteader or Hasidic Jew, but someone else in his thirties, annoyed looking, in a dark raincoat, dark trousers, dark porkpie hat. Burl glanced at him a couple of times as the man desultorily fingered the fruit, examining a piece now and then unconvincingly, until the guy started looking back— brazenly, Burl thought, or weirdly for such a person, as if on the make, or in the know. Burl had an instinct to call him on it, face him down, but heard the express approaching along the open-air cutout that carried the subway in this part of town and decided as a little test to duck into the station. He hurried down the stairs but thought better of the turnstile and so ducked into a shadowy niche just large enough to hold him. As if looking at a movie, he watched the man in the raincoat run past for the train. Then Burl hurried back up the stairs—huffing and puffing now, he was unhappy to note—and walked off into the crowded side streets to thread his way unhappily home. He decided, en route, that probably it *had* been somebody on the make, some chance encounter that meant nothing. It was so easy to see yourself at the center of the universe, as if everything that happened had you in mind. What foolishness. You too shall die, he reminded himself. No one will even notice.

The fast continued. He tried to avoid Norma at first, out of embarrassment and an unarticulated desire to present himself suddenly transformed, but she wouldn't leave him alone, which delighted him. Neither of them was sure she wanted him to succeed, but this at least made it seem as if she did.

"are you mad at me for putting you through this"

"Are you kidding? The real question is, are you getting cold feet?"

"my feet are warm you may someday learn"

"Really, what will you do if I succeed?"

"everything"

In person, they were less frank, of course, but she still took an avid interest.

"You see this?" Burl asked, holding his pants out to show how much room there was already.

"That's very impressive, Burl," she said, looking away. "How do you do it? I've been trying to lose 10 or 12 pounds for years and I just can't keep it off."

"It takes motivation. I'm highly motivated."

Norma blushed. She sat primly on the sofa while Burl was heaped in an armchair nearby. His bulk was already visibly diminished, yet he was still a great distasteful mass, his hot breath palpable even several feet away, his aroma not unpleasant but detectable. The whole room felt warmer, damper for his presence.

"But what do you eat?"

"You live on the stuff you used to leave on your plate, the green and white things that seemed like garnish. That's my bread and butter, nowadays. Lettuce, cabbage, watercress. And I walk. I traipse all over town. You should come along one afternoon. I do miles and miles."

"Maybe I should diet with you."

"Don't be silly, you don't need to be dieting. You needn't lose a pound."

This was true, but there was calculation in it. Burl had begun to fantasize about Norma more seriously than ever before. It gave him chills. What a different life he would lead! He began calling her in the mornings, just to talk. He always said what he ate, and how much he lost, and she offered praise. They never alluded to her promise except on the screen, where both felt freer, but their talk had an exuberance that was missing from all their chaste dinners. A ritual imitation of courtship had become a genuine intimation of sex.

"Don't you ever get tired of being a copyeditor?" Burl asked one day. They were walking idly down the ramp at the Guggenheim Museum, an act of devotion for Burl, who found it hard to walk on any gradient and in whom this particular institution brought out the worst. It was too much like a parking garage for his taste, a place where they parked paintings no one could understand, or perhaps it was a huge and indecipherable DNA molecule of twentieth-century culture. Maybe eventually some grand gene project would explain it all.

"What?"

"Copyediting. Doesn't it bore you?"

"No, why?"

"All that minutiae. Don't you ever want to write something from scratch, toss out the stylebook, hyphenate from instinct? You know, let down your hair."

"Burl, I like editing copy. It's like doing puzzles. You find mistakes, deviations, and you make things conform to the rules. The rules themselves change, adapt, require interpretation. I love finding new cases, or helping make new rules to cover changing circumstances. What's wrong with copyediting?"

"Nothing, nothing. I understand a couple of copyeditor families have moved into my neighborhood. Some people were worried, but I have no problem with it. Some of my best friends, you know . . . "

"That's very reporter of you, Burl."

"Hey, live and let live, that's my motto."

"And a strange motto it is, for a man who writes obituaries."

"D'ja hear the news? Death rate's up in Queens. I just saw that in *American Cemetery*. You probably don't read that."

Burl was beginning to act as if Norma were his girlfriend, and she went along, until they really had grown closer. They began to take it for granted that they would see each other on Saturday nights, their one day off in common, and people around the office began to talk. They spent hours together; Burl thought he tasted the faintest flavor of domesticity, like some new herb he couldn't quite identify. After a while they had everything but sex, aside from food.

Sometimes they even had food. On the blustery first of November Norma lured him to her apartment on the pretext of needing his help to move some furniture and confronted him there with an elegantly set table and elaborately prepared vegetarian dinner.

"Burl, I stir-fried all this without oil. The salad dressing is just soy sauce, ginger, and lemon juice, and this over here is just potatoes, rutabaga, onion, and garlic, whipped in the food processor. With a little salt and white pepper."

The food was clever and delicious, and it filled him with hope. This, he thought, is what it would feel like married to Norma. You would gain a whole new set of skills and experiences. Things that used to matter wouldn't. New things would matter more than anything. Day after day, as a matter of routine, you would sit across from her at a table like this one. Life would have texture, interest.

"Now Burl, sometimes you have to reward yourself, you know? I mean, you can't be an absolutist about things, because sooner or later we all falter in some way." Norma talked as she carried the plates into the kitchen and then pulled on a padded glove. "So you're entitled to a little treat once in a while, aren't you? Because I made it myself, and we'll only have a little. Burl? Because it is your birthday, after all. No no, stay right there."

When she came back through the swinging door it was with a deep and glowing pan of chocolate fudge cake, whose aroma blended with that of the percolating coffee to surround her as she emerged. Burl realized that the glow was from some lighted candles.

"I can't sing, Burl. I'm sorry."

He was nearly overcome. The fragrance reminded him of his love for food but also made him think of Norma sweating over the kitchen counter, sifting and stirring and beating, worrying about how it would come out, with him in mind the whole arduous time. The woman, the cake and the candles somehow suggested the tragedy of the human condition, the anonymity of God, the existence of the soul and its noble perdurability. He swallowed hard.

"Now make a wish," said Norma, setting the pan down.

The lights were dim, except for the dinner candles and the birthday cake, and Burl didn't have to think what his wish should be. But doubts came in a flock. What right had he to wish for something so narrow and ultimately meaningless in a world abundant with suffering? Shouldn't one wish for an end to hunger, peace on earth, a cure for cancer? If one is really granted a single wish, how could one possibly waste it on something as trivial as a component of personal happiness? Sex or money or talent felt sacrilegious in the context of wishing, and it seemed that one should be rewarded in any case for wishing so unselfishly, although of course to wish altruistically in hopes of a reward would be pointless. Yet to ask for world peace seemed to Burl a conceit, as a wish and an impulse. He rubbed his chin as the candles burned. A drop of pink wax fell on the shiny mahogany surface of the cake.

"We are giving this a lot of thought," Norma prodded.

"Well, it's kind of a dilemma. Okay."

He wished for worthy loves to be requited, and blew, but there were only 14 candles and thus no guarantee. Alexander meowed jealously in the corner, and Burl realized he hadn't even considered animal rights.

"I was going to invite some people over, but then I decided it would be better without them. Happy birthday, Burl."

They clinked wine glasses full of flat seltzer.

Norma sometimes tried to feed Burl less wholesomely—less innocently, perhaps—but except for his birthday he stood firm. Was this some nurturing instinct at work in her? Guilt that she was depriving him? A secret wish to subvert his diet? He was puzzled but not worried. Why shouldn't her motives be mixed? What does it mean to be pure at heart in any case? Dripping, the muddy self will always intrude.

Since Burl was sheepish about sharing a meal with Norma, they often went to the movies, a rediscovered pleasure now that he was slim enough to squeeze into the seats, and this became their new regular date. By unspoken agreement, they chose harmless comedies and commercial epics with characters and plots that could never be mistaken for real life. He especially liked theaters where there was sure to be a wait. Flushed with anticipation, movie lines were some of the happiest places in New York. There was much animated chatter, the men looked over one another's dates, and Burl for once didn't feel left out. It was like trying out a new identity. He liked being with an attractive woman in public, and as if understanding this, and wanting badly to make up for things, and what (this unspoken) she still insisted on if they were ever to be lovers, Norma took pains about her appearance. This pleased Burl, who always did likewise with his own, but didn't see that she looked perhaps a little too much at pains, her face a little white with the extra makeup, her lips a vivid, cakey red that made them even larger when she opened her mouth to laugh, the whole edging however slightly toward the harlequin.

Their relationship had its discontents. After his initial steep slide, Burl began to shrink more gradually, and as the struggle grew more strenuous his euphoria gave way. Losing weight became harder still as winter took hold, his body conserving energy as if in hibernation. He still tried hard. He made spaghetti with vegetables and no oil. He boiled sandy fresh spinach, onions and potatoes into a kind of eggless, creamless, crustless pie. Every day he poured on lime juice, pepper, cilantro, costly cardamom, licoricelike fennel: a harvest of spices. He seasoned salads with basil and mint. He ate apples, carrots, so much silky lettuce he began buying by the crate. Eventually he came to see this process as a trial whose edge should not be blunted, and so Burl mortified his tastebuds with uncooked pasta and plain rice cakes, lo-cal matzoh and seltzer water. Like a knight preparing for battle, he conducted a wary vigil against flavor.

"Got any ketchup?" he asked Norma electronically. "These function keys are starting to look pretty good to me."

"du calme burl" she messaged back, which annoyed him. He wanted her to feel guilty. The diet was quite painful now, and Burl became irritable, prone to self-pity. He still shrank, but with more suffering, his body battening down for famine by increasing its efficiency against itself. He was forced to heighten the embargo, eating less and less until finally he stopped eating altogether.

"Not even unbuttered?" They were at the movies, and eating alone for Norma was the same as drinking alone for other people. "Popcorn doesn't even have any calories."

"But it's a slippery slope, you know what I mean? For me, all food is like potato chips. I can't eat just one. Besides, right now I'm in starvation mode. You're looking at a machine that could run for a week on a bag of popcorn. Get some for yourself, I won't mind."

"No. It's okay." Norma looked like she was about to cry.

"I'll be right back," he said, returning, as the feature began, with the largest size of popcorn they had. "But I'm not having any. Two fifty-five and counting."

Norma made herself think neutral thoughts and resolved somehow to make amends. Later, when Burl walked her home, she insisted that he come inside for some seltzer, which she stocked just for him. They sat on the sofa with their colorless drinks, talking aimlessly about the movie until Norma found her moment and kissed him. She thought Burl might faint at first, but he came to his senses and kissed her back.

Both parties were shocked at what a pleasure this turned out to be, and they kissed for a while. Burl thought he knew at last what heaven must be like and vowed to himself never to eat again, if this might be his reward. His face took on a look of such grateful beatitude that Norma was moved still further. Standing, she pulled him to his feet and led him into the bedroom, where she gently pushed him down onto the bed and began, with his shoes, to undress him.

Burl didn't know what to do. He thought perhaps he should reach for her buttons and zippers, but when he tried in his haphazard way, Norma moved his hands.

"Here," she said. "Let me for now."

With great care, she opened his shirtcuffs, removed his necktie, and slipped off his shirt and suspenders. Burl's chest was hairy and large, but his stomach came in folds and obscured his waistband. Later she would remember thinking that he looked better without clothes, but only without all his clothes. She bade him stand, and looking straight into his eyes, undid his pants, which fell heavily around his ankles. Embarrassed further, he moved to slip them off, but she quickly slid his undershorts off and then pushed him down again. The bed groaned in protest. Lifting first one foot and then the other, she removed his pants and shorts, disguising her dismay at their great size. It was really only a matter of getting used to it. He was a big man, but what difference did that make? She let him help her strip to her underwear and then, when he couldn't do it, she undid her bra. Burl looked astonished.

"My poor boy," she said.

And she offered him one, which he kissed ineptly but with a hunger so ravenous he could not conceal it. He didn't want to conceal it. Norma and Burl had many of the same thoughts. They wished she had milk. They wished he were thin. They knew that Burl was experiencing one of life's rarest and most dangerous events, which was to have one's deepest longing fulfilled. She pressed him down and, lying beside him, did something out of sight that made him moan, loudly and continuously, until she whispered "Shhhh!" as gently as she could. Looking at each other, neither could quite believe that she held his livid penis lightly in her hand.

She wanted to make him come that way. Being with him was erotic, but she didn't want to make love. She was ashamed that she didn't, and would have forced herself for that reason alone, but she had no birth control and was sure Burl didn't. And what if he tried to get on top? It seemed no easy matter to make him climax in her hand, which was growing tired after her increasingly vigorous efforts. But she wanted to please him, and watching him, feeling him in her hand, made Burl seem so needy and vulnerably human that she ached for him in almost the same way he ached for her. He was less repulsive now, despite his hairy folds and pinkish mottled skin heaped across her bed. He was becoming almost familiar.

Norma decided to try some more direct action, and having done such a deed only in her imagination, wondered whether it would make her gag. She moved her shroud of hair aside to get some air, and slid down to get comfortable. Didn't men come instantly when they had this done? She tried to figure out, from Burl's sounds, the right things to do. She was fascinated. She had always wanted to do this. It was like some tiny person, or a living sausage salty and slightly rough at the top. That part felt almost like a tongue. When she sucked a certain way, it stood up straighter. Looking up, she was amazed to find her field of vision filled by the swelling dome of Burl's abdomen. Without raising herself, she couldn't see beyond it. It was like being invisible.

THINGS CHANGED, OF COURSE. Norma hadn't intended to initiate a sexual relationship and avoided a repeat performance. She continued to spend time with Burl but kept him out of her bedroom. She ignored the double entendres in his computer messages and changed the subject when he talked about how beautiful she was, or how he longed for her. She could still taste his salty semen and feel it sticky in her hair. The whole world must smell it on her breath.

Burl felt cast into his wildest dreams, only to be awakened when the good parts began. When he tried to embrace Norma, or when he circled her shoulders with his hefty arm, she slipped away, and her intent wasn't lost on him, even if she kept smiling and took his arm in her hands. The strangest thing was that his night with her had made him so hungry. Instead of helping alleviate the suffering of his fast, sex exacerbated it. Burl was living now on seltzer and vitamin pills. The lack of food and his bewilderment over Norma had made him moody, almost paranoid. He worried about Joey Gem. He fretted over his pills—was there enough potassium? enough zinc? Might he drop dead suddenly of a heart attack? Slowly, painfully, he continued to lose weight.

Feeling himself dying, Burl became morbid. His image of himself was fatter—grander—than the reality, and so when he worried about who would bury him, and how, he became convinced that a big enough coffin would never be found. He decided to take the funeral arrangements into his own hands. How lucky that Steinways are made in Queens! Burl called the company to find out if piano cases really were useful in burying the huge and, learning that they were, ordered one to be held until necessary. It crossed his mind—fleetingly, fleetingly—that he might have it delivered to his place, where he could try to get used to sleeping in it. A worthy habit to develop, but he wouldn't like that smell of cut wood. He was relieved to find subsequently that, unlike airlines, which sometimes compel very fat people to buy two seats, two burial plots wouldn't be needed. A standard cemetery space was large enough. "We had a situation once in the mausoleum, but as long as you're not interested in a drawer, no problem," said the patient man who explained it all.

That settled, Burl set to work on his own obituary, searching in an orderly fashion through the materials he had saved obsessively throughout his life. He had always been a borderline packrat, saving not just his college diploma but his sixth-grade report cards (one for each term), not just his Scholastic Aptitude Test scores but fever charts of his blood pressure over the years, reports of an occasional urinalysis, boxes of ancient credit card slips, long-since expired half-price coupons. The documentary record looked fairly complete: his passport, for his travels, his old appointment books, for what he'd done, and his birth certificate, a strange-looking copy given him by his mother, for the exact time. He appraised himself ruthlessly. He would never merit more than a few paragraphs, even given the premium accorded the paper's own current and former writers when they died. Still, to win just a mention implied something. Few people managed even that. But it was cold comfort against the morbid thoughts that filled him instead of food. He had written dozens, hundreds, of writers' obituaries, discovering with a certain horror that some long-forgotten scribbler, dead at 93 in a Torrington, Connecticut, nursing home, was the author of 27 books and innumerable articles, and that Burl had never even known the person had lived. But what good does it do the dead to be remembered? Never mind posterity. Burl wanted to be known even by one person. Ultimately he realized he could write the piece right out of his head, and in a single bleary hour, he did so.

Burl G. Bennett, a staff writer at *The Tribune* and the author of several books on a variety of subjects, died WHERE, WHEN, HOW. He was AGE years old and lived in Brooklyn.

Mr. Bennett held a variety of positions at the paper, most recently serving as the chief obituary writer, where he achieved prominence for his essayist's ability to encapsulate a life, often under a tight deadline

LAUDATORY QUOTE HERE

Mr. Bennett was born in New York City on Nov. 1, 1953, and attended Columbia University, where he obtained a bachelor's degree in English literature. He was a copy clerk and eventually a reporter at the now defunct *Long Island Press* and worked in Albany for the *Staten Island Advance* before joining *The Tribune* nine years ago.

A prolific writer with diverse interests, Mr. Bennett was the author of eight books, including novels, biographies, and, with a well-known expert, a dog-training manual that quickly became a classic in its field.

"Although it assumes a belief in the perfectibility of dog that is at variance with my own wretched experience," wrote E. C. Hedgecock in *The Tribune* when the book was published, in 1985, "the authors' knowledgeable, thorough, and often hilarious approach is enough to instill confidence even in an owner faced with some latter-day Hound of the Baskervilles badly in need of paper-training."

Mr. Bennett was also passionate about food. An accomplished cook, he was a gourmet of catholic tastes whose love of cuisines both high and low was reflected in his ample waistline.

He is survived by his parents, Stuart and Betty Bennett of Secaucus, N.J.

There. Like a man who has purchased sound life insurance, Burl felt a load off his mind. He was coming to think that he hadn't finished a minute too soon, either. One busy night, churning out ill-framed proclamations of decease (it was never a good idea to die on a busy night), Burl began feeling dizzy. The last thing he remembered was the image of a sled-pulling husky staggering forward, the snow pierced by paw tracks and stained with blood, until finally the creature dropped in his traces. Then things went black, and Burl landed with a thud on the floor, his left side striking so that he twisted his arm and bruised his hip. The misery did not last long after that. Down 53 pounds, he resumed eating.

He gained weight as if walking magnetized among canned goods. Burl didn't tell Norma right away. Instead he just avoided her, and confounded with guilt, pity, and indecision, she was silent. A dread grew up between them. Burl lived in terror of a chance encounter and hated thinking about her, yet saw reminders of her everywhere. An item about the sale of a Rembrandt referred somehow to her Dutch roots. An actress in a television commercial looked like her. The bottles of Montecillo Riserva in his cupboard spoke powerfully of their dinners.

Finally Norma got to work early one day and stopped at his desk. Burl was embarrassed but glad, and she flirted to show that she still liked him. They said they missed each other, and Burl got a lump in his throat. Later, he sent her a message saying he was still trying to lose weight but that he was eating again. "Fasting made me feint," he explained, proving there are no accidents. "im glad you stopped its dangerous," Norma replied. They went out for a light meal, which became their new ritual, and afterward Burl would walk her home, a little nervously or at a distance somehow even while right beside. She never failed to ask him in, and he never failed to decline, hurrying off into the dark feeling lighter of foot and freer of heart when gone. Their outings ended early, and there would still be time to stop at Sal's, or at the little Mexican takeout place, and then home, where he could satisfy himself fully, and privately, with no one to observe.

Life resumed its accustomed timbre, although Burl often thought of his night with Norma, and seeing her was sometimes overpowering. Still down 39 pounds, he tried to keep off most of the weight. Studying his reflection clandestinely in shop windows, he almost looked decent to himself, and he considered getting a mirror at home. But the delis and restaurants of Brooklyn welcomed his return and set about fattening him up like a son of the neighborhood who has survived internment in a war.

"Hey, put a little back, 'anh? 'S a bad number, 39."

"Really?"

"Sure, three times 13, 's no good."

"Ah, Sally, I missed you. You remind me of someone, a poet."

Sal knit his brow and jerked his head.

"His comment about guys like me: 'The grave doth gape for thee/Thrice wider than for other men. 'See, 13 wouldn't be enough for me anyway. I need all 39 if I'm really gonna have any bad luck."

Sally smiled politely and waved a floury hand in dismissal.

"So how 'bout some anchovy today, eh Mr. B?"

"Loaves and fishes? Why not? Fish oil is supposed to be good for you."

He heard nothing from the police for a while and, now that he was eating again, had begun to forget the whole thing—Louie was right, why mix in private business?—when Shields called, sounding chipper. Burl was at work, knocking off "a licensed undertaker" (the paper was obsessed with such credentials) who was also "a longtime Democratic activist" from Queens.

"We heard from his lawyer."

"Whose?" Burl said distractedly.

"What are you doing, taking this down?" Shields could hear the plastic clack of Burl's typing.

"I'm just finishing this paragraph. Stay with me a second."

Burl hit the save button.

"There. Now, what are we talking about? Whose lawyer?"

"Implamenti's, okay? We heard from him this morning, says his client's been traveling on business, and he wants to know what is this stuff he's been reading in the papers."

"So what does that mean?"

"It means he's coming in, big man. He's not gonna take any kind of permanent powder on us. You gonna get your chance."

"Does this mean he thinks you have no case?"

"No, his lawyer's a smart fellow, the prosecutor must'a talked turkey with the guy, let him know his client's gonna be invited before the grand jury."

"I am too, I suppose."

"You bet your ass."

"That's what I'm worried about. I'll probably testify and he'll get off anyway. Then I'll really be in trouble."

"You testify and Implamenti's gone. Then we get Joey."

"But I thought these guys never ratted on one another. What about the code of silence?"

"You watch me, big guy. I'm like Nelson Eddy. I always get my man."

"More like Dudley Do-Right. Do I still have to watch myself?"

"Nah, nobody's gonna bother you. But lemme ask. Anything unusual happen lately? Anything queer, out of the ordinary?"

"I lost 39 pounds."

"You're kiddin' me. You on a diet?"

"Not anymore. Thirty-nine, that was it."

"God bless you, Burl, it's a lot of weight. But there's plenty more, isn't there?"

"You got eagle eyes, copper. I gotta run."

"Now that's something I'd like to see."

"Will you listen to this stereotyping?" Burl groped for a tone of injury. "From a black man! Do you have a boombox, Godfrey? Do I offer you watermelon?"

"No, you just live in some honky ghetto where the cops'd stop me just for walking the street. Listen, man, you're the saint, not me. We got enough black martyrs already."

Burl went before the grand jury in January, it having been explained that firsthand, nonhearsay evidence was crucial for bringing a charge such as murder. The air was stale, the heavy chairs of that shiny bent wood that always reminded Burl of old libraries or film noir private eyes. Burl's appearance was brief and to the point. He testified as to where he was on the night of the killings, how he happened to stumble into the restaurant at that particular moment ("I was hungry"), and what he'd seen. Then he identified three of the four photos he was shown as the man he saw leaving the restaurant. "Let the record show that the witness has identified one Gianni Salvatore Implamenti," said the young prosecutor, in characteristic regional drawl. A crucible, this port city. Her accent was Catholic to his careful ear, probably Italian, certainly not Jewish and not likely Irish either. "Known to reside at 300 East 79th Street in the County of New York." Against the motley and unkempt jurors, a collection of dragooned New Yorkers as weary as Muscovites in winter, she seemed larger than life in a sleek oyster-gray dress and matching pumps, the frosted hair falling around her face, her cheekbones emphasized through careful shading, her lips shiny with gloss. The faint rustling of her movements was audible in such close quarters. She was a lawyer and a law enforcement officer, but she also felt the need to spend 90 minutes getting ready in the morning and to turn herself out this way because a degree from a local college and one's prowess before the bar were laid atop old habits that die hard. He saw a large diamond on her left hand and knew that she and her husband lived in a house her own age in a Long Island suburb, and that this was good. Why should she apologize for her aspirations? The thought of her in such a house—its Haitian cotton sofas, pale carpet, the young couple's shin bruises from the unseen corners of a glass coffee table—filled Burl with wonder and envy. He shared her kulak's dreams. What else is it to be human, if not to have bourgeois aspirations? All our longings seemed predetermined to Burl, like his desire for lasagna, or puttanesca, and in this respect not even the weightless can escape their mortal destiny.

It was hard to breathe. He woke disoriented and then flopped about in the king-size bed that took up most of the stuffy room until finally he gingerly turned the knob, lighting the three-way lamp to its lowest level of illumination. You could almost see the stuffiness in the room. Perhaps he had drunk too late. Alcohol after a certain point in the evening tended to spoil Burl's sleep, to wake him at ungodly hours and ruin his attention for the entire following day, killing a morning's writing and making him cranky, without focus at work. Let not Margaret Thatcher shuffle off this mortal coil without I've had my rest, he thought. Feed me no nightcap on the eve of DiMaggio's death.

He reached down for a magazine and lay back in bed, thinking to read himself back to sleep, but sensed immediately the futility of this. His stomach was making noises, and he felt a burning emptiness within himself. There was no denying it; he was hungry.

This was a fairly chronic condition since the humiliating diet that had failed to win him Norma's hand. Such diets condition the body to starvation, Burl knew, and so when food becomes available one tends to store up calories like a bear before winter. In restaurants he had allowed himself to regress. He was ordering two entrees again, in sequence: creamy carbonara thick with pancetta and peas, then chicken à la francaise all tang and meat, followed by Caesar salad heavily anchovied. Tonight he had consumed four appetizers at a favorite place near the office: gnocchi with frogs' legs and garlic, risotto with quails, scallops sautéed with truffles, and a grand slam of oysters and asparagus sautéed in champagne and butter, arrayed with a dollop of glistening salmon eggs at the center. O! The first bite took him to the brink of tears. Burl skipped dessert in a spasm of penitential restraint, but really it was out of respect for the oysters, so he finished with a glass of sauterne and sent one to the chef with his compliments.

Now it was 4:30 in the morning and he was hungry again, hungry and oppressed by the stale air in his bedroom. The middle of the night was nothing to Burl, and his hunger was profound, insistent, ineluctable. It compelled him to rise. He dressed quickly, hating the silence and solitude of the hour and feeling grubby, unshaved, and unwashed in keeping with the soiled-linen feel of the guilty pleasure he was intending to indulge. He was like someone about to do something he never admitted—to anyone—that he really liked to do, some secret sex act or other embarrassing impulse of appetite. Stumbling downstairs, he glanced through the window at the landing and stopped. His car was just visible, but there was something odd about the old Checker. Burl looked again and saw that the hood was lifted.

This fucking city, he thought. He began to hurry down the stairs, vowing to strangle the thief with all the rage accumulated from years of missing radios, stolen batteries, broken antennae. Once someone sawed through a pipe and stole his muffler. But Burl stopped before he got outside. Wouldn't such a person be armed? Shouldn't Burl be armed too? He had a length of stainless-steel pipe from an old vacuum cleaner, but he kept that in the car. He turned around. There was an old softball bat upstairs, and then he could also call the police. Who knew, the guy could have a knife, an accomplice. What a place this was. You had to worry that some weasel auto-parts thief might have a gun.

"Tell them not to use the siren," he cautioned on the phone, peering from his kitchen window and munching a slice of Arnold's white bread with Hellman's mayonnaise. "I wanna get this guy."

Impatient, Burl crept back downstairs, treading lightly, trying to keep his breathing under control and armed with a bat that was for him light as a furled umbrella. When he peered through the glass door of the lobby, the car was visible but the thief was not. He might be anywhere, Burl thought. The street was dark, but there were sodium vapor lamps at the corners that made it seem almost daylight at both ends of the block. There was no moon.

The explosion came as a sudden stinging shower of glass. It was a short-winded clap, scary but quick, barely noticeable as noise for the way the panes from the door leaped out at Burl, falling all around him with the sound of flung beads. He stood transfixed, and as he began to realize that his hands and clothes—and his face!—were covered with little glass darts like acupuncture needles, he saw the hood of the car, blown clear into the sky, come crashing to the ground with a fearful lingering clatter that echoed off the building fronts. A second or two later, a single light came on in an apartment across the way.

Crunching glass underfoot, Burl threw open the door and looked all around in a black foaming rage. His heart beat so hard it shook his whole body. He felt wet and saw that blood dripped from the heel of the bat, below his hands. He pulled a couple of slivers out and realized that he could taste blood, too, could smell its iron fragrance. His face was a mess. Burl was a fearsome sight, in fact, a bloody, club-wielding giant coruscating in the yellow glare of the streetlights, thanks to his earlier immersion in glass, like some macabre, inflated Elvis, like a giant Liberace back from the dead.

"Drop it!" the police demanded as they came screeching to the scene, their arrival heralded by sirens audible in New England. Both officers had their guns drawn.

By then the Checker was a charred corpse. Burl reached it just in time to see a fire flare briefly in the engine and interior. The paint blistered and blackened, the upholstery smoldered, and the dashboard was torn apart. In the cab, wiring sprang crazily in every direction and rusted-looking springs were exposed here and there in what had been the seats. Grinding more glass beneath his great, wide feet, Burl looked through the passenger window to see a few audiocassettes melted Daliesque onto the floor. As wreckage, the car seemed much bigger than it had before, and the ramifications of its destruction seemed to spread all around. The hood, when it was blown free, had apparently glanced off another vehicle, the roof of which was badly depressed. In this respect it was not alone.

The first officers on the scene, when they realized Burl was the victim, seemed impressed by the wreckage and behaved solicitously, although they still wanted to see a license and registration. They radioed for an ambulance, which materialized instantly, and they called the bomb detail. The truck, when it finally came, looked like a giant wicker hamper painted some kind of military green just a couple of shades removed from black. Two men dressed in police armor stepped out and surveyed the situation with studied casualness. They peered into the car, prodded it here and there, and finally left, by which time the earliest hints of dawn had bled the night gray, and Shields was on the scene. Was the morning as chill as his shiver made it seem? It was always hard for Burl, who was usually hot, to judge the weather for others.

"Pretty exciting, huh?" Burl said, as a couple of paramedics worked at him with tweezers and gauze. He felt as if he'd been up all night. "I've always wanted to feel wanted. This is like the old Chinese curse: 'May all your dreams come true.'"

"Dry to hold steel," said one of the paramedics in a lilting accent. He was dark, with a turban and black beard, and Burl realized that the man must be a Sikh. *Still*, he meant. *Try to hold still.*

"Second thoughts?" asked Shields.

"I see you're still twisting my arm to testify."

"You're a stubborn motherfucker, ain't you?"

"How did you guys ever get started with that oedipal stuff? Anyway, it sounds funny from you, too literal or something. Your diction is too precise."

Shields sat on the edge of the gurney as well as he could in the ledge left by Burl's girth. An image flashed through his mind: of his son shot with a thousand slivers of glass, the life draining out of him in a thousand places. Shields could stand the sight of blood on anyone else.

"Listen. This little blastoff was a warning, okay?"

Burl looked at him.

"Do you guys go to school for this?"

"I mean it, Burl. Only reason you even came close was you hadn't eaten in 15 minutes and went out foraging. But there's no sense ignoring it. Look, I'll put a couple of men on you, we'll take you where you want to go, whatever. No more worries, okay?"

"Are they gonna be with me forever? Is this lifetime protection?"

"Eight to four, right through the trial."

"Eight to four?"

"Write an article. Budget's so tight it only allows for one shift."

"Then why bother? If somebody really wants me dead, they can find someone who works nights. And what about after the trial? I mean, they'd rather kill me sooner, so I can't testify, but if necessary they'll kill me later, right? At least it sends a message."

"Okay, look. Just get out of the apartment. Okay? Is there somewhere else you can stay, somewhere out of town maybe?"

Burl considered. All this was strangely exhilarating, like being a younger and thinner reporter and chasing after some story. American journalists working in this country were rarely in any personal danger, although few of them owned restaurants like Gardenia's. But the prospect of being turned out of his home was not a happy one.

"How long will this last, do you think?"

"Couple of months at most," Shields said. "No big deal."

Accommodations were a problem. Most of Burl's friends were married and in no mood for a long-term house guest—even a long-term phone call seemed an imposition—and Norma was surely out of the question. Hotels were prohibitive. Burl made a decent salary and earned a modest second income writing books, but his finances were always a shambles, and he lived forever at the brink. He was a shameless user of credit cards, a dandy when it came to clothes, and a gourmet as much as a gourmand, which resulted in enormous food and wine tabs. His closets were full of fine wool suits for every season and in every size, the result of fluctuations in his weight. He owned three tuxedos, nine pairs of shoes. Most of this attire was custom made. Even his socks and underwear were expensive. Repelled by the notion of the fat slob, he was fastidious about his person, and his dry-cleaning bills were terrible. Auto insurance, parking, rent, all were burdensome. And he always owed back taxes; none were withheld from his profits on the restaurant or his book advances, most of which were customarily spent long before they were earned. His apartment was always stocked with good wine, cognac, beer, cheeses, coldcuts, and prepared foods harvested from the polyglot shops in the neighborhood. Dearth in all its guises was repellent to Burl. He routinely carried one or two thousand dollars in his hip pocket, just for walking-around money, and a clump of singles in his suit coat for beggars and bums. He gave away $50 a week just walking to and from his car.

But he had to go somewhere.

ON HIS WAY TO New Jersey Burl found himself pay-
ing inordinate attention to the rear- and side-view mirrors as he
nosed the aging vehicle through traffic. The police had packed
him and a few of his belongings into a cruiser and then transferred
the lot to what Shields proudly presented as Burl's new car. It was
a mixed blessing. The department had arranged the use of a
weather-beaten olive-green Dodge of indeterminate vintage and
untraceable registration. It was free, but cramped. And it did little to set Burl's mind at ease. On the expressway in Brooklyn he
drove distractedly, swiftly yet not altogether purposefully, so that
he often caught himself wandering across stripes, or just about to
miss a turnoff. In Lower Manhattan he was more alert, although
it would be hard to say that he really noticed the chaos in the
streets. It was slow going, like wading through a swamp or writing
a book. The traffic pattern implied some great natural disaster.
Scarred and rusting cars with "no radio" signs were double-parked
next to hydrants, even next to legal spaces, and other cars triple-
parked next to them, until traffic was forced to crawl along on

avenues constricted to one or two lanes by this creeping vehicular arteriosclerosis. Burl struggled against an obstacle course of delivery trucks, taxis stopped helter-skelter, drivers who blocked intersections rather than miss a changing light, and the general accretion of selfishness that made the city torture. Such heedlessness. The drivers of New York lived in a state of perpetual anger and humiliation, perplexed at a universe of incomprehensible tie-ups, cryptic signs, and random stoppages, even in the middle of the night. Like rats subjected to sharp and unpredictable jolts of electricity, they were jumpy, bellicose, suspicious. Worse, they could never look you in the eye. In some small way they had abandoned civilization, and so beyond everything else they were ashamed.

He drove north on Hudson Street, squeezed past a backup at the Holland Tunnel, and headed up Eighth Avenue. Waiting to pass through the Lincoln Tunnel, which would take him to New Jersey, he was stuck in traffic. Up ahead, a driver emerged from his car, walked a few paces to the tunnel's great mouth, and emptied his bladder against the wall. Fastidiously, he shook the last drops from his penis and returned to his car. Eventually traffic began moving again. Burl decided that if nothing else his watchfulness was a convenient way to keep his mind off his destination, which he knew would rush upon him without his thinking about it. He could find the place in his sleep, and in fact he often did, waking with a grumble from a dream of that hellish kitchen table cold against the soft undersides of his bare arms.

The Dodge's brakes squealed and its engine rumbled as Burl alternately stopped and started in passing through the smoggy tunnel, which moved cars in a kind of peristalsis until finally they staggered out into the light and accelerated in their joy at having the entire continent spread innocently before them. Burl himself experienced this feeling, however fleetingly, right up until the turnoff for his parents' place.

He pulled reluctantly into their condominium complex, which was set with Cartesian precision in the middle of a parking lot. Even in summer the winds tore through the tiny trees and low-maintenance shrubs to buffet the Oldsmobiles and Toyotas that clung to the development like barnacles. Pulling into a visitor's space, Burl's outsized Dodge gave an unseemly rattle when he shut off the engine. In the row of neatly parked compacts and midsize sedans, it looked like a big kid left back in class.

"Welcome home, son," his father said, beaming blankly. He looked embarrassed, watery eyed.

"Great to see you, Burleigh," his mother added, as he began the ritual of removing his shoes before entering the fussy apartment. Burl had been sure that morning to choose a pair of socks without holes. "Don't lean on the walls, honey," his mother pleaded sweetly. "You know how they are here."

It was like getting off an airplane among the Japanese, a people tidy, insular, rigid, and hopelessly foreign. Yet here he was, and here, for a while, he would stay. At the urging of disparate voices—Norma's, Shields's—whose agreement should have raised alarm, Burl adopted temporary residence with his folks, attempting to share their refuge until things calmed down. Against his every wish and instinct, he moved into a small, hot room on the second floor, the lights of a far-off power line twinkling outside his window at night.

The dwellings in his parents' complex came in standard interior configurations and were built in long rows, but each unit was designed to look different from its neighbors, so that a Tudor townhouse was attached to a Gothic Revival, followed by a Cape Cod of white siding and black shutters, a Victorian bristling with gewgaws and battlements, and a squashed California bungalow of jutting beams and dark shingles, all anchored at the end by what looked to be an imitation Russian Orthodox church, complete with onion-shaped dome. Preferring simplicity, Stu and Betty had chosen a faux-brick and aluminum Colonial wedged between a stark New Mexican adobe and a thatched hut loosely suggestive of the Cotswolds. The whole place was carved from an ancient wetland, and beyond the edges of the asphalt the rushes still stood like wheat, so that the builder chose to call the place "Council Bluffs." Indeed, when the complex was first erected, the vistas had seemed limitless, at least until the far-off rise of the Palisades on one side and the next row of Jersey hills on the other, but since then development had gradually filled in the marshes. The sky was still huge and empty at night, yet the low-slung industrial buildings and newer townhouses that had begun to crowd their lonely landscape made these neo-Iowans feel at once less isolated and less happy. Their uniqueness eroded, they began to speak sadly after just five years of the way things used to be, until another sedimentary layer of nostalgia was added to the feelings of loss that refugees from old-fashioned communities brought with them in their exile.

Burl's stay began with the customary formal visit around a Formica table with a gold-flecked surface, his father fussing occasionally and his mother worried about the chairs. "Sit up," she would urge, patting her son on the back as if in concern for his posture. Burl had long ago stopped trying to sit in the living room, and it was never any longer suggested to him.

Stu and Betty were quiet people of thin lips and fair skin whose default expression was pained, at least as far as their only son would ever know. Until Burl's father started to let go, they'd been very careful, Betty's hair always delicately coiffed in a short, plucky wave, Stu's close-trimmed and combed back neatly from his face with a little Vitalis. They both had light, watery eyes and, with age, had developed a diffident manner out of the house. Stu had been a plumbing-supply salesman and so prospered during the decades after the war when the woods and cornfields of New Jersey began to be covered by new houses. It was hard to believe that this was the man who, as a young Marine, had his forearms tattooed with anchors that he could make ripple by clenching his fists, the man who went to the brig for smashing a noncommissioned officer, the man who won his pretty wife by vowing to carry her everywhere and who did so until finally she gave in and agreed to marry. A powerful man who tolerated no slight, who filled his clothes and had a certain dignity. He had wanted to be an actor, and even in his decline he carried more the air of tragedian than real tragedy. He had become prosaic. Instead of loosing his demons, alcohol simply diluted them, until finally they were so watered they became something else.

Betty worked in a chiropodist's office and retained a hygienic, scientific air that blended nicely with her self-conscious lack of learning.

"Do you ever listen to Rolly Richards on the radio?" she asked, carefully placing a hand on Burl's thick forearm, which stretched his Speidel watchband so that the wrong side of the inner links was exposed. "He's quite a brilliant man, and he had a doctor on—what was his name, Stu?—who said the reason most people can't lose weight is they don't have enough, oh what was it? I wrote it down here somewhere—ketones. That's it. Their ketones aren't working properly, and if they ate a diet high in citric acid and low in carbohydrates they . . ."

"I missed that, Ma," Burl said, looking toward his father. You could see each gray hair rising oiled from his scalp.

"Too bad about the Checker," Stu said. "I liked that old heap. Valves, huh? You want to have my mechanic take a look?"

"I don't think so, Pop. Sometimes you just have to let go, know what I mean?"

"R.I.P., huh? I gotcha. Where'd you get this old thing?"

"From a friend, for a song."

"Oh, Burl, imagine all this going on at the same time, first that flood in your apartment and then your car dying all of a sudden," his mother said. "On top of that awful stuff at the restaurant."

"Isn't it incredible?" Burl marveled. "When it rains it pours, huh? Cats and dogs."

"Well, if it means we get you back home here for a while, it's okay with us," Stu said.

"That's right, just make yourself at home. I made up the spare room, and there's clean towels in the second bathroom. If you need Q-Tips or anything just go in the medicine chest."

"So how's your Uncle Lou holding up?" his father asked, clearly hoping for the worst.

Betty shot him a look. The brothers-in-law were not on the best of terms. Burl's father was convinced that Lou ran the restaurant more for his own benefit than that of the owners.

"Pretty well," Burl said warily. "I've only been back a couple of times since then. He's been too busy to chat."

"You're still not ready to sell that place, are you?" Stu demanded reproachfully. "Is the food really all that good? I haven't been back there in years."

It was hard to believe he'd ever been there, but Burl was living evidence. Stu liked to say it was because of Kim Il Sung. Thanks to Kim, as well as to Harry Truman, Stu Bennett and Gene Gardenia spent a miserable winter in Korea, where, as Burl had heard the story, his father pulled his wounded compatriot to safety and carried him a day's walk through the snow back to their unit. Everyone thanked God that the Marines had got Gene's weight down; he was always chubby as a civilian, and after the war reverted to form, eventually swelling to a size not unlike Burl's. Stu meanwhile swore he never liked the man, even before his Korean heroics, and Burl could see how this might be. His father had simply done what seemed right, probably even relishing the feat for its own sake, thinking as he trudged that he would be damned before he would give up. The whole time, Gene said later, Stu tried to cheer him up. Gardenia and his family were not the kind to forget such extraordinary altruism, and they practically adopted Stu when the war was over. He claimed he had avoided their gratitude whenever he could, but the family's restaurant was good and the food was free, so he went. Gene eventually took over the place and, after Burl was born, became a kind of Dutch uncle to him, always there with some good food or bad advice, not to mention a little money anytime he needed it. He was a little too warm for a family friend, almost nosy, but he always had time for Stu and Betty's boy. Besides, Gene and Burl had something big in common: their weight. Gene was fat for as long as Burl could remember him, and for all his glad-handing in the restaurant always struck Burl as lonely. He married late and un-happily and died childless, which was assumed to account for his surprising will—surprising especially because as Burl got older he spent less time around Uncle Gene. As a teenager he found Gene a little too willing to abet youthful subversion, which only made Burl feel the pettiness of his defiance. And truth be told, Burl didn't like to be around fat people. It was embarrassing. Gene died of a heart attack before Burl ever had a chance to form an adult per-spective on him.

But he was not the sort of man Stu would like, Burl could see, trying to imagine the two of them on some frozen battlefield and then afterward, in the New York of those years. Stu put himself through the Gardenias' hospitality that first time in order to cele-brate the safe return of their only child, who would have come home in a box, if at all, were it not for Stu. Not that Stu had a bad time at the party. He danced with so many pretty young women that night, all of them dark-haired relatives, that he couldn't recall any of their names. When it was all over, the only one he remembered was the waitress.

"Betty. You like to gamble? Why'n'tcha take a chance on me?"

And so she had. Burl's image of New York in those days was black and white, like Norman Parkinson's photo of that young couple dashing excitedly across the Brooklyn Bridge, all woolens and smiles, their faces aglow with postwar optimism. He tried to see his parents in the city of Feininger and LaGuardia, swollen cars gliding like hippos up and down the streets, masonry everywhere, the glass boxes and violence still to come.

"At least they didn't shoot up the whole place," Betty said. "His business still okay?"

"His business," Stu scoffed.

"Yeah, fine, I think. Good. People find all this exciting."

"Your uncle always lands on his feet," Stu said, shaking his head. "Don't worry about him."

"You talked to him, didn't you?" Burl asked, hoping Lou had kept his promise not to say anything beyond what was in the papers. Burl had told him about the car, about everything.

"Just right afterward," Betty said. "I spoke to your Aunt Hattie, who was all upset and scared half to death. But forget about your uncle. It's you I'm worried about, Burlie. Don't you get mixed up in this kind of thing. It doesn't pay."

Burl sipped gingerly from his mug. Anything ingested here was taken with guilt, even this penitential wastewater. Instead of the cappuccino to which he was partial, he was forced here to drink instant coffee with artificial sweetener and "nondairy creamer," while his father gamely drank the same from a garish German beer stein, the souvenir of more freewheeling days.

"You're right about Uncle Lou. Remember, this wasn't random. Just the opposite."

"That's exactly right," his father said. "I find it hard to believe this just happened in Lou's place, just out of the blue."

"Stu, for God's sake, my brother is many things, but he is not a murderer—"

"Nobody's saying he's a murderer—"

"Ma, Ma. How 'bout some more coffee?" Burl asked.

"I got some extra packets of Sweet 'n' Low," she said, tossing a few of the little pink rectangles before him like a gauntlet. "You can take some home if you want."

"Coals to Newcastle, Ma."

"I know they make it in Brooklyn, you tell me all the time. Take it anyway."

Burl felt bad. Even Gulliver came to terms with the Lilliputians. His parents were not small, merely normal. His mother had added a few pounds as she got older, and perhaps went up and down a bit depending on whether she was "watching," while his father shrank gradually as his drinking increased and his other reasons for living did not. Between the two of them it seemed about a wash.

With relief Burl saw his father take out a deck of cards, shuffle them casually, and without a word begin dealing. Betty rose and got a box of toothpicks for chips, and they settled down to poker. When Burl picked up his hand, nothing matched, but that was okay. The three of them could pass a pleasant evening this way; Burl's father had taught his mother to play even before he was born, and Burl had taken solace in his skills with a deck for as long as he could remember. He was grateful for this skill, like the others he had learned from his parents. Picking up some new cards, arranging them in his hand, he felt more at home now. He remembered his mother doggedly teaching him to type, even though that wasn't supposed to be for boys, because it was always good to know things, and his father teaching him to do plumbing, and to shoot, patiently and without the posturing he'd seen in other fathers. Burl appreciated these things; he was never comfortable under a sink and so came to take pride in being competent with a gun, a skill he had kept up over the years.

They all got along during cards, but he learned more about them separately, on the phone. He would get some real news from his mother, for example, who would fill the wine bottles halfway with grape juice and water to cut down his father's drinking, or empty a can of regular coffee so she might fill it with decaffeinated, hoping to soothe his stomach and help him sleep. The main thing, she said, was that "Your father mustn't see."

The strange thing was that, living with his parents, he hardly ever saw them. He worked nights and slept late in the morning, so that for days the only sign of them was the notes his mother left him on the kitchen table. "There are apples in the fridge," she would write. "Eat some Jell-o when it gels. It's lo-calorie!"

Burl began to wonder where his folks really lived. The house was clean to the point of sterility, for example. There was never a single newspaper or magazine, no article of clothing or open book, no dish, pile of ripening fruit, marinating roast, blinking phone machine, errant mail, bank statement, or other sign of life, except for the night lights of a couple afraid of the dark and the redundant kitchen notes describing items in the refrigerator. And of course the occasions, once or twice a week, when Burl came home and caught his mother wandering the house asleep.

He was terrified that first time. It was late, and he was trying to be quiet, which was difficult for someone who breathed noisily. He opened the door gently and his heart skipped a beat. There was a presence in the living room, and for an instant he was reminded of Gardenia's. When his eyes got used to the dark he began to see a strange apparition, muttering and dusting, its movements jerky and accelerated. He wasn't even sure at first that this tricot specter was his mother. It was like seeing a ghost, the spiritual remains of some departed loved one. She seemed possessed, whirling and moving about in a frenzy instead of the stately glide he somehow expected from a sleepwalker, or a shade. Occasionally she would break into a violent round of twitching or flailing. Sometimes she would seem to be warding something off, other times attacking an unseen foe. His father had complained for years of her somnambulism, but Burl had never before witnessed it. Later he noticed that her arms and legs were blotched purple with bruises, and sometimes she broke things.

"Dad, what are we gonna do about this?"

"Nothing you can do," Stu said. "I told you, she's been at it for years. I used to try and stop her, but the only way to do that is to sit up all night."

"Won't she hurt herself?"

"Nah. I used to worry, but it's a funny thing. Some part of her is awake. She sees, know what I mean? That's why we leave all those little lights on at night. She bruises herself because she moves around so fast."

"Something must be bothering her."

"Nothin' bothering her. It bothers me."

Weekends were the hardest, because Burl and his parents were home. He tried staying out day and night, driving around, but this only aggravated his sense of homelessness, and in any case he was under instructions to avoid wandering in the city.

Burl's weight had always made dinners a problem, and the ordeal resumed now that he was back. He was the only fat person in the family, and his mother regarded his weight as a moral failing of her own. Each pound was a sign of her inadequacy, each forkful a stab at her heart. Sending him into the world this way was an advertisement of her unworthiness. Yet for Burl, eating her disagreeable food was both mandatory and forbidden; Betty couldn't stand to watch him take in calories yet was disappointed if he didn't finish the small portions she served him, hurt if he wasn't there at all.

"Have some more salad," she urged, pushing the bowl toward her son. "I got some Weight Watcher's dressing for you."

These dinners took him back. Burl had merely been chubby as a child, a somber, irritable boy, moody and alone much of the time, dressed when it was warm in a striped polo shirt stretched tight over his chest and belly. Food had already become a forbidden fruit, dark and freighted with consequence, the subject of subterfuge and pretense. His mother hid it from him. His parents talked about it obliquely, avoiding the subject and, when he was little, spelling it out like the name of a god that cannot be said. "I-c-e-c-r-e-a-m," they would spell. Or, telling him they had decided to skip dinner that night, explaining to one another, "We'll e-a-t-l-a-t-e-r, after h-e-i-s-i-n-b-e-d." But he always found excuses to wake up and wander in, even when he was forbidden to do so, and he began to imagine them eating whenever he wasn't around, especially behind closed doors in their bedroom, their hushed moaning provoked by fried chicken or angel-food cake.

When he was a little older, the amphetamines began. Burl's mother took him to a doctor who prescribed them, a man she had heard about from a patient at the chiropodist's office. They helped; Burl's weight was down when he was taking them, but he couldn't stay on them for long. His heart would race ahead sometimes, and after a while they seemed to make him even moodier than usual, even more lethargic. His blood pressure soared. Eventually the pills were dropped. There seemed no alternative to dieting. Burl spent years in a great, gnawing hunger until, as an adolescent, with more chances to feed himself, he embraced food and guilt in equal measure. He got terrible pleasure from a hot knish or cheesy calzone, consumed alone at some stand-up counter with a drink of yellow- or orange-colored sugarwater, gulped happily from a paper cone set in a plastic base shaped like an hourglass. But eating was never an unalloyed pleasure because he was never supposed to be doing it, which both heightened and perverted the satisfaction in it, and by then he knew that a fat person wasn't wanted in the way that others were, so that when he ate he must blame himself for the increasing pain of his own isolation.

As a teenager, entertaining seemed such an easy way to win friends and influence people that it became habit for Burl to sing for his supper. He mainly did food tricks. He learned to inhale beer, swallowed hotdogs whole, right out of the package, and could stuff a dozen eggs in his mouth without breaking any. (The trick was to use the small ones.) He took pride in his ability to eat strange things: mustard-covered ice cream, a heaping spoonful of coffee grounds, a fistful of lard. This was sickening sometimes even to Burl, but he took a perverse pleasure in mortifying his senses thus, as if he had it coming. It didn't really make him friends, of course. Some people were embarrassed by it. Others wanted to see how far it would go. In high school one day, in the lunchroom, Burl inhaled cartons of milk and ate some other weird things for a couple of girls until finally a guy chewed up a Twinkie and put in an ashtray. "Eat that," he said, looking around for approval. "Eat that and I'll give you $5." Burl judged this not to be in the spirit of the event and after a moment's shame—he considered walking away, relying on his exaggerated sense of dignity—rubbed his mocker's face in it. He had long ago discovered the physical power that came with his weight and knew that the world hates nothing so much as a weak fat man.

Impelled by the need to prove his willpower—another form of strength—Burl expanded his repertoire beyond food tricks to include feats of self-control. It was just an extension of his native stubbornness. He challenged and beat all comers in breath-holding contests, and on camping trips could go days without moving his bowels. At home he practiced expanding his bladder capacity; eventually anyone who joined him in consuming pitchers of beer quickly found that Burl was the last to rise for the men's room. And no one could go longer without blinking. Years later, long after he'd abandoned any hope of grace through stamina, this was one feat he still made sure to practice.

BURL PRAYED ALL DAY long that no one impor-
tant would die, and by late afternoon it appeared that his fervent
wishing (for this was all the prayer he knew) had shielded the
mighty from their own mortality for a little while longer. When
the coast seemed clear, he left work early and drove north
through traffic to a large old house in Riverdale. It had been a
while since he had made this pilgrimage; not since August, in fact,
when it was still light for his drive and the sun was low over New
Jersey as he edged patiently up the Henry Hudson Parkway, its
every crevice sprouting weeds in frantic obeisance to summer.

The trip was made now in the dark. As on earlier occasions,
on the seat beside him rested a large brown grocery bag, usually
stuffed but sometimes intriguingly roomy. One bag; those were
the rules. When Burl arrived, Frederic's house was always airy and
yellow with light, surrounded in the summer dusk by moths beating against the screen like sparks around a Roman candle. It was
a stony gray pile atop a hill distantly overlooking the Hudson,
standing aloof in the middle of a broad brown lawn. The evening
air smelled of the river mixed with New York exhaust.

"Bonsoir, mon ami! Comment ca va?" Frederic welcomed him with a theatrical hug. "Let's see what you have brought for me today."

Frederic spoke English in that French way of giving all the syllables equal accent, except for a few important words he accented wrongly. A dark, stocky man with an invincible Gallic stubble, he was always eager to know what was in the bag so that he might turn over in his mind the possibilities as Burl settled himself and complained about the traffic.

They would have a glass of wine, some one-sided conversation, and then they would begin, Burl perched uncomfortably on a kitchen stool and Frederic pacing rapidly if unevenly back and forth before his giant steel range. It was their game. On the appointed day, Burl would appear at seven in the evening with a bag. Frederic never knew the contents in advance but must instead improvise a meal from whatever was inside. He loved it. He said it kept him "on my tippytoes, *oui?*" When Burl wanted to include obvious staples but didn't get around to buying any, he simply enclosed a slip of paper that said "flour," or "cream," or at the very least "butter," and Frederic would draw on his own seemingly bottomless stores.

In gastronomic circles, Frederic was famous. With manic fervor undiminished—perhaps even increased—by the mild disability of having legs unequal in length, he lectured, wrote, and sold cookware with his smiling likeness in each pan, posed in a white smock with a kerchief around his neck in the very picture of culinary banality. But on these challenge days with Burl, his public was ignored, his wife and children banished if not spared, and the hyperactive bird dog boarded if necessary so that Burl's visual test might be met and mastered. Sometimes it was easy; the things fit some dish he already knew or Burl perhaps had selected them based on a menu lurking already in his own subconscious, and although they ate well on those occasions, Frederic was vaguely disappointed.

But more often he was challenged, and sometimes, with a wave, commanded silence as he paced, brow furrowed, chin in hand. He was never stumped; he could always make something, but the trick was to make something special. Each time, he had the right to exclude a single ingredient, a right he exercised on this occasion with unusual swiftness. A plastic squeeze bottle of Hershey's chocolate sauce didn't go over. Frederic merely lifted it out, clucked his tongue, and tossed it in the trash. Had he never heard of sauce molé? But he accepted the tangerines and raspberries, the red potatoes and (obviously defrosted) shad roe, the sesame and fennel, the watercress and leek. It was as if to say that everyone, everything, has limits. No thing can expand itself indefinitely. Burl, who loved chocolate sauce, was too sheepish to rescue even a virgin bottle from the pail.

"Your New York—a city of foulness," Frederic said with sorrow of Burl's encounter with the underworld. "One expects more of organized crime. For what is it organized, after all, if people like you can fall across it like a body in the street?"

"Un bon question, mon vieux," said Burl, who loved harrumphing and exclaiming in French. "It seems to me a sign. Advanced societies need the mob, you know?" This struck him as a very French idea, and he expanded on it. "They require some organizing principle to contain and channel their darker instincts. Organized crime is a sort of Las Vegas without a country, a diaspora of lust and greed—"

"Ah, Burl, very good!" Frederic was still unpacking and had found the Laphroig. "Yes, yes, Las Vegas, I love this place, all the lights."

"Who runs the mob, after all? *Evidenment*, a collection of conservative elderly gentlemen, the most bourgeois individuals one might ever wish to meet."

Frederic nodded thoughtfully and topped Burl's glass with red Bordeaux.

"Evil? *Biensur. Certainment.*" Burl shrugged, gestured; he was becoming French. His accent broadened, his eyebrows leaped. "*Mais sans lui*, who knows? Prostitution, drugs and so forth would get out of hand, *peut d'être*. If they didn't run the construction business and inflate costs so effectively, Manhattan would be even more overbuilt. And at least one knows where to go to get something done. Eh?"

"My friend, I think you are holding my leg," said Frederic, arranging the shad roe with a smile. He looked in the bag and pulled out Burl's staple sheet. "Ah *bon!* Uh, I cannot believe you defend these people, *monsieur*, who prided himself for so long on raking across the muck."

Frederic owned two restaurants, one a shrine of French cuisine in midtown Manhattan and the other a country inn in the upper Catskills. He was also, of course, Burl's partner in Gardenia's. He loved Italian food, especially in the American–Southern Italian style, but knew nothing of business and relied on Lou as much as Burl did.

"Louis is worried about you," Frederic said over their first course, a cold leek soup garnished with flecks of tangerine rind. "He hardly hears from you since the night of the killings."

"Hmm. I guess I have been a little uneasy about returning to the scene of the crime."

"Well, but now Louis feels the sadness, as if they shot you, because you don't come anymore. He says we won't even charge you for a while; you get food and profits both, *oui*? I told him I would call a jurist for the bankrupting."

"*Oui, oui, tres drôle, alors, faire de comique.*" Burl, sounding Quebecois, imagined himself a gap-toothed hockey star. He really did miss the place; it was as close to paradise as he had come, a place where he could eat as much as he wanted of whatever he wished, all free for the taking. He thought with sadness of the days when veal piccata seemed to grow on trees.

"Burl, seriously, it remembers him of the damage, your not being there at all."

"Funny, I haven't been in the mood for that sort of food much since," Burl lied. Damage, *domage*, could they be connected?

"Well, perhaps you should go and just see him."

"Get back on the horse before I build up an aversion."

"*Un cheval? Je ne comprends pas.*"

The soup was followed by shad roe scalded in Irish whiskey and raspberries, served with boiled potato and fennel. Afterward they had a watercress salad doused in sesame walnut oil and tangerine juice.

"Honestly, I am *orrified*," Frederic said, without the h. "I make food which gives life, *oui?*" They were on their second bottle. "And now we have three deaths in one of my place. *Incroyable!* I am very depressed for this."

"I've been happier myself."

"You worry also?"

"A little. I'm kind of down about Norma, though, too."

"*Ay*, your *paramour!* What's happening, what is your news?"

"It's over, finished. Kaput."

Burl told of his inability to lose weight and the romance his girth had strangled.

"So that is why I didn't see you for all that time, eh? You were starving yourself, *et pourquoi?*" Frederic reached over and grabbed a handful of Burl's shoulder. "You must find someone who love the total Burl."

"*Tout le* Burl, *vraiment. Absolument.*" Burl searched his mind for other French words of assent.

Frederic was right, and so Burl went back. He owned the place, after all, and he missed it, missed his uncle, the food, the table all set as if for royalty. Gardenia's, as much as any place, was home.

"Burlie, son of a gun!" Lou greeted him. "Where are you keeping yourself lately?"

"Enough guns," Burl said with a smile as they hugged. "I've been busy, you know, the job, the book, the cops."

"Have the portabella mushroom, it'll knock your socks off."

His uncle excused himself to take care of business and Burl enjoyed one dish after another, although he was distracted somewhat by the handful of diners around him. He eyed the men suspiciously, wondering about their connections.

By the time he was ready for dessert, Lou was finished with most of his work and sat down with his nephew for coffee and grappa.

"Who are these people, Uncle Louie? I mean, do we really have any idea?"

"Who are they? They're customers. What are you talking about?"

"For a long time you'd hear rumors about this place. You know, that it was frequented by a certain kind of character."

"Burlie, the only characteristic I care about is whether they have enough money to pay for a good meal."

"Hmm."

"Look, it's an Italian restaurant, it's in Brooklyn, what do you think they're gonna say about us?"

"So we don't have any dealings with anyone we wouldn't want to bring home for Thanksgiving."

"Burlie, let's not kid each other here, okay? We pay the inspectors, even though our kitchen is spotless. We pay the trashmen, even though our contract is with the hauler. We buy peace with the unions. We give a certain number of free meals to those who can help us. That's life in the big city."

Burl smiled uneasily. "We bribe city health inspectors?"

Lou looked at him fiercely.

"All this comes as a surprise to you, right? How the hell do you think you run a restaurant in New York City? Listen to me, mister, you're happy to enjoy the food, enjoy the profits, but you don't want to get your hands dirty. Well, that's okay with me, but don't try to play dumb, Burl, it's unbecoming in a man of your age and stature. How do you think that newspaper of yours keeps its distribution system running nice and smooth? You think they aren't taking care of the people they need to take care of?" Lou looked over his shoulder and quickly downed the remains of his grappa, exhaling heavily. "Listen, my friend, it's hard to be a saint in the city."

Burl asked himself to what extent it was a game that he was playing. Hadn't he known all this was going on, in a general way? Wasn't his ignorance about the specifics just the result of his own unwillingness to sully himself? He left the dirty work to his uncle. He preferred to eat.

"I'll tell you something else, Burl, I don't know what kind of halo you think you're gonna earn helping the police with this thing we had here that night, but it's time to knock it off, and I mean it!"

Burl felt the remains of his appetite melting, and he pushed away his cannoli.

"What happened? Did somebody talk to you about this?"

"Never mind that, I'm talking to you about this, and I'm telling you to mind your own business. You're my own flesh and blood, kid, and you're playing with fire."

When Burl was at work the next night, Shields called to say that Implamenti and Joey Gem were both about to be indicted.

"Any day now, okay?" the detective said. "So it's all gonna be over soon. You can even give it to what's-his-name, let him put it in the paper. Joey's lawyer knows already anyway. You know, the prosecutor tells him, kind of under the table."

"Sotto voce."

"Yeah. These lawyers are birds of a feather. They got more loyalty to one another than anybody else."

"When do you think it'll come to trial?"

"Oh, maybe two, three months, maybe not at all. Who knows, maybe they'll plead after all. Either way, won't be long now."

Burl did not share these feelings. He saw his great bulk stuffed into the witness stand and felt that now it was really just beginning. For all their bravado, he knew that there was actually very little the police could do to protect a witness, except for a very short time, and even then they weren't always successful. Joey Gem did not exist in a vacuum. Connections, associations, "friends" were the man's raison d'être. He was corporate where Burl was merely corpulent. A horde arrayed against a party of one.

Often at times of great stress Burl needed salt. Was he sweating more lately? Running through electrolytes at an unusual rate? Hypochondria was a side effect of weight gain for him; good sense was not. He would make sandwiches of smoked mozzarella, Italian salami, and prosciutto, which he would salt and eat with calamata olives and ridged potato chips. Black lumpfish roe piled glistening on a bagel with cream cheese, sprinkled with lime. Softshell crabs, scampi. Tempura dipped in wasabi and soy. Belly lox instead of Nova. Burl had been on diuretics for years to restrain his blood pressure. In the past he had tried Draconian measures to control these briny impulses, at one point banning salt from his home because of a tendency to sprinkle some on his palm and lick it. But for one whose pleasures in life were largely gustatory, this was stringent mortification indeed. It couldn't last.

Today he went to Chinatown. Why not? He felt safe. Joey Gem, his lapidary antagonist, understood that Burl could be eliminated whenever he wanted and apparently felt the time was not yet at hand. Most men might be struck dead at any time, whereas Burl had specific knowledge that his own fate was in abeyance.

So he went in search of sodium. It was a good time for it; early in the afternoon, deep enough into winter to forget the fetid nadir of summer in Chinatown. When he slipped into the booth at Ho Lee's, where he knew the tables weren't nailed to the floor, he rattled off his order without looking at the menu.

"Shark fin soup. Fried meat dumplings. Singapore noodles— what? Okay, how 'bout pork lo mein? Some of that hacked pigeon with vegetables. Kung Pao shrimp."

When the dumplings and the lo mein arrived, Burl would drown them in soy sauce, banishing the low-sodium kind if he spotted it on the table. That was another nice thing about being a marked man. You could stop worrying about blood pressure, cholesterol, and all the other tedious medical constraints on physical enjoyment. Even money. What was debt to a dead man? For whom should he accumulate an estate? He had written an obituary once of a philanthropist who gave away millions, vowing not to be the richest woman in the cemetery. Who might have guessed that Burl's time would be, if not at hand, so predictably close? It was relaxing, in a way. No more flossing. He could eat and drink, and these things in themselves implied a certain merriment.

His appetite grew, and he, of course, grew with it. Burl was without his mechanical scale in New Jersey, but dieting for Norma had left him within the limits of his mother's icy bathroom weighing platform. He weighed himself daily, noted the steady increase, and vowed to stop when he hit 279 pounds, which was as high as the scale went. He reached that level in no time, and according to the scale, he held it. Betty was appalled.

"Burl, honey, are you maybe putting on a little weight?"

"Me? No."

"You do seem awfully hungry lately."

"It's this country air."

These exchanges inspired in Burl hours of sulking restraint followed by outbursts of vengeful consumption. At work, now, with his evening tea, he took three pieces of the cherry pie at the deserted cafeteria. The cashier gave him a look.

"Are you pulling my leg?"

"C'mon, Marella," he said. "I'm wasting away over here."

"I shouldn't even ring you up."

"You want to embarrass me? Okay, I'm embarrassed."

"I'm not gonna say another thing."

When Burl arrived at his favorite Indian restaurant, for example, he came in a state of high expectation. The place was always dark, the waiters courtly and sleek. Every surface seemed covered with fabric or upholstered in some way. When the food began to arrive, he felt his mouth water. The garlic-and-potato nan was light and slightly elastic, the curried mussels spicy, orange and soft, the lamb tikka salty and succulent. Burl became euphoric. He experimented with sauces he couldn't identify—green, red, brown. He relished the yogurt-cucumber dressing and the chili garlic hot sauce together on bread. He called for more mango chutney. But the same thing always happened. Because he was compelled to continue, to plod grimly on against all reason, comfort, and physiology, his pleasure in eating was soon followed by increasing discomfort, a feeling that mounted as the food rose in his stomach, until together the feelings and the fullness coincided in despair. He had to try the shrimp vindaloo. A sucker for dumplings, he couldn't resist the samosa. And what would an Indian meal be without tandoori chicken? He ate so much it made him dizzy. His breath came short, his knees were weak. He felt faint. Brooding and embarrassed, he would stagger away from these meals in confusion, stupefied by food and dumbfounded by his own capacity for it.

As soon as he felt less full, he was hungry again. It was as if his body feared a shortage and demanded to be kept at absolute capacity. Spicy foods slowed him down a little, so he demanded them hotter and hotter, until finally the inside of his mouth was blistered and his lips were shadowed in red. He looked like a pistachio fancier.

Burl knew he was getting bigger. With every reason for furtiveness, he returned to his apartment in Brooklyn to get his medium-weight set of clothes (medium referring to Burl's weight, not the fabric's). His weight had fluctuated enough—and his tastes were traditional enough—that he just kept several sets of garments, each tailored to a different Burl. big, very big, enormously big, and so on. The suits and shirts were made in Hong Kong and entailed surcharges for extra material and postage.

It wasn't just the clothes. His movements were slower. Bathing was becoming more difficult. His neck seemed on the verge of extinction, replaced by what looked like an incipient goiter mottled in red and white. Capillaries began to define themselves. He was always wet. People were beginning to take notice. He found ways to decline movie invitations from Norma, and since meals together were still somewhat taboo, they saw less of each other.

"are u avoiding me" she asked.

It took him a long time to figure out something playful to message back.

"Don't be silly. Where does a guy like me hide?"

She came by his desk to say hello now and then, and he could see her jaw muscles tighten—imagine such a thing being visible, instead of larded with fat!—and her face set in guilty sadness. She looked old and distinctly mortal at such times. It made him feel awful; he was sure he had triggered all this just by eating, and thus had splashed graffiti on his own worshiped idol. He felt such a failure.

But what is to be done? Burl wondered, thinking of Lenin. It was his own collectivization he was carrying out, with a ruthlessness of which the conscious mind wasn't capable. This came from somewhere else, the depths of the soul or the gene pool, an inner impulse little understood but in command, its secret police cruel and irresistible.

Burl grew and grew. Once a kind of light heavyweight, quick on his feet and quiet as he moved through the world, he now felt the air itself impede him. His cocky walk was replaced by a labored roll, a hurtling rather than a gliding when he had no choice but to walk somewhere, his arms held out from his sides in grotesque parody of a big-screen gunslinger, except the look on his face was not that of a hunter but of some prey. Every step was painful. His skin and clothes chafed, and he was sure people were looking. The fatter he got, the faster he tried to move. He began to look like a man rushing to meet a curfew or, moved by sirens, fleeing to avoid an impending air raid.

What did he make of this while it was happening? Ashamed, he withdrew. Secretly, though, he was relieved. Surrounded snugly by himself, sheltered, exempt from his unessential obligations, Burl felt cosseted and secure. His own amplitude began to seem voluptuous to him. He washed more carefully, lovingly soaping the folds of his flesh, its vibrant precipices and curves. Betty and Stu had a "California" bathroom that came with an extra-large whirlpool bath, and Burl took to spending hours in it, seduced by his buoyancy in this other medium. Fat floats. He was no good at land sports but swam like a seal. He was big enough now that he need only run the bath a quarter full; he displaced so much water the level rose right to the rim as soon as he sat down. He made further trips to Brooklyn to fetch ever-larger clothes. He stopped using shoelaces.

In the tub he read literature from the Fat People's Defense Council, or catalogs with names like *Mr. Big*, selling products specially designed for the fat: Desk fans. Remote controls. Reaching tools. Extra-large hangers. A two-foot shoehorn.

Water churning, Burl surfaced like a submarine, in a cascade that drenched everything around him. He dried himself cautiously—a fall here would be disastrous—and then applied deodorant, first under his arms and then in all the major folds. He flapped around a little to let this dry, and when he felt ready, dredged himself in cornstarch. A myth that fat people are insensitive: with all this skin, Burl had more sensors pointed at the world than most people, and no one's flesh could be softer. Imagine the lucky cannibals who might catch me for their dinner, he thought. Long pig, isn't that the name? What more fitting way for me to go? But do not eat my cowardly heart, for courage then will leave you. Try and *find* my heart. Nestled in whiteness, canned in lard. How nice the world had been before we invented cholesterol.

Dressing was not a project, just a pain. He would drop a pair of clean underwear on the floor and, leaning against a hollow wall, step into it. Then he'd pull the elastic, a small lasso, up to within reach using the hooked handle of a furled umbrella. Pants went on about the same way, except sitting down. He'd hook one of the huge front pockets—what did they think fat men carried? —and then stand up, the pants rising with him. Sadly, propriety forced him to abandon—for now, only for now—his beloved neckties, which were ridiculous on a man who looked like a horny frog, his neck puffed with desire. It's hard to be formal when you're fat.

Socks, of course, were the hardest, until he got a contraption from one of his catalogues that made it possible, if no less embarrassing, to abolish his huge, bare ankles. Shoes were relatively easy. Burl just stepped into these, and moved his feet around until they were firmly on.

He stood with a sigh. How exhausting! Perhaps a snack, to revive himself. He lumbered down the treacherously carpeted stairs, breathing heavily. Peeking into the kitchen, he saw his mother embalming a series of foodstuffs in layer upon layer of Saran Wrap.

"I made you a lunch for tonight," Betty said. "It's all good stuff, all very fresh."

It would be largely cruciferous, he knew. Cabbage. Broccoli. Probably carrot sticks and celery as well.

"I've even included a treat," she said, with a smile that would have to be called brave.

It would be an orange, a pear, maybe a banana. Of the lot, the only thing he would eat. He must carry this brown bag like an emblem of sin, or an amulet against his own peculiar lust. Sooner or later, covertly, he would throw it away. Meanwhile it must be borne.

He toted the bag upstairs, where he went to retrieve his briefcase. He wasn't due at work yet, but it was time to go. In his bedroom, he decided to open his briefcase to make sure he had everything, and so tucked the paper sack under his chin. It promptly fell to the floor. Damn! She should have hung the thing around my neck, Burl thought as he struggled to pick it up. Bending was now impossible, he saw; he was really quite a large operation balanced on a pair of size 10 triple-Es. Just a little more. He was huffing badly, and his face was mottled and shiny with sweat, which he felt also coursing down his flanks and in his folds. Just as it seemed within reach, he heard a loud tearing sound and knew his pants had split. Son of a bitch! Furiously, he kicked the bag under his bed, closed the door, and began the arduous process of changing clothes.

Burl was now wearing his largest, and even these massive gabardines and flowing worsteds strained to hold him. It began to dawn, as he struggled damply into a new pair of pants, his shirt drenched, his bath already pointless, that he was now as big as he had ever been. He sat down from the exertion, breathing heavily. His chest was massive, and it heaved as he gulped for air. *As big as I have ever been.* A surfeit of Burl. Amplitude upon amplitude, yet the more there was, the harder he found it to manifest himself. Thrift upon thrift, the body husbanding itself so efficiently that its savings, its very stores of energy, make it harder and harder to spend from its reserves, until this miserly fanaticism, paid in pound upon pound of flesh, makes any effort at all unlikely. Burl felt himself silent partner to some mad banker. Maybe he could find an anorexic who needed a loan.

BURL FINISHED HIS SHIFT and dined temper-
ately in the cafeteria, where the food wasn't good enough to eat
for three anyway. After dinner, on the way home, he drove downtown for a nightcap at one of his favorite places, in the West 20s.
Emerging well oiled an hour later, he was approached on the way
to his car by a soberly dressed man in a porkpie hat.

"You Burl Bennett?"

"Who are you?" Burl felt he had seen this man before.

"The Grim Reaper."

The Reaper stared for a moment, smiling, and Burl felt his
bowels beginning to liquefy. The mango mauler! The subway
chaser! The Reaper pointed thumb and forefinger like a gun.

"Bang." He blew across the top of his finger, his breath on Burl
like garbage in summer. "You're dead."

The man made a clicking sound with the side of his mouth,
poking his finger-gun into Burl's flab.

"Be smart, big man. We know all about you."

He walked off with a swagger, got into a large, night-colored
car, and sped away.

"It's intimidating a witness," Burl said into the phone the following morning. "How long do I have to put up with this?"

"We'll nail 'em any day now, you'll see," Shields said. "Just do me one favor, keep this stuff out of the paper. We don't want anything that might jeopardize our case."

"Okay, but if I drop dead of a heart attack it won't help, so let's get a move on here, huh?"

The Reaper's admonition made his skin crawl. That night Burl went over to a Thai place where he'd come to know the owner, and had them make up a few things for him. He ate ground pork mixed with onion, garlic, mint, hot pepper, lime juice, and cilantro; thin-sliced cucumbers in rice vinegar; a kind of jumbo-shrimp curry with avocado, coconut milk, and peanuts; and octopus with noodles in a rich coriander sauce. On the way home he stopped for a little whiskey at an Irish bar he knew downtown and couldn't resist the bacon cheeseburger, juicy and good because they added fat to their ground meat, with a side order of the onion rings cooked brown and crisp in lard. Still in the mood, he stopped at another place afterward and ate three slices of creamy, sweet lime pie, each melting in his mouth with the consistency of flan.

Burl felt a little woozy after all this, and without thinking very much drove over the Brooklyn Bridge and cruised gingerly past his apartment building. He circled the block a couple of times and then parked in a space mysteriously open right in front of the building.

Upstairs, wheezing, he gathered up clothes by the armful. The apartment felt musty and unused, its air heavy and rank. It was amazing how quickly dust settled. From a desk drawer, Burl grabbed his passport, checkbook, a couple thousand dollars in loose cash and a few dozen credit cards that were too bulky to carry all the time. Stuffing these in his pockets, he seized his typewriter and lumbered back down to the car. When he'd shoved everything in back, he decided that he was attached to the place seriously enough to ape the forms of sentiment, even if he was nauseated from food and exertion and had no real interest in a lingering last look. He knew that if he were going to die it would happen in those extra seconds taken for no good reason, and so it was irresistible to spend them. He went back and looked around. He wasn't considering the long term, but the silence of the place insisted somehow that he think beyond the next 15 minutes. Burl trudged back to the car and returned with the type-writer, which he uncovered and replaced on his desk. Then he went from room to room, systematically ransacking the place.

He was tentative about it at first, respectful of his own things and whatever they represented, but it goes fast when you're not looking for anything, and gradually he became freer, until before long he was tossing papers wildly about, cushions were thrown across the room, every cabinet and drawer was open or pulled out and cast to the floor, and the disarray began to seem authentic. He swept the tops of tables, sending clocks and radios flying as far as their electrical tethers would take them until they landed with a plastic crack on the floor. *Mustn't be too noisy.* Stumbling through the debris to the bookshelves, Burl shoved a thick arm behind each row and pulled the volumes down. After only a sec-ond's hesitation, he did likewise with his own manuscripts, his own published works, and even, finally, the unfinished epic into which he'd poured so much effort. That called for a drink, and Burl took down a bottle of Irish whiskey that stood undisturbed on a shelf. After a healthy swig he tossed it into the corner, where it landed softly on a sofa cushion. In the kitchen, he opened all the cabinets and drawers and pulled out pots, pans, and utensils. He emptied the refrigerator shelves onto the floor. He worked faster and faster until finally he stopped, sweating and exhausted, his life a shambles around him. Burl stood for a minute, trying to compose himself. When he reached for the doorknob he was trembling. Outside, he closed the door meekly and wondered if he should turn the lock. Of course.

He drove quickly, his foot heavy on the gas. There is a diner on the lower West Side, among the tunnels and warehouses and tattered remains of the elevated railway, and when Burl slipped into a parking space outside he could taste the salty breeze of the Hudson River, which lay before him. It had the flavor of a voyage.

"Three regular coffees, please."

Without responding, the exhausted-looking Greek behind the counter filled three blue containers decorated with amphorae, columns, and discus throwers. The counterman, dressed entirely in white, walked to the cash register and rang up the sale.

"One eighty."

My ideal weight, Burl thought. He took his bagful of coffee out to the car, pried open one of the containers, and began to drink as he gazed west through the windshield across the shiny river. The coffee was very hot and sweet, the way he liked it, and he began to feel rejuvenated as the land across the way gradually grew light. He wasn't sleepy but he was tired, and he had all the signs of not having slept. His flaccid cheeks bore stubble, and he wasn't sure he was looking at things entirely rationally. His stomach growled. Burl drank almost to the dregs and then replaced the lid, tossing the empty container onto the floor of the car. Taking up the next one, he carefully tore a small opening into the plastic lid, just enough to sip through, and then backed away. He wanted to be far from the city by the time rush hour got serious. There was a cassette sticking out of the tape deck, and without looking, he pushed it in. It was the Motels.

Emerging from the Lincoln Tunnel, he could see the cars already backed up to get into the city and a stampede of buses hurrying toward him in the special lane on his side of the barrier. Burl leaned left against the centripetal force as he ascended the giant helix that enabled traffic to close a huge vertical space in a little horizontal one. When he saw it from below it made him think of Crick and Watson, so that driving it was like spinning out of one's own genetic material, rising up from it onto a plane of purest possibility. The roadway seemed dirty and clouded with exhaust, but as it curved he could see the darkened skyline back-lit by the dawn, and it moved him.

What difference did it make, what he was doing? A few people might care, for a little while, but life goes on. A sea of cars waited at the tunnel, their headlights still lit, as he accelerated into the straightaway. He moved into the left, the lane right next to the on-coming buses, whose path was delineated only by some flexible rubber markers. Burl loved this, loved the accentuated sense of movement it gave to .eel their speed next to your own. When the roadway met the New Jersey Turnpike, he headed south. The air was chilly when he rolled down his window to take a toll ticket. The sun was almost up, and on the Turnpike everything was mo-tion. Cars, buses, and trucks sped along several elevated spans, while overhead a jet pulled itself aloft from Newark Airport. Steam rose from a distant power plant. Commuter trains moved almost out of sight, lit cozily from within. The highway straightened and Burl opened a new container of coffee, holding the wheel with his stomach while he tore at the lid. It wasn't as hot now; he gulped quickly, spilling a little on his shirt, and adjusted himself in his seat. He was glad when the roadway bifurcated and trucks were segregated from cars. He kept the speedometer on 75, where he was comfortable, and didn't even bother looking for state troopers until suddenly it came to him that traffic citations, to someone with a computer, were as breadcumbs left by Hansel and Gretel. He slowed to about 70, the same rate as everybody else.

"Shame on you!" the Motels sang. *"Shame on me! Shame on every little thing that we see!"*

Elizabeth, up ahead, looked quaint and foreign with its bricks and treetops and church spires, like someplace in the Midwest or Scandinavia, someplace that didn't get much sun. Burl imagined it a provincial city in the Ruhr Valley, a Hanseatic port, or like-lier still, a community founded by nineteenth-century utopians in upstate New York in which, today, the young people always move away. Elizabeth. Never before had it seemed so filled with prom-ise. Imagine what must lie ahead.

Coffee and sleeplessness had this effect on Burl. He became emotional, saw poetry everywhere. But he didn't stop. He didn't even pull over until he was good and hungry, and by that time he was in Delaware. Outside of Wilmington, he stopped in a pricey-looking shopping mall and, within, moved toward the illuminated directory with a certain delight. The place had just opened for the day and was virtually empty. A few people were looking, he knew, but nobody could possibly know him here, and it was good to get out of the car, get that steering wheel out of his midsection. He felt lightheaded and a little unsteady on his feet, as if he'd been out fishing since dawn. On the escalator, he surveyed the atrium at the center of the building with satisfaction, and on the upper level he took pleasure in the texture of the fake brickwork under-foot. Welcoming. That's what this mall is, Burl thought. In the bookstore he couldn't resist a cursory check for some of his own works and happily took down the dog book, smiling like a cus-tomer with a beloved German shepherd at home. But what he re-ally wanted was a guidebook; he bought three, after assuring him-self that each gave proper attention to the nation's culinary dimension.

He sat down on an ornate wooden bench at the bottom of the mall to study his guidebooks. Before him a glass elevator rose and fell with stately ease, and potted spathyphylum sprang up unnaturally green all around. Water burbled somewhere. Thumbing through the first volume, wondering what life was like in Alabama—did it ever get cold? did they wear sweat-stained Palm Beach suits in summer, with straw boaters?—Burl realized to his increased stupefaction that he had no idea where he was going. He looked around. The young woman at the information desk drummed her long red fingernails against the glittering counter and stared off into mall-space. Burl continued thumbing until his eye was caught by an extraordinary-sounding restaurant near Salt Lake City called the Holy Grail, and as he read about the radicchio and terrines, the coullibiac and berried fishes, it struck him that this was the Smithian journey he had always hoped to find time to re-create. Thanks to Joey Gem, Burl was at last following in the footsteps of his own protagonist. He would re-create the flight of Joseph, more or less, then take up the path of Joseph's successor and carry on, like Brigham Young and all the rest, into Utah. Looking down at his book, Burl decided he might as well head for the restaurant.

It was a long way off, of course, and in the interim there must be food, drink, and rest. He would drive a while longer—it would be depressing to hole up in a motel too early in the day—and then have a good meal and a good night's sleep. The mall he was in turned out to have three levels, its top consisting of a Food Court boasting "Snacks and Delicacies from the Four Corners of the Globe." Could I be indicted in the Food Court? Burl wondered. Did they deal harshly with culinary offenders in this state? If I were well connected, might I make judge?

The mall wasn't crowded, so Burl decided to chance the glass elevator. The only others waiting were a young mother with a baby in a stroller and a little girl holding on.

"Mommy, look at—"

"Shhh."

Burl blushed.

"But—"

"Be quiet, now, we're going up to Chuck E. Cheese, so just be patient."

Burl smiled. Emerging onto the upper level, he surveyed the Food Court for signs of promise. A couple dozen restaurants, snack bars, and fast-food joints fanned out on opposite sides of an eight-screen movie complex. Burl strolled around the atrium— quite a drop, this—and was pleased to discover a Japanese restaurant. Passing through the flags that hung from the lintel, his suspicions—that this was a real restaurant stuck amid merchandisers of comestibles—were confirmed. He was delighted. There was no one else at the sushi bar, and the magouro looked fresh. The place was just opening for the day.

Burl fared well at sushi bars, as long as they weren't crowded. The Japanese tend to be polite, and at least they have sumo wrestlers. In this case, the sushi master soon realized he was in the presence of an aficionado. He worked hard, preparing elaborate concoctions of pickled cabbage, diced mackerel, cucumber, seaweed, rice, and so forth, and Burl bought him a beer. The experience was only marred when, as one of the things the chef provided such a valued customer for free, he presented a couple of squares of cold egg sushi, which Burl always found revolting. Smiling grimly, he ate them anyway.

He went forth from the mall, an ice-cream cone his scepter, to see firsthand how the latter-day saints had come to be. His agenda was to follow the route of the Mormons west, soaking up ambiance as he went, but his truer self approached the country much as he might a giant deli counter, tasting wherever his fancy led him as long as he covered the bases Smith had covered.

Burl had been to Sharon, the White River Valley town in central Vermont that had been Smith's birthplace, and so instead he drove for upstate New York, traversing the state's southern tier to reach Manchester and Palmyra, where Smith, who had gotten into trouble before for claiming mysterious treasure-hunting powers, finally discovered gold. He saw the clearing in the grove where the Father and the Son were supposed to have revealed themselves to Smith in 1820, and he saw the monument to the angel Moroni on the crest of the hill outside Palmyra, where Smith said he found the gold plates that contained the Book of Mormon. Except for the sprawl around Canandaigua, it wasn't hard to picture the area as it must have been when western New York was still the frontier.

He got the hang of long-distance driving, so that 300 miles soon came to seem nothing, and he was thankful that he wasn't Dutch or Sri Lankan but was born instead in this sprawling, unfathomable place where you could drive hundreds of miles daily and live a life of green interstate signs with rounded corners and beaded lettering, a place so enormous and incomprehensible to itself that it could absorb anything. Burl felt it consuming him, as he got out into the great unknown center of the place, just as he seemed bent on consuming it. He tried hard, eating six or seven meals a day and always between them in the car, so that really he ate continuously, and to distinguish one meal from another required only a sense of geography, which he did not have. It was a large undertaking; he was like Thor, trying to drain the ocean in a single draft and doing a creditable job, given the circumstances. Except for the coullibiac and berried fishes, the 50,000 bottles in the wine cellar, and the waterside setting, he felt no great tug from his destination and so decided to take his time. America was a great place to get lost in, and in any case to stop would have raised a host of unsettling questions that, like most important queries, could have no real answer. Dissembling would be required. An approximation of everyday life would have to be arranged and time's insistence (like that of a little child, with its constant needs) satisfied. The pull of the quotidian would be like an undertow. He'd have to buy a couch.

It was much, much easier to drive. Through the wintry heartland he made his way across Indiana and Illinois, ignoring the bigger cities and passing instead through Ft. Wayne and Peoria and Galesburg, skipping the Tippecanoe Battlefield and the Wyatt Earp birthplace and moving with determination until finally he reached the Mississippi and turned south, where he followed the old road on the Illinois side to Nauvoo.

The town smelled of cheese. Burl pegged it as a blue of some kind, and learned that it was made in abundance at Nauvoo and stored in some of the large wine cellars built by Swiss, German, and French settlers and converted during Prohibition. He wandered amid the old brick homes, with their low windows and broad lawns, and tried to imagine a time when the scale of life was so much smaller. About 20 miles east—how long was the trip in those days? he wondered, gunning past the rows of corn and soybeans—he went in some awe to the Carthage Jail, a tiny structure of yellow limestone where Smith met his end. Burl had to pass through the narrow doorway sideways, and peering into the second-floor room in which Joseph and his brother Hyrum were felled by musketballs, he thought it seemed tiny. There had been threats, violence; Smith and his followers probably had some idea they were in for trouble. Much of it they had stirred up themselves. But Smith by then must have been the person he'd striven to become, the prophet and organizer of a great fraternity, with a bureaucracy and secrets and its own private militia, all of it existing in the name of God but answering to him, proof of how easily faith can generate its own truth.

Burl wondered if a lack of faith might be his problem on the epic front. Calculatedly, he had left what there was of the manuscript back in his ransacked apartment and now wondered with equanimity if he might ever return to it in any sense of the term. This question had been in his mind even as he followed Smith's trail, but the journey had by then become something to do for its own sake, apart from any literary ventures. Maybe what was needed, he began to think, was a different way at the story, an approach less literal, the invention of some other, latter-day Joseph Smith of the kind heading cultlike organizations all over America nowadays. Any of these groups could be the Mormons of tomorrow. Who knew, perhaps he would write it as a novel. Think of Elmer Gantry. Or perhaps Shields had been right. Perhaps he should write it as an opera. It was the least of his worries for now.

After Carthage, driving became hypnotic for Burl, the spiritual equivalent of food. He wasn't much interested in the rest of the Midwest and needed to feel he was moving in the right direction, so he drove fast through the flat central states, conducting along the way an informal survey of the nation's hamburgers. At a place called Mom's—he couldn't resist—the beef was so rich and smoky from the grill it was like meaty chocolate, and Burl ate four double cheeseburgers there, rare, each with a fizzy lime sort of drink that was described as a local specialty. The girl behind the counter was polite but nervous, her great Saxon jaw muscles bulging as she worked over a wad of chewing gum.

"Have the next one with fried onions, if you like. They're the sweet kind, and she cooks 'em in real butter."

"Mmmm, you're on."

"'Nother double?"

Burl nodded blissfully, the little knob of his chin disappearing into the mass of his fleshy neck. There was grease at the corner of his mouth, and a little ketchup. Her gum chewing made him wonder if some vestigial impulse was at work in this young girl. Had her ancestors masticated venison until it was fit for a baby's gums? He imagined that she was selected for child bearing and tried to see if she had broad hips.

When in doubt, Burl discovered, the safest food in the American heartland was pie. There was good pie everywhere, with or without ice cream. It always seemed homemade, its sweetness unabashed, its flavor intense. All through southern Illinois Burl ate cherry pie, once almost cracking a tooth on a pit in a diner with a sign that said, "Real Cherries! Watch for Pits!" It was lost amid the other signs; one showed a drawing of a coffee cup, curving lines rising from it to indicate steam. "Try our Coffee!" it said, and underneath: "We Brew it Fresh!" He wondered what it might be like to be accustomed to such a community, to feel it as familiar as he felt the streets of New York to be, their texture satisfying, almost subconscious, like a familiar song on the car radio.

The desert took him by surprise, a great unanswered question not nearly as hot as he expected, but emptier, scrubbier, without the dunes Lawrence of Arabia and Laurel and Hardy had scampered across. For miles around the only interpretable mark was the highway, and in the distance were always mountains, their shapes and colors shifting with his progress, and the sun's. He wasn't ready yet for his destination—the Mormons had taken months, some of them, dragging handcarts all the way—and he felt there was a side of Smith that wasn't much understood by his descendants, a hustler side that Burl wanted to know better too. He was in Arizona, wandering now, well past his ostensible target, when the Dodge started seriously burning oil.

"None?"

"See for yourself," the kid said, offering a gleaming dipstick.

"These rings are done, mister," the mechanic said a little while later, as if the pistons had fallen from grace and lost their halos. He had magnificent gray sideburns flecked with dirt and a face lined with grime that didn't look as if it came out with a shower. He might be a coal miner. You could count his pores.

"Will it get me to Salt Lake?"

"If you keep a bunch of oil in the trunk."

Burl cursed the name of Gemignani. The Checker would never have dribbled its lifeblood away so carelessly. Burl decided he would give the poor devil a rest in Las Vegas, where he'd been hoping his travels would lead him. Besides, he was running out of cash and was loathe to use credit cards for fear of giving himself away. This was a hard habit to break, but he was determined. Vegas beckoned like a giant bank. Burl was a disciplined card player and resolved to play only with the cash he'd taken from the drawer at home. The main thing was to avoid Circus Circus, where he was always afraid someone might mistake him for a part of the show.

Arriving at night, the Dodge's air conditioner faltering ominously even in the cool evening air, he had trouble finding a room until finally he checked wearily into Spengler's Alcazar, an elaborately skewed postmodernist wedding cake a block off the strip. Lit narcissistically from the perimeter of its lot to show off its angles and aspects even at night, it tried to appeal to a new generation of gamblers with black-and-white advertising and Gershwinesque music. The Alcazar dressed up its tawdry mission in good taste. The hostesses wore little, but it wasn't polyester, and there was a vegetarian restaurant off the lobby. Fortunately for Burl, young sophisticates proved immune and the effort backfired. The Alcazar's real target audience thought the Strip hotels were campy and fun, while the toupee and Sansabelt crowd considered

Spengler's the height of sophistication. As a result, there were plenty of fat people around, and Burl felt comfortably at home.

His arrival was always bad news for the gaming industry. Burl had all the wrong appetites. With his heavy-lidded eyes and expressionless wattles, his face was impossible to read, and in five patient days he managed to accumulate nearly $10,000 playing twenty-one with just a $1,500 stake, walking away from each session in the middle of a streak that might have led lesser men to ruin. Greed had no hold on Burl, and besides, he couldn't resist the buffets, where he gave new meaning to the phrase "all you can eat." Sometimes he would go twice for dinner, once when the buffet opened and again just as it was closing. Or he would stay through the dinner hour, reading Richard Wilbur or Emily Dickinson between courses the way some people take sorbet. The food was good too, although it made him wonder if there was some animal unique to Nevada that provided the ubiquitous electric-red "prime rib," which he never saw in quite the same form anywhere else. The men in toques behind the counter were accommodating, and to save everyone a lot of trouble served Burl three or four pieces at a time. Lunches were best. He would sack the buffet and then stumble back to his room, change into tentlike bathing trunks, and go out to the pool. There he would ease himself into a lounge chair (steady, steady—it was embarrassing when they collapsed) and sprawl immobile like some beached walrus or human solar panel, acres of epidermal cells supine beneath the desert sun. Burl was pale as well as vast, and he ran through half a bottle of suntan lotion each time he lay out in the sun. The sweat poured off in rivulets, leaving a shaded puddle all around him. People sometimes splashed in it, assuming it was from the pool.

Burl was comfortable in Las Vegas. Freaks can find a home there, and he considered staying. The weather was nice, the food plentiful, his plush room cheap and air conditioned. He could come and go without exciting too much fuss. In the parking lot one night he gave $100 to an old woman trying to sell him a ring. "One-and-a-half-carat diamond, you can see for yourself, 24-karat gold band." Tugging at his sleeve, gaptoothed, cronelike, she was on the verge of hysteria. "It was my wedding ring, you know? But I gotta have the money. What am I gonna do?" Burl winced. Would it be worse if this were true or false? "Keep the ring," he urged. At the hotel newsstand he picked up a copy of *The Tribune* for the first time since leaving New York and read it with pleasure. He even noticed a Whitney among the wedding notices. Like the ghoul pool—in which bets were made on which figure from the advance-obituary list would die first—counting Whitneys had been one of Burl's favorite pastimes. You'd bet on the number for the month of June, say, or the entire year. Last year the number of Whitneys whose nuptials were noted by *The Tribune* got up above two dozen; toward Christmas the Whitney watch became a big deal around the office. Burl was almost nostalgic. But he was satisfied to see nothing of himself in the paper.

He even learned to say Nevada properly, like a New Yorker saying "she *budda*." But buffets get boring, and he began to feel unsettled by the cynicism of the place, its naked appeal to avarice, ego, and lust. Vegas was an extraordinary city, but it managed to make human appetites uninteresting. After a while Burl wasn't even very hungry. In his hotel room, on his final night, he wished for Norma, and then for the nerve to use some of his newfound riches to pay a woman for sex, even if he knew it wasn't in his nature. What would a prostitute say when such a man opened the door? Perhaps they've seen everything. But the whole idea seemed pathetic, like paying for your own birthday party, and with a sigh he tossed a bit and finally fell asleep.

In the morning he drove northeast, wandering through the orange deserts and black mountains, saving his great restaurant for

later the way sometimes, eating spaghetti as a boy, he would segregate his meatballs and keep them for last. Even away from Las
Vegas, Nevada was a big, bleary reprobate of a state, its base di-
versions thrown into high relief against the general topographic
emptiness as if someone had blasted a Mt. Rushmore of naked
women and slot machines, lit at night with lamps powered by
Hoover Dam. Burl stopped for sustenance in Dry Wells, a collection of mangy trailers surrounding a couple of saloons and a legal
whorehouse.

His skin felt strange, excessively smooth or without pores.
The bar was raw but friendly, its walls covered with baseball caps
sporting the names of fertilizer companies and tractor makers, interspersed with bumper stickers saying things like "Shit Happens,"
or "Make My Day" under the barrel of an outsized handgun.

"Let me have a couple of drafts."

"You want both of 'em now?"

"Yeah, it's better that way."

Burl inhaled the beers and signaled for two more. This time
the bartender stood by, watching unabashedly. Feeling better already, Burl did it again. The bartender was impressed.

"Next pair's on me," he said.

"Thanks, but I'm just gonna sip these, if that's okay."

"Take your time."

Looking around without moving too much, Burl could see that
the place was really a trailer, or perhaps two trailers, and that Dry
Wells had a unique sort of architectural consistency, like those
New England villages with white-paint laws. He shifted gingerly
on his stool, testing. Stools were usually stronger than chairs but
less comfortable. He pulled another one closer and, with some relief, sat himself on both.

A muscular older man in a white T-shirt and khakis sat
down next to Burl and ordered a soft drink and cigarettes in an

odd, old-world accent. He smoked voraciously, until he was surrounded by stinging haze. Burl was lonely and intrigued. The beers, inhaled so fast, made him forward.

"Where you from?" he asked, stifling a cough.

"New York," the man said quietly, with only a sideways glance.

"New York? I'm from New York!"

The man raised his eyebrows briefly, out of politeness.

"But where are you from originally?"

"Poland." He looked startled and shrugged. "I'm Polish."

"What are you doing out here?"

The man smiled a little.

"I got some business out here."

Suddenly Burl's stomach began to flutter. He felt his heart racing. The old guy looked scarred and tough, with fingers like swollen frankfurters, thick arms, and no fat under his spotless T-shirt. His left thumb seemed flattened at the top, as if he might have been using it for a ball-peen hammer. He gave the impression of a walking callus. Would the name Gemignani mean anything to this man? Just what "business" was he in? Perhaps it was time to go, change directions, zigzag.

The man's story, when it emerged, was stranger than Burl's. He was a survivor of Hitler's camps, with a scar on his right forearm where the numbers had been until he grew tired of them and had them cut out. His family was wiped out, his wife was newly dead, and he had no children. He lived alone in a trailer in the middle of nowhere—Dry Wells was downtown for this guy—and kept his own counsel. In the desert, he was mining plutonium or uranium or some other mysterious metal, for rather mysterious purposes. He was passionately convinced that God had given the Jews the land of Israel—all of it—but only after the trials they'd had to suffer first.

"I shed blood in the Holy Land. I got 400 acres of desert when I was shot in the War of Independence."

"Four hundred acres?"

"Of desert. I was wounded. Here." He slapped a hard thigh. "Bartender." With a knobby hand, the man pushed his money forward and pointed aggressively at Burl's place. "For my friend. Whatever."

Burl got two more yellow brews, glasses sweating onto the bar.

"What do you do out here for fun?"

"Read. I read a lot."

Burl wondered if this anchorite was a harbinger. Perhaps Burl would stay here in the desert too, reading, thinking, living a life uncluttered and unencumbered. Uninterrupted.

"Did you—have your experiences affected your beliefs? Do you believe in God?"

"Sure. Absolutely. *Tohu va'vohu.* Chaos and desolation, like in Genesis. Only I lived through it."

"Do you ever wonder why He does these things?"

"He doesn't do these things," said the man, smiling through his gray mustache and quaint-sounding accent. "We do them."

"But he allows it. He lets people do these things."

"Yes, well, but it's up to us."

"To whom? And why does he let them do this to his chosen people? Who says the Jews have to suffer so much?"

"Because we didn't obey him." Silence, and a sip of soda. "Look what happened with Moses. As soon as they got out of Egypt, they had the golden calf."

"Obedience always seems to be a godly demand. How did that get started, I wonder?"

"He's the Father, that's why. For the rest of you. For us, we made a deal. There was a contract."

"I don't see Him that way." Burl gulped some beer. "I think of Him as a dead composer of music to which we all must dance, even when we won't dance, even when we can't dance. His works are enigmatic, atonal, or maybe they only seem atonal because we can't hear the melody. They're infinitely complex but ultimately self-absorbed, even narcissistic. Art for art's sake, except for His sense of irony toward posterity, His sense of humor—"

"Vicious it must have been."

"—in making the dancers self-conscious. By getting them to spend all their best efforts trying to understand the music, He's won a kind of worship He never could have wrested any other way. That's what an angel is, by the way: one who understands." Burl drained one of his glasses. "But I don't believe in angels, and I can't pretend to comprehend His music. Just hearing it seems to me an accomplishment. At the heart is always mystery."

"For you maybe. Depends what you expect. Depends even who you are."

Pushing north, Burl drove up into the magical state of Utah, which he entered toward the end of day. The sun was near the horizon, and the ferrous rocks around St. George glowed prime-rib red and Play-Doh purple. He passed through Zion National Park at night, sensing only the outlines of its lunar formations, but was flabbergasted during the day when he stopped at Bryce Canyon, which he considered a revelation, the most beautiful thing he had ever seen. He passed through little towns with names like Manti, strung along U.S. 89 like silent little havens of camaraderie and oppression, and drove through miles and miles of picturesque farms and undulant meadows backed by snow-capped peaks.

Despite Mormon fecundity, there was open space everywhere. In the glassy clear air, which seemed as if God himself had scrubbed it with ammonia, huge vistas stretched extravagantly in all directions, and the sun's progress over the course of a day, along with Burl's own steady movement, made for an infinite variety of lighting and color. New York seemed so rainy and ragged by comparison, so hopelessly muddled and sunk in human arrangement. Burl felt he might have stumbled into paradise.

He didn't realize until he arrived in Salt Lake City that he'd failed to add any extra oil—"Ten dubya forty, thirty weight, it don't matter," the man had said—and hadn't even checked the dipstick since leaving Las Vegas. Miraculously, the mark was right between the lines. Somehow the car had stopped hemorrhaging, and whatever was in the engine had lasted the whole time.

LEGENDARILY, BRIGHAM YOUNG was drawn by the seagulls.

"This is the right place," he supposedly said on July 24, 1847, when he first saw the Great Salt Lake and the radiant, mountain-ringed patch of desert that would become his home. In the grip of a powerful idea, the saints had arrived by horse and by handcart from as far away as Europe, many of them dying in the open spaces far short of their destination. Burl had never been to Utah before but was taken with the strange, sober, scrubbed little metropolis right off. It was large enough to get lost in but small enough to feel comfortable, if you already felt like a space alien, and remote from anyplace else of note. Unlike Brigham Young, he arrived in winter, when the air was clean and bright, and was struck by the plainspokenness of folks, their straight-ahead, firm-handshake, look-you-in-the-eye manner, and their loopy religion. He couldn't imagine anyplace more different from home.

When he first arrived, Burl went about leading a relatively normal life, considering that he was hiding in a motel room 2,000 miles from home in a city where he knew no one. Outside, the days had a fairy-tale clarity that was painful. Salt Lake City struck him as a place with a halo over it; there was a celestial quality about the very air, so that the mountains and buildings seemed lit by a divine light which gave credence to the wacky claims of the proselytizing Mormons whom Burl was always delighted to meet on his rare excursions from the Chrysalis Motor Lodge on the edge of downtown (where he had had to accustom himself to mirrors, not just in the bathroom but on the ceiling). He met them often at first, because he couldn't immediately figure out the city's bizarre grid system and so kept having to return to what is literally, in Salt Lake, square one, the grand temple at the center of town.

Burl emerged from the Chrysalis occasionally to drive a couple of miles west, over a viaduct that reminded him of the Brooklyn-Queens Expressway, and then north, in order to do his laundry, which would accumulate on the floor of the closet until finally he hauled it out and sat it on the vinyl bench seat of the Dodge, reminding himself every time he did so that he must get another car. The dirty clothes sat next to him like a stack of molted skin.

He was surprised at first. Salt Lake City seemed homogeneously filled with fair, fit-looking people of Anglo-Saxon origins, but the laundromat was in a neighborhood occupied mainly by short, stocky immigrants with jet-black curls and, under the fluorescent lights, faintly purple skin. Like the poor almost everywhere, there was a diffidence about them that was perhaps exaggerated in the laundromat, where, like Burl, they were wearing their very last and least likely clean clothes. Sartorially, it was a journey back in time. Burl's fellow patrons wore, besides the glassy look of late-night laundering, form-fitting shirts in bright honeydew with big collars; "Western" shirts with diagonal plaid yokes and fake-pearl buttons, and even the odd pair of bell-bottom jeans without pockets. But for their clothes, these people were quiet, except for the young man in the dry-cleaning section, who made change.

"Hey, hey, hey," he said when Burl first approached with a five-dollar bill. Burl stood amazed as, arms straight up, the guy bowed thrice down in ostentatious worship. Burl was even more astonished to see him wearing what looked to be a knee-length skirt, bright with flowers, and a navy-blue T-shirt with a roll of bills in the breast pocket. His hair was cut short and pomaded so that it stood up in tiny needles all over his head, which as a result resembled some expensive tropical fruit.

"What a man!" he said to Burl, with what seemed genuine admiration. "Geez, you must come from kings."

"Kings County," Burl said. "Rex Bennett is the only title I can claim."

"Rex, far out." Pointing to himself, he said, "Engel."

Burl held out a massive hand, which the younger man seized and shook with surprising strength.

"Where are you from?" Burl asked.

"Where am I from? I'm from Tonga, man! Where you think?" Engel glanced from side to side. "You think I'm some kind of a Samoan or something? A Chicano?" Pointing at the floor of the laundromat. "This is Tongan turf you on now."

"Tongan turf?"

"Don't kid yourself, man, we all oppressed peoples. You already got some Tongan Crips in this town. Don't believe all that LDS bullshit you read in the papers. Mormons ain't everything around here no more, and those Latter-Day Saints ain't so saintly. Someone's buying all these drugs, right? You can't have no contract without a buyer; I had B-law."

"I need change."

"Welcome to the club, man. Quarters?"

His first name was Filipu, but to everyone, it seemed, he was just Engel. "My great-grandfather was German, the sonofabitch. All kinda people came through in those days. They acted like it was one big Gauguin with brown bimbos everywhere."

Engel was lean, sharp, angular, quick. By Tongan standards he was hopelessly American. He reminded Burl, with his babyfaced bid for toughness, of the young Chicanos he'd seen in zoot suits in '40s photographs, even though Engel made a point of wearing a traditional *tupanu*, or men's skirt, around the laundromat.

"Nobody laughed at the Romans, right? They outlawed pants. In Scotland, kilts are macho. Over here nobody wears the *tupanu*. Tongan men wore skirts because they had too much balls for pants. Pants couldn't hold them."

To Engel, that was what great girth implied. He was a wiseguy, but endearing, and Burl decided to let himself be called Rex. Why not? It might not be a good idea to use his real name too freely anyway. And it was nice to get out of the Chrysalis now and then. Engel would go eating with him, squiring Burl to extraordinary diners and favored Chinese restaurants late at night, just the two of them. He'd eat, but more than that he would revel in Burl's eating, watching with grateful awe as Burl ran through triple bacon cheeseburgers in three bites or left the waiter dumbstruck by demolishing a heaping dish of moo shu pork as if it were a petit four. They would go through an entire meal at Wasatch Mandarin, and then Burl would signal.

"That was very good. Would you ask the chef if he could do that again?"

The waiter looked confused.

"Sure, anytime. You come back?"

"No no, now." Burl looked at their waiter innocently. "Right now. Again."

Engel shaded his eyes. He could barely contain himself.

"You teasing?" the waiter pleaded. "You still hungry?"

"Well, yes. We've taken the edge off. Now we'd like a more leisurely supper. That's why we didn't want any dessert. We didn't want to spoil our appetite."

The waiter would pad off, unsure if he was being made fun of or was abetting some form of self-abuse, and the meal would be repeated. Engel was surprised at how much more he could eat around Burl, although he never seemed to gain much weight. His disappointment in this was dramatic. He regarded his leanness with the tragic sufferance a midget might have for his dwarfism, and he blamed it on his grandfather's European genes, which had deprived Engel of his rightful birthright of fat.

"You think it's a joke, man, but in our culture, big really is beautiful. *'Oku 'ikai ke kovi 'a e lahi.* Even the current nitwit, King Taufa'ahau Tupou IV, is well over 300 pounds, and he's a light-weight. The jerk-off."

"The king is 300 pounds?"

"You bet your ass," Engel cackled. "They've all been big; this guy is nothing, really. Truth is, they're getting smaller as time goes on. We've polluted the gene pool, man. And I'm a prime example. Look at me. A hundred and fifty pounds of Tongan wimp, unfit for the throne or even the royal entourage, all thanks to some old-time German sun worshiper and his taste for *zaftig* women."

Engel showed Burl the ropes in Salt Lake City. He explained the confusing street system and promised to smuggle him into one of the temples, whose worship halls were off limits to non-Mormons. Burl enjoyed the weird combination of deference and affectionate disdain showed by his self-appointed retainer and did a few food tricks in return, always fending off Engel's curiosity about his past. But mostly he tried to be a good influence. Engel tolerated his reform efforts good-naturedly and always called him Rex.

"We Tongans have an affinity for royalty," he said.

On their nightly outings, Engel explained that Tongans revere their royal family even more than the British do theirs. The islands have never been colonized, except by Christian missionaries of various stripes, and even today there are only 100,000 people in the whole place, all of them fairly closely related.

"You know what that means, right?"

"Inbreeding?" wondered Burl. "Idiocy?"

"It means we're all related to the king, asshole."

"Hell of a name for a king in any language."

"My grandmother was really close, like second cousins or something; she and her family had a place at court, and everybody hoped she might land one of the young princes—"

But love is unpredictable, and she stained the family name forever by taking up with Engel, whose moniker she defiantly adopted. The latest Engel and all who followed were condemned to wander.

Burl saw that, like all true believers, Engel was a lost soul. At once obsessed with Tonga and hopelessly removed from it, he fought assimilation with the double-edged weapons of his adopted culture. He tried to make himself listen to tapes of Tongan melodies as he drove around in a garishly clean midnight-blue Pontiac Firebird, purchased with his skimmings from the laundromat, which was owned by the Mormon church and entrusted to Engel by a local bishop who hoped oxymoronically both to exploit his obvious savvy and set him on the straight and narrow. He always started with Tongan music but sooner or later lapsed into one of the local top-40 stations. He found Madonna irresistible.

Engel lived in a small furnished apartment not far from the laundromat. He and Burl would drink beer and watch sports on the snowy color television, fiddling with the ancient rabbit ears until the picture was tolerable. Sometimes, while they were watching a game, Engel would work with the bench full of weights he kept on hand. He was slim but strong and kept trying to lift Burl, who guessed that he weighed perhaps 330 pounds by now.

"You'll give yourself a hernia. You can't even get your arms around me."

Obsessed with Burl's size, Engel would challenge him with little pokes and slaps, which Burl brushed off the way a horse might shoo a fly. Finally, once, he grabbed for Engel to teach him a lesson; Engel slipped free, circled him energetically, and they began to wrestle. Engel was quick, and it was all Burl could do to spin around and keep facing him. He tried upending Burl by attacking a leg, and using his speed to get behind him and jump on his back, but it was no use. They wrestled regularly after that, whenever Engel could provoke Burl into it, and most of the time Engel held out only by dint of his quickness and Burl's forbearance until finally Burl's overwhelming size and strength prevailed. It was exhausting for Burl, who in the car culture of the West no longer walked as much as he had in New York, but it was fun and made him feel all the more connected to his elusive subject, Joseph Smith, whose father had been a big man and a wrestler so strong that supposedly he was bested only once. Engel loved it, wrestling Burl again and again on the brown shag carpet of his living room. The outcome was always the same. Burl was too strong; Engel tried a headlock, but Burl grabbed a leg and lifted him upside down. It was true. Engel couldn't get his arms around him.

That was when they got the idea for sumo. Late at night, on public television, they watched a little of it on a Japanese news show, with two great *yokozuna*, or champions, squaring off for what seemed an eternity until the smaller of the two, grasping his opponent's heavy belt, managed to fling him out of the ring.

"That's it!" Engel shouted, leaping from his chair. "See the way that little guy beat the big one? He used the big guy's weight against him."

"Everybody's always used my weight against me," Burl said, draining his beer. "What are we gonna do, throw salt on the carpet?"

But Engel was already rooting around in the closet.

"I used to deliver supermarket fliers," he said. "We always got this great chalk. Gimme your belt."

"For what?"

"A compass."

Emerging with a piece of lilac chalk the size of a kosher pickle, Engel inserted it into Burl's belt buckle. He took a cheap pen from his pocket and gave it to Burl, who was by now standing up.

"Here, hold this end down. Use the pen, through the hole so it'll turn freely."

With Burl's enormous belt as a radius, Engel chalked out a circle in the middle of the floor, hastily nudging the furniture out of the way.

"There," he said, removing his pants. "Now strip."

"C'mon, Engel, not now. I've just had a dozen beers."

But Engel was already hopping around in the circle, and Burl knew he would have no peace until he wrestled at least once that night, sumo-style.

"Okay, Engel, but be gentle," he said with a mocking laugh. "I'm not altogether up to snuff right now."

"No excuses, big man."

They stripped down to their underwear, which they hiked up in back in imitation of the sumo wrestlers they had seen on television, and after formal bows, circled each other warily, Engel hopping from side to side looking for an opening and Burl staggering slightly in an effort to keep up. Catching the bigger man off balance, Engel rushed at Burl sideways and from behind, hustling him toward the chalk. Burl caught himself just in time, leaned back, and was about to swing his opponent around and out of bounds when Engel, realizing he must elude Burl's grasp at all costs, let go, ducked, and attacked Burl's left leg, attempting to topple him backward and out of the ring.

Burl was just too big. By now they were both grunting and sweating, Burl stalking around the circle, Engel pursuing his own brand of guerrilla warfare.

"I'll be the world's lightest *yokozuna*," he boasted.

Ducking and feinting, he dashed around behind Burl, grabbed the waistband of his massive briefs, and with his shoulder low against his back, drove him once again toward the chalk. Again Burl stopped himself in time, but when he tried to swivel around, Engel ducked. As soon as Burl's arm passed overhead, he drove his shoulder into Burl's exposed flank with all the strength of his legs, giving him a final nudge that carried him over the line.

"Aiiiiayah!" Engel shouted, in imitation of some imagined samurai. "Haaeeioh!"

"You're supposed to just bow," said Burl, whose laughter further winded him. Rivulets of sweat ran down his body. His shorts were drenched and stretched beyond recognition; leaning against a bedpost to catch his breath, he kicked them off. The workout felt good, like the air on his nakedness. Engel meanwhile gathered himself into solemnity and bowed deeply from the waist.

"Hey man, this is great! I can wrestle with you this way, it evens things out."

"You wanna even things," Burl huffed between each word, "widen that ring. Regulation is 15 feet across. You used a 60-inch belt for the radius. The smaller the ring, the better for you."

"Nuh-uh, smaller helps you, man. We ain't got room for 15 feet in this place."

Sumo wrestling became their passion. Engel would use his quickness and compact strength to tire Burl out, hit from weird angles, and avoid a clutch. Anytime Burl got hold of him, he simply lifted Engel off the ground, carried him to the perimeter, and deposited him beyond the line.

"You lose," Burl would say as soon as his opponent fell into his grasp. Engel would howl in protest, knowing the match was over.

Sometimes Burl would throw him all the way onto the bed, where he landed with a *sproing*. Engel always wanted one more match, no matter how many they'd had and no matter how often Burl defeated him, in part because his chances improved with the number of contests. Burl just got too tired to keep up. He tried simply planting himself in the center of the ring, but it was too small to avoid the perimeter altogether if Engel maneuvered him even slightly and then managed to topple him in one direction or another. This was a favorite trick of Engel's, who proved himself fairly reckless. Once Burl fell on him, not entirely but at least partially, catching himself against the ground lest he crush his opponent completely, and they still had to go to the emergency room, where Engel had a pair of broken ribs.

"We better take it easy," Burl said on the way home. "If I'd landed on your arm it'd be smashed."

"Ribs ain't bad," Engel said in some pain.

He had grand plans. He thought Burl had real sumo potential, if only he would train, and he felt there might be a market for an American sumo circuit.

"We go where all the Japanese are, you know, Los Angeles, San Francisco—"

"Ft. Lee, New Jersey," Burl added helpfully.

"—wherever. But we also try for the domestic wrestling crowd. We even lay some money, get Vegas to post the odds. I could be your manager."

"Why not league commissioner?"

"You're a wiseass, but you'll see. The idea is to get legal betting, like on jai alai in some places."

"You shoulda taken care o' me," Burl said, in a kind of samurai Marlon Brando. "I coulda been somebody. I coulda had class. Now all I got is a one-way ticket to Nagoya."

Engel's ribs were mending, and soon enough he wanted to resume wrestling. Burl missed it too but vowed to be more careful.

"Wait, I got something here," Engel said. "Close your eyes."

Burl reluctantly complied and felt a light, cool pressure on his head. Engel was covering him with styling gel, attempting to arrange his thinning sandy hair in the traditional sumo manner.

"We gotta change your diet, too. No more fatty foods. We want high protein, lots of complex carbohydrates. You got a long way to go."

Engel recognized in Burl a fellow displaced person, or perhaps someone to admire for the genuineness of his displacement, and he did what he could to help. One night, at a diner with an all-you-can eat salad bar, Engel tried hard to grab for the check.

"Hey, you don't always have to pay."

"Don't worry about it," Burl said, at the same time wondering if he had enough cash. He was resolved not to leave a paper trail by using his credit cards.

"Look, how do you live, man? I make plenty at the laundromat, but you don't even have a job."

Thus was launched Burl's new career. He became assistant manager, keeping an eye on the place and making change while Engel looked after a bunch of LDS vending machines put in his charge. "Push products," he told Burl. "Bluing, Tide, all the little packages. We make a bundle on those things." Burl liked the laundromat. It was always warm and damp, like a greenhouse in the middle of the Utah desert, and the constant tumbling sound after a while became a comforting white noise, although afterward at the Chrysalis his ears rang and he felt lightheaded. Burl pretended the fluorescent lights were something special, for plants, and they seemed less depressing. Engel was irate that he wouldn't skim.

"Look, man, otherwise it's only gonna go to the church. They get 10 percent of everything anyway. At least if we keep it, it stays in the community. We can support wholesome vices, like drinking and weed."

"It's stealing."

"What *they* do is stealing," Engel pleaded. "They convert ignorant islanders, they get tithes, they don't pay taxes. It's a racket."

"Everything's a racket."

"Exactly! They own the newspaper, the big department store chain, all the land, they do it tax free and secretly. How's an entrepreneur gonna compete around here?"

"You're an entrepreneur?"

"You bet I am. I'm taking a loss here, man. I'm not around to take my cut, you let it all go downtown."

Burl was immovable. It wasn't so much honesty, although there was that. But he remembered the outcome when he'd acquiesced in corruption at his own restaurant. It was time to go straight, do no more harm. Besides, the idea of petty theft made his position in the laundromat seem not funny but humiliating. If he stole, he was some bum working with washing machines, and he wanted to avoid that feeling at all costs. Anyway, he rightly anticipated that Engel would make it up elsewhere, and he didn't object when Engel insisted on paying him a high hourly wage, "in keeping with your training and experience, like they say in the ads."

The job made certain minimal demands. When machines stopped working, Burl had to slap on an out-of-order sign, and he cut himself once trying to open a roll of quarters. Most of the time he just read.

After a while they developed a routine. Engel would come in just before the banks closed, collect the day's receipts, and cart the money off for deposit. Later they'd go eating.

"Trouble with vending machines, man, is inventory. Income's gotta match. Here, we sell service. Long as we can pay the gas bill, we're all right." Engel was feeling expansive, counting change and pocketing the largest bills. "Listen, we're having a feast this weekend. Come over. You can taste all the Tongan delicacies, eat as much as you want. When they see you they'll be pushing food at you."

"What kind of food do Tongans eat?"

"Besides tacos?"

"Yeah. Is there a lot of poi? Or pineapple?"

"Nah. Dole brought that shit into Hawaii. We don't eat no pineapple. Come and see."

CHAPTER 11

ENGEL'S PARENTS LIVED NOT far from the laundromat in a tan stucco cottage with brown trim and parking where the lawn might have been. When the front door opened, Burl was greeted by a shy, smiling woman barely over five feet tall. She was so fat Burl couldn't possibly get past her into the house, and so he gallantly signaled with his hand that she might precede him. Inside, when she got a better look at him, she beamed shyly and held her face with her fingertips. Burl imagined himself shirtless, a kind of Tongan Clark Gable.

"Mom, Dad, this is Rex," Engel said in Tongan.

"Speak English," the father said. "Rex?"

"Like the dog," said Burl, extending his hand.

Engel's father smiled uneasily. His grip was shocking. He was not a big man, but he was thickset and powerful looking, with a brooding quality perhaps owing to his forehead, which hung low over his eyes. His demeanor was respectful but wary. Burl guessed that anyone associated with Engel was suspect, no doubt rightly so.

"Hey everybody, this is my friend Rex," said Engel toward what Burl now saw as a crowd of shy faces surrounding a large table. "Say hello."

There was a murmur of welcome, and Burl detected a complicated smell, like old cooking oil and the folds of his own body. The room was lit warmly by candlelight. Everyone was quiet at first, and Burl felt hugely shy and self-conscious, until a large elderly woman extended her hand in welcome. "Come. Sit." When room was made for Burl and Engel, it became clear that the places left open weren't altogether suitable. Burl was faced with a slight, delicate-looking chair with a triangular seat and straight, anorexic back. The house was full of such furniture, all brightly colored, with hard, glossy surfaces and spindly black matte legs. There was something sad about it; it was yesterday's too-hip stuff, its makeup smeared, its stockings askew from too many dances. He was relieved when someone thoughtfully produced a steel folding chair.

"Mickey Mituoulu," the man next to Burl said cheerfully, thrusting out his hand. His wiry hair stood out around his head like a helmet or a crown of thorns. "Fili's sister is my wife. He's told me a great deal about you. You ever been to one of these before?"

"Never."

"You're in for a thrill. I can see you like a good meal, but you haven't feasted until you've eaten Tongan. Did Fili tell you anything about what we're having?"

"Hamburger Helper," Engel interrupted. "What does he need to know? Rex is cool, man, you should see him pack it away."

Burl was delighted to see that the table was covered with huge Tupperware bowls and Styrofoam coolers filled with food, almost none of which he could identify. Now that he was settled and the food had begun to be distributed, the chattering resumed in earnest. Some spoke in accented English and others in a staccato-sounding Tongan.

Glancing around, he realized that except for Engel and some of the men, everyone was fat. The older women especially were pyramids of flesh, their forms widening rapidly from top to bottom. The men and women smiled and laughed readily, yet their faces bore some indefinable sadness. The older ones were heavy lidded and stolid looking, but young and old alike had mouths that in repose turned down at the corners. Burl had the sense of people dancing on their own graves.

"Were you born in Tonga?" he asked Mituoulu.

"Nah. I was born here in Salt Lake. I got my own law practice downtown. Personal injury, divorce. What line are you in?"

"Uh, I'm between jobs right now."

"Well then, dig in."

From a large platter before them he served Burl what looked to be an extraordinarily well-prepared rollatine of some kind, perhaps of a small bird cooked in leaves. On his plate it had a sharp, high odor that he was suddenly able to distinguish from all the other dishes moving around the table.

"Mmm, thanks," said Burl. "What is it?"

"Taste it," Engel urged, perhaps too eagerly. "It's a delicacy, you'll love it."

Burl cut into the heart of the thing and heard the crunch of bones. A pigeon? He loved squab, done properly.

"Do you eat the leaves?"

"Not if you're smart," Mickey said. "Eat the meat. The taro leaves are just to cook it in."

From within its nest of taro he extracted a large, dark, stringy piece of flesh. He moved it up and down once or twice—it was dripping—and then thrust it quickly into his mouth. He smiled. A shock of revulsion swept over him far worse than from any late-night mouthful of sour milk out of the carton. The suspicious smell he'd detected earlier was matched by a stingingly high flavor.

Engel and his brother-in-law regarded Burl intently. He tried to chew, but the meat was resistant, gristly. He must somehow swallow and, with a gulp of root beer, did so.

"What is it?" he asked evenly.

"Bat," said Mickey.

"You like it?" Engel asked.

"Very interesting flavor," Burl said, feeling faint.

"See, I told you," Engel said to his brother-in-law and parents. "Rex loves bat. He's royalty, man."

Engel explained proudly that he had gone to elaborate trouble to obtain a brace of bats, which his mother prepared according to a recipe passed down from the days when the family *was* somebody. Skinned and seethed in coconut milk, the bats were then wrapped in taro leaves and baked. In Tonga, bats were traditionally restricted as food to members of the royal family.

"They didn't really like it either," Mrs. Engel confided, mercifully removing his plate. "But it's a big deal for Fili."

Engel protested, but she clucked and waved.

"Enough bat. He's having lu pulu and steak and lots of other good things."

"Oh, man," Engel moaned. Sotto voce, he said to Burl, "Rex, you don't want any of that lu pulu, it'll kill you."

"Don't be silly, that's easy to like," Mickey said. "They make it the American way."

Burl drank some more soda, swishing it around pointlessly in his mouth in an effort to erase the flavor of bat, which seemed to have spread through his sinuses into his ears, eyes, and brain pan. He thought of Frederic and imagined handing him a mystery bag containing potatoes, butter, eggs, white wine, and bat.

Engel's mother returned and set before him an even larger plate laden with Tongan delicacies. Lu pulu, however it was prepared back in the islands, was at the moment a striking concoction of mayonnaise, half-and-half, chopped onions, and canned corned beef, cooked in spinach. There were also plaintains, tapioca, taro root, and ufi, a root dish something like candied yams. None of it was much to Burl's taste, but he was hungry and polite and managed to swallow enough to save anyone from losing face—except perhaps Engel, who was disappointed that his friend wasn't able to display his largeness of spirit by consuming as much as he usually did.

"You should see him when we go for Chinese or Italian. You can't stop the guy."

Burl made up some lost ground by eating two steaks.

"Save some room, Rex, we got something really special coming," Mrs. Engel called from the end of the table.

Burl thought briefly of escape, but at that moment the kitchen door swung open and a pair of pigs, hooves sticking straight into the air, were carried into the room, borne high like conquering heroes on admiring shoulders. The beasts were enormous; when they were set down Engel's father slapped their bellies admiringly and then, with an electric knife, began to carve.

Suffused with smoke, it was perhaps the best meat Burl had ever tasted, slaughtered fresh that very morning in the Engels' backyard and pit-roasted for hours. It made up for the bat.

"Hey, you think this is a feast, wait till Fili gets married next month," Mickey said.

Everybody but Engel nodded and laughed.

"I didn't even know you were engaged," Burl said to his friend.

"I'm not engaged, and I'm not getting married. I don't know how many times I have to tell you people."

In the corner, a chubby young woman with a sad, pretty face got up and left, squeezing with considerable force past her protesting aunts and uncles. Engel's father waved his electric knife at his son, and a restive murmur went up from the table. The two men glared for an instant before the younger Engel turned away.

"Later," his father said gruffly, tossing down the knife. "Now we eat."

A couple of the women waddled out after the young girl. Engel seemed to be sulking. Burl elbowed him as the celebrants busied themselves with food.

"So I guess you're not too eager to tie the knot right at this particular present moment."

Engel rolled his eyes but said nothing. He looked like he was about to cry.

"It's an arranged marriage," Mickey explained. "The two families worked it out, but he doesn't wanna go along."

Engel looked away in disgust and Mickey pointed at him with his hand as if to say, "Can you believe this guy?" Burl put a dish into it. Melmac bowls in avocado and persimmon kept going by, laden with taro root, plaintains, and the like, but Burl was on the lookout for some ribs.

"Mr. Tongan Culture," Mickey chided. "The Frantz Fanon of the islands, and he rebels against the single most important tradition at the core of *kainga*, the Tongan extended family. See, *tauhi vaha'a* is everything to a Tongan. It means keeping up relationships, and the whole thing is perpetuated by the family's role in choosing its new members. This goes back a zillion years. I have a car phone, but I'm in this family because his parents chose me for his sister. Okay? And we went along. Why not? You think I could have done better on my own? You know how many divorces I handle? I added a room onto the house with a coupla months' worth, big-screen TV, everything."

Tauhi vaha'a. That was why Tongan had seemed so familiar. He thought back to the desert: *tohu va'ohu.* Chaos and desolation, like in Genesis. How Tongan it sounded. Burl looked sympathetically at Engel. He wished that his friend and Mituoulu weren't sitting on opposite sides of him. He had to turn his back on one to pay attention to the other.

"*Kainga* is how we preserve our culture," Mickey persisted. "We're all Mormons at this table. We're immigrants too. Aliens. And that's how it feels. You know what it's like for a culture that reveres its elderly to find that the children have all the power, because they're the only ones who speak English?"

Burl tried to take Engel's part.

"Well, wanting to preserve one's culture doesn't mean everything about it was so grand. That's why we all came here in the first place, right?"

"No mistake, Rex. We came here because Tonga is really shitty," Mickey said.

"Not enough ambulances to chase, right?" Engel spat.

"He's never even seen the place," Mickey said. "He was born here; he'll go when there's a Tongan Club Med. Meanwhile there's no land, no jobs, everybody's dirt poor, and the royals take everything. There's not five miles of good highway, but they have a Rolls Royce. The weather sucks; it rains all the time or it's hot as hell. You get to the capital by boat from someplace and the humidity hits you like a ton of bananas.

"The place stinks of rancid copra, which is everywhere. The bugs are bigger than the king, and day and night you hear this constant, oppressive pounding, all over the place." Mickey beat the table noiselessly.

"It's the women. They're pounding away at mulberry bark the Tongans strip off the trees. They have to work round the clock sometimes to make their quota of *tapa*—barkcloth—for the village chiefs. The country is one big Excedrin headache."

Afterward, there was a tea ceremony. Two large, smiling women poured water into an enormous wooden bowl, while a third kneaded the contents, which looked suspiciously like sawdust.

"Kava root," Mickey explained. "Very important Tongan ritual, like a sacrament almost. They fly it in from the islands, grind it up, and make a drink from it. It's bitter."

"Nice symbol, huh?" Engel said.

When the kava was steeped and strained, the first cupful was offered to an elderly man who sat quietly in a corner, but he waved it away and pointed at Burl. When the cup was brought, Burl smiled and pretended to drink. The woman who brought him the tea was enormous and looked at him coyly, her painted fingernails brushing his hands, her massive hips a giant censer as she walked away. He should feel at home here, he should even be flirting, but it was like being in a house of mirrors, and he felt himself recoil from these fat people, the deep-voiced women, the heavy breathing, the air damp with their exhalations. Almost stranger than being a misfit was the experience of landing on a planet full of misfits. Maybe the answer was time.

From Engel's point of view, the whole thing was a disaster. He had lost face, and the next time Burl saw him he was black and blue. His father had hit him with a chair.

"You're not in love with this woman, is that it?" Burl asked.

"That's it."

They were in Engel's apartment, smoking marijuana. The peppery-sweet smell of burning weed filled the room, and they had already been through a couple of six-packs of beer. Now Burl was getting a massage. Engel had done this before, and it had made Burl uncomfortable, but he had learned, eventually, to relax.

His eyes were closed, he was drowsy, but he could tell Engel was standing behind the chair, bent over him.

"Well," Burl said, almost mumbling. "There's something to what Mickey said. I mean, as well her as some other, right? She's Tongan, she's fat, she's willing. She seems awfully sweet. And you get your *kainga* or whatever. What more could you want?"

"I'm just not attracted to her."

Burl opened his eyes. His feet were bare. Engel was squatting, doing something exquisite to his left leg, kneading the big calf.

"Wait. She's got a pretty face; you mean after all this talk, all this Tongan *ga-bragh* night and day, this endangered species rap, you don't like her *because she's fat?*"

"You like fat women? I seen who you stare at."

"Yeah, but I'm not Tongan."

"Well, I'm not fat."

Burl pondered this for a moment.

"Okay, you're right. I hurl no stones. I guess we're both hypocrites."

"Not really."

"No?"

"I like fat men."

"Sure, you like our power. Our regal bearing. The nobility with which our flesh presses back against the world."

"I like all those things," Engel said, rising. "Very much."

Burl felt himself being looked at in a way he hadn't been looked at before. Perversely, it reminded him of his encounter with the Grim Reaper. Engel leaned over the chair, squeezing fistfuls of Burl's upper body. Burl was pretty well stoned; he knew what they meant in computer books by "real time" because that was exactly what he felt he no longer inhabited. He was floating, tingling, Engel's hands functioning as clamps atop his trapezius muscles to make the rest of his body below feel like a puppet's, or a dummy's.

"Strings," he said in wonder, lifting his fingers lightly.

Now Burl wasn't being touched. He felt hypnotized, unsure even if his eyes were open, and as he lay there in a trance he felt the beginnings of ecstasy. It took him what seemed to be forever to discover that his penis was engorged and that Engel was moving it rapidly in and out of his mouth.

The Barcalounger was in a position of deep recline, as if Burl was to be launched into outer space, and in that situation, for Burl, gravity was a mighty adversary. On his back, he struggled with the chair and the determined young man who pinned him to it. They wrestled, sweat bursting from every opening in Burl and dripping from Engel's nose. Burl was dopey with cannabis and alcohol. Engel tried to calm him by rubbing the sides of his huge neck.

"You want it, man. Admit it."

"Get off, Engel, I'm not kidding!"

But Engel reached down and rubbed Burl's burning crotch.

"You like it. Why fight it?"

"Engel, I don't want to hurt you."

"Me neither," Engel said.

Burl screamed and moved to strangle Engel, to crush his throat with a single deadly squeeze, but Engel only squeezed harder, and Burl knew he was lost. Engel had him literally by the balls.

"Just relax, man, I said I didn't wanna hurt you. Don't make me."

"You'll pay, Engel—"

Burl screamed as Engel squeezed again, harder. He thought he might pass out, which would be just as well. The sucking resumed, much more expertly than Norma had done, and before long Burl had to admit to himself, to the extent that he was conscious, that he was no longer struggling against Engel but with him, until he was making noises again, involuntarily, as he came he knew not where.

"I know you like that," Engel said, catching his breath, still clutching Burl's scrotum. He gave it a squeeze, just as a reminder. "Now, Rex, I want you to do me. All the way down, just like you do with those hotdogs."

With a short, sudden motion, Burl drove his fist into Engel's face with enough power to knock him off the chair. Burl sighed deeply, scrambled off the recliner, and went for him. His balls ached. He grasped Engel's neck in his big left hand, soft as some weathered mitt, and pinned him to the wall. Engel's face was hideous, the lower half covered with blood from his nose. He was strong and he struggled angrily, but his eyes looked to Burl like those of a steer bound hopelessly for slaughter.

"You liked it man, admit it!" Engel shouted.

This was perhaps the trouble. Burl felt his strength coming back through the beer, the pot, the orgasm, but it made him madder still to know that he could not—would not—bring himself to harm Engel. This fact was unknown to Engel, however, who wailed in fright as Burl slammed his right fist again and again into the wall beside his head, knocking a framed poster to the floor and leaving a depression in the wallboard. Engel tried to reach for him, but Burl clamped down on his throat and pulled back his fist as if to strike. With a sudden exhalation, Engel began to hyperventilate.

"I give, man," he said finally, hiccuping for air. "Enough. You too big."

With one hand, Burl lifted him by the belt and hauled him, coughing and wheezing, to the bed, where Engel moaned gratefully. Burl fell into the Barcalounger and rolled himself another joint. His right hand hurt.

This should be a lesson, he thought. Some of us are meant to travel alone and carry our own baggage. His face burned. He was steaming with exertion and shame, furious at Engel but also feeling guilty and suspicious of himself.

"Listen," Burl said. "I'm sorry if I got a little rough."

"Should be," Engel panted.

"Don't you think you should be too?"

"Wrestle with an Engel, what do you expect?" His breath was gradually slowing. "We fierce."

"You shouldn't have done that, Engel. I'm not interested in men."

"You loved it. Why don't you do me, see what you're missing? Don't be selfish, Rex."

"Stop calling me that. The name's Burl. Burl Bennett. Rex is just something I said, on the spur of the moment. Kings County made me think of it."

"You never been with a man before?"

"Or a woman, really."

Burl lit the joint he had rolled, took a deep drag and passed it over to Engel.

"So now you know why I ain't getting married."

"Now I know," Burl agreed mildly, looking toward Engel through drooping eyelids.

"So you don't want to do me?"

Burl shook his head.

"So I'm f.a. So shoot me."

"You're what?"

"F.a. Fat admirer. I like to eat the stuff. You and me both."

Burl snorted halfheartedly, unable to muster much derision. He held out his hand for the joint, which Engel slowly passed back.

"Burl. Man. So now you know my secret. Why don't you tell me yours?"

Burl told him, although in the telling it was hard for him to make sense of it. It was a story he had never told himself and whose holes therefore hadn't become apparent until he tried to convey to Engel what had happened, and why. In telling the tale of his flight, his trek across the desert and his arrival in the place the Mormons knew as Zion, Burl tried to construct an orderly narrative, but there were paradoxes, mysteries, lacunae. He wished that he had cultivated the habit, whenever anything important happened, of trying to encapsulate the events in a newspaper story that a complete stranger could read and understand, just as he tried to encapsulate whole lives in his obituaries. In trying to explain it all to Engel, he found himself speculating, fudging, even forgetting. Our own lives are invisible to us.

"Man oh man," Engel said at last. "So what's next? You gonna stay around here?"

"I don't know," said Burl, getting up to go. "I don't know."

"Stay over, man. You too high to drive."

Burl said nothing.

"Don't disappear now, man. You still the king."

Burl said nothing. As he moved toward the door, Engel threw a shoe at him.

"C'mon, Rex. Don't be a stranger. I won't tell no one."

Already a stranger, Burl stumbled out into the cold night air. On the way, he remembered something Engel's brother-in-law had told him. "Only one important thing I know of comes from Tonga," Mituoulu had said after a good many beers. "We gave you the word *taboo*."

CHAPTER 12

BURL STOPPED WORKING at the laundromat.
He still went there sometimes, bantering uncomfortably with
Engel while he ran his clothes through the machines, but it wasn't
the same, and pretty soon he took his wash elsewhere. He hoped
sadly that Engel wasn't really necessary. Maybe, by virtue of the
flesh alone, one could have nobility without him.

Yet he thought a lot about his friend, for whom ethnic libera-
tion took the place of what would have been a lonely and embarrassing struggle for personal and sexual freedom. Here was subli-
mation close to home. Burl had still never had intercourse with a
woman, and although they were attractive to him and the perennial object of his fantasies, Engel caused him to question his own
sexuality. Coming in his mouth, that grip on the scrotum at just
the edge of pain, the scary feel of teeth—it was all troubling and
a bit confusing. He couldn't get it out of his mind. Perhaps he
protested too much. Why had he reacted with such violence?
Well, the compulsion; no one should be subjected to that. But
what had he been thinking, with all that wrestling and massage?

What a fool he had been! It was upsetting too that the only person who had ever lusted for him was a man with a fat fetish.

Burl had not weighed himself for a long time but could tell from the pinch and erosion of his biggest clothes that he was well over 350 pounds. He was gripped by contradictory impulses about this. His diuretics were running out, and he was loath to leave evidence of himself by refilling the prescription. Then again, without his job at the laundromat he had no income. Financially, the bleeding resumed. He could return to Vegas, but that was always an iffy prospect; one might just as likely lose as win, although food and accommodations were cheap and superior. But Burl was beginning to feel the comforting pull of inertia at the Chrysalis, the emotional gravity of security. He shifted himself to monthly rates, which were cheaper, and tried to work on his poem, starting fresh, working only from memory. Writing felt good, and he also kept a haphazard journal, wrote unmailed letters, made notes for stories, plays, scripts. It was a particular pleasure to write with no thought of an audience, as Emily Dickinson or Kafka might have done. Never had he written so freely, or worried less about revision. Without thinking about it, he started saving things again. The growing accretion of newspapers, books, magazines, empty bottles, too-small clothes, and his own scribblings had begun, like ivy, to mount and cover a single wall, with similar softening effects. He felt himself slipping, but it was not so terrible. Mostly he was just lonely, which was nothing new. Engel's departure left him bereft, much worse off than before, conscious this time of the fullness of his plight, which was also, of course, his remedy. Without money or succor, how long could he continue to hide out in a down-at-the-heels motel room on the edge of downtown Salt Lake City? What, after all, was next?

Burl had begun to grow suspicious of the Holy Grail. Although a shrine to food cultists, who would steal a day from skiing to ride down for its legendary cuisine, the place actually was run by a cult, one revolving around a prophet named Janet David Witness, who claimed to be descended from Christ, Buddha, and Christopher Columbus. In a state where men once routinely practiced polygamy, Witness ran a kind of matriarchal subculture in which it was rumored that women actually had several husbands. Burl wondered if polyandry could be legal in Utah. Witness and her followers were something of a problem for mainstream organized feminists, who were divided over whether to defend her as an example of womanly self-sufficiency in the face of persecution or denounce her for adopting the militaristic and authoritarian posture women were supposed to know enough to oppose.

The Mormons were alarmed, of course, and the largely Mormon authorities were said to keep a close watch on the whole operation, which was a sprawling former sheep ranch that Witness and her followers had turned into a utopian ashram and entrepreneurial free-trade zone marked by dozens of metal quonset huts staked out in the red and orange Utah desert. Among the things Witness was careful never to unequivocally deny was the allegation that her group had stockpiled tons of sophisticated armaments ranging from automatic rifles to antitank weapons, which was a problem for a number of celebrities who had allowed themselves to be associated with her. There was also some kind of running feud with the Internal Revenue Service over the distinction between taxable profits and other forms of "church income." The Mormons, who seemed to control a healthy chunk of the state's business activity and had long ago settled the tax status of their operations, were not happy about any of this either.

The food at the Holy Grail was another thing; in certain circles it was held in the kind of awe that aficionados in other walks of life reserved for the hitting of Ted Williams or the poetry of Yeats. The chefs, all women, were said to be divinely inspired; the lambs, reared on site, were rumored to be raised on the finest marijuana. Knowledgeable food lovers talked about the place with reverence, and Texas oilmen, at the height of the boom, would fly in for lunch. *Newsweek* reported that an unnamed tycoon had sent his jet just for takeout.

"That'll be for just one," Burl said on the phone. "But you should know that I'm very large. I'll need an extra large table, and an easy chair would be better than anything else. I can sit in a dining-room chair as long as there are no arms."

The menu was arranged in advance and was rather literally heartstopping. Burl had anticipated this experience for some time, but it would not be an unalloyed pleasure. His reservation, for a Thursday night instead of a crowded weekend, meant the end of any pretext that his stay in Salt Lake City had a purpose; he anticipated spending most of his remaining cash at the Grail, which was notoriously expensive, and he had planned no further. The meal began to take on the character of a last supper, after which he wasn't sure what he would do. Except for fruit juice and sparkling water, he fasted for three days beforehand to prepare for the feast.

It was certainly that. The Grail was housed in what had once been a church. Burl followed sheepishly as he was led by a handsome young woman in flowing skirts through a large room centered around a fireplace and then past a series of plush private dining rooms, the last of which would be his. There, she bade him remove his shoes, and he noted with pleasure the uninterrupted blackness of his feet; one sock had only the beginning of a tear above the big toe.

Had there been pillows on the floor instead of a comfortable, high-backed, overstuffed chair, the place might have been too much. There was shiny wallpaper with a whirling pattern in felt or velour, and the light came from silver candelabra on the sideboard, which were reflected in a large wood-framed mirror on the wall. On the ovate table, which was covered with a starched white cloth, a silver saltcellar, a black plate edged in gilt, and a formidable array of silverware rested.

When Burl was comfortably seated—the chair was mounted on spherical casters and rolled as if on ball bearings—another young woman appeared, with the same glowing complexion and hypnotic smile but a more interesting face.

"Hello. I'm Wanda. I'll be serving you tonight. Welcome to the Holy Grail."

Her green eyes shone, and her introduction signaled the onset of a silent choreography of attendants ministering subtly to their guest. Women in white tunics, black trousers, and short hair glided in and out to add glasses and further silver to the daunting armada already in place. He felt a sybarite at the eye of this courteous storm. A basket of rolls appeared; next to it, a bouquet of butter sculpted into hibiscus floating on a bed of ice. Tasting it with his pinkie, Burl confirmed that strawberries had been used to make the flowers pink. A pillow was brought for his feet, and another for his back, which he sent away. It was like Eunuchs' Day at the seraglio. Someone lit two small candles, and the striking of a match, as if restoring his power to hear, made Burl aware that there was music in the room, soft but not faint, in the voice of a woman and in a language he did not know.

"Those are Spanish *cantiga*, from the thirteenth century," said Wanda, as if reading his mind. "Settings of stories from the Bible. Love poems. Folktales. Shall we begin?"

They began with the champagne, a frothy 10-year-old half-bottle made from French chardonnay grapes that showed lemon and oak and went perfectly with three slender wafers covered with creme fraiche and striped in orange salmon roe and black sturgeon eggs. The cool complex of flavors exploded in Burl's mouth as he chomped down on each of the matzohlike wafers, the eggs bursting with brine, the creme fraiche poised between sweet and sour. Each of these crackers was like a potato chip to him; he looked forward from this auspicious beginning to what might appear next from the swinging door in the corner.

This time Wanda placed before him a glistening snowcap of scallops set atop what turned out to be a tomato *concasse.* "The scallops are seared over wood coals, and the tomatoes are grown here in our own greenhouse, vine ripened, and dipped for just seconds in boiling water before they're peeled and mixed with fresh basil from the same garden."

Unconcerned with sacrilege, Burl ground some pepper onto the scallops; they should be fed on the stuff in the ocean, he felt. He was always suspicious of scallops, especially in Utah, but these were tender enough to make the hardest heart weep, and they took to the acid and intense concasse like a twin separated at birth.

Moments later, Wanda reappeared.

"A whole foie gras, again from our own farm, in a sauce of Armagnac and quince, sectioned by slivers of the fruit crisply sautéed. And this is the lobster, poached live from Maine, shelled and reassembled in beurre blanc scented with ginger and lime."

As she spoke, one of the tunics hovered in the shadows, bearing a bottle of wine. Wanda took it and ceremoniously displayed the label.

"Wanda," Burl said. "I trust you. You may dispense with that."

It was a spicy, long-necked California Gewürztraminer, which carried over into the next appetizers: a cool avocado soup garnished with cilantro followed by medallions of salty raw salmon seared on the outside and served with the lightest dill vinaigrette on a bed of arugula.

After that, Burl had a few moments of peaceful contemplation to finish his Gewürztraminer, which, warmed a bit in his hands and on his tongue, had the taste of dessert after what he'd eaten so far. He took a little bread and strawberry butter. The music, noticeably louder, began to sound like Palestrina, and the candles on the sideboard shone murkily in reflection on the polished wood floor.

The next wine, a brooding, formal, inky 1970 Bordeaux from the Pauillac region, heralded the onset of the entrees, in the ordering of which Burl felt he had shown great restraint.

"Ah," he said, eyebrows arching, when the first was brought in. The fanned slices of meat shone with heat upon the plate.

"Aged, trimmed filet of Utah beef," pronounced Wanda, "coated in olive oil, sweet basil, and peppercorns."

The meat was rich, salty, and delicious, with a risotto Milanese, in which Burl savored the grated truffles, and kale braised in garlic, butter, and white wine. This was followed by an intermezzo of lemon-mint sorbet, very cold and intense. Burl was beginning to feel full. When he rose it was with difficulty; he had to be still until he could regain his bearings. His head swam, and he reached out for the tabletop with his fingertips. In the bathroom he threw up with violent, hacking, flowing sounds that he hoped were contained by the wainscoted walls. He had not induced himself to vomit in some time and was glad the skill was not lost. Brushing his trouser legs and examining his coat for spots, he combed his hair with water from the sink and returned to his place, where one of the smiling tunics stood ready to tuck his chair beneath him.

He felt clear and refreshed for the crucial next course, which began with rather too much ceremony surrounding the wine.

"This is the 1970 Chateau Lafleur, Theresa Robin. It's another Bordeaux, but from the Pomerol region, and mostly of soft merlot grapes that make it very deep, fleshy, and warm," Wanda said with a certain smug appreciation. "It's very rare."

When Burl tasted it he could only sigh. The fragrance spoke of thyme, chestnuts, and some dark fruit he couldn't name. His eyes grew wet.

"Black currants?" Wanda supplied.

She was beginning to grow on him. There was a dignity about her, a silent self-sufficiency in her movements, as if she were beyond struggle. Burl knew this was only possible as the result either of greatness or a deep belief in a single insane idea, and he wondered, assuming the latter, whether it was worth it. The wine in his mouth blossomed and evolved, caressing his tongue as it warmed and mixed with his saliva. Swallow and it's gone, tingling the gills with its memory: tannin. The pleasures of the flesh are so fleeting. What could compare to a single mad falsehood, thoroughly embraced? Conventional religions were such pale palliatives by contrast. How sad that he could accept no low-calorie alternative to anxiety and confusion. Wanda seemed in the candlelight so clean and beautiful, so ruddy, so mature yet so flushed with her own enormous future. Why must she give her bounty to the dead?

"Wanda, please get a glass and have some of this."

"Oh no—"

"I insist; it's obscene for me to sit and consume this amazing distillation alone. Especially after the black currants. That you should know the black currants."

She would only pour herself a mouthful. Inhaling the fragrance, she was already changed, if only for a moment. With her eyes closed, Burl noticed the small scar that interrupted her left eyebrow and left a space hairless. It dawned on him that her entire face was charmingly asymmetrical. Her fine nose twitched as she breathed the grapes and earth, the sun and the rain, as if they were on her skin. When she took the wine in her mouth she held it there and stood very still, her eyes closed, and kept it on her palate until it might become something else. Then she swallowed noisily.

"Please, Wanda, for God's sake have a glass. It's not that big a deal."

Flushed and smiling, she shook her head and swiftly fled. But Burl was still happy.

When she returned, it was with what looked like a small missile or time capsule, rolled out upon a trolley. With mallet and chisel she smacked the thing along the top until a large crevice appeared and then pried the casing apart by inserting a pair of tongs and pulling at the handles.

The room was instantly suffused with an overwhelming scent of thyme, and Burl raised his eyebrows again in greeting toward the centerpiece of his dinner. Dodging steam as she pried the cask further apart, Wanda set down her instruments of torture.

"This is the leg of a young lamb," she said, "grown here and fresh slaughtered this morning. We seal it in this capsule of kosher salt, flour and thyme, roast it in an open hearth, and let it finish cooking away from the fire."

"Bravo!" said Burl, who was anticipating its flavor with the Chateau Lafleur. He knew that normally this dish could only be ordered for four, so he expected there would be plenty.

Wanda expertly carved the leg and arranged some meat on a plate. It seemed impossibly rare and bloody beside the "garlic-scented roast potatoes and pencil-thin young asparagus in lemon and butter." Burl was skeptical. He had been served cold, near-raw lamb before by zealots fearful of overcooking, but in this case it would be difficult to rectify. The mortar that had contained and cooked the meat was shattered. He wondered how or even whether he could break the news to Wanda that he was in no mood for thick hunks of lamb carpaccio. As the plate was placed before him, he recognized that the music was Beethoven, one of the later string quartets, tragic, enigmatic, irresistible.

The lamb tasted like the music. From the very first rare slice it was a revelation, a deep, ineffable feeling not contained by the mouth. The flavors were salt, smoke, and almost—did he imagine it?—somehow the freshness of the Utah meadows which must have sustained this creature in its brief life. The texture was soft as uncooked salmon. He understood the rumors about marijuana; the thyme was strong and pervasive, and the meat was intoxicating.

"How is everything?" Wanda asked. She was flushed with exertion from carving.

"Oh, Wanda," Burl said, swallowing and reaching for his glass. "Oh, Wanda."

She nodded that she knew, she had seen this before, she was the worldly but patient courtesan who understood the great pleasure she brought (but did not share with) her esteemed clientele.

"Tell me," Burl said. "I must know."

"I can't."

"Please. A hint, at least. Is it really grass? Is that why the secrecy?"

"It's grass all right. But that's all I can say. Except that nothing is illegal. We couldn't. Not the way they watch us."

"Grass. Hmm. Grass. Will you share some of this? We've enough for four; surely I don't need all of it."

But Wanda was gone, already, her manner claimed, having said too much. Burl saw that there was some mystique at stake. What if the lambs fed on free-growing marijuana—it was a weed, after all—just hours before they were slaughtered. There would still be cannabis in their blood; the meat would be suffused with it. Burl was beginning to feel intoxicated; who would ever be able to distinguish what came from food, wine, a great meal, or even the expectation of hallucinogenic meat from what might actually be a heavy dose of the stuff?

And who cared? He ate on, through three portions of the lamb and most of the wine, pacing the two, each evolving as he ate, the lamb seeming to grow saltier, the wine bigger, grapier, more voluptuous if perhaps looser and sloppier too. He thought of Frederic and wished he could be present for this meal. That was the trigger. He thought of Frederic, and he had the answer.

"Salt grass," he said. Wanda blushed. "As in the south of France. They feed them salt hay. The lake is right over behind us, right? You graze them right here?"

"You know a lot about food," she said quietly, busying herself with more carving.

"Only from personal experience."

Burl wondered if she was humoring him. Perhaps the salt was just from the mortar the leg was cooked in. Perhaps she was trying, by the flattery of feigned belief, to throw him off the scent?

"Besides," he said. "They've tested the meat."

Wanda froze.

"Right," Burl continued. "I know about that."

"How? You can't be with the police!"

"Of course not. You think this flesh is a disguise? But wouldn't you test it, if you were suspicious? Kidnap a lamb, or slip in for a great meal on the cuff and put a slice into your pocket? Take home a doggie bag?"

"They didn't have to. They came into the kitchen with a search warrant."

"And found nothing."

"We told them it was the grass," Wanda said, smiling.

"But better that it doesn't get around. The panache that accrues from the other rumor is priceless."

Burl ate all the lamb, savoring every bit even as it grew cold. He would have eaten the tailings, the little burnt pieces shed in the carving, and he longed to run a moistened finger across the casing and see what that tasted like, but after four portions Wanda took it away. He respected her sense of propriety.

In truth, he was growing weary. He greeted the salad—leaves of red lettuce, sorrel, and arugula perfumed with orange, yellow, and purple flowers of the sort he felt he'd seen in the meadows on his way from Las Vegas—with relief. The olive oil was light and infused with oregano and raspberries, the perfect accompaniment for the taste of photosynthesis. There had been enough meat for one night.

Cheese came next, to finish off the red wine: imported gorgonzola, goat cheese right from the Witness farm, bel paese, and parmigiano-reggiano, all ringed by warm almonds and slices of beautiful ripe American persimmon, which he found as insipid as any other persimmon that had ever crossed his path. A trio of sorbets followed—mango, grapefruit, and boysenberry—after which were sweets: a hot blueberry custard tart with mint leaves, accompanied by a glass of the fabulous 1955 Chateau Y'Quem, a golden nectar of sauterne deep in flavors from peach to fig; and finally a cold crepe of apricots and ice cream, with cappuccino.

The candles were beginning to burn low, and a few strands of hair had worked loose from Wanda's bun. When a glass of brandy was set before him, Burl grinned and pushed back heavily from the table. Lighting the Miami cigar he had brought for the occasion, he would bask in the afterglow of his last great meal.

His thoughts turned to final things. He had always felt bad about having to wring an account of so many lives from a handful of objective facts, however carefully collected. But looking back over his own life, he saw that there was little consistency, and that lives, like poems, are not much susceptible to summary. They skulk or caper in the shadows of understanding, casually and without awareness. The objective facts are perhaps best after all, like a skeleton for the reader's imagination. Or perhaps the newspaper obituary is a form unsuited to the inevitable shape of a life. And why had he bothered to write his own? If the facts were all, could not someone else do as well? Why should he care, once he was in the grave?

Afterward he toasted Wanda with a glass of Armagnac older than himself and persuaded her to drink one with him. Both, it was announced, were on the house.

Wanda's style was that of the interviewer who says nothing, so Burl tried drawing her out. Her life was a mess before she found Mother Witness, or rather was providentially guided to her. She had been a heroin addict, the child of an abusive father and the victim of an abusive husband whom she lacked the strength to leave. Burl now saw the asymmetry of her face differently, imagining this pale visage colored by blood and bruise, disfigured by swelling and tears. It made his bowels clench. But she was more interested in Burl. Who was he? Where was he from? More Armagnac appeared, and Burl realized he was a prospect of sorts. Of course. From the meal they would think he had money, from his body and intake he was clearly an addictive character, and for his insight they would want to know more about him in any case. Wanda was persuasive about this, gazing into Burl's eyes with the rapt attention of a new lover. He saw that she was a true believer.

"I'm nobody," Burl said.

"Nobody? You must have been somebody at some point. Who killed you?" Wanda asked in all seriousness.

"I did, I guess."

When he left, Wanda pressed a pamphlet on him and wrote down a phone number. Burl copied it onto a slip of paper in his wallet and threw the pamphlet away.

Back at the Chrysalis, there was a void. After all the plotting and anticipation that went into his meal at the Holy Grail, it was a letdown to find himself living on in the same way as before. It took him a couple of days to recover from the feast, yet he didn't feel much changed by it. The transformative power of food was gradual, after all, and cumulative. The Holy Grail had made it hard for him to face the frozen macaroni and cheese he cooked on his hotplate, or the all-you-can-eat early-bird spaghetti and meatball dinners at the Tic Toc Diner. Lesser foods now lacked taste for him. He ate huge quantities still, but almost out of duty, and meals lately induced not euphoria but exhaustion. He plodded nevertheless grimly forward, plowing into desserts as if digging a foxhole, opening cans like K-rations. The enemy being tenacious, victory came slowly. Soon, though, he would be vanquished, and then, at last, there might be peace.

IT WAS NO LONGER morning, and her stomach fluttered as she thought of the evening ahead. Perhaps she had had enough coffee. Focusing with effort, Norma saw that the pot was almost finished. Why could she not just stay there, reading the paper in that opaque light, moving her arm now and then to a cool spot on the table top? She glanced nervously at the clock on the wall. The dry cleaner would be open for another hour at least, and there was still enough time to do some laundry. She knew she must stir herself, yet she sat on, finally rising only on impulse to fetch a pen. She would make a quick start on the cross-word puzzle.

She was practically finished with it by the time she dashed out to the cleaner's, which was long closed when she arrived—she had miscalculated how late they were open on a Saturday—so that she couldn't retrieve the dress she'd counted on wearing. And it was already too late for much in the way of wash. On the way home she berated herself for what she felt was her compulsive need to put things off to the very last minute and in fact beyond,

and plotted what she might wear instead. By the time she got upstairs she had decided she didn't need the scoop-necked blue
dress anyway.

See, she thought, I shouldn't even be going out. Burl was
dead, she knew it, she could feel it somewhere in his absence. She
had tried to reach him; she'd left phone messages, written letters,
tried through his parents, through the police, but still there was
this loud silence, like a reproach. He had left without a word,
which after a decent interval of great guilt had made her furious.
She had loved him, or she hadn't loved him, either alternative was
cause enough to feel terrible, but she also *missed* him, missed having someone to show the latest outrageous thing she'd just read,
missed even having someone familiar to go around with. Norma
hated dating, had never understood the thrill for her girlfriends
when she was young, but she was lonely now, and her world was
coming to seem more and more like Noah's ark, as full of couples
as if everyone's survival depended upon it. And so here she was.

In the bathroom mirror the harsh light made her look at least
50 to herself. Small wrinkles had collected under her eyes, and
when she wasn't smiling the flesh along her jaws loitered in jowls.
She was on the downward slide; nobody would ever want her.
How could she do her makeup under these circumstances? Her
life spun onward as if Burl had never existed, as if her brother had
never lived. One could forgive the dead, one knew that their departure was no real choice, but if the thing she hoped but did not
believe—that Burl was alive—were true, than it was just vicious of
him, inconceivably vicious, not to give her even the comfort of
a postcard.

She tugged at the skin of her neck and sighed. No more
putting it off, it was time to get ready. Resignedly, Norma went to
work on her face, surrounding her eyes with makeup and covering
her skin with powder, desiring to be desired but applying her

mask without enthusiasm. She wished things had been different with Burl, wished there was some state between fraternity and matrimony, some halfway house that took account of the unavoidable revulsion one could feel in a person's body even while allowing a couple to form and endure for the more important reasons of compatibility, comfort, fun.

At least Hanks ate normally. You could go to a restaurant with him or fix him a meal without worrying about whether you were making him fatter or embarrassing him with any assumptions about what he should be eating.

The doorbell rang at the appointed hour, and Norma looked out at him through the peephole. She couldn't get over the idea that he moved his lips when he wrote, and when she made a joke that he didn't get, or a reference that was beyond him, she imagined Burl snickering behind her, his hot breath annoying on her neck.

"You see they posted the obit job?" he said, testing.

"Yes, I saw that," she said.

"Looks pretty clear they don't expect any kind of comeback by our friend." They were at dinner. He pretended to look down at his food, watching her the whole time. "Maybe you should apply for it."

"Oh no, I couldn't fill his shoes." She blushed at her own unconscious bad taste.

"You can say that again," Hanks laughed.

He talked on about office politics, and Norma thought about Hanks during dinner, about how it was hard even to use his first name to herself, and how he was perfectly reasonable and presentable and stirred in her no feelings whatsoever. She sized him up while he ate. It was the third outing they had had that was unmistakably a date, and there was no reason not to sleep with him, she supposed. She couldn't very well turn down everybody, although it was surprising to her how frequently men asked for dates once Burl was out of the picture. She usually said no, settling in this case for the devil that she knew. She sighed inwardly at Hanks's eagerness, his efforts to impress. Afterward, she invited him up for coffee, but when she'd served it to him, sitting lightly as he was on the sofa that Burl had so often stressed, she retreated to the loveseat that was cluttered with pillows and yarn, pattern books and the other accoutrements of her knitting, which for some reason she had returned to after years of knitting nothing. As Hanks talked, she settled in, put her feet up on the coffee table, and took up her needles, surrounding herself with balls and skeins and instructions like a mouse arranging a nest. If he seemed to be getting too comfortable, she decided, she'd have him hold a new skein out with his hands so she could wind it into a ball, and if he persisted she'd give him another skein, and another. Eventually, she felt certain, he would go away. She didn't have any coffee, either. It was hard enough sleeping without it.

―――――――――――

All because they want to get away from us, Shields thought. He had emerged from the Lincoln Tunnel, driven the helix, and now rode west. Incredible. Office buildings, highways, shopping malls, all filled with white people. Want to get away from crime, drugs, and so forth. But they hated us long before all that. People forget. How do they think about this, in their most rational moments? Maybe they figure we're kind of their Frankenstein.

But wasn't the doctor named Frankenstein? Hard sometimes to sort out the offspring from its maker, which was shaky ground for so early on a Saturday morning. Shields had some Puccini on the radio but was suddenly annoyed by it. Pressing buttons, he found Abdullah Ibrahim on that good jazz station in Newark, at least you can get it over here, but he took no pleasure in it. He felt taut, edgy in the way he got when he went without sleep too long. His heart was a lump in his throat. His son was back home after a bad episode, bad enough for the thought to cross Shields's mind that they might someday lose him. Since he had trouble banishing this thought, he began to worry that it was actually a wish, one of the involuntary kind that seemed likeliest to come true and for which one might reproach oneself forever after. Shields felt guilty a lot, even when he reminded himself that guilt was conceit and indulgence compared to what Adam must feel.

It made him nervous just having to drive someplace new. It reminded him of trips to new doctors, different medical facilities, always wishing for some magic words to say to the patient boy on the seat next to him, the boy who accompanied him in such resignation to these affluent white neighborhoods that harbored all the best physicians. What a sweet kid Adam was. The weather always seemed so nice on those days. Shields objected for a while that his wife took such pains about dressing their son for these excursions. It felt like putting on a show for white folks, as if the Shieldses worried that they weren't good enough. But when she said, in exasperation, "Okay, Daddy's gonna dress you, honey, 'cause Momma can't do nothin' right this morning," he couldn't decide what the boy should wear. Shields himself was a little neater than he might be otherwise on a day off, and what did that imply? That was the kind of time he hated having to live with white people. For what they had done to people's minds. For how they made it impossible to know yourself, separate from what they did to you. Maybe he should have shucked the slavemaster's name, the way some of his college friends did. They seemed mostly to choose the names of Arab slavemasters instead. Hemophilia isn't even that common among blacks, who bleed in enough other ways. *Never mind what the doctors say about a colorblind disease,*

Shields's mother had insisted. *We even got their genes. A long time ago, they did us that favor.*

The day was clear, except for some tough little clouds, and cold. Shields took the Meadowlands exit and pulled the scribbled directions from his shirt pocket, reading as he drove. There were a series of turns involved, and he kept the scrap of paper in his mouth, where the papery taste made him salivate, reminding him that he was hungry. He'd used to like eating with Burl and wondered whether the Bennetts would press breakfast on him.

The house was so spotless Shields was almost suspicious. Did they really live here? The place made him feel crummy about the modest disorder of his own home, but he did not become truly suspicious until they offered him coffee with artificial sweetener. There were no Danish, no bagels, no oily smoked fish, nothing. Finally he put his finger on what had seemed strangest from the moment he walked in, which was that these people were thin.

Drawn, in fact. They looked worried to death, sick at heart. He felt for them. He felt terrible, a parent who knew too well the suffering of parents, and he fell to encouraging. He'd been assured.

"I know it's hard to look beyond what we see," Shields told them. "But there's no sign Burl's come to any harm. Believe me."

"Then how come you're here?" Stu demanded. It must be strange to him, a black man at the kitchen table. It must look funny. "From homicide, right?"

"It's just a missing-persons case, but because Burl may have been a—a witness in a homicide, I have to check out every lead."

There was silence for a moment as that answer sank in. Shields asked, "Have you had any communication from your son? Anything at all?"

"Nothing." Betty seemed to bite the words as she spoke. "Not a word."

Shields sighed.

"I want to tell you—I've been at this a long time, and I really, truly believe he's all right—"

"How can you say that?" Betty asked. "How can you know?"

"I have a lot of experience. Ma'am, sometimes this job involves a lot of faith."

That seemed to make things worse.

"Look, I'm a father. I know it's pointless telling you not to worry. But it's my professional and personal opinion that the big guy's okay. I mean, he may be worried and upset or something, or going through some kind of episode. But he's physically unharmed."

"You said on the phone you knew Burleigh."

"Yeah, knew him real well when he was a police reporter. We worked together on a book about the Stalker case. Remember that one?"

"Do we ever? We lived in Brooklyn in those days, and I made him—" Betty nodded toward Stu "—put up all kind of new locks."

"I told her, he only wanted dark-haired young girls, right? He wasn't gonna bother any of us. And if me and my son got ahold of him, he wasn't gonna bother nobody ever again."

"You really can't be too careful," Betty said, trying through emphasis to surmount the cliché. "Our neighborhood started—well, and we wanted more space, we just got so tired of that dingy old place, so we moved out here. Our rooms in the city were small and, you know, so dark. Dusty all the time."

Shields again told them he was convinced Burl would pop up.

"Bawl him out when he calls," he said, shaking his head sympathetically. "Worry a parent half to death this way. I got my own. I know how it is."

He left them smiling weakly, even charitably, and hurried back to his car. The hard plastic steering wheel was freezing, and Shields turned the heat up as soon as he started the engine. He was an orderly man, and he could never fail to notice that the beige bench seats of his city-supplied Oldsmobile wore bloody purple blotches on the passenger side, as if the vinyl had a rash. Amazing that you could get used to such things. Leaving the Bennetts' in search of the highway, he took a wrong turn, and then another, until he was lost. There seemed to be no signs. He drove for a while until he was in some kind of old-fashioned neighborhood or town, with regular streets and houses, wintry shrubs, and the grubby moraine of former snowfalls and melting ice in the gutters. He passed through a pleasant little shopping district and then a neighborhood of neatly kept old apartment buildings, some with nice dark canvas awnings. He saw knots of people walking leisurely but dressed up, the men wearing hats, and children scurrying in knots of their own or scampering from one pair of grown-ups to another. He knew he would come upon a synagogue soon and abruptly turned onto a side street. It made him ache sometimes to see children running happily about, without fear of bleeding to death from a scraped knee, and under the circumstances the Jewish Sabbath could only depress him.

It was Adam's circumcision that had given it away. The young doctor had joked that perhaps they should get a *mohel*, it's an era of specialization, and at first they had wished they had; the bleeding wouldn't stop and he seemed to have muffed the job, Shields was aghast that his baby's penis had been harmed, but then of course they thanked God they were in the hospital. The doctor tried the sinus spray; he said it was a trick the *mohel*s used, handy for constricting blood vessels, and harmless. But a little Sinex was no match for this, this inborn failing handed down generation after generation. They hadn't even known they were carriers. His wife took comfort in the Bible, but on that day she read that blood as the handwriting on the wall. The two of them since then had felt they'd been found wanting.

Shields drove what he guessed might be north, following bigger and bigger streets until he saw signs for the New Jersey Turnpike, and finally found his way home. He thought guiltily about Burl again and felt he'd accomplished something. He already knew there was no friend or vacation house, no old haunt that Burl might have fled to, selfishly failing to tell anyone. He was pretty certain Burl was scared but okay, off somewhere just waiting for the heat to die down. He'd slip up sooner or later, leave a record of himself somewhere so at least Shields could tell where he'd gone. No law against moving, after all. It's not a right in the Constitution, Shields remembered from his bleary nights in law school. But it's assumed.

In truth, visiting Stu and Betty was more for their benefit than his own. Shields knew that when a man is past a certain age, his friends and associates probably know him better than his parents do, and the police had interviewed all of them. Shields's pilgrimage was motivated less by his search for information than by his need for absolution, since guilt was a powerful drive always with him, guilt so well mixed with paternity it was hard to distinguish them from one another. Acting as a dutiful son to a father he could never truly know, he felt in a way he had fathered Burl's flight. Now he felt responsible.

The worst thing about fatherhood, Shields always felt, was not knowing things. You could not always be there to protect your children, and you knew this, so at some point not knowing became a blessing. Bad things happened all the time. You couldn't stand to know, so you rested with assumptions. You tried to make it very clear to all concerned that things shouldn't go past a certain point, but it was disconcerting when, as a father, you didn't know as much as a stranger. A perfect stranger.

Thus it was with doctors. He had learned a good deal about his son's disease since it all began, though, and he was no longer entirely at their mercy. *Lover of blood,* it meant. But it also meant, in Shields's case, that you didn't know your own family. The gene was recessive. Shields hadn't known his father; that entire side of him was a mystery to this day. His wife hadn't known of any hemophiliacs in her family either. The whole thing was a surprise. They had no more children after Adam.

It was expensive too. The hospital bills, medication, transfusions—if you really wanted the best, it was far beyond what his health insurance could handle. And because Adam needed her, or she needed him, Linda had stopped working.

Since then, Shields had made a fetish of being in the know. He knew what his colleagues on the force were up to, the petty corruption, the corrosive sea of drugs and other commercial offenses from which so many police officers supplemented their income. He didn't interfere—you couldn't interfere—but he stayed away from it. It was demeaning, he felt, to think of yourself as a chiseler in this way. You didn't even need it. You did it because it was in the air; the culture made it almost mandatory. You were suspect if you didn't. Shields's basic honesty was a problem for many of his colleagues. They knew by now he wasn't going to turn anyone in, but it made them feel bad. It was a constant reproach, his silent judgment enough to make everyone nervous. He worried when he was a patrolman that someday someone who couldn't stand the soiled bedclothes of a guilty conscience would shoot him by accident, sort of. It had happened before.

The way Shields saw it, you didn't want to know about most of the little things, but you had to know about the big ones. Knowledge was what he traded in. You had to give some to get some. You had to accept that some things in the world were a certain way and weren't going to change. You had to look out for your family, because the world would remind you again and again that it wasn't going to do that for you. And so when a chance came for Adam to get into a promising clinical trial at a famous New York hospital, and when one of the institution's major benefactors let it be known that he would be happy to help a police officer's little boy as long as there was no publicity about it, that was something you accepted. Who was it who said the ends don't justify the means? Someone who never had surgery. Someone whose little boy had no trouble with clotting. The experiment seemed to be helping Adam; except for a couple of bad episodes he was better, and that was what counted as long as Shields could walk the tightrope without letting anyone's competing interest make him fall. Besides, if the hospital considered Gemignani good enough to serve as a trustee, why should Shields object to his efforts on behalf of a little boy in desperate need of help?

So Shields made the phone call he had to make, happy that he needn't dissemble, glad that he had no knowledge in which to trade, relieved that neither Burl's family nor his friends had the slightest idea of where—or even who—the big man was.

"Plus we had the fire inspectors. That's why it was more this month."

"*Ohlala*. This city."

Louis Naumann and Frederic LaChaise met in the office. Through the open doorway they could hear chopping and the sounds of dishes being stacked as the restaurant prepared to face another day of dining.

"Money talks and bullshit walks in this town, know what I mean? That's why we have this little category, with the invoices from the East River. Truck drivers, inspectors. You name it. There's no single taxing authority here. Anyone in a position to cause problems takes a bite."

They were going over the accounts, an exercise for Frederic like his morning walk, good for him in some way he would never understand.

Lou droned on. He insisted on these sessions, wanting Frederic to hear of every expenditure as much as Frederic didn't want to hear, as much as Burl refused to hear. But Lou insisted, because he didn't want all the responsibility. If things went bad, he didn't want the blame. It wasn't fair for the partners to dine out year after year on his worry and not share a little of it, maybe gaining some appreciation along the way of what he went through in running the place. It kept them off his back. Frederic knew all this only as openness, but even when something extraordinary arose, there was always an explanation. So what was the point? He would never have detected anything amiss anyway and so during these sessions always did his best to distract his businesslike manager.

"You'll see the payroll is down this month," Lou said. "It was a short one, first of all, for pay purposes, and remember we were down two busboys for a week or so, which was okay in the end because it was a little slow anyway."

"Louis!" He shouldn't say anything, but he would, he had to. "Can you hold a secret?"

"Sure." Lou's poker face gave Frederic confidence. With a sidelong glance, he proceeded in confidential tones.

"I hear from Burl. *Vraiment!*"

"My nephew? You're kidding me!"

"Unbelievable, huh?" Frederic dropped his wrist and used it to shake his hand. "But he is well, I think so."

"I hope so. We've been worried to death about that guy. Jeez, his folks'll be glad to hear he's still alive at least. But why doesn't he call somebody or write or something? Where is he?"

Another sidelong glance.

"Las Vegas. Perhaps he is losing at cards. He send this note."
Lou read it quickly:

> *Frederic,*
> Everybody has to trust somebody sooner or later. I have
> always trusted you. I need you to draw as much cash as you can
> from my checking account using the enclosed ATM card, pin
> no. 0731. I think there's some daily limit, maybe you can go two
> or three times a week. There's only a couple thousand in the
> account, so it shouldn't take long to empty. Send me the pro-
> ceeds at the enclosed address. And please don't tell anybody—
> I mean *anybody*—where I am, at least for a month or so, until
> things cool down. Then just tell Louie to let my folks know I'm
> all right. Please don't ask questions, I'll explain it all later.
> *Burl*

"You send it?"

"The money is his." Frederic shrugged. "He send me his plastic card, secret number, I go to the machine and send him the
cash. It's a post office, the address. After that I hear nothing."

"Jeez. That's amazing. Ain't that a shame, the way he took off?
He musta been really scared "

"Don't tell anyone, you understand. He asked at least for a
while."

"Oh no," said Lou. "No no no."

"Because a big secret here. He made me promise"

"I got you."

"Between us, *oui?*"

"Hey, *certainment*. Listen, that whole business with the dead
men gets my nerves on edge. C'mon and have a drink. I got some
Calvados, make you feel like you're back in France. Right back in
your grandfather's garden that you used to talk about."

Frederic smiled uneasily, regretting his need to tell and thinking of his childhood home outside of Paris. It was all asphalt and

concrete now. When he was gone, Lou called his sister to let her know that Burl was okay.

"He doesn't even say a word? Just takes off? And when he needs money he turns to a stranger?"

"Freddy's not a stranger, they're good friends. We're partners."

"He took off without a word."

"At least he's safe. Betty, he was scared. It's not rational. You'll hear something soon."

"He's like his father. Like nothing's more important than the obligations men have to one another. It's a big show they put on for one another. It's convenient. That's all it is. Convenient."

"Betty, what can I say? I'd wring his neck if he was here."

"Have you told the police?"

"Nope."

"You want me to do it?"

"Nope."

"You just want to keep quiet? They're supposed to be looking for him."

"Better they don't find him. I hate to disillusion you, sweetheart, but I don't trust the cops. I got too many on my payroll."

"Oh, for God's sake. Sometimes I rue the day you ever got us into that place. That goddamn restaurant."

"You gotta take the bad with the good. That's my philosophy."

"Good-bye, Socrates. Keep me posted."

IT WAS MARCH. The sun had melted rivulets on the window, fogged to opacity by the heat inside, but it was still cold, and the radiator clattered ceaselessly each day until the management at the Chrysalis turned off the heat at night.

From above, it wasn't immediately clear that the pinkish flows and undulant mounds were those of a person. The impression was of a huge, ductile mass, organic but without scale, like some alien mountain range, or a pile of shaving cream or pudding up close. Burl would pass the time by squinting into the mirror on the ceiling over the bed, spying like a god on the fleshy landscape below and succumbing in an excess of self-love to a certain satisfaction. He created it, after all. A firmament of Burl. *This huge hill of flesh.* Seen through narrowed eyelids, there was something obscene here, or voyeuristic, he felt, like watching a man with two lovers snuggling tenderly in his arms. His massive breasts, furry with hair, could be their heads, sensitive to the movements of their host. His great thighs, his round arms, his mighty stomach, all implied a host, except despite the vastness of the flesh there were not several people but one, and Burl, like a god who suddenly sees himself, felt not love but shame. As each day passed into evening the light dimmed, and groggily he would watch his immobile form lit blue in the twilight of the television set, which was on all the time. Often he was amazed; in less organic moments, he could pass for a Henry Moore sculpture. I am large, he would think. I contain multitudes.

His image was stable now, which was a nice change. Sometimes when the sex upstairs got out of hand the ceiling shook, and the mirror set Burl's image aquiver. He worried that it might fall on him, and covered his private parts. He had had enough of broken glass.

Maybe his private parts were not in danger. He reminded himself of a eunuch in the mirror; he was so fat his sex organs had virtually disappeared, absconding with his libido. He could barely reach his penis and no longer experienced more than the casual arousal that comes from rubbing against his own pants or bedclothes. He'd stopped caring; it was difficult enough merely to breathe.

He knew that he was fatter than he had ever been, fatter than he had ever dreamed. If he stood or even sat for too long, his lower back became a torment. He lived on cash; he had still not had to use his credit cards, and as long as Frederic kept his word, people should continue to think their quarry in New York. One must always rely on somebody.

Burl tried not to think beyond his present suffering, which was ample enough, although increasingly it was hard for him to think clearly about anything. He was sleeping a lot, yet he was groggy all the time, and his snoring was so bad that the neighbors—a new set every few days—occasionally complained. Breath came only with mighty rasping noises, which at night sounded complicated and wet, the way he imagined a death rattle, and he often woke from dreams of suffocation to find himself in actual respiratory distress. Sometimes he just had to sit up and catch his breath.

He worried. His arms and legs twitched annoyingly, and sometimes he felt an unpleasant flutter in the center of his chest, as if a bird were imprisoned there. Some part of him suspected that by existing on such a grand scale, by expanding the quantity of life associated with Burl so that many and larger cells came increasingly to be, he was flirting with some natural threshold that threatened to reverse the whole process, perhaps radically. He might strangle on himself, choke, burst, die, and then wither into nothing.

He began to feel the first luscious, Ptolemaic stirrings of paranoia. It came in the increasing certainty that someone knew about him, knew and cared where he was. There would be a signal, a sign. But where? How? After much puzzling, he decided it would be in the newspapers. Of course. Thank God he'd kept them all! The stacks in his room were a complete archive of the Salt Lake City papers almost since the day of his arrival; this place really is a morgue, he thought. He began studying them, wondering if the message would be in code, or among the obituaries. Every morning he bought the papers afresh, dressing as well as he could to drag himself past the pool and into the glass-walled lobby, an air-conditioned 1950s aquarium with orange vinyl chairs in the Danish modern style and leafy plastic plants sprouting from kidney-shaped end tables that bore these bogus tropics to the desert.

He found nothing except a few items beneath even his level of suspicion: one day, for example, there were obituaries for the president of a meatpacking house, a bread-company executive, and one of Geronimo's great-grandsons. Amazing. A butcher, a baker, and an Indian chief, all in one day.

Perhaps what he was after was in *The New York Tribune*. Wouldn't that be the place to put a message for Burl? But no, that would mean someone who wanted to reach him didn't know where he was. Although there could be such people as well. He wished he could call Norma, or write his parents, but he didn't dare.

Burl soon stopped going out altogether. Why leave his room? Dressing was almost impossible, walking an ordeal. He certainly didn't relish being seen, and from this reluctance, like some redolent nightsoil, sprouted the rationale that someone might be watching. He'd given up bathing long ago.

So he spent his days in his undershorts, studying the papers until he dozed off, watching television, remembering his former life. Almost everything could be brought right to his door, and all of it was supplied by people born in another country. He grew accustomed to the waxy, cardboard taste these takeout foods seemed to share, or the hollow sound of his plastic fork against aluminum when he slipped slicing the lasagna that came in a disposable metal dish. By afternoon the little Formica desk in his room was covered with an array of empties: round tin containers like pie plates, their lids white on the outside but coated with aluminum to keep the food warm; squares of styrofoam that, rubbed the wrong way or scratched with plastic utensils, were like a nail on a blackboard; and a whole fleet of white Chinese food cartons, flaps open like sails on some Asian sea, their insides smeared with congealed sauces of khaki and orange and tidbits of onion or pepper, which Burl picked at after meals with chopsticks. He didn't notice it anymore because he no longer went out, but the room had a sweaty fragrance of sesame oil, body odor, and moldering newsprint. Every couple of days he'd cover himself and let the cleaning lady in. She cleared out the lot with her lips drawn up in distaste, as if she wanted to hold her nose. Burl remained in bed.

The stacked newspapers now lined every wall, diminishing the room by about a foot all around but perhaps functioning as insulation. Maybe that was why it seemed warmer lately at night.

Burl couldn't tell if it was the season or his weight. The room was getting sunnier in the mornings, and hotter, until finally he remembered one of the laboratory buildings at college and taped aluminum foil over the single large window, which darkened and cooled things considerably.

The more his accumulating newspapers shrank Burl's living space, the more compulsively he pored over them in search of he knew not what, studying the wary reportage of the church-owned daily and its dreary morning affiliate for some message from beyond. His fingers and soon his clothes were stained with printer's ink, and by the end of a morning's work his face was streaked with black as well. Over the months even the brown carpet grew visibly sullied. He paid special attention to the classifieds, of course, and as his money began to run out his desperation increased, his powers of concentration rising to a pitch he had never known before. He spent hours puzzling over the most mysterious items, sure at first that they were intended for him. He was looking for a sign.

About to doze off in an armchair, he spotted it.

WANTED
OBESE MEN & WOMEN
Major Salt Lake City research facility seeks obesity sufferers who are at least 100% overweight for experimental weight-loss program. Not a diet. Those accepted will receive payment, free treatment, and in all likelihood a longer life. Call Dr. Stringer at 832-6161.

A longer life indeed. Burl was attracted mainly by the very presence of this notice in the newspaper, which he read like a seer parsing entrails. And of course by the money. He'd spent most of what he had left at the Holy Grail, and he would cut his wrists with his credit cards before he would use them.

Could this be the message? A ploy? A code of some kind? He dialed cautiously.

"St. Ferdinand Medical Center. Hello, St. Ferd—"

He hung up. Consulting the yellowing white pages stuffed in the drawer with the Bible, he found that 832-6161 was indeed listed as the hospital's switchboard. Burl examined the pages for tampering and found none. The phonebook, with an overwrought Western motif on the cover, was two years old, meaning the listing was an established one. In the hall, the ice machine shuddered into action. Burl called again and made an appointment.

When the time came, he rose nervously and opened his closet for what seemed like the first time in weeks. He wanted to dress carefully, to approach this with dignity, but putting clothes on reminded him of how truly enormous he had become. His pants didn't come close to closing, and his shirts, buttoned only under the most strenuous resistance, clung like an uncomfortable skin. He felt trussed, suppressed. Seams sliced his flesh under the arms and across his neck, while his pants, zipped as high as possible under the circumstances, compressed his thighs and buttocks mercilessly. The crotch made his scrotum burn.

Burl wanted to sit down and cry, but the image of himself, shoulders heaving in his ridiculous outfit, would have been worse. Besides, it was obvious that sitting would be impossible.

He tried to move around. The plan now was to leave his shirt-tails out, more or less covering his unfastened trousers, and hope that things held together long enough to reach the car. He would just have to drive with his pants down, and he moved toward the bathroom for a towel to cover his lap. In reaching for it he tore what sounded like a gaping hole in the back of his shirt, and his efforts to twist around and get a look at it were rewarded with yet another clawing sound, for a second tear. Furious now, he tore the shirt open, sending buttons popping against the cheap tiles, and stalked back into his room. He pulled the topsheet off the bed, used his clipping scissors to slice a rough hole in the center, and then pulled it over his head. It made a perfect toga, reaching just down a few inches below his knees. There was ample material at the sides, which he folded up and fastened with safety pins. He felt comfortable, but in the mirror he resembled that repulsive Pillsbury Doughboy, dimpled and giggling. Maybe a sash of some kind. Certainly the Romans wore belts; he tried to recall Richard Burton and Laurence Olivier. With his scissors he cut the length of another sheet, slicing off a foot-thick swath, which he rolled and wound around his waist a couple of times, tucking the end in.

Much better! Except for the faded ink of the Consolidated Laundry label, which even lent a certain postindustrial cachet to the hem, he felt himself not unreasonably presentable. He donned his huge, dark woolen coat, beating the dust and must out of it first, and looked at himself again. Elegant! Almost elegant! How different from his usual look! Why should fat people keep trying to shoehorn themselves into fashions made for an entirely different body type? Why should they not have their own style, as befits their own special needs? Perhaps he might write something about this. But did togas have pockets? Or did the Romans carry some kind of pouch or sashlike purse diagonally across the chest? Well, for now the coat pockets would suffice. He looked at himself again, skeptically. The dark wool, draped open, conferred a certain dignity; against the pure white of the sheet, it was almost formal. Burl was transformed. Smoothing his hair, breathing heavily, hot but not completely humiliated, he waddled for the door.

Approaching it sideways, he was startled by how narrow the frame now seemed. It was sobering. He tried to pass through quickly, dismissing the doorway and its implications, mentally leaving it behind, but it tugged at him embarrassingly. Annoyed, he dragged himself through, or perhaps halfway through, and was even more embarrassed at the effort it would clearly require to drag the entire corpus entirely past. He pushed painfully, harder, and then harder still. It was like straining at the bowels. Burl's face reddened, and establishing a grip on the lintel with one hand and digging in with his back foot on the carpet, he pushed with all his considerable might until it hurt, until he could feel the strikeplate from the lock in his back. He was drenched. Sweltering, he was certain he could make it without the coat, but when he tried to withdraw he couldn't move. In growing panic he scraped and pawed, grunting with exertion, but to no avail. Stuck! It began to dawn that he would remain here until set free, and he blushed to recall the taunts of childhood:

Fatty, fatty, two by four,
Can't fit through the kitchen door.

A short woman in her thirties, tan and blond, with small features pushed together toward the center of her face, was approaching with a toddler of perhaps five. They wore swimsuits and flopped along with towels, sandals, sunscreen, and other pool paraphernalia, the mother's spreading bottom demurely covered by a little bathing dress, her thighs rippling with each watchful step. They both hung back a bit and leaned toward the far wall, the mother instinctively taking her daughter's shoulders, the little girl reaching for her mother's hand.

"Stuck," Burl panted. "Ridiculous. Isn't it? Stuck. Fast. They. Say. Stuck slow. Really."

The little girl was awestruck. As they moved off, she regained sufficient composure to ask, "Mommy, if he's too big to get out, how did he get in there?"

"Shhh, I don't know, honey. Watch the stairs now."

"And the smell—"

"Shush, I said."

Burl cherished the dim silence of the windowless hall, so soothing compared to a subway station or fast-food restaurant, places where unyielding environments had arrested him before. My womb undoes me, he thought. The fire department came fast, a cadre plodding down the hall with those rubber sounds, coats and boots squeaking and scraping. Their Anglo-Saxon uniformity, their uninflected speech, and all their equipment, which Burl heard more than he saw, gave them an air of seriousness that was upsetting to him. He wanted to take this lightly, wanted it to be taken so.

"Sorry. About. This." He paused for breath. "In a. Kind of. Spot."

He was breathless. He couldn't find a way to stand comfortably; the pressure on his abdomen was almost like a punch, and he felt stabbed from behind by some part of the jamb. "Located individual stuck in doorway," one of them said into a handheld radio, with matter-of-factness bordering on ennui. They all seemed bothered by something, the air perhaps. "About to extricate. We think an ambulance, ah, Chrysalis Motel? Right, same. Ten-four." Why do we have to medicalize this, Burl wanted to ask, but he was too embarrassed. Besides, the clank and thunk of axes, sledgehammers, and so forth as they dropped to the floor made him feel like a dental patient, and in fact his rescuers insisted on holding an oxygen mask over his face for a while, and would have left it had the strap been big enough to reach around his head. It was immediately clear they couldn't pull him out, and virtually without consultation—had they done this before?—they attacked the wall behind him. He felt the power of their blows, conducted perhaps by the doorframe, right down to his fillings. When they had a big enough hole—it was only drywall, after all—they found the framing still unwilling to release him, and so Burl heard the

unbearable scream of a power saw, at least until better sense prevailed and a hand saw was inserted. Someone behind Burl worked
it aggressively—zip-zap, zip-zap, *zip*-zap—until the frame began
to bend against its burden. Finally the frame snapped and with a
yank he was out, freed suddenly in a cloud of gypsum dust and
debris. Deprived of support, he nearly fell over and took a couple
of firefighters with him. Lilliputians, they seemed.

"Easy, now. Lean against the wall for a minute."

"I'm. Okay."

"You look kind of blue."

"Not happy. Experience. Being stuck."

"Your skin." He was a healthy young man with perfect teeth.
"Sally, what do you think?"

"He's blue all right. Sir, I want you to just relax and take some
more oxygen."

Burl inhaled gratefully, with noisy rasps muffled by the plastic mask. It tasted cold. Blue? Could the light of the television
have dyed him somehow? He was always ruddy, hot pink where
people could see and a kind of parchment on the rest of his body.
He wasn't *feeling* blue.

A gurney was brought sliding through the debris, but it was
laughably slender and spindly legged, as if designed for speed
rather than strength, and to the relief of the cavalry that had
come to his rescue, Burl waved it away. He rode to St. Ferdinand's
on the ambulance floor.

————————

Burl sat perched uncomfortably on an unusually generous examining table, wearing a flimsy cotton medical gown that didn't
seem to fasten in the back, so that he felt shamefully naked and
compelled to keep trying to cover himself. Finally, a couple of

nurses began to work him over, sampling with jaded cheer his blood and urine, standing him gingerly on some kind of industrial scale (whose reading—493 pounds—they recorded without comment), and measuring his blood pressure with the largest pressure cuff Burl had ever seen. At this result at least their eyebrows rose. Burl was already tired and irritable from his morning's adventure and the endless forms they'd had him complete with an uncomfortably skinny pen that felt, in his hammy fist, like writing with a length of wire. Medical histories were tiresome for Burl under the best of circumstances, since his was so long and complicated. Then he was left alone in his medical gown, humiliatingly open in the rear, until one of the nurses told him to dress.

"The doctor will see you in just a little while."

Burl donned his toga and adjusted it as well as he could. On his way down the hall, he had the feeling he got just before going for a haircut, when it came over him that his hair now looked just right and didn't need cutting. The world that had seemed too small for him no longer was so. He noticed the generous doorways, the wide halls scuffed here and there by gurneys and wheelchairs. Why couldn't the rest of the world be cut to such generous proportions?

He was wary of the unseemly haste surrounding his presence and wasn't altogether buying the program. He rejected an intravenous line as treatment for which he had not signed up, and along those lines he insisted on walking to the doctor's office, refusing the extra-wide wheelchair that had brought him to the examining room in the first place. It reminded him of those Taft chairs in old hotels, extra-wide antiques made to order for an anticipated visit by America's biggest president. On the elevator—extra-wide doors again—Burl felt the tiny diamonds stamped into the steel walls. He was no inmate yet.

Upstairs he found a tall, slender man in a brownish plaid shirt, beige knit tie, and white coat. His forehead was as high as it could be without blending indistinguishably into his scalp, his brown hair combed across the top. His nose was long and sharp, an accusatory finger, and his eyes shone without warmth.

"Mr. Bennett?" he said with a cold smile, extending his hand.

Burl shook it and read the little white tag on his breast pocket.

"Dr. Stringer."

"That's me. Have a seat, Mr. Bennett."

Burl settled himself in a loveseat in the center of the room, and Stringer took the armchair perpendicular to it.

"You know, of course, that you have a weight problem. Do you have any idea how severe it is?"

The wall behind Stringer was covered with laminated diplomas in dead languages and incomprehensible typefaces.

"Pretty severe?"

"I want to be frank, Mr. Bennett. In my opinion your condition is life threatening. Your blood pressure is sky high, you have diabetes, and from your blue skin and the symptoms you describe, you suffer from Pickwickian syndrome."

"Like in Dickens?"

"Like Fat Boy, exactly. Textbook case. Obesity, cyanosis, obstructive apnea, somnolence, respiratory acidosis, low alkaloids, muscular twitching, heart failure practically any minute. In plain English, you're eating yourself to death, and your bodily systems are about to collapse under the strain."

He was silent for a moment; the only sound was the rasp of Burl's breathing. In measured tones, Dr. Stringer continued.

"Cyanosis is blue skin, from insufficient oxygen in the blood. Obstructive apnea means you stop breathing now and then, mainly during REM sleep. You snore like a buzzsaw. You're sleepy all the time. Breathing's labored the rest of the time too."

Burl felt small again. It was embarrassing to hear this account of himself. It was like being warned for masturbating, like carrying the smell of semen on his hands.

"Still," Stringer continued, speaking with what seemed deliberate slowness, "you're fairly strong, under the circumstances, and there are no other abnormalities that aren't weight related. For all these reasons, you'd be an ideal candidate for an experimental weight-control program we have here at St. Ferdinand's."

The two men sat in silence for a moment until Burl felt able to mimic full consciousness.

"Tell me about it," he said thickly.

"It's a pilot project, a twist that I've developed on a very well-established medical procedure called a banded vertical gastroplasty, which I hope solves certain problems, the low incidence of which has plagued this field for some time. It's a surgical procedure, basically, in which we partition the stomach, walling off the great bulk of it so that only a small pouch remains available to food."

"Isn't that dangerous? How would I live?"

"It's not terribly dangerous anymore; certainly it's not nearly as dangerous as allowing your weight to continue increasing, or even maintaining its current level."

"I'm not usually this fat," Burl said. "This is kind of an aberration."

"How about your parents? Are they the same way?"

"No. Quite thin."

"Other family members? Grandparents?"

"No, just me. I'm the lucky one. I just haven't had the will to take any of this off lately."

"But you've been seriously overweight a long time."

"Yes. Always, really."

Stringer leaned forward.

"Burl, over the years you've accumulated some very serious weight-related medical baggage, which, if left unchecked, will have devastating consequences. Consider your breathing problem. Alveolar hypoventilation. Without treatment, pulmonary hypertension, maybe even pulmonary embolism. Right ventricular hypertrophy, erythrocytosis and so forth. Or the chronic backaches you no doubt suffer. I think you indicated that here somewhere . . ." He shuffled through Burl's forms.

"I do, I uh, have had back troubles."

"Probably incipient intervertebral disc disease. Your spine can't handle all that weight. You're grinding it into dust, Burl. Or your blood pressure. Hypertension as pronounced as yours will kill your kidneys. You already show signs of gradual collagenous fibrosis with marked luminal narrowing. And uremia; I smelled it as soon as you walked in."

Burl flushed, but Stringer continued.

"While we're in the neighborhood, your inadequate testicular function comes from sky-high estrogen production, which looks"— he flipped through the papers again—"maybe 15, 16 times normal. It exaggerates the formation of fat cells and throws your hypothalamic-pituitary-testicular system completely out of whack."

"I haven't had much use for any of that stuff anyway," Burl joked weakly.

"I think you understood when you called us that you had to do something. I'm fairly certain we can help you."

"One problem is that I don't have any money, and I don't have any insurance. Your ad said the program is free."

"That's correct. We're trying to build this institution into a center of bariatric surgery based on some of my research, and for certain qualified candidates it becomes worthwhile for us to perform our work for free and even pay a modest follow-up stipend where warranted."

"Would this be permanent? The surgery, I mean."

"Preferably. It can be undone in two distinct ways. We can reverse it surgically for medical reasons, which is rarely indicated. Or you can eat your way out of it."

Burl enjoyed the feeling of looking up at the ceiling going by as he was wheeled along.

"Do you have a wide-load sign for this thing?" he asked.

He had expected to move through the halls faster, but what after all was the rush? Surrounded by orderlies who nudged and tugged to help the slow-moving vessel negotiate corners and avoid obstacles, he felt like an oil tanker brought home by tugs.

He really wasn't nervous until they put the mask over his face and told him to breathe deeply, counting backward from 100. Even then, he decided, there are worse ways to die.

IN THE MONTHS THAT followed, Burl lost him-
self. Back at the Chrysalis, where the insurance company had paid
for the broken doorway, Dr. Stringer had prevailed upon the management, and the kindly owner was charitable, even amused. Burl
had only to pay his rent in advance and show daily, by his appearance at the front desk, that he could get through the door of
his latest room. "I know," Burl said, in his tremulous postoperative
voice. "Before it was like a camel through the eye of a needle."
There would be no more sending out for food.

It is not a pleasant thing to feel yourself liquefy. "When the
body converts fat into energy," Stringer had warned, "a great deal
of water is released." Burl was literally pissing himself away, in the
early weeks wearing a coat of paint off the wall on his way to the
bathroom. That was until he got thin enough finally to stumble
into the john unscathed.

At the beginning it was difficult because there was still pain
from the surgery, as well as vomiting and diarrhea. He hadn't
much wanted food and thought of himself as convalescent, a

pleasant idea that gave him a clear goal and excused him from his own harshest judgments. His circumstances put him in mind of Saint Nicholas von Flüe, fifteenth-century sufferer of a stomach-ache so bad that he went the last 30 years of his life without eating. He dispensed wisdom from a mountaintop, living on thin air.

Burl's early symptoms for the most part disappeared, but they left a chronic weakness that he could not shake. Beyond that, there was the knowledge that he really was losing himself. In the span of a few months he lost an average man's body weight, and even though the transformation he saw was gradual, it came upon him with the force of a death.

The hospital's compulsory counseling sessions were no help at all. Members of the group sat in a circular arrangement of Barcaloungers and other large and sturdy chairs, since it would be catastrophic for someone's seat to collapse while sharing his or her pain about being fat. Several of the dozen participants, like Burl, had already had weight-reduction surgery; one had had it twice. The rest were candidates, as was evident from their enormous bulk. Some were even fatter than Burl had been at his peak, and one of these, a black man named Earl, was certainly the fattest person Burl had ever encountered. He was brought into the sessions in what must have been a custom-designed wheelchair, which he almost entirely obscured by pouring over its edges like a melting sundae. Burl liked him. Earl spoke shyly and, perhaps because there was no question of establishing credentials, didn't seem to vie with the others to see whose suffering was greatest. Burl was interested to hear that although Earl had long ago stopped leaving his house, he'd had the doorways widened anyway, in case of fire.

It was hard for Burl to fit in. Aside from Bob, the group's wan and passive leader—his look of alert sympathy, his droopy mustache, his leg over the chair arm all so maddening to Burl—and Earl, there was only one other man in the group, Andrew, who seemed unable to settle on the right expression for the occasion, his face alternating between embarrassment and defiance. Beside him rested a large stuffed rabbit.

The rest of those in the group were women, and their sense of grievance over society's insistence that they be thin and beautiful gave their comments a legitimacy that made Burl's own troubles seem paltry by comparison. But he also detected an accusatory energy that he felt was directed at himself, which only increased his desire to be elsewhere.

Edna was speaking. She wore proper clothes instead of caftans, but the obese, in dressing themselves, always trod the edge of parody, Burl felt, and Edna seemed to have crossed it, looking in her huge khaki wraparound skirts and paisley scarves, her billowing alligator shirts and flat pink slip-ons, like some country catalog reflected in a funhouse mirror. He was reminded of his own former fastidiousness. She must have spent hours on her looks; her lush and pampered hair was swept neatly back to bare a swollen face of moist and unblemished skin anointed with all the right creams and oils, burnished golden brown by the sun, and set off against sticky red lips. But it was a thin skin, easily bruised by the climate of opinion it encountered.

"We moved a lot when I was a kid," she said, thin lipped. "You can imagine, it was, well, very traumatic. It was hard enough to make friends in any case."

Looking bravely at the ceiling, she seemed to choke with emotion, but with a show of courage carried on.

"Every time we moved to a new neighborhood, my mother pulled something new. She wasn't fat, you see, but her sisters were. Once when we moved she left behind my bicycle, because she didn't want me riding it around outside. She, um, she hated the idea of this fat kid on the bicycle. I mean, what would the neighbors say?"

Burl tried to arrange a sympathetic look but was embarrassed at this public outpouring and secretly worried that his own carefully nursed grievances were just as banal. Edna must have read his mind.

"I feel you're judging me," she said suddenly, shifting her bulk effortfully in his direction, like a battleship turning broadside to bring all guns to bear. "Your silence is very aggressive."

"Silence is assent," Burl said nervously.

"Not here! Not here! Here it's an aggressive act. You never share with the group." They both glanced toward Bob, himself a veteran of stomach surgery.

"Perhaps Burl just needs to become a little more comfortable in the group," Bob said. "I don't feel he's judging."

"We're always being judged by men," Sylvia retorted. "Even your role here is that of a judge, and Bob, you're a man too."

"Exactly!" Edna agreed.

"I saw that in my family all the time," Jeanette said. "But the women were worse. They bought the whole program. My mother would never go to a restaurant with me. She never wanted anyone to see me eating, and I still feel the same way about myself."

Another woman, who had the deflated, melancholy look of one who'd had stomach-reduction surgery about six months earlier, said everyone in her family hoped that after the operation she might find a man and marry, but that she had since discovered she was a lesbian. Jeanette, who was black, sympathized, but Sylvia challenged her. Obesity was more acceptable in black women, she asserted.

"Well, that kind of stereotype is exactly the problem," Jeanette said. "You see what I'm talking about?"

It was all true, horribly and obviously true, Burl felt guiltily. Worse, he felt as he had among the Tongans, their fat feet slapping noisily on the linoleum; he felt cast among life's losers and anxious to get away. Feeling this way shamed him further, but not as much as the idea that someone might think he belonged here.

"You're too concerned about your dignity," Bob chided after one such session. "I'll bet you don't dance either. Right? It's amazing what you can do when you stop worrying about looking foolish. Let it go, Burl. You're among friends here."

Burl felt mocked by this and decided to mark the death of so much of himself in more traditional ways. He'd had plenty of grief, but his direct funerary experience was slight, and so he borrowed. Already thin enough to wear his largest, darkest suit, he rent its sleeve at the shoulder and then covered the mirrors and windows with other dark suits, until the room was draped on all sides with masses of brooding fabric. It was startling to go into the bathroom and not see himself, but perhaps for the best; his new room at the Chrysalis fortunately had no mirror on the ceiling, but the place still mocked him. There was a kitchen this time instead.

He lived on tablets and water at first, vitamins and diuretics, Tylenol and Prozac, a whole pharmacopoeia of multicolored pills and capsules spaced throughout the day to avoid giving offense to his vastly diminished stomach. These he swallowed.

But food was something else. All he took at the beginning was water, then a little lemonade, and finally a bit of orange juice watered to dilute the acid. As time went on, though, Burl began to recover his health and his appetite. One night he visited one of the Chinese restaurants he'd used to frequent with Engel. He ordered a few appetizers, hoping he could just take a little taste of each, but the fried meat dumplings were so good, the wonton soup so salty, that he got a little carried away and was almost immediately violently ill. In the shabby men's room, with its tiny sink and continuous towel roll, Burl bore suddenly the full, pathetic weight of his tragedy: no more food. The sole tactile dimension of his prior life was a thing of the past, sacrificed to science and the promise of thinness. Now he really was a eunuch, stripped of the power to achieve gratification, deprived of the only way he had ever known how to reproduce. He must follow Paul's advice to the Romans: "Spend no more thought on nature and nature's appetites." But for what? To prolong his life? What was that without the capacity to taste and consume?

It did not take him long to discover that only the power to consume was gone. The ability to taste lived on, cursedly at first, and like a stroke victim who has suffered brain damage and must relearn the basics, Burl rediscovered the pleasures his tongue could hold. Few things were more profoundly satisfying than a palmful of salt, licked at like a doe, or a single damp cherry tomato (he spent afternoons searching out the very ripest) dipped in the glass saltcellar he kept at his writing table. A spoonful of fruit preserves, or sour yogurt perhaps mixed with a tad of vanilla, he would hold in his mouth like a sip of Bordeaux until his tonsils tingled.

It was an interesting discipline, relearning to taste. He tested sections of his tongue, mingled flavors two at a time, concentrated like an oenophile on the flavor of a glass of water, reaching to sense iron and chlorine, noticing for the first time its slippery finish on the palate. Who knew what the stuff had been through to make it fit for human consumption? He became like those monkish early gourmets who, limited only to bread or other simple foods, sought perfection within the narrow confines of their culinary world. It's only natural to substitute quality for quantity under the circumstances.

Monkish though he felt, Burl still couldn't be satisfied with bread and water. He soon busied himself cooking up minuscule sections of chopped beef, filet mignon, salmon, or potato, each just a mouthful. Quickly graduating to more elaborate dishes, he took deep satisfaction in a kind of gustatory scrimshaw: puttanesca sauce with half an anchovy, an olive, one caper, and the barest sliver of garlic, for example. He used the same Lilliputian proportions to prepare other favorites: chopped liver, lamb vindaloo, moussaka, steak and onions with old-fashioned mashed potatoes.

Ingredients never come in such small packages, though, and pretending to be horrified by the waste, Burl soon began cooking in full. He tried eating just a single mouthful at first, but this was torture, and so he decided to eat larger portions, entire meals, without swallowing any. With much painful practice, he trained himself to "eat" a meal this way, spitting each mouthful into a bag at his feet until at the end of his meal he could carry its queasy weight to the trash. He only stopped out of boredom or fatigue. He was, after all, full when he started.

The worst thing is to grieve alone, and so Burl sought the company of other mourners. In the newspapers, which he continued to read compulsively and not without a glimmer of hope, he studied the death notices. On weekday mornings, when he could rouse himself early enough from his torpor, he went to Catholic masses for the dead. He liked these well enough, with candles glowing at either end of the casket set beneath the soaring ceiling, the priestly vestments and holy tone, the incense swinging back and forth, the deceased consigned to the angels in paradise, his soul borne off by winged cherubs as in those paintings. Sometimes he even took the sacrament, which he hadn't done since childhood. He wondered idly how many calories the Host might have, and whether the Blood could be fattening at all. It was intoxicating on an empty stomach. But Burl was the other kind of catholic, heterogeneous in his funerary preferences, and he attended any death rites that happened to come his way, so that he watched Protestants coping bravely with loss and Jews offering ancient prayer in remembrance of the departed. He would fall in among the mourners sometimes and bask in their condolence, and he understood then, in a way, how it might be meant when people said someone else had died for their sins. Yet it was a sorry thing for Burl to find his own grief discharged through the sadness of these strangers, because it reminded him of his circumstances. After all, whose death might so directly move him? And who might mourn him so if he should die?

Today, as on so many days, there was grave Pachelbel, who was to funerals now what Brahms was to weddings. Burl sat sore-assed on a copper-colored metal folding chair, narrow and hard, "Samsonite" decal peeled partly off the chair back in front of him, as the room gradually filled with mourners. He judged them mildly, aware of his own sad departure from his former care with dress. Some were in neutral flaxen sportcoats, white socks, loud ties or dresses, too much hair spray. Brimming with nerves and emotion, a middle-aged man rose to remember the dead.

"We were associates . . . partners . . . friends . . . for more than 30 years." The man's hair was white, slicked back from a low hairline. "Thirty years. We built a business together. First for Avery; then for Dataprint, when they came in."

He stood beside the lectern, leaning, his dark tie short on his protuberant belly, his suit brown and shiny.

"Gene was there." He waved helplessly. "He was there every step. Every step of the way. He was a salesman. Boy was he a salesman. He knew pressure-sensitive labels inside and out, nobody better. Company used to call him on things; he knew more than they did. And he knew people. We had some hard times, Gene and I. He stuck by me—" Burl felt a lump forming in his throat at this "—through thick or thin. His word really was his bond. And I don't know how—"

The tears came then, and Burl felt his own eyes dampen as well. He adored the banal eulogy of loving friends, the paean to the dead man's extraordinary accountancy, what an honest golfer he was, how much he knew about brassieres, how well he drove a car, his unswerving devotion to Little League. A husband and father. In cracking voices they spoke of his affection for dogs, his modest and always humorous pennypinching (tearful laughter at this), inevitably so in contrast to his well-known generosity. And it really was moving; the very banality of it brought tears. "Goodbye, sweet prince," a dopey niece bids the indifferent dead. This was what a life was.

"Snowy fields. Strong arms. Your hairy squeeze."

A loving daughter, at the podium, peered through glasses like goggles beneath a floppy hat with upturned brim. She was moved to a form of funereal free verse that Burl knew well by now, one best delivered in earnest fragments to convey the inchoate nature of the sensitive eulogist's response to this tragedy.

"Whirring engines. The fragrant oil, your skillful socket wrench clicking in the driveway . . ."

It wasn't a particularly emotional funeral—Burl guessed the man had been dying for a while—yet our hero sat quietly blubbering, the grandest mourner present. Afterward, when most of the others were gone, he felt a hand on his shoulder and saw a box of Kleenex thrust before him. He took one and nodded warily at the carefully attired stranger.

"Take two. I buy them in bulk."

Burl took another, and when he was finished blowing the man stuck out his hand.

"Mort Allen," he said, fingernails buffed bright. "You haven't been in for a while."

Burl shrugged and looked around, fearful of a trap.

"Hey, hey, we've missed you," Allen assured smoothly. "You add something to the proceedings. Kind of a hobby of yours, isn't it?"

"I'm mourning a loss myself," Burl ventured. "It helps to be among others."

"That's the name of the game, my friend."

"I'm about over it," Burl said, sensing a good time to go, but Allen seized him by the arm.

"You know, you've really contributed something around here. What better way to remember a loved one than to give something to others?"

"My feelings exactly," Burl said, rising.

"Look, this can be very rewarding, I mean in ways you might not have thought of. Are we beginning to understand each other?"

Burl was running out of money anyway. It hardly seemed work, attending services at the Allen Funeral Home, and at $35 each, how could he say no? To Allen, apparently, it was worth it; he felt people would come away from one of his funerals with the sense of release that only a public display of grief could provide, without themselves having to muster that display. It was Allen's hope that this would fix the experience in their minds, so that when they needed to make funeral arrangements themselves someday they would remember the place favorably. Burl was most useful when someone died virtually alone; he helped the few on hand feel less lonely, less put upon.

He was good at the job; he got a new dark suit (he was down to a svelte size 48) and quickly learned the ropes. And he tried not to let it turn altogether into work, picking and choosing funerals to avoid those certain to be too much for him. Allen preferred that the deceased's family not have to minister too much to the professional mourner. Burl avoided the funerals of women for that very reason; they were just too sad, the whole place stumbling and weeping, graying sons, haggard and fleshy, supporting wobbly aunts who knew they were next. The saintly descriptions of dead women always seemed more accurate, their selflessness less conjured by those who remembered them, often those who were given life by them. Maybe he was jealous. No dead children, either. He stuck to grown men and wept modestly, in dignity.

It was a strange thing to learn one's way around a mortuary. The dead here, at this remove from their habitat in life, seemed more like mannequins, wax dummies merely modeled after living people. The thought crossed Burl's mind that he could help out with the obituaries, phoning them practically written into the local papers. What the heck, even start a business: a wire service, of sorts, offering obituaries on everybody in the county and celebrities coast to coast. Free the papers from these awful funeral directors, careless news clerks, the annoyance of being late reporting on one.

But it finally started to strike him as morbid, and much as he needed the money to pay his rent at the Chrysalis, he quit. Mourning for a living didn't make death less sad, only less emotional, which was worse. Burl had been starting to professionalize the thing. An element of calculation had crept into his mourning, and he felt, in encountering the families of the dead, an unctuous look beginning to spread across his face. You could not always weep for the dead, Burl discovered, even when the dead one was you.

So gradually he withdrew from the mourning business, much to his employer's disappointment. The Chrysalis was depressing in warm weather, and rather than slip back into his former eremitic state, Burl tried to get himself outdoors as much as he could. It was late summer, and the dry heat struck him with a mocking blast whenever he left his air-conditioned cocoon. But it was a pleasure. The natural environment, however urbanized, seemed an effective balm for the changes wrought in his body by technological artifice. It was also a pleasure compared to the oppressive summers he was accustomed to in New York, whose streets were soupy with humidity. It was strange but pleasing not to sweat for a change; the desert air made your skin feel papery, and walking around in it hatless for hours on end was like taking a drug. It made Burl lightheaded, sometimes even dizzy. Dr. Stringer warned him about it; his stomach wouldn't hold much water, so he was supposed to sip slowly all day long to avoid dehydration. Needle or no, he was the opposite of a camel. He took to carrying a canteen.

Thus equipped, Burl went daily into the streets, wandering all over the city. He worked his thighs to exhaustion roaming the tantalizing hills of the Marmalade District, its charming streets named once upon a time for fruits that Burl couldn't eat: Apricot, Quince, Almond, Grape, Strawberry, Currant. When he tired of the chockablock dollhouses, bright palette, and fussily tended flowers, he tramped east on South Temple, out past the great mansions, up through the gracious Avenues district, toward the university. There was shade in these leafy precincts, respite from the windswept avenues of the central city, and he enjoyed the old polygamy houses, with separate wings for a man's two families. One day when he awoke tired of the city, unable to face slogging through it again as if it were his job to survey the place on foot, he hitched a ride out to the great and eerie Salt Lake, which alone among bodies of water could offer him the buoyancy he had once felt whenever he was wet.

He arrived early in the day, the high desert sun already hot on his bare skin, the air filled with the sulfurous stench of plants choking on too much salt. A hot, briny wind blew in off the water, which was defended by a cloud of tiny flies, but other than the insects, Burl was alone. He quickly stripped off his clothes and forged ahead, hurrying through the brine flies to wade into the cool lake, his breath coming short as it rose against his trunk, until he gave himself over to it. With a great effort, he dunked himself completely so he could later feel the salt drying all over himself. May it pickle me, he thought, fighting his way down against this otherworldly buoyancy, his eyes pierced as if by needles. He bobbed up panting, teary eyed, and finally gave himself up. Propped on these magical waters, chest hairs powdered with salt, Burl did the backstroke now and then but mainly just reclined, floating blind under the sun in what seemed to him a vast baptismal font from which one emerged stinging and encrusted but clean. Maybe Engel's brother-in-law was right, Burl thought, remembering that epochal feast. Maybe it really does make a new man of you.

PART Two

And homeless near a thousand homes I stood,
And near a thousand tables pined and wanted food.

—*Wordsworth, "Guilt and Sorrow"*

HE AWOKE SMELLING DAMP and eggy, his face cold, his body sore. You couldn't cover the grate too thickly if you wanted to feel the heat; thus, when Burl rose it was with a grillwork design pressed into his flesh, right through the blankets and clothes. When he woke up, it itched.

The advantage of having no useful stomach to speak of, its great indisputable virtue, is that you really can live on virtually nothing. You had to. Burl was used to it by now. He received a supply of vitamins and liquid protein during his periodic visits to see Dr. Stringer, who followed his case with rapt medical attention and never stopped trying to enlist psychiatrists in the cause. Of food, clothing and shelter, Burl marveled at times that he now seemed able to dispense with two of the three.

He traveled light. Everything he owned nowadays fit in a single suitcase, which one of the hospital maintenance men kept for him. St. Ferdinand's had become something of a way station for Burl; it was on a hospital vent that he slept and in the hospital that he showered occasionally and groomed himself. Because he enjoyed the hike and nursed fond memories, he sometimes walked out to the LDS laundromat he'd used to run with Engel, but each time he went the other man was missing, until finally he learned that Engel had moved up in the hierarchy and was now in charge of several laundromats. One day Burl got up his courage and trekked over to the one he'd been told Engel used as a kind of home base. Burl found him in the back, making change and selling soap as before.

"Hey, Engel," Burl waved a five, expecting to surprise his prey. "I need a box of Tide and the rest in quarters."

Engel looked annoyed. Without the faintest hint of recognition, he plopped down the little box of detergent and 16 quarters. Burl stared at him.

"There you go, take it," Engel said. "What are you looking at?"

"Engel. C'mon. Let's let bygones be bygones."

"Hey, man, why you keep calling me Engel? Do I know you?"

Burl stared and stared until he realized, with a certain awe, that Engel had not the faintest notion of who he might be.

"Rex," Burl said. "Remember me? With a beard."

Engel was dumbstruck.

"As a sumo, I guess I'm kind of off the fast track," Burl said.

"Holy shit," said Engel. "Holy fucking shit."

"What? C'mon, Engel, this is creepy, there are people around."

"Rex, what happened?" Engel looked him up and down. "You decided to starve yourself? You get cancer?"

"I had my stomach stapled. I eat like a bird. It's handy when the economy gets slow."

They sat in a little room behind the counter and off to the side, where they could have some peace and quiet. Engel couldn't get over it.

"You know your voice has changed? You're completely different, a different person."

"C'mon, Engel, I'm not that different."

"Totally! I mean, unrecognizable, man. Everything about you."

"So you had no idea at all. When I walked in, I mean."

"None. I thought you were some kinda homeless person, some transient."

"Well, you had that right. But you had no idea it was the king?"

"It's not the king. Listen, man, I'm gonna call you Burl from now on. The king is dead."

And so he was. Engel was somehow the one in charge now and Burl a sort of ward, prodigal and incompetent. But this shift only reflected reality, and Burl was grateful for Engel's loyalty and help. He arranged for Burl to do his laundry for free and slipped him some cash, with no questions asked—and none answered—about its provenance.

Waiting for the bus back to the heart of the city, where he felt more comfortable, Burl tried on for size the notion that he was completely and unrecognizably different. It had happened a little too slowly for him to grasp it while the transformation was occurring, and now that it was evidently complete, it was hard to accept that he was in fact someone else.

It was tragic, in a way, but a relief as well. And why should it be surprising? Looking at the person he saw in the plate-glass windows of the city's shops, reflected against rows of women's pumps and lurid travel posters or lost in the frantic titillation of the latest videos, it was hard for him to recognize himself, even if he was more or less used to seeing a wan, bearded, brooding stranger enter the same looking glass at precisely the same moment. *That man is always with me*, Burl thought. As he passed the shops of downtown, pedestrians giving a wide berth, he glanced furtively toward the walls of glass and caught that man again, slouching along next to him through the phony transparency with what seemed sure foreknowledge of disaster.

This foreknowledge seemed the only thing that bound them together. Certitude is the wretched handmaiden of paranoia, and Burl was strangely without doubts, all his old uncertainties sloughed off like so much flesh. That was why he'd had no qualms about leaving the Chrysalis one fine day when his money ran out, honorably making sure his bill was paid and then simply strolling out as if for fresh air. He'd stashed a fold-up suitcase, one of those hideous plaids his mother got somewhere with King Korn stamps from the supermarket, in some bushes the night before. Presumably they still expected him to return.

He felt like an escapee, and acted like one too, except for his strange love of routine. Perhaps it was the packrat in him, manifesting itself in this way now that there was no place for him to keep things. Thus, he slept on the same vent every night, in the same position, finding comfort in being someplace familiar, backed up against the familiar vent-warmed brick of St. Ferdinand's, the only place in the world where he was known.

And so he awoke, pushing away the cardboard that he slept under to keep off the dew. The day was cloudy and threatening, with that sweet taste of good tap water in the air, which had the flavor of snow. He rose stiffly, aching from his iron pallet, his body scored like a slice of grilled swordfish. He was anxious. Cloudy, windy days like this, days that made everyone else glad to be indoors or determined to arrive there, dreaming of hot tea and loved ones en route, made him especially nervous, not so much because he had no home, although that was bad enough, but because he felt so left out, the kid who didn't get a valentine, the boy not chosen in stickball, the fat guest at the party.

Always meticulous, Burl felt the need to clean himself today especially, and also, without admitting it, to see familiar faces and be acknowledged in their eyes. The squeaky corridors and patronizing workers of the hospital, its shiny floors and formaldehyde smell, its gurneys and scuff marks, all seemed inviting under this sky, in this wind, and sickened by the eggy breath of the unfiltered vent, he hurried inside.

In the shower room, for the umpteenth time, he examined himself. Certainly he was a different person. He was no longer fat, in the normal sense of the word, but he would not be mistaken for a thin man either. He felt lost in himself, his flesh as loose and baggy as a Russian novel, skin hanging in wattles not just from his jaw but from his upper arms, so that at night, lit shirtless from behind by the old-fashioned streetlamp, he could raise his arms and cast the winged shadow of a bat, or a pterodactyl, depending on the state of his hair. His flesh was everywhere this way; he was draped in it like a tutu or a toga. It hung skirtlike from around his waist, yellow and flabby, chicken skin covering even his private parts, falling as well from his upper legs. Stain it black and pass as a beefeater in pantaloons. But it was all over. He looked like a melting candle.

A part of him remained fastidious and in love with himself, and he soaped and scrubbed accordingly, relishing this tactile interlude, running the shower hot and hard because the needles felt especially good against his checkered flesh. Washing his stinging anus, he groaned delicately; it always itched now. It was hard, without a home, to find a comfortable place to use the bathroom, impossible, often, to wipe oneself properly, and anyway his robust bowels, driven in Burl's great heyday by volume, had never been the same since the surgery, running too fast or too slow, issuing only irregularly and painfully, veering neurotically between recalcitrance and capitulation.

Grunting loudly, he dried himself and then grimly put the same clothes back on. Nothing clean this morning, although there had been worse days. He left the hospital through the sliding front doors, which he rarely used, and walked down the driveway to the bench at the bus stop out front, his hair at least feeling clean, beard damp, ears itching with melted wax. The bench was wet, so he stood next to it, waiting, until he saw the car drive up, slow down uncertainly, and then, a bus looming right behind, accelerate again even as he tried to wave. The car turned the corner and evidently circled the block, because a couple of minutes later it came back into view.

Wanda Bildung arrived to fetch him in a little white import, which she drove carelessly and fast. To Burl she seemed to glow, her eyes wide, her cheeks ruddy, her ever-so-slightly lopsided face radiant above her turtleneck and parka. In the way she spoke and acted and handled the car, there was a quality of euphoria he hadn't seen in her at the restaurant where they had met.

He couldn't say what exactly had prompted him to use the phone number she had given him after the big meal, except that he'd kept it all this time and without Engel found himself increasingly lonely. Perhaps also, now that he was so much thinner, he was enamored of his new self, wanted to show it off, test it out. He had thought of Wanda often since meeting her that one and only time. One night he dreamed of her, held her image in his mind all morning, and finally picked up the phone and called, just to see what would happen.

He tried to open the passenger door, but it was locked. Through the glass, he pointed at himself and mouthed, "It's me. Burl Bennett."

Wanda popped out on her side and regarded him warily.

"It's me," he repeated over the traffic. "Burl Bennett."

"Burl? My God, how incredible!"

"It's the beard."

"Why didn't you say something when you called? You must have lost 100 pounds."

"A hundred and fifty, since you saw me. Even more from my peak, which was after that fine meal you fed me. I've been living on that meal for months."

Wanda laughed and covered her eyes.

"What?" Burl asked. "Everybody's weight fluctuates."

"I'm just so relieved. I was worried you'd never fit into my car."

"Maybe in back, with the seat folded down. You got heavy-duty shocks?"

They went to one of Burl's favorite diners, where they spent the morning talking in what seemed to Burl the startled way that people do when they have found each other against all odds. Emboldened by this instant rapport, he explained about his stomach-stapling and boldly inquired about the Witness movement, a topic he at first regarded as taboo.

"Have you ever thought of leaving? I mean, do you see yourself spending the rest of your days there?"

"The rest of my days? Burl, who knows? We all think about other ways of life, don't we? Can you really say that your choices have been any better—or even more rational—than mine?"

"My choices have been entirely rational. That doesn't mean they've been good."

"But they were taken in what seemed your own best interest."

"Exactly."

"And how did you know what that was?"

"How does anybody?"

"Indeed," Wanda smirked. "A very good question."

"And they were made freely. The choices, I mean."

"Really? So you chose to be fat and live in the Northeast and have lead in your drinking water as a child?"

Lead? Burl decided it was better to humor her than to argue.

"Well, within certain constraints," he said mildly.

"Mother Witness teaches that islands only dissolve. You're nothing by yourself except the victim of a cruel hoax. None of us are—"

"—Is."

"Look at yourself, Burl, the helpless slave of your own destructive desires. That's not free will. That's genetics, advertising, chance, radioactivity—"

"Radiation?"

"Don't give me that crank stuff; there's ambient radiation everywhere, electromagnetic fields, a million and one physical and biochemical factors working on us all the time. You're smiling. I did everything but the dissertation for a doctorate in biochemistry and you're smiling. Because I'm a woman? But who are you—you!—apart from all those things?"

"No different from you, I suppose. No more capable of taking arms against a sea of electromagnetism and childhood, uh, psychodynamics than you."

"Don't make fun, Burl. Doesn't that coffee cake look awfully good? I'm gonna get a slice. You mean to say you never eat anything?"

"Not really. Not solid, anyway. I live on liquids, vitamins, that kind of thing."

"Wow. Is it worth it?"

"Well, they told me I wasn't going to live if I didn't do something, and as you say, there was something in me I couldn't control. I'm comfortable with a little asceticism; it's kind of refreshing after the life I've lived."

"I'd think you'd be interested in the Witness movement, Burl; compulsions are a specialty of many of us who're involved. Mother draws heavily on Confucius, the Bhagavad-gita, the Jewish sages as well. We study all the religious books. We aren't bound by any prejudices in our search for enlightenment, because we all know that the truth is making us free."

Burl blinked, watching for some nonverbal cue that never seemed to come.

"Do you ever get there?" he asked.

"Only in the perfection of the afterworld, but you should understand that for us freedom is a disciplined process, since only in a state of becoming can we live harmoniously in the human condition. 'We must not seek to be anything, but to become everything.' That's our motto. Becoming is an essential part of Mother's teaching; Mother shuns abstractions and teaches us to shun them too. Nothing could be more abstract than the here and now."

"And being?"

"Is kind of a joke, don't you think?"

"Can't argue with that," Burl said.

Wanda reached across and took his hand. "Poor Burl; it must be brutal not having any home, always wandering the way you do."

"You'd be amazed what you can get used to."

"You know, we offer accommodations. It's not like some giant shelter, they're sort of small rooms, quite clean and private. How long can you stay on the streets?"

Burl began to feel the need to be elsewhere.

"You don't have to become a part of anything, Burl. You can just spend one night, if you want, get yourself cleaned up and be on your way."

Out of politeness, and maybe something more, he vowed to think it over.

The university library was open to the public, but a homeless man is an interloper in all public places and Burl moved through it on psychological tiptoe. Lacking the nonchalance of those who know their night's ultimate retreat, he stood out. It was a style that

that gave him away as much as anything else, an attitude. He wasn't more than slightly dirty or bedraggled, on a par with some graduate students, for example, or one of those well-known figures who haunt the corridors of learning and seem chained to the campus like ghosts. Being homeless was not so different from being fat, Burl had discovered, only without as many places to hide. Of course, no place was mandatory, either; there were no compulsory appearances at work or family functions, but without refuge or rest—real rest—the day hung heavy as flesh.

So he had adopted the university library. It was virtually empty this early, but still he moved with anxious haste along the edge of a reading area and through some stacks toward his goal. The staff knew him. One of his pant cuffs dragged, leaving a subtle trail on dusty floors, and his shamble felt oppressed.

He spent the morning in the microfilm room, straining his watering eyes to read whatever he could find in the newspapers on the Witness cult and its founder. It seemed a nasty business, although it was hard to sort out the truth from all the cult hype that seemed so prevalent in the press for a while, in the heyday of the Moonies, and also from the untrustworthy hectoring of the church-dominated local papers. Everybody hyped cults, it seemed. How were the Hasidim in Brooklyn any different? Or the Mormons, for that matter?

Janet David Witness was the widow of a Reno, Nevada, bathtub-enclosure salesman who really was named Witness, and who died under mysterious circumstances. He now functioned as a kind of saint for the movement he and his wife had begun together and spread throughout the Rocky Mountain states. Janet claimed to hold regular communications with her late husband, the movement's ascended spirit, who was regarded as a kind of pioneer of the afterlife.

Witness theology was essentially apocalyptic. The world was coming to an end fairly soon, it was believed, probably as the result of nuclear conflagration. The cult was said to have burrowed an elaborate network of radiation-proof shelters into the mountainsides abutting its sprawling encampment, and these reportedly were stocked well enough to last a decade, by which time it was hoped the earth might be habitable again. The world emerging from this earthly womb would be different because it would be shaped and guided by women. Violence and oppression would be unknown. Inequality would be banished. Strange that their only saint should be Herbert Witness, who reportedly struggled all his life against temptation and most of the time lost. Herb gambled compulsively on and off for years, and for months the newspapers reported with thinly disguised glee on the trial of a lawsuit, brought by someone identified as the daughter of a well-known Reno chorus girl, claiming a share of Herbert's modest legacy and the empire that grew from it. Financial information that emerged during this embarrassing episode showed that the holdings of the Witness cult, which extended to fast-food franchises, daycare centers, weekly newspapers, and a small ball-bearing plant, were worth as much as $275 million. The plaintiff eventually settled for an undisclosed sum.

Like all modern religions, the Witness cult sounded preposterous, and Burl felt that this explained why a body of well-aged dogma had to be at the center of any ongoing ecclesiastical enterprise. You've just got to have an accepted body of lore, ancient magic and miracle, some long-ago interaction with your deity that doesn't happen anymore. Anything that appeals solely to modern understanding is just too funny. In that sense the old-line religions have quite a franchise, Burl thought, just as right of way was the essence of a railroad. This was why it seemed so much easier to fit one's desire for faith into one or another of the existing forms. They might not be any truer—what made Abraham or Paul any more credible than Janet David Witness?—but they had a kind of tenure, a grandfathering past the barrier of credibility that permitted them to propound myths and rituals impossible in a newer church.

Witness joined God in her sleep. It seemed simple enough. Witness's sleeping habits, and sleeping generally, took on sacred overtones. "Sleep well" became a kind of shalom for cult members, and in sleep all were said to commune in some way with the spiritual power of the universe. Waking was a daily rebirth, living a cycle of death and resurrection that helped sanctify one's existence. Of course only Witness had the ability to communicate with the Lord in her sleep and to interpret the sleep—the dreams—of others, in accordance with Her wishes. God's gender—even Her femininity—was self-evident in the Witness cult, given the Spirit's fecundity, but She too was a jealous God, which was said by some to account for Her taking Herb Witness. She wanted him for Herself.

In any case, the universality of sleep was convenient. It allowed everybody access to the godhead, it was the territory of dreams, and it was eligible for all sorts of religio-mystification. It was also handy for indoctrination. One long article based on the account of a former cult member said that tapes of "Witness thought" were pumped into every room in the compound, and on a weekly schedule all members of the cult took part in directed dreaming exercises. Special goggles detected rapid eye movements and flashed pulses of light to alert sleepers that dreaming was under way; through earphones, dreaming instructions purporting to be from God Herself were delivered in Witness's voice.

With his whole body, Burl understood exalting the role of sleep. He never got enough sleep anymore, and he never stopped feeling bleary eyed, grubby, and dazed. No one without a place to live ever did. Burl had read about the homeless and seen them daily on the streets of New York. Slipping into a reverie of his former cosseted and nourished life, it was inconceivable it would ever come to this for him. But knowing the depths of exhaustion that the homeless feel, which is a kind of nausea that comes over you on and off throughout the day, he felt that sheer sleeplessness must be a factor in the aberrant behavior he'd observed for so long among them on the streets, and which the man in glass who followed him everywhere must be starting to show. Truly satisfying sleep requires periods of unguardedness that the homeless can never afford. We ought to do it in shifts, Burl thought, taking turns looking out for one another.

"I'm sorry, but you can't sleep here." A bearded librarian, a clean version of Burl, shook him awake. When had he dozed off? "This is only for reading."

Burl rose stiffly, stiffly, his tailbone compressed, his genitals still asleep, his neck stiff. Even standing, it was hard to resist the somnolent drag of the yellow table lamps, the shiny old oak, the quiet and the blanket of white noise thrown across the whole by the fans of the microfilm machines. Heavily, Burl shut his off and left. At this point, he too worshiped sleep.

It was dark when he emerged, and chilly, with a few large snowflakes gliding in stately diagonals onto the pavement. He observed with relief that rush hour—what there was of it in Salt Lake City—was mostly over; he hated being out in all that darkening hustle and bustle, feeling like the only one with no place to hurry off to. He never felt more homeless than during the afternoon rush.

It crossed his mind that he was just waiting to let a decent interval go by before he called Wanda again. Why not? As he tramped sullenly around the city, the streets and buildings began to seem so weary, the place so small and confined. How many times had he seen these buses, this downtown mall, the arena where the basketball team played? The houses too lost their charm. The wavy sidewalks, lifted by tree roots, were almost unbearably tiresome, like an itch that one can't stand another instant. What kind of a life was this? Where was he going, walking and walking day after day? He knew the city's public restrooms by heart, knew he could always find clean toilets and comfortable temperatures in the Zion Cooperative Mercantile Institute, knew that around the Statehouse he was liable to be rousted. After a while he came to see that homelessness was inevitably monotonous, for he never got to see anyplace private from the inside. Aggressively ignored wherever he went, he felt himself shading off into unbeing. Never before had the bearded man in the glass seemed so completely an illusion.

It was overcast again, a Saturday, and the tempered light and quiet streets enabled him to sleep a little later than usual. By the time he got cleaned up—his toilet was scrupulous that morning, his songs lusty, his tone rested and firm—she was waiting for him outside the hospital, wearing an air of contained triumph.

In his previous life, Burl never would have accepted an invitation such as the one he was accepting now, but in the days since he had received it, he'd thought of nothing else. He was smitten with Wanda and curious about the Witness movement anyway. It was like wanting to see if you could be hypnotized. What could it hurt to spend a day and perhaps a night? It was a relief, really. The winter was proving harsh; he was already suffering chilblains on his hands and feet, and his shoes were wet so often they were brittle and grey, scratchy against his toes.

Since he had read about the Movement, it didn't concern him that he passed through a metal detector when he first arrived and that he was asked, as if at Customs, whether he "had anything to declare."

"It's just the way they do things around here," Wanda said with a smiling shrug.

But when Burl answered no, his suitcase was searched anyway, and later he submitted to a physical examination, medical history, and blood test (the Movement had a lab on the premises). He even had to give a urine sample and take an IQ test. He liked all this. He wanted the full treatment and, as he had as a newspaper reporter, tried to bend over backward to give the most far-fetched proposition an unprejudiced airing.

The thing he hoped for most during his early days at the Movement compound was a good night's sleep, but this was the one thing he was hardly ever permitted. From the very first hours, when he watched a video about Mother Witness and the Movement's accomplishments in an overheated conference room, there was hardly a moment of unguarded thought, never mind rest. After the video there was discussion. Members of the Movement described the horrors of their lives before they discovered Mother Witness and talked of the miraculous changes wrought since. Addiction, gambling, and despair had been commonplace. No one's life had had any meaning.

He was rarely left alone. On his very first night, when at last he retired to what amounted to a partitioned cell in a quonset hut for the evening, ready to collapse with fatigue, Burl discovered that the door didn't lock. He looked out and found that nobody's did; they were all slightly ajar. He had spent a few nights in missions and shelters and was glad not to have any valuables. What was there that anyone might want to take from him by now? What could be left?

The room was spare and without a mirror, which was just as well. There was no place here to know yourself except through the eyes of others. And although he had planned to stay only one night, that idea quickly fell by the wayside. He didn't even get to see Wanda during his first week—she had warned him she would be scarce—until finally one night, his Movement-issue shirt unbuttoned, Burl sat on the edge of his cot to remove his battered shoes, his back to the door. He stiffened with fright when he heard it creaking open, but to his delight it was her.

"I came to see how you were doing," she said.

He told her about his first day, how strange it all seemed, and how glad he was mainly just being warm. He felt himself babbling as she moved closer, her eyes holding his, until she gently pushed his shirt off and he found himself draped in the softness of her arms. The heat on his neck was from her mouth, he knew, and it distracted him a little from the chill of embarrassment he felt at having her hands on his supremely flabby torso, the capelike flesh of his chest and stomach hanging flaccid all around him. He was like a fat man on some other, larger planet, where the gravity is vastly greater than earth's.

But Wanda seemed unperturbed. Her lovemaking was narcotic and sure; she ran her hands through his hair and pulled it by the fistful, so that his scalp tingled, and she dug her fingers into his meatier portions and then kissed the places she kneaded. He didn't know what to say, or do. Reaching for her under her flannel nightgown, he was struck by the solidness of her figure, and its amazing smoothness. Unlike his scarred and amorphous body, hers had definite volume and seemed held together by some fibrous structure missing in his own. Most of all, he couldn't believe he had a woman in his arms, and when he suggested, with his hands, that she remove her nightgown, she smilingly complied.

He was immediately and hopelessly in love, running his hands up and down Wanda's sleek, thick-waisted fullness and kissing her forehead whenever he could allow himself. She seemed impossibly precious, and as he drifted off into what seemed to him his sweetest ever sleep, Burl's head danced with plans. He must shave, straighten out, behave as if the future were real. And he must take his love away from these strange, strange people.

BURL WOKE AT DAWN, feeling Wanda rise smoothly and determinedly from him like a spirit leaving the dead. He tried to sleep after that but couldn't; he was too wound up, and the room was flooded by the rising light of day, which passed bluish through an uncurtained window and the sheet of plastic taped over it against the cold.

He had never regarded the Witness Movement as something he might possibly join, but to the extent that he was enamored of Wanda, he was seduced by it. More than that, in the light of subsequent mornings it began to seem hard for him to segregate his love for her from his attitude toward the religious orthodoxy—for that is all it came to seem—which was so much a part of her.

He stayed, of course. It was his own decision; compared to the misery and exhaustion of the streets, the happiness and exhaustion of his new home were overwhelming. Quite sensibly, given his experience, he was put to work in the laundry.

It was comforting to spend his days amid the hum of washers and dryers, dressing lightly in the steamy warmth, the damp and

bleach suggesting to his unforgetful senses the humidity and chlorine of the pool where he'd used to swim as a child. It was a non-
political job too, he liked to think. He wouldn't have done anything that actively furthered the Movement's cause, but everyone
needs clean clothes, and working in the laundry, Burl could indulge what was rapidly becoming a fetish for warmth. Salt Lake
City, which once seemed so cozy, was unspeakably cold and dry
now that he had shed his lifelong coat of adipose. Only indoors,
in his small portion of the Movement's sprawling complex, did he
realize how cold he had been.

Working in the laundry also gave him time to read, but since
there were no books aside from the writings of Mother Witness—
access to other works, even Bibles, was strictly controlled—he
read these densely printed ramblings as well as he could until he
fell asleep. (He was always sleepy, no matter how much he slept.
Could it be something in the water?) The other nice thing about
this laundry was that there were no customers to keep him awake.

Wanda brought him Witness books and pamphlets she said
were particular favorites and candidly steered him away from
tracts she considered "immature," "opaque," or "not fully realized."

"You can see that some of these were written by Mother herself, and have the freshness and candor she somehow manages to
bring to everything she does," Wanda said. "Others, obviously,
were written for her to cover points that needed to be made, but
that for one reason or another seemed insufficiently crucial for
her to make personally."

"Kind of like Rubens, or Titian, leaving the background for his
students to fill in."

"She's a real person, and her frank and practical advocacy
brings more good to more people than the kind of shopworn asceticism lesser mortals invariably think they have a right to expect
from a religious leader."

"So she doesn't drink urine or hike barefoot through the snow. I'm not going to hold that against her. Just because I don't eat doesn't mean no one else should."

Wanda combed his hair a little with her fingers, and he blushed.

"It's a big joke to you, Burl, but mockery can never substitute in a life for faith, and that's really what this is all about."

As if to affirm this by example, she kissed him gently, letting his lower lip slide reluctantly through her teeth. Burl, who reached back for her lips with his own, now saw what she meant.

Later, he reflected with a certain unease that he was beginning to feel this way more often. He began to doubt his initial view that Wanda was the victim of some elaborate, institutional brainwashing, or that she suffered from what might be called battered-apostle syndrome and thus was no longer the best judge of her own situation. (She confessed that the leaders occasionally imposed corporal punishment, in her case for marijuana, a chronic weakness of hers.) He tried to think of her allegiance to the Movement in terms of faith. Has there ever been any faith without coercion? Does anyone come to God without indoctrination, or the insistence of human misery? Universally, it seemed to Burl, faith was a response to mortality, the ultimate duress. And faith was invariably blind in some way. Why then should not the faithful, in the desperation of their adherence in such a lonely world, accept within reason the authority they have vested outside themselves? To question or reject was the opposite of faith, and meant drifting through time like a dust mote.

"It's not blind, Burl, that's the point," Wanda said the following afternoon, with some exasperation. "We accept Mother's teachings as the way to know God and participate in our own becoming, and we accept her leadership for our own good. Which we all sooner or later admit she knows better than we do."

He saw her little enough that he didn't seriously want to argue. She worked days and most evenings at the Holy Grail, considered a position of privilege within the organization (aside from the leadership posts, of course), but at night she returned to what Burl understood now was her cubicle (despite the absence of any personalizing elements), and he could stop his reading.

At night they made love. Wanda taught him how, had begun teaching him on that very first night and continued, on all the nights that followed, with what seemed to Burl boundless energy. She taught him that the sexiest thing is really a quality of attention, and to be able to pay such attention as well as to properly receive it. He learned from her that whatever was done pleasurably to him might be done likewise to her, and when it wasn't quite right she showed him how, which he found sexier even than the thing itself. She made love with her eyes open, and firmly; there was a disarming quality of directness and strength to much of what she did, and she taught Burl this too.

"We're not made of china," she said, thumbs in his back muscles. "See?"

He did see, and as he caught on he could participate more fully. Sometimes one or the other would do everything; Wanda could admit at times now that she was tired and lonely and wanted to be made love to. Burl never had to say such a thing of himself; she always knew.

Like any pupil, no matter how devoted, he sometimes wanted to cut classes, but Wanda wouldn't let him. They made love every night and every morning; she saw to that until it became his habit too. More than habit; it became the thing he lived for, at least at the Movement. They made love sometimes during the day as well, during breaks, on piles of laundry, with their clothes on, or if Wanda had brought high heels, standing up, leaning against the table meant for folding things, her big hands spread atop the tiny gold and green boomerangs that covered it.

The Movement began to seem something Wanda might grow out of as their attachment deepened. She became more relaxed about her own view of it, and traces of ambivalence seemed to sprout like weeds in the cracks of a sidewalk. Burl did his best to nurture these, partly by making a great show of open-mindedness. He was forever placing the Movement, without judgment, in historical context, even if for Wanda comparisons were inevitably "value laden." But under the influence of desire he was becoming more unsure of his own attitude toward the Movement as well.

"Nothing can be judged in a vacuum," Wanda insisted, reasonably enough. "This religious movement is the work of people as well as of God, and we are an imprecise implement. It must be frustrating for Her having to work with us. But in the context of its times, and in comparison with the waywardness and illusion and cruelty of your life—every modern life—it's a shining star. It's a beacon, Burl, above a great and tragic mire."

"Freedom has its price."

"I'm gonna treat that seriously and assume it wasn't sarcasm directed against a variety of freedom you can't quite accept, even if it's the only legitimate kind. But what has been the price of freedom as you understand it? First of all barbarism, which is everywhere, and second acquiescence. The legitimization of barbarism. The contextualization of any and all behavior, no matter how reprehensible. The question, of course, is who gains? Who benefits, ultimately? And whether or not the answer is 'us,' is that a just outcome? Is that any good for everyone in the long run? And is anyone really terribly happy with the way things are? Even the beneficiaries aren't much pleased, it seems to me. But do you notice something about the people here, Burl? They're happy. It's that simple. They've found a just framework for living a happy life."

"Everyone in Utah is happy, practically, except some of the Tongans, and even they're mostly glad they came."

"The Mormons are happy, that's true, and I respect them for it. Their patriarchal system isn't for me, but it has great efficacy for its adherents, it seems to enable them to live their lives, and I'm not going to minimize that. Our way's better, that's all. Truer. I should say truer."

Love made Burl susceptible. Their discussions would stop when Wanda placed a hand lightly on his thigh and gently squeezed. He understood Pavlov's drooling dogs. Merely for her to look straight into his eyes—she was tall, so this wasn't difficult—made him aroused, sex so often having followed her gaze. He told her this, and she would do it sometimes from across the cafeteria, where men and women were segregated by velvet ropes like those in a movie theater, as if in an Orthodox synagogue. It worked. Sitting with a cup of tea and his pills in the morning, he felt a swelling at his crotch, even as he thought how strange it was that no other couple ever showed such open fondness.

There was a strange chill about the whole place, in fact. No one ever showed much of anything, and Burl concluded that with no place of their own people made privacy into something portable. It was a paradox: such closeness, and such secretiveness as a consequence. He didn't even know much about Wanda. She lay naked beside him, enjoying the brush of his fingertips on her back, her buttocks swelling mightily and bare. It was like the emperor's new clothes, in reverse. The empress only seemed naked, but what was under her cloak? Burl kissed her and his heart fluttered at the touch of her lips. For the first time, he felt he knew the human impulse to reproduce.

"Did you ever want to have kids?" he asked.

"Actually, I had one before I ever really knew that I wanted children. I'd had dolls, of course, and—"

"Wait a minute. You have a child?"

"A girl, 16. She lives with my folks back in Colorado. It's okay. She comes down to see me now and then, but they mostly raised her. She doesn't belong here."

"She's not the only one."

Wanda said nothing, because Burl was very carefully grazing the tiny blond hairs that spread across her powerful lower back. When he did it just right, as he was just now, she would grimace and suck her breath until she couldn't take it anymore, and when she shouted this he rubbed her there and took her in his arms.

"Did you ever want any more?"

"Oh God, yes, but it was just too much. I could feel the hair standing up all over my body."

"I meant children."

"No. Maybe." Wanda said. "I don't know. I don't think so."

"So are there families here or what?"

"There is a family," she said carefully, "of which we're all a part."

"And what place does love have in all this?"

"Love is what holds the whole thing together. The love of God and of one another are what this place is all about." Burl felt himself flush with adrenaline.

"But there are no permanent couples."

"There are couples, but what does permanent mean? In this context or any other?"

They seemed so relaxed together that Burl's incipient panic went a notch higher.

"So what is this?" he asked. "What am I doing here? It sounds like in your world we have no possible future."

"Burl, that's ridiculous, the future is what this is all about. Every future becomes possible, if you stay. We'll always have each other here, and we can change the world together. I don't want to lose you, Burl."

These words were spoken so evenly that he was up most of the night in anguish. But what was to be done? It made no sense to leave. As long as he remained, there was hope, and surely Wanda had some real affection for him by now. He was inexperienced but clever. He could see it in the way she was sometimes after making love—even during, sometimes. She seemed surprised occasionally, and she squeezed him so hard it hurt. Burl's skin was thick and baggy as a turtle's, but it bruised easily.

And as a practical matter, he hadn't anywhere in particular to go. Wanda said he only now seemed to be recovering from life on the streets, the loss of some 300 pounds, and so forth.

"You're playful now," she said. "You were so somber before. And you've come alive intellectually. I don't think I've seen you reading a newspaper yet."

"There aren't any here."

"Oh, there are. That stuff gets in. But it's discouraged. It's just stress and distraction."

Maybe he would just stay. Was this system any worse than any other? He could publish a newspaper for the compound. The *Witness Eye* or some such. Too bad the Jehovah's Witnesses got *Awake!* first; it seemed perfect for a sleep cult, and subtly subversive too. Maybe he could publish it underground. He could write an opera column; "Awake and Sing," he'd call it. A cult wasn't much different from a newspaper anyway, or any other bureaucracy. It was working the oars on a comfortably appointed galley. One rowed and rowed to ends so obscure that all that mattered was rowing or not rowing. One didn't want the ship to sink, but mainly because one was chained to it.

He could always leave. They didn't appear to be keeping any-one here "against their will," whatever people in such a place might take such a concept to mean. But perhaps that was the na-ture of the thing in any case; like everyday life, one invests one-self, one ages, and then what? He saw himself washing the dirty linens—could he air them in his newspaper?—of this cult for the rest of his days, living out his life like some old foot soldier in the barracks with the rest. What then? Would Wanda have others? Would he?

Staying didn't seem a bad idea, in the abstract. No more ex-temporizing; one's existence beelike. The Witness organization functioned like a hive, he noticed, and he might fit right in: man your post, serve the queen, and die. Where else but Utah, the Beehive State? He realized with a start that the Witness cult had built Deseret, the powerful state the early Mormons had pro-posed, its name taken from the Jaredite word in the Book of Mor-mon for honeybee. Now Deseret was Utah's headache; today, Burl saw, even the Mormons have Mormons.

One afternoon Burl was out walking under the brilliant Utah sky, almost cobalt all around, trying to puzzle things out. He had been with the Movement for a couple of months. He and Wanda were evolving a certain domesticity, as much as was possible in the midst of all these others and considering that meals were not only communal but, for Burl, irrelevant. What he couldn't figure out was what to do. He could just go along this way, or he could try to make some change occur. He thought of New York, his for-mer apartment, his family and friends. To the extent that he could remember them, he missed them, but they seemed so far away. He really was a different person now.

He returned to the small room he shared and found Wanda home early with a thermometer in her mouth. She thought to hide it at first, he could tell, and she quickly thought better, but the move didn't escape him.

"Are you sick? What's the matter?"

She nodded and held up a finger. A minute later, she read the thermometer up against the light and smiled.

"I was feeling kind of faint, maybe a cold coming on, so I came home. I missed you, Burl."

Then, before he could say anything, she grabbed for him. She looked flushed too, and felt a little warm.

"Wait a minute, sweetheart," Burl said, freeing his mouth to speak. "You're not well. You want me to get you some tea or something?"

"You're the cure for what ails, Burl; just stay right here with me."

And so they made love. But to his dismay, he noticed that their lovemaking had begun to change, to become more routinized, even purposeful. Wanda no longer seemed interested in sex standing up amid the piles of laundry, or straddling Burl on her knees to make herself come atop him. She also took on a strange wifely interest in his underwear, unilaterally discarding the cotton briefs he'd worn all his life in favor of some new boxer shorts.

"I don't understand these," Burl complained. "There's no support. You might as well not wear any underwear at all."

"Ooh, there's an idea. Look, your old shorts were full of holes, and those things are for little boys anyway. A man like you needs to give his equipment some air. Let it breathe, Burl."

Soon after, he was mysteriously transferred out of the laundry. They put him to work driving a delivery van, carrying packages and people all over the compound.

"It just means they're starting to trust you more," Wanda explained. "Get used to it. Besides, this place is like the army; they move people around all the time."

That was Burl's new job, moving people around. The compound was so big and tightly organized that it had a regular shuttle service, like a university. Burl didn't mind. He'd read all the Mother Witness works he could stand, and he liked being out and about, although he sorely missed the warmth of all those washers and dryers. Even with the heat on, the van always seemed cold, the door always opening to admit a blast of frigid air with the latest strange lot of passengers.

But they impressed Burl. He liked the evidence they provided of humanity's consistency and of the unvarying nature of everyday life, which had the same quality of general repose wherever he happened to observe it. In the early morning and late afternoon, when he was busiest, he might as well be ferrying commuters in Baltimore, except instead of the morning paper there were the works of Mother Witness. And of course the obligatory Walkmans—Walkpersons?—whose earpieces leaked Mother's exhortations tinnily throughout the day. Perhaps the only difference between driving a Mother Witness van and driving a city bus was that, here, Burl very quickly came to know everybody, at least by sight. He grew to like the job, the life, the conjugal duties he came to feel he fulfilled. He and Wanda seemed to settle into a more quotidian kind of arrangement that was quieter but probably more sustainable, Burl felt. They didn't argue so much about the Movement, and the assumption that Burl or Wanda might leave anytime soon went away. Wanda began to smuggle home copies of the *Deseret News*, and through his acquaintance with another seeming skeptic on the van, he managed to snag some marijuana for Wanda's birthday. He was rewarded with an old-fashioned night of love. Otherwise sex was on a schedule.

Burl saw no reason not to further the dual cause of justice and sexuality by providing Wanda with more dope. He liked it himself, and it was somehow plentiful in the area. Maury, his likeminded passenger, was happy to provide it gratis, out of fellow feeling and some long-standing instincts for subversion.

"I'm a CPA," Maury confided. "Most people don't realize it, but we're very independent-minded. This place works, from a financial perspective. Believe me. But as a way of life, it doesn't add up. No way José."

"Strikes you as funny too?"

"Hey. Was I born yesterday? Where you from? The City?"

"You mean New York?"

"Where else? Listen, I worked with all of them, Fortune 1000, mom and pops, entrepreneurial geniuses. Lotta medical men too. This is one hell of an operation."

Maury shook his head. It was the slow time between the morning rush and lunch. There were just the two of them in the van.

"So what are you doing here?" Burl asked. "Why do you stay?"

Maury made a sputtering sound with his lips.

"Horses. I liked the horses a little too much and got into a little trouble. I had a problem, know what I mean?"

"So you're here."

Maury shrugged.

"Are you still with that nice-looking woman I've seen you around with?"

"Wanda."

"Ain't that her? There, by the infirmary."

Burl barely caught a glimpse of her, hurrying out of the clinic and away from the main road. What was she doing there? Was she still sick? She hadn't mentioned anything.

"Maybe this is it," Maury said with a little smile.

"What?"

"The occasion for you to join the rest of us over at the barracks for a while. It's not so bad. By the time my last one got pregnant, I was glad to get away."

"Burl," Wanda spoke very carefully. "Burl, listen to me."

He wouldn't listen.

"Listen, Burl. I need to explain some things to you."

Wanda sat down in front of him on the bed and grabbed his face to stop his turning away.

"You just want me to get you pregnant, right? Or is that what they want you to have me do? I can't decide whether to blame you for this or for merely following orders. I can't decide which is worse, either."

"Yes, Burl. Yes. I wanted to have your baby. Is that so terrible? Is that so shameful? Do you think I want to bring a new life into the world with just anyone? It's what you wanted, remember?"

"But you're the one who kept it secret. Why the fuck didn't you just tell me?"

"Not just because you love me," Wanda said in that same wary tone Burl hated, as if she were waiting for him at any moment to become violent. "Mainly, it was because I love you."

"Oh, for God's sake."

"Burl, listen to me for a minute. I want a baby with you because I love you, and I didn't tell you for the same reason. Burl, we have ideas about mating and parenthood that you might not have been ready to accept. I understand that, but you have to understand that I am absolutely dedicated to these ideas. They are a part of me. I can't imagine living any other way. It's inconceivable that I could ever embrace the unitary patriarchal family system we've sought to replace here. But I do want kids. And the Witness Movement requires them. The alternative is Shakerdom. People would remember us for our furniture."

"So you enlist the lame and the halt and homeless, and when you're done with us it's off to the barracks with the rest of the proud fathers."

"As opposed to what? How many of us can really say we know our fathers? How many of us wish fervently that we did not?"

"You can justify anything, can't you? But why don't you just buy sperm and use artificial insemination? Why all this untidy rutting?"

"Precisely because we do not regard men merely as a source of semen. See, we can't objectify you that way, even though you've done that to us. Can't you understand? Men and women both have a place here, and fathers do know their children. They can be as involved as they wish; we encourage it. The funny thing, though, is that they aren't. Most pay no attention at all, once it's clear that's allowed. But the point is, we've just chosen not to organize our society according to the artificial structure you and I inherited from our unfortunate parents. That's all. You don't own me, Burl, and you won't own your child—"

Burl blinked. "You're pregnant."

"I was speaking hypothetically, that's all."

"You're pregnant, an idiot could see it in your face."

"I'm not pregnant," Wanda said with some exasperation. "The point is that 'people aren't property'; that's one of Mother's main mottoes."

"How about 'Thou shalt not steal'? Does she have that one?"

"What are you talking—"

"About me! Who the hell gave you permission to take my love, or my seed?"

"You gave those things, Burl. You never asked about contraception, you didn't say I shouldn't love you unless I could meet some abstract standard like *forever*. What do you want from me? You were living on a steam vent, for God's sake."

It was shocking to Burl, who had no experience of close relations, that such a transformation was possible. It hit him like an earthquake. If one could not know a loved one, how could one pretend to know anything at all?

"Who are you?" Burl asked.

"Who I am isn't the issue. The issue is who you want to become."

Yes, thought Burl. Who am I becoming? One answer, if he stayed at the Witness compound, was: a father. Wanda wasn't pregnant yet, but surely it wasn't from want of trying, and for all his protestations, Burl was perfectly willing to help. He was in love, and God knew he was old enough for fatherhood. The timing was never ideal, after all. Besides, it was hard for him to believe things wouldn't work out, that Wanda wouldn't come to her senses, flee with him, resume life in the real world.

And what if she didn't? Would it really be so bad? Was it worse to stay in this community of like-minded positivists than to go back to the streets and be separated from the woman and baby he loved? Maybe staying was not so different from living in suburban Dallas, going to the mall, drinking Diet Coke, watching movies on HBO. Burl thought of the place he had traversed in the old Dodge he'd been given to replace his beloved Checker. America was a kind of cult in which individuals were replaced by consumers and amusements supplanted satisfactions. Why, the followers of Mother Witness were better off! No wonder they wanted to stay, Burl told himself with the shallow conviction of necessity.

So he tried to change not just his behavior but his beliefs, an exercise he knew to be in keeping with Witness teachings. His relations with Wanda were infected with the same artifice; toward her he grew cordial, which made him sad when he thought about it, but it was unavoidable against the backdrop of what was at stake. What else could he do? In the event of a baby his rights, he knew, would be slight. The courts were unlikely to uphold the claims of a bum off the streets against the child's mother, even if Burl could prove paternity and find the money to pay the lawyers for his fight.

As Burl's attitude toward the Witness Movement changed, so, it seemed, did the Movement's attitude toward him. This was re-flected not just in Wanda's comportment, which became less guarded as she came to think Burl might come around, but in a subtle change in his status in the larger community. Whereas once he had felt very much the guest, even if he did work to earn his keep, now a shift began to occur. Somewhat to his horror, he could feel himself becoming accepted. He found himself included in some formal gatherings in which members were encouraged to share their doubts and fears but at which these sins—Witness sins—were always overwhelmed by the testimony of the faithful as to their inspiration and redemption as a result of the Move-ment. And he knew enough to keep his own doubts and fears to himself.

Burl noticed that they let him sleep a bit more now, perhaps in deference to his sperm count, and when he awakened in the middle of the night in the grip of some vestigial hunger that lin-gered like a phantom limb after amputation, it was often to the sounds of Mother Witness's incantatory voice accompanied by New Age music. She chanted Witness thought—an Orwellian form of Protestantism, it seemed to Burl—in a hushed, theatrical style verging weirdly on *sprechstimme*. He wondered how long this nocturnal indoctrination had been going on, and to what extent it might be working. He was torn over whether he hoped that it was.

"It's because of our fallibility," Wanda explained. Was he dreaming, or was her body already changing? Her breasts were larger, he felt sure, and she seemed to need the bathroom more often. "It's so easy to get distracted, or confused. Personally, I find that it helps me sleep. Almost like you holding me."

"So you find my caresses brainwashing, huh?"

"Burl. A better word is *cleansing*. Like the world around us, our souls become soiled—by despair, by doubt, by cynicism. It's like exercise. It clears out the cobwebs."

Burl decided it was a good sign that the powers that be—that Wanda?—trusted him enough to allow him to hear Mother Witness's night-time maunderings. Thus, he regarded it as an especially good sign when he was invited to hear her in person. Wanda made it seem a very special occasion. "Mother hasn't directly addressed the entire community in over a year," she said. "It's very exciting."

The nights were still cold. Burl and Wanda walked quickly to the community center, bent like the hundreds of others around them against the chill wind. They passed the Dream House, where Witness followers bound for guided dreaming entered beneath the motto, "In dreams begin responsibilities," and filed into the hall. The relatively small group of men in attendance was directed to the balcony; by the time Burl was seated on a backless, bleacher-style bench, he had lost sight of Wanda and couldn't locate her in the sea of female heads and torsos below. But how many were pregnant! They squeezed sideways past one another into their seats, waddled up and down the aisle, knitted patiently while waiting for the show to begin. Why had he not taken notice of this before? Was it some seasonal thing? Burl looked up. The room was like a giant high school gymnasium, large and warm and dimly lit except for a raised platform in the center, which was suspended in a cone of light like an old-time boxing ring.

Gradually a silence descended on the hall like a blanket of snow; everyone just seemed to know to stop talking. Then the lights were turned down until the hall was entirely dark. Finally, almost imperceptibly, light began to grow in the center, revealing a figure at a podium. She began speaking long before the deep twilight lifted and continued in the semidarkness that persisted for the rest of her talk.

"Like so many good things," she began, "it came to me in my sleep. Or should I say, in Her sleep? Or best of all, our sleep—the sleep that we all share."

Mother Witness stood like an apparition, dressed in luminescent robes. Burl strained in the dim light to see her face.

"You will wonder, when I describe it to you, how it is that I can call this thing good, because it is so terrible. And it is terrible. Yet you will see immediately that it embodies Her truth and that, characteristically, Her truth is revealed in metaphor, by indirection, by means of one thing standing in place of another. For that is the way of Her world."

Mother moved out from the podium slightly and said with some passion, "I had a vision of the desert. I was in flight." She spread her arms, each bell sleeve forming a hypotenuse to the upright of her body. "It was warm, breezy, and I could glide to my heart's content, though there was no joy in this flight. I soared over the landscape, and the landscape was empty. At first this seemed natural. The land around us is desert. And I looked for the signs of our settlement. But I realized that the desert I saw was not our desert, which is not empty, but the baked and hopeless desert of a much larger world. I saw then that I was no longer gliding but flying at great speed, at high altitude, across miles and miles of earth, seeing only emptiness and desolation, a desert that could not bloom, a land blasted and parched and ruined for any earthly purpose!"

Mother Witness took a breath, composed herself.

"I knew where I was. I saw the great harbors of New York and San Francisco, the Great Lakes, which should have our mighty cities of industry arrayed on their shores, the flowing rivers whose confluence is always marked by a center of commerce. But it was the landscape that gave these places away. The cities were gone. The buildings were gone! The *people* were gone!

"And I knew then that I had been vouchsafed a look at the world to come. I had seen the desolation that Mother Earth will suffer, her barrenness at the hands of her children, and my heart was heavy with the sorrow of this knowledge. My heart was heavy, yet I had no fear. I was sad but calm; cruising through the skies across the vast emptiness, I knew in my heart that all of us, here, were safe."

Mother Witness smiled at her audience, which let out a great sigh of contentment, and then she drank some water. Burl fidgeted thirstily. The room was hot with warm bodies, and Mother Witness's apocalyptic delivery bored him. He felt sleepy.

"During my flight, I could not get the word for what I was seeing out of my head.

"*Desert*. It ran through my mind, again and again and again, like the echo of something I had always known.

"*Desert*. And I was puzzled. Because it has been no secret to us, to all of us, that the world would come to this. It was a sorrowful experience, my children, to be granted the chance to witness in such a graphic way the truth that we have prophesied. But in some deep way it was no surprise, until I turned over in my mind, over and over, the word that I could not let go of.

"*Desert*. And finally it came to me. The desert we live in, the desert all around us, comes from the Latin *desertum*, for deserted. Think of it. Bereft. Abandoned. Forsaken.

"For that meaning, in English, we emphasize the second syllable, but spoken that way, *desert* has another meaning as well. It speaks of something earned—a just retribution, for example. The root in that instance is the Latin *deservire*, meaning thoroughly to serve.

"And then I saw, then I saw what the Goddess was hoping for me to see: that this barren Mother Earth was what mankind had earned. It was what the people of this planet had coming and would inevitably receive as the fruit of their wicked ways.

"But those who truly serve, who rise above the here and now to reach the heights of spirit that we can in our sleep achieve, they will find themselves spared in the final battle in which the Mother's children eat one another, and the Mother herself shall fall to their care—"

Burl awoke with a start, an elbow in his ribs. He realized he'd been asleep for some time. Perhaps he had embraced the Movement more fully than he knew. Or perhaps some Pavlovian force was at work; he was accustomed to hearing Mother Witness in his sleep, and so now that he tried to listen to her while conscious, he dozed off. He spent the rest of the lecture passing in and out of wakefulness. At the end, wiping the saliva from his chin, he accepted the snickers of the other men with a sheepish shrug.

"You were snoring, for God's sake," Wanda complained when they were reunited in her room. She'd been too embarrassed to wait for him in public after Mother Witness's talk. "You disrupted the whole event!"

"Don't be silly," he protested. "If I'd been snoring all that much, someone would have kept me awake. I only got elbowed once or twice, that I can recall."

"That's just the men! They got a kick out of it, they're like the boys in junior high, sitting in back cutting up. They loved it!"

"Well, boys will be boys."

"You thoughtless ass, I was mortified. And you can bet Mother knows who disrupted her teaching too."

"She doesn't know much of anything," Burl said crankily, "judging from her interpretation of that dream. Sounds to me more like a commentary on her demesne, or maybe her life, than anything else. What a place. How can anyone get in trouble for falling asleep during a talk by the leader of a sleep cult?"

Burl soon found out. Wanda didn't simply forget about the incident. She went to bed angry, didn't sleep, and continued worrying about it the next day. She said little, and her expression seemed forced whenever her features departed from the look of worried distraction that most of the time now beset them.

Then one day he came home from his shift on the van and found their room locked, his cloth-and-vinyl suitcase standing, packed, outside. A folded slip of paper was stuck to the door.

> *Burl,*
> I'm sorry, love. It's best for everyone if you go. May all your dreams be true.
> *W.*

He couldn't find her, of course. He wandered the compound for a while, tried to get into the administration building, began asking strangers at random. Finally some of the Movement's security force escorted him to the gates. He didn't struggle. A part of him was relieved. It all seemed so maniacal; even from Wanda, whom he still loved, he felt set free.

He tramped along the roadside with his little plaid valise— cursorily searched at the gatehouse when he left the Witness compound that frigid night—until someone driving by picked him up and dropped him near downtown, off the freeway. People are neighborly in the West, Burl thought, his eyes tearing from the cold. He scanned the deserted streets, wondering where to go now.

"BURL, THINK FOR A minute," Dr. Stringer urged. "You're in better health, you can breathe, you're able to function. You're running up against some of the abrasions that are inevitable in life. It's just that you were insulated before, from the good as well as the bad. You have a life now, so you're upset."

"You're like Frankenstein. You're playing with people's lives here. I want you to kill the monster you created."

"Burl, who's to blame here? If you'd continued on your prior course, you'd be dead in no time. Then you'd have killed the monster neither of us created."

"Fine, you're right, undo it anyway."

"When we did this procedure, we warned you, didn't we? That there would be a transition, that for many people being thin was very, very tough at first, that there were pressures to deal with? And we offered counseling, which you—"

"—didn't want, right, so shoot me."

"—didn't think you needed, despite our best efforts. And the irony is that you've been through the worst. You've had the surgery, you've had your big heartbreak, let us finish the job and help you get back on your feet."

Reluctantly, Burl went along. He knew somewhere inside that the answer to his sorrow wasn't to get fat again, but he also wondered whether thin people always had such troubles, or if there was some quality of tyro about him, whether he was a pigeon in a sophisticated card game and thus could only lose his shirt.

He wondered this again later, after the plastic surgery to gather up and excise his cloak of empty flesh, to create more of a waistline, to place his nipples about where they seemed to belong. It was painful; he was doped up for a while but off the streets, at least, and not thinking so much about Wanda.

"You're fortunate," Stringer told him later. "It wasn't that big a job, because you weren't morbidly obese for all that long. You'll just have a few seams, but otherwise it should be fine."

Stringer kept him in the hospital for as long as he could, but the surgery went well and Burl healed quickly in body, if not in heart. It was still cold, but winter's grip was broken. The faint taste of spring in the air, clear and cold as snowmelt, made Burl think he might go somewhere afterward where it was always warmer than winter in Salt Lake City. Especially if he was forced to live on the streets, which held no terrors for him now. He wrote to Wanda, pined for her, and fretted over the child she might even bear, but he never got any response. He grew tired of haunting the hospital, where they were devoted to keeping people alive. He felt like a shade on the wrong side of the great divide. One day, with no particular notice, he walked away.

———————

Approaching the abandoned-looking scrubland beyond the railyards, Burl took solace in the durability of cliché: where there's smoke, there's fire. His legs ached from the hike down the hill from the university and all the way across town, and his face felt weathered by the cold wind, which seemed to grow stronger, and the glittering city darker and more hurried, with each step.

He had adjusted rapidly to life on the streets again, was even better at it, perhaps, than before his stay with the Witness Movement. Losing Wanda had hardened him. But tonight he was almost too exhausted to gather the offering of firewood that protocol required from each who would warm himself, the society of the homeless functioning like any other in the need for all to produce in order to consume. The sound of weeping, which was the first thing he heard from the group, told him that Abe must have taken a turn for the worse.

"Hey, Burlie's brought us some nice firewood," Lester said cheerfully as he approached.

Johnny, Otto, and Karsten greeted him hopefully, but when it was clear that he hadn't brought a bottle, Johnny slipped back into his characteristic sulk. He didn't like Burl. "Don't mind him," Lester insisted, but Johnny's tone toward Burl was always sneering. He viewed Burl with the special contempt that some would heap on him who falls the furthest, and he grumbled about Burl's getting to sleep on a grate outside the hospital when any of the rest who tried such a thing were kicked off, roughed up, their possessions confiscated as a lesson or for spite.

Burl looked at Dee, who wept loudly, and then at Lester, who shrugged. The others looked away, and Dee bellowed, with a renewed outburst of tears, "He's dead, Abie died, O God you bastard!"

"Dee! Don't say such things," Lester cautioned almost primly. "He's better off anyway, ain't he?"

"That's right, Dee," Otto said in his reedy, maudlin voice.

Burl knelt and laid a hand on her shoulder. It frightened him a little. Everybody knew Abe had had AIDS, and now Dee was alone with her own probably similar fate, without him to take care of her.

"I'm sorry, Dee. I'm so sorry."

Her weeping deepened and outran her breath until she began coughing. Burl rubbed her back and looked at the others, hoping someone had a bottle or some money for one. Lester shook his head, the others shrugged or looked away. They were ashamed, these drunks, that they couldn't even produce a drink on demand. Maybe that was why they hung back from her: they couldn't console her even the least bit, and it freshly demonstrated their failure.

Burl felt a chill for the nearness of oblivion, the uselessness of these companions. Dee was already badly broken, toothless, bloated and alcoholic. She had lost much of her strawlike hair, and her skin was the color of dirt. A swollen foot in a ragged open-toed shoe stuck out of her skirts—she wore most of her clothes simultaneously and her legs, hidden most of the time, had sores.

"He was the love of my life, Burlie, you know?" She wiped her nose on her sleeve. "He's the reason I was put here. Nothing makes any sense without him around, except suffering."

"His suffering is over," Burl said, glancing around for support. "We can be grateful for that at least."

"Sure, that's right," said Lester, whose black skin shone in the firelight. A couple of the others nodded perfunctorily. Johnny, always pale, looked away. Knots of homeless people dotted the embankment, huddled around fires, stamping their feet and clutching their rags about themselves as the day's light and warmth drained away. They looked like a medieval army, some rabble bound numbly for the Holy Land.

"He suffered so much, but my suffering is only beginning," Dee wept. "What am I gonna do? I can't even bury him right. That was the only thing he wanted at the end, cremation. So the worms wouldn't eat him, and we'd always be together."

"It's all right, Dee," Burl said without conviction. "It'll be all right, you'll see. Maybe we can get you a drink, huh? Lemme see if I can find you something."

Burl looked around to see if he might bum some alcohol from someone. Going from fire to fire like a beggar going door to door, he got much the same response, until finally someone took pity and offered some cough medicine.

"Not just Robitussin. It's prescription."

Burl took it and Dee drank it eagerly as the others again looked away, jealous or embarrassed that they had begged so much booze their credit was no good. None of them had much liked Abe anyway; many had been intravenous drug users at one time or another, and watching him had been like watching themselves die.

"Where is he?" Burl asked the others.

Lester signaled with his head.

"I'd like to pay my last respects," Burl told Dee. "Will you come with me? C'mon."

With Burl's help Dee stumbled heavily to her feet. He forced himself to put his arm around her. He was still clean, for a homeless person, and the smells of the others were hard for him. He clung to some fastidiousness that persisted long after his weight was gone. Dee reeked and was fat too. Burl wondered with alarm whether he had smelled so bad.

Abe didn't look as bad as Burl thought he would. He was laid out straight, so you could tell right away he was a person and not one of those piles of brown rags you had to sidestep in a doorway, and which shocked you by having a head. He'd had AIDS, sort of, but that didn't appear to have killed him. He drank insatiably, enough so that dementia set in long ago. He was kind of wasted, for a normal person, and they all assumed he'd had pneumonia lately, although once he learned about the virus he wouldn't go near a doctor. He was afraid to end up in the hospital, where he couldn't drink.

"Astrophysicists, right?" he'd needle Burl sometimes. "Dentists? Miracle workers at tax time. Heh heh heh. But whoever heard of a homeless Jewish alcoholic stevedore? Hah? From Corpus Christi? They wanted to name a submarine for it, remember that? The body of Christ with nuclear missiles. Heh heh heh."

Abe. A stevedore in the desert, his muscles starved and atrophied and now the whole of him disbanding. "L'chaim," he'd say sometimes with a twinkle, happiest when he slurred it most because then he was really safest from himself. He and Burl would talk sometimes; Abe had seen and read, knew the world a little, understood that life meant more than survival for some people. No one had any pennies, so they used a pair of small stones to keep his eyes closed, and this above all Burl found sorrowful, for it had been done by those who could not waste a penny on the dead and knew nothing of the Jews, but who knew and in one case loved Abe, and who left stones on his eyes the way Jewish mourners everywhere left pebbles on a gravestone whenever they visited the departed.

Dee had begun to cry again, petting her poor lost love as if to console him.

"Is there anybody we should tell?" Burl asked. "Did he have any family?"

"I was his family, Burlie. He had nobody. I used to ask him, maybe a daughter who could help, or sister or brothers or something back in Texas. It was just the two of us. We were all we had."

Burl began to feel around the dead man's hips. Amazing what you can get used to, he thought. Cleaning corpses again, just like back at the paper.

"What are you doing? He's got no money, Burlie. You looking for money on a dead man?"

"Not money. Papers. Information."

Dee reached into her skirts and handed Burl a tattered brown leather wallet, melted hide gluing together the empty glassine sleeves intended for photographs. Several yellowed library cards attested to his wanderings, and other odds and ends revealed his blood type, draft status, and prior membership in the Knights of Pythias. Among these things, stuffed in with inexplicable clippings bent round where the wallet folded, was a Texas driver's license.

"Abraham Alter," it said. "D.o.b. 9/17/54."

Burl looked up in astonishment.

"He was 37? Abe was 37?"

Dee nodded gravely, her mouth trembling.

"And I can't even bury him. Not right. They'll put him in the city cemetery in a pine box when all he ever wanted was to stay with me."

Burl looked at her solemnly and then looked down at the dead man.

"I can arrange it, Dee, but you'll have to help. It'll have to be our secret."

"A secret?"

"A big secret. You can't tell anyone, but once it's done you won't mind. Abe will have what he wanted. You'll be able to keep him with you."

A lot of it was luck. Burl always kept a couple of virginal credit cards for such an occasion and decided that the time had come to use one. In three trips to an automated teller machine, he managed to get $750 in cash on a previously unused Visa card.

"He drank himself to death, basically," Burl told the men who came to collect the body. "He used to be real fat. But I think it's only right for me to tell you that he was HIV positive. So be careful."

Burl was hoping to avoid any mention of AIDS on the death certificate, and the local authorities were obliging enough to put it down as pneumonia. Probably Alter had had cirrhosis, which they'd see if they took the trouble to open him up and find out. There were no next of kin, just a couple of his fellow hobos, as they were still sometimes called in places like Salt Lake City.

It was as if Burl had been planning all his life for this. Mort Allen was happy to help, sort of. Burl called his former employer, gave his name as Bo Charon, and explained in a haphazard Australian accent that his good friend Burl Bennett had died, virtually penniless, of AIDS.

"Above all, he wanted to be cremoyted," Burl said sadly, hoping for a break on the price and trying hard to keep from falling out of accent. "He left a little money, but I dinno if it's enough, and I frankly don't have anything I can contribute. He said he used to work for you. Some kind of official mourner."

"Burl? Heavyset guy, kind of lost looking?"

"That's the one, only he ain't heavy"—Burl pronounced it *hivvy*—"no more. He's wasted. The AIDS et him up."

"Oh gee. Oh, I'm really sorry to hear that. What a shame."

Allen agreed to cremate the body for $700, a price Burl knew to be somewhat below retail, if somewhat above cost. He spent the remaining $50 on a cheap motel room and the use of a laundromat in an effort to get Dee cleaned up. When she looked nearly presentable, he dispatched her by bus to deliver the $700 to Allen's funeral home. Then she took possession of the death certificate and, at Burl's instruction, had the body sent directly to the crematorium. Allen would never even see it.

Afterward, Dee wept with gratitude. The urn said "Burl Bennett," but the ashes, she knew, were Abraham Alter's.

———

Godfrey Shields did not like to leave the ground. You were no closer to God up there. The stewardesses were pretty, but this came to seem a small thing as you got older. Air travel was wearisome, confining, and, worst of all, incommunicado. When you landed, in case of an emergency you were far away.

He didn't travel much; the West was very strange to him. On the way in from the airport, trying to follow the map markings the woman behind the counter had made with a felt-tipped pen, it crossed his mind that this was just what came, eventually, after that place in New Jersey where Burl's family lived. It was all of a piece.

The beauty of money, Shields thought, is that it's like a common tongue. Everybody uses it. The best thing Shields had ever done was getting into Burl's apartment and taking the time to go through all his junk for some bank account numbers. He couldn't figure out who might have trashed the place that way; they swore it wasn't them.

Sure enough, withdrawals. It was a relief. Burl was right here in New York, Shields thought smugly. Found out, just like that. Up in the Bronx, ATM withdrawals from the same machine every time, at erratic intervals. But why interfere? This was good. He would just have to figure out something for the parents. Maybe confront the insensitive sonofabitch and make him send them a message. At least everybody was safe. Godfrey Shields did not like the current equilibrium, but he could see it resolving itself harmlessly.

Then, out of nowhere, Salt Lake City. The report from the credit card company—$750 in cash advances from a bank there, obtained by someone who knew Burl's four-digit personal identification number—did not itself seem creditworthy. Maddeningly, the report was six weeks late. Shields felt sure the card was stolen, although it had never been reported stolen.

He decided he'd better figure out what was going on, and so he looked everything over and saw that the withdrawals in the Bronx weren't just in the Bronx. They were in *Riverdale*. How stupid he had been. Louis Naumann wouldn't say anything, but Shields had wrung the truth out of Frederic LaChaise without too much difficulty. He'd been using a branch just blocks from his house.

So Burl had been in Vegas. That wasn't surprising; he was a good card player, and the town was a magnet for transients. And then, judging by the $750, Burl had for some reason moved on to Salt Lake, where Shields now landed.

In his rental car, he drove out into the city. With his right hand, Shields snapped open his briefcase on the car seat beside him and rooted around for the address of the bank. He didn't expect them to know anything; the $750 was obtained using an automated teller machine. But there was always a chance someone there might know Burl; they might turn up some other transactions, even other accounts, that Shields didn't know about. Something. Mrs. Bennett was so sad on the phone, he just couldn't stand it. All he needed was a little something to report back to them, learned legitimately.

But the bank proved a poor place to begin. No one there knew anything, no one had seen anything, the money had simply been drawn from a machine in the wall outside in the middle of three different working days. The transactions were just three of hundreds occurring every week at the branch.

Next stop, the local police. When they checked on the Dodge he'd given Burl to replace his immolated Checker, police records showed it to have been abandoned at a downtown motel, the Chrysalis, where Burl hadn't been in months.

"Oh, I remember. Very fat. Many problems. Just disappeared one time. Poof."

The owner of the Chrysalis hurled some of these words over his shoulder as he struggled to deal with a busload of tourists eager to check in. Shields pursued him along the counter and called into the office.

"You never saw him again?"

"Never. Even left his car." The man cradled a phone in his ear and, from a bursting Rolodex, dialed a number. "Just as he was losing weight, some kind of crash diet he was on. Hello, Royal Oaks?" He stressed "royal" in the name. "This is Vikram at the Chrysalis. I'm overbooked. Do you have anything? Yes, I can hold."

Shields persisted: "Did he get a lot thinner?"

"Yes, thinner. Then *poof*."

The dates of Burl's tenure at the Chrysalis were interesting. He was there while he was also supposedly in Las Vegas. Then again, Frederic had simply posted to a mail drop in Las Vegas. Burl must have gone down there to pick up the money.

People were nice, yet Salt Lake City was a funny place to be black. A difficult city to fathom too, except everything was so close together that all you needed ultimately was a sense of direction. Since Shields did not have this, he kept getting lost.

It was strange to his wife that he'd even made the trip. Much of this stuff could be checked by phone. But the district attorney's office insisted that he go. Go on to Las Vegas if necessary. Follow up. There was heat from *The Tribune*. Everyone wanted Burl.

And he had a feeling. He was certain Burl was alive and well somewhere. He didn't want to find him, exactly. He just wanted to prove the proposition. So he went in person to learn that the local police had no reports on Burleigh Bennett, robbery or otherwise. He wasn't registered to vote in Salt Lake City. He certainly didn't own property. There was no record of earnings from the Social Security people.

There was only, when Shields perfunctorily touched base, a record of his death.

"That can't be right," he told the man at the counter.

"It comes in from the medical examiner's office. They don't usually make mistakes."

"You got one here. It's not him. You got the weight at 150. He weighed twice that."

The clerk craned his neck around to read the form.

"Cause of death says pneumonia, which at his age probably meant AIDS. He might have been wasted."

To avoid being wasted, that was the whole reason Burl took off. Shields felt sick. He sensed a little animal eating at the bottom of his stomach, a creature too familiar from some of his son's worst episodes. He tried to remain focused on guilt, but selfish thoughts intruded. If Burl was dead, there would be some very serious consequences. The district attorney's office would open one hell of an investigation. *The Tribune* would likely do the same, which would only make the DA even more frantic. Everything Shields had done would come under scrutiny, every move. He was careful, had always been careful, didn't even talk to his wife about things, but one slip and people would start to look more closely. His stomach burned. He could not see how any of this might redound to his benefit. Then again, if Burl really was dead, and the causes were natural, well, that was that. How could Shields or anyone else be blamed for pneumonia?

"Date of death on here is March 15," Shields said.

"That's what the paper says," the clerk replied.

Shields made a mental note: someone had used Burl's credit card *after* the guy died. But how in God's name might Burl have died? Maybe he was gay after all. Shields had never heard anything about him with a woman; Norma had insisted they hadn't been romantically involved. Couldn't have been drugs. Assume AIDS; then Shields's actions were irrelevant. If not AIDS, it must be someone else. How could he lose all that weight? Shields searched his memory, trying to figure out what he might have done differently, hoping not to find anything. He'd tried to protect the guy, to keep an eye out for everybody's interests, to keep things in balance. He had never taken a life. It didn't seem fair that this one should be taken from him.

"Where's he buried on here?"

The clerk craned again.

"Cremated."

The word filled Shields with a kind of awe as consequences tumbled through his mind. Exhumation not possible. Can't make positive ID. His heart jumped to the longed-for conclusion: Burl not likely dead. It was just a feeling, but these were so important, Shields knew. They came from knowledge one couldn't always articulate. Who would pay for cremation? Must have been someone close to him. Maybe they used his credit card? Damned ATMs.

At Allen's funeral home, Shields learned that the ashes were released to Diane Stiggs, no permanent address. She had paid the bill, in cash. Shields had to come back later in the day to catch up with Allen, who had been at the dentist.

"A sweet guy, heavyset," Allen said later. "He used to work for me."

"Doing what?"

"He was kind of a welcomer. He attended funerals, basically. He was good at it, so I paid him to help out a little."

"Did you know he had AIDS?"

"Not a clue, until he died. Though in retrospect, he did say he'd lost somebody himself. That's why he started coming here. It helped him, I think, kind of like a therapy. In my opinion."

"Who made the funeral arrangements?"

"For Burl? There was no funeral. He didn't have anybody. Just an old friend, from Australia. Lemme look through my calendar here . . . Bo Charon, said his name was. From Australia. 'The land down under.'"

Shields knew that the next step ordinarily would be finding Diane Stiggs and Bo Charon, and by now the thing was taking on the fascination of any good investigation. How would it all come out? You always wanted to know. It kept you going. Back in his hotel room, he sat down to consider the possibilities.

Someone, not pneumonia, killed Burl and stole his credit cards, using them—only once—to pay for cremating the corpse. Or something killed Burl, and then this Diane Stiggs used the dead man's credit card to pay for Mort Allen's services. Then who the hell was Charon? Shields understood that Charon and Stiggs would have some answers. He reached for the local white pages but, as expected, neither was listed. They would be hard to find, even assuming their names were real, and although Shields wouldn't have admitted it, that was a relief.

On a hunch, he went back to the Chrysalis that evening and caught up once more with Vikram, who apologized for being so harried.

"You know, he really was quite a bit thinner. The first time, he got so fat, you're not going to believe this, he was so fat he got stuck in the doorway."

"Here in the lobby?"

"No, no, to his room. The door to his room. I had to have the fire department; they sawed through the frame and everything. What a mess."

"Stuck in the doorway? He wasn't that fat. You got narrow doors?"

"Thirty-two inches, right according to code, you can look for yourself. He was really, really fat. Then he went away for a while. I think they took him to the hospital. Then he came back and got thin very very fast."

"You remember what hospital?"

"Um, wait a minute, let me think. The doctor called me when your friend wanted to come back. I think it was St. Ferdinand's. Out toward the university."

The hospital would tell him nothing—not even whether Burl had been a patient—without a written request from local law enforcement authorities. Privacy, they said. This was his reward for straightforwardness, Shields stewed on his way back to the hotel. He might have just called, claiming to be Burl, and concocted a billing inquiry. He probably would have learned quite a bit that way. One of these days, he resolved, he would actually do it.

Meanwhile, he was loath to involve local authorities more than was necessary. It was too easy then for things to get out of hand. Shields wanted to know everything first, figure things out, and then decide what to do. Events had already gone far enough beyond him.

He switched on the radio and moved the dial around in search of the local classical station, hoping that there was one. When he found it, it was playing early music of some kind, he thought perhaps a madrigal, and later, poring once again over the paperwork on the disappearance, he listened with satisfaction as the announcer confirmed that it had been a madrigal, "one of the lesser-known but nonetheless delightful earlier works of that much-loved Italian, Claudio Monteverdi."

Shields looked down at the name of that burial arranger from down under, Bo Charon, and gave a yell. Then he burst out laughing. He thought of Caronte ferrying Orfeo across the river Styx—or as Burl would have it, Stiggs—in pursuit of Eurydice. "Burl, you loony fuck," he said to himself, wondering if his quarry's choice of names was for his benefit or just the result of some literary gene whose influence the guy couldn't control.

Burl had obviously staged his own demise somehow. There did not appear to be a crime that needed solving, at least as far as Shields was concerned. And if Burl wanted to bury himself and be somebody else, that was okay too. Shields decided that Burl's parents must already know, or that they would soon find out. He'd worry abut that later—much later. There might be official heat back home, but hey, whose fault was pneumonia? Whose fault was AIDS?

The day was fine, and with a sudden sense of freedom Shields set about killing the afternoon. How nice that its death would go unremarked, its mortality foregone with or without him. He walked around the city center, looking over the Mormon institutions, checking out the citizenry. He smiled at everyone. He felt generous, expansive. His eyes were nearly wet with relief.

Thinking he might buy something for Adam, he crossed the street to go into the Zion Cooperative Mercantile Institute, which appeared to be a department store. He pulled open one of the heavy smoked-glass doors just as someone was pushing against it to leave.

Shields stood face to face with a bearded, bedraggled soul who looked so astonished he might have just killed someone. The man stared wide eyed as if Shields were the angel of death. He made no attempt to move aside. Shields finally shouldered past him disdainfully, just as the guy's lips started to move. You'd think he'd never seen a black man before. Some nut with a little red valise, in the kind of plaid you used to get for opening a new savings account. Probably a shoplifter.

But it wasn't enough to spoil Shields's mood. Before boarding the plane home he bought himself a tape of *Orfeo* and listened to it as he flew, using the little Walkman he'd brought for self-administered dosages of opera whenever he felt the need. When he got to La Guardia he made the phone call that he knew he had to make and baldly lied. When he got home he hugged his wife and son, and at work the next day he took a deep breath and filed a report concluding the obvious: Burl Bennett was dead.

"FRIENDS AND FAMILY. Coworkers and loved ones. Dear parents."

The man spoke loudly, deliberately invoking each phrase.

"All of you *knew* Burl Bennett. It is fitting, therefore, that we gather here today to share—for that was the essence of our friend, was it not? How sad that we've come to share our sorrow.

"We *must* do that, but to do that alone would never suffice, not for this large man, large in every way: large in body, large in spirit. Even more important than sharing our sorrow, and I know this isn't easy, we must also share our joy—our joyous remembrances of this man's very special life, and in doing so perhaps inform our grief, together."

It was so quiet. At a fine old church too, with no casket cluttering up the place with all its funereal bulk. Still the dark clothes, the balding minister, red faced and meaty, row upon row of somber heads and shoulders. Déjà vu. The pastor always seemed so clean.

"It is never easy accepting death, in all its implacable finality"—a sob burst forth from the audience like the bark of a dog—

"and every death seems senseless, except in the light of the life that preceded it, the quality and direction of the journey, no matter how brief. In this case, the one we mourn has himself shown us the way. That was one of the great wonders of Burl's time with us." The minister looked around in mock amazement. "He shed so much light, his life was so full of meaning, and one of the ways it derived its meaning was leading the way to understand death by looking to the life."

In the audience, behind his beard, he was moved. He swallowed heavily. His eyes were wet.

"The life of Burl Bennett is full of such ironies. He lived alone, and yet he encompassed all of us here in this room, a host within himself. He loved fine food, fine clothes, and fine wine, yet couldn't be less a materialist. Wags at the paper he loved so well called him St. Burl, yet he was a lovable rogue—"

Elephant. Rogue elephant. The look of indomitability these guys invariably mounted. A little smile. Almost smug.

"—who always went his own way and never failed to indulge his appetites. Fortunately for all of us, his hunger was never just for food. It was also for decency. Integrity. The meaning of each and every life. It was the hunger of a seeker, one who has worked up an enormous appetite wandering in the desert or, more aptly, working hard in the vineyards of life."

Always the boilerplate. This guy didn't know Burl Bennett. Burl never went to church unless somebody died.

"I believe that Burl reaped a bountiful harvest during his short time with us, a harvest that nourished him more than any of the meals he so heartily enjoyed. Burl also left us a much larger legacy. For we discover that the seed he planted in each of us is no briefly blooming annual but a hardy perennial that will bear luscious fruit year after year after year."

The turnout was shocking. The paper must have arranged this. The minister was good too, he had to admit. And such a gathering; row upon row assembled in tribute. He looked down and tried not to listen for a second. It sounded such a wonderful life. Was it sadder that it ended, that it was never so wonderful, or some especially pathetic combination of the two? Like the old Catskills joke: "The food was terrible. And the portions were so small!"

Abe looked sadly toward Burl's modest collection of relatives, clustered together on one side as if huddled for warmth. Aunts, uncles, cousins, grandfather Bennett posted grimly on the end, all of them fitting easily into the pews. Seeing them all together struck him forcefully, as family gatherings always had, with the anomaly of Burl Bennett's weight.

It was like being a ghost. Practically everyone he had ever known, except those he had known most recently, was in the room. Even Shields! Abe quickly looked away. His sinuses were clogged with suppressed crying. It was tragic that people never got to experience this while they were alive—everyone, all together, dwelling however momentarily on the meaning of one's life. This must be the essence of prayer, this collective outpouring of wonder. That's what it was, wonder. How was it that he never felt more than sorry at all those other funeral services he'd attended in Salt Lake City? Perhaps, though, one can only mourn oneself. We are like sailors bobbing in shark-infested seas. Treading water, the men cling together even as they are picked off one by one by the greedy jaws of death.

"—and so most important for us today, I think, is to make of this memorial the thing Burl himself would have wanted it to be, the thing he tried to make all of life, which is a feast. We shall have today a feast in celebration of Burl Bennett."

It was horrifying. The minister explained that Burl's good friend, the renowned chef Frederic LaChaise, had supervised the preparation of a veritable banquet following the service, and in honor of the dearly departed, they were all to eat until they were stuffed. All, of course, save the one who knew and no doubt loved the dead man (and Frederic's cooking) best. He was condemned only to watch.

Abraham Alter, swimming fashionably in the slimmest suit Burl had ever owned, had finally grown comfortable in his own much-tailored skin when, shaken by his department-store encounter with Shields, he resumed reading *The Tribune*, which arrived in Salt Lake City by mail. A week later he turned to the obituaries, and what he saw there seemed to make time stop. A little giddy, he read the obituary he had written for himself. His own material was there, mostly, with an italic introduction explaining that he had "left" the piece before his mysterious disappearance following his grand-jury testimony. And it was much expanded; he never would have claimed so much space for himself. Oh for God's sake! At least two mistakes already. Somehow they got his high school wrong, and they fell into that classic obit trap, failing to update; it was no longer true that he had joined *The Tribune* nine years ago. Time passes. He also realized with a start that the obit ran next to the jump of a story reporting his death as news.

He was aghast to find that it began on page one:

JOURNALIST FOUND DEAD IN UTAH

A former *Tribune* reporter who mysteriously vanished nearly two years ago was reported dead of pneumonia in Utah, authorities said.

Burl G. Bennett disappeared after stumbling into the immediate aftermath of a gangland-style killing of three men reputed to be members of organized crime. Mr. Bennett, who spent nine years with *The Tribune*, was known to have testified before a grand jury investigating the slayings, where he was said to have identified the gunman (obituary on page B16).

Mr. Bennett's life was subsequently threatened, forcing him to move from his Brooklyn apartment, but a police department spokesman said yesterday that Mr. Bennett had rejected offers of protection even though at one point his car was dynamited.

Mr. Bennett's death was shrouded in no less mystery than his sudden disappearance late in January 1990.

The Utah Medical Examiner's Office in Salt Lake City listed the cause of death as pneumonia. Mr. Bennett's body was cremated at the request of Diane Steggs, who has since dropped out of sight.

They can't even spell a phony name right, Abe thought with some satisfaction.

Mr. Bennett's disappearance stymied the investigation into the triple murder in New York, which occurred Sept. 13, 1989 at a Brooklyn restaurant called Gardenia's that Mr. Bennett partly owned. The investigation is known to have focused on Giuseppe Gemignani, a reputed underworld figure who is said to have consolidated his powers as head of the city's Mandoli crime organization, or family.

He couldn't read the rest. His first impulse was to go to New York and put a stop to all this, but he recognized that this is merely what he told himself he ought to feel. The skin of the dead man was beginning to get comfortable. Eager to get back in any case, he had turned to Engel, prepared to plead for enough of a loan for a plane ticket and a little walking around money once he got to New York. But no pleading was necessary. Engel understood completely his desire to go home. "I only wish I could," he said, handing over $2,000 in cash. Alter got back just in time for the funeral.

It was a fine day, bright and cool, the kind that had always made Burl anxious. Alter's stomach was heaving. He'd nibbled crackers on the way East to try and calm it; often at such times it felt better with a little something in it.

His run-in with Shields in Salt Lake City had scared him half to death and revived his long-standing paranoia, but it also gave him confidence that even those who knew Burl best would not see him in Abraham's countenance. Yet there was certainly the chance that somebody would—the merest thought of his parents made him cringe with guilt—and he had no idea what he would do if the circumstance should arise.

He couldn't even say for sure why he had decided to attend. His plan, if that's what it could be called, had worked so well that he expected it would be easy for him to live out his life as someone else if he chose. He must miss Burl, he decided. He must feel the need to mourn not vicariously, as he already had done, but personally, and among others. Perhaps they might confirm with their presence the identity of the dead man, an identity so painfully shed.

They did just that. For Alter, it was like being one of those movie ghosts who at first runs up to the living and proclaims himself, until he realizes they can't see or hear him because he's dead. He'd had to rush to arrive on time, and when he got there—early—he couldn't stop his heart's pounding. His hands shook, and he felt a line of sweat trickle down his flank from beneath his left arm. But he soon relaxed. No one knew him. Abraham Alter was one of those strangers who round out every funeral, one who is assumed by the relatives to be a friend and by friends to be a relative.

A short, dignified woman sang *Der Kindertotenlieder* in good voice. Good grief, Abe thought, Mahler's songs for his lost child.

Everywhere he looked he saw people Burl had known. In each face he expected to see the shock of recognition, and at times it was all he could do not to embrace somebody. He reminded himself again not to call anyone by name. Selfishly, guiltily, he had made a full circuit of the nave before finding a seat for himself. His mother and father looked right through him and even to Alter seemed like strangers. Betty, prim and sorrowful, her lips thin and tight, looked all around, everywhere but at Stu, who didn't seem to be looking anywhere at all.

After the minister's synthesis, which made of Burl's life so much more sense than there was in it, came Borman, the executive editor. Hypocrite! He could never stand Burl, it was well known. A stolid, self-satisfied sort with cold blue eyes and ruddy cheeks from all those chamber of commerce functions, he had banished Burl to the obit desk in the first place, however wise the decision might look in retrospect.

"Mea culpa," he began, so obviously pleased with himself. "I admit it, Burl was right. 'Why can't we get some more space for obituaries?' he used to demand whenever I passed him in the hall. 'Why can't we make more room for the dead? It's a measure of how much we value our readers' lives.' Well, I see now that Burl was right, and I hope that when he read our obituary (and rest assured that wherever he is, *The Tribune* is delivered) he found it to his liking. In fact he wrote most of it himself, and editors at the paper learned long ago that it wasn't wise to tamper with Burl's copy."

Flatterer! He feels no grief. The dead are nothing to those who haven't lived.

"I'm smiling. I joke. How is that possible?" He worked his eyebrows rhetorically. "Well. The real question, in dealing with the life of Burl Bennett, is how could it be otherwise?"

The drape of his suit. The rich blue of his tie. Unseemly.

"Burl brought all of us at *The Tribune* too much joy, in his work and in his presence, as a colleague and a friend, for me to do anything but smile." Borman showed his teeth. "Burl was the nicest guy in the whole wide world, but as a reporter, he was a holy terror. He was a wizard with public records, which he proved to the rest of us can include telephone records and credit card bills under certain circumstances, as well as the usual array of deeds, liens, and so forth. Burl Bennett had no hesitation about going through your garbage either. I mean, watch out. And he never filed mush. This is one case where both the reporter and his copy sang. Burl kicked and screamed at first when we told him we wanted him to write obituaries, but he was brilliant, and we all know how well he came to love it. He had just the right skills, which are rarely found all together. He was a terrific, sensitive writer. He loved and respected people. And he was a subtle and imaginative interviewer."

Damn right.

"One of the ironies about all this is that we could sure use Burl right now. Burl would have an awful lot of questions about his own demise. And Burl was pretty good at finding answers. So if there's one thing I wanna promise you here today, it's that we're going to make like Burl. We're going to try and live a good life. And we're going to try and find some answers."

Abe wept noisily, prompting sympathetic looks. He felt like a killer. But perhaps Burl had not been his to kill. Looking at the misery on his mother's face, he felt a growing panic, an intestinal distress that came with the idea that Burl had taken a life not his own. He wanted to embrace her, to make up for her suffering with the miraculous resurrection she must have dreamed about. Embarrassingly, he couldn't stop sobbing. He wept for what he had done, what he had thrown away. Somehow the ones he barely knew especially broke his heart, but when he spotted Norma, at last, after looking and avoiding simultaneously since his arrival, he nearly fainted.

Nobody knew Abraham Alter at the restaurant either, but he hid behind sunglasses anyway. Sipping Scotch, he was almost immediately drunk, which made available to him the ironic cast of mind necessary to get through the proceedings.

"From college," he said when people asked. "We were at school together."

He mingled. What would have been a subdued hubbub anywhere else here rose like the surf, bouncing off the walls and pipes and pouring through the larger portion of the cavernous space that was unoccupied. What had this place once been, in the days when sweat poured off the men who worked here smelling of tobacco and leather and hair oil? A brewery? A printing plant? Stables? Surrounded by all these soft people, he tried to imagine the darkness and flies, the smell of dung, the hay, the big arms and mustaches and collarless shirts of the men. Now it smelled sickeningly of perfume and faintly, generically, of food.

Past the elegant women in black stockings—more bounty wasted on the dead—and the men unused to keeping their suit coats on, he made his way to a table laden with beautiful things, foods it would take some thought, or some tasting, even to figure out. As soon as he saw them, Abe turned away, as if in modesty before a naked stranger. Someone urged him to dig in; Hanks, he realized. "That's what Burl would do." All around the table he could see the hard core, men and women from the paper who acted as if they never ate, hanging around the food.

"Sorry, I can't. I can't."

"Were you very close?"

"At one time."

"Gee, I'm sorry. It's a fitting tribute, though. You know how he was about food."

"Yes, but we never ate together. I'm kosher, you see."

"Oh," said Hanks, putting up a respectful look.

Alter had the thought that people shouldn't eat in public. Seeing them struggle with plates and forks and drinks, their jaw muscles working obscenely beneath their skin, the women's careful daubing at their sticky red lips, the napkins then grease stained, it was all as dispiriting as someone else's hairy, sticky sex. Abe was glad to be free of it.

He felt impervious. If knowledge was power, then he was like a god with his secret. It helped him understand the strength people derive from faith. He thought of Wanda. Faith is a form of knowledge, really; belief so strong that something arbitrary becomes true. Cloaked in the shroud of what he knew, Alter sidled up to little knots of people and just stood listening. There was little talk of Burl Bennett, he discovered with some disappointment, although there was some fascination with the mystery of his disappearance and death. (AIDS was the favored explanation, and Alter felt Burl would have liked the myth of martyrdom, with its hint of illicit love, growing up around his memory like a vine. He thought with a start of Engel, alive and well, thank God.) Mostly, though, the talk was of the here and now, of whatever people were concerned about, of the surging and seething of hope and ambition at the paper, of sharing cabs. People only mourn for themselves.

Yet they need one another. Seconds after Alter appeared at any gathering, a speaker would make a nod in his direction, a glance of admittance to these instant tribes of discourse. Generosity.

"From college," he'd say, laconic in his grief. And to the mystery: "Such a tragedy. I can't believe we're standing here."

As someone young spoke to him—"He taught me to use a pencil covering fires. 'Cause ink freezes, you know? In winter I mean"—Alter spotted Stu and Betty moving wearily toward the exit. He followed them outside and waited for the other mourners, their concern so plainly a burden to the truly bereaved, to clear away.

"Mr. and Mrs. Bennett." Alter suddenly was at a loss, not Alter. But they stared blankly, Stu nodding slightly, almost smiling, as if to say, you needn't find words. They didn't know him. "I'm so very sorry."

They both nodded.

"From college," Alter pressed on. "I knew him at Columbia. We were very close over the years, even though I lived in California. Your son was a wonderful talent."

"Yes," said Stu. Betty remained silent. She seemed to hold herself together with great effort. "What was your name?"

"Abraham. Alter." He held out a hand. "Abe Alter."

Stu smiled and shook it, but Betty's silence unnerved him. He couldn't let them go yet.

"We met. Years ago, when Burl and I were at school. You probably don't remember."

"Alter? Yes, I think so. I think I remember you."

"I didn't graduate."

Betty nodded.

"I just wanted to say that you must have faith. Burl is somewhere safe. It's not what you think."

"I'm sorry, I don't have your faith," Betty said turning away. "I don't have any faith."

When they left he felt unlike Alter again, for Alter, he imagined, never would have done such a thing. But it must have been in Alter's character, because after Burl's funeral—at what he enjoyed considering the Feast of the Assumption, where so much was assumed—he did the same song and dance again and again and again.

Back inside he felt freer, and so did everybody else. With the family gone and the crowd thinned, the hubbub perversely grew, or rather shook free, with the help of drink, the artificial bonds of propriety. Alter, no longer peevish, was glad to see the gathering become more of a party whose excuse was someone's death. It was more momentous than somebody quitting, at least. The food seemed great, and even the very young who hadn't known Burl particularly well understood that it was a worthwhile place to be. Fortified by additional Scotch, Alter did what he regarded as his duty. He was growing cocky that no one would recognize him, but there was always the chance; he was uneasy. And it was unsatisfying to succeed, because there was no one to share the secret. Knowledge bestows power, but it isolates, he saw. He thought this might have been a consolation to Burl, who had fretted about not being Tolstoy. Imagine the loneliness of genius.

But to be a genius of loneliness was something too. Norma wore black, not a silky black but something like corduroy or velvet that absorbed light, cut into a kind of bell shape that hung modestly on her pearish frame. Her hair was pulled back and held with a large black bow that gave Alter a lump in his throat, and her face looked drawn and aged by unwanted proximity to death. Yet on her shoulders she wore a kind of lace mantle in white that looked to be made by knitting loosely together hundreds of snowflakes. Alter pictured her getting ready that morning, her dress perhaps laid out the night before, the thought crossing her mind that it was tragic to think of looking nice at such a time. And ultimately that was what passed like electricity through his guts, setting them unpleasantly atingle: not only that she was so pretty, but that she should be pretty. The bow, the lace, the makeup were all sacrilegious and touching as well. Like breathing, they refuse to stop for any death but one's own. The beauty and ruthlessness of life is how ultimately unconscious it is. Alter's intestinal distress—he imagined he could feel the staple biting his stomach—nibbled the edges of panic at the idea, which seemed to rise up through his feet, that Burl's death made no difference at all.

He took a healthy gulp of Scotch.

"You're Norma. He spoke often of you. You were very special to him."

"He was very special to me," she answered as if startled, her voice deep inside her. Her eyes held him, but searchingly, like a blind person's following the sound of a voice.

"I knew him at school. I live in California, but we'd talk."

"I'm sorry, and your name is?"

"Alter. Abraham Gabriel Alter."

She was forced to take his outstretched hand and he saw that she misunderstood the way he searched her eyes. He let go of her reluctantly. Her hand felt clean, almost talced. She couldn't tell by looking, and she couldn't tell by touching.

CHAPTER 20

SHE IMAGINED SHE COULD feel the seams even in bed, snuggled as she was in the hollow of his chest and knees. She dreamed that she was sleeping with somebody else, someone familiar whom she couldn't name. In the hot morning light this lover awoke and, careful to keep his hairy back turned, pulled on a new skin like a suit of clothes. Zipped into himself, he turned then and greeted her. The person she saw now was irresistible.

The dream, which recurred with dismaying frequency, filled her with dread. Sleep had seemed someplace Norma could forget the nearness of her lover's mortality, as irritatingly ubiquitous the rest of the time as a jealous stepchild bent on spoiling their romance. Maybe that was why she thought she felt the seams even when he wore a nightshirt. It was her way of refusing to forget, a string around her psyche's finger: worry, it reminded.

Who wouldn't? His very survival was a miracle. No wonder he had that brooding, blinking quality she found so endearing. "I'm the groundhog who's seen his own shadow," he liked to say. Like some hostage fresh from years in a dungeon. Lying this way in his arms, she would pretend to be asleep while she listened for his heartbeat, felt for it against her back or in the wrist of his hand cradling her breast, her own heart thumping faster as she waited for his to skip or stop.

He had survived so much that she wondered how he had any energy left for living. Lymph cancer, stomach cancer, the operations, chemotherapy. He wouldn't talk about it. But from the scars it was clear they'd had to open him up like a coconut, or a pomegranate. It made her cringe. She couldn't get the image out of her mind: the tearing sound of stria splitting, the tight pack of the body filled with organs and ruby juices spilling like claret. Seeds of cancer everywhere. A miracle.

They had just happened, Norma and Abe, she couldn't say how. She had never been to bed with anyone she knew so little. Maybe these things were largely circumstantial; she wondered sometimes if it might have been the same with anyone who'd come along, or had she been waiting all this time for this one?

"How did you get my number again?" she asked as if in a fog.

"I called you at the paper, remember?"

It was right after the funeral. Morbid, almost. She was appalled at first, but he was so persistent, and a friend of Burl Bennett's. As it turned out, Burl had been pouring his heart out to this man for years.

"He would call me. I didn't know from where." Abraham spoke quietly, portentously. "He talked about you all the time. He hadn't had a lot of lovers, you probably know that. You were kind of somebody he mostly admired from afar."

It made Norma uneasy. How much had Burl told him? She felt Abraham had the advantage of her, and was using it.

"He gave his life for us," Alter said, nodding slightly. "Literally, for us."

It was strange to be called Abe. He thought of Lincoln but felt like a dog who has learned to respond to Rover or some such, because it has come to understand that this arbitrary sound is a reference to itself, or even just some audial correlate. This was very different, he saw, from the feeling expressed in the sentence "I am Rover," or "I am Abe." It was shocking how accustomed he had been to being Burl, the extent to which he identified with the concept. This new feeling, not of Abe-ness but of being named Abe, was disorienting. Even as he grew accustomed to his new identity, adjusted it on his shoulders like a new suit just back from the tailor, some part of him felt, when called Abraham, a sense of shock, even outrage. People are confusing me with "Abraham," some deep part of him protested, using quotation marks in his mind like clothespins to hold this abstraction at squeamish arm's length. It contributed to the feeling of invisibility that he still, somehow, couldn't shake.

Most of the time he was astonished at the extent to which he was a new person to Norma, and at the ease with which one might wear identity's costume. He put so little effort into it. He didn't memorize his social security number and hardly bothered to change his signature. Perhaps he really was someone new. Regarding himself in the mirror, it was hard to see much of Burl in that bearded face, its hairy colorlessness, its timorous fatigue, its tall, sad mirthful upper lip all suggesting, rather than Burl Bennett, Burt Lahr's cowardly lion.

"Where did you come from?" Norma asked sometimes, in amazement at her newfound circumstances.

"A stranger and a sojourner is all I am. California."

"You don't sound like someone from California."

"Los Angeles. Honest Abe."

Listening for his heartbeat, wrapped in his arms, Norma let out a sigh of equal parts contentment and despair. How could she sleep thinking she felt the ugly raised scars that girdled her lover's midsection, his arms, his thighs, his whole body, it seemed, when he was finally willing to show it to her?

And he lived on nothing—liquid protein and vitamins, liquids of all kinds. He was always sipping. But he never ate, never anything at all. He'd explained having lost much of his stomach to the cancer yet seemed never in danger of starvation. How could anyone repose in the embrace of one who had suffered so, and who was so surely bound for an early grave? Was this why he seemed so appreciative, as if all his life he'd wanted Norma and no one else?

No, it hadn't just happened. There had been something from the minute they'd met, in the way he held her hand when they shook, even in his eyes. She felt known around him, as if he could see through her, into her soul, all the clichés that seem just that until it happens to you. He spoke and gestured so familiarly, he seemed at times to read her mind. It was often hard to remember that as an old friend of Burl's he'd picked things up from him— words, manners—that Norma also shared, perhaps even originated. It was spooky.

Norma realized now how vulnerable she must have been, but if that was what it took, she was glad. She had consented to meet him for drinks, any friend of Burl's after all, and of course she had seen it as a chance to learn something about what had happened to Burl, perhaps even what he had said or thought about her, although it would have been hard to admit to herself that she did all this in search of forgiveness.

After that he called her for what he obviously intended as a date. She put him off again and again, pleaded that she worked nights, that she had a boyfriend, that she was unwell.

"Don't you get it?" she finally blurted. "I loved your friend. Have a little respect."

He started sending flowers to the paper, and people began teasing her. Gradually, her resistance broke down. Her memories of Burl became less hagiographic. She pretended to be affronted, but she enjoyed the blossoms and the teasing both. "Burl would have liked nothing better," Abe insisted. "He always wanted me to meet you, he said so himself. Besides, you haven't seen him in over a year. Are you going to avoid men forever?"

Well, why change now? Norma had always hated dates; all the possible outcomes (boredom, embarrassment, sex, heartbreak) seemed bleak. And she was still mourning for Burl, or herself, or perhaps the idea of the two of them together. That first morning, the name of Abraham solemnly inscribed at the bottom of her calendar, she rose early, nervously, and examined the paper word by word, so intently focused that she found it difficult to make sense of what she read.

Since the funeral, Norma had troubled herself. She did this with the kind of ruthless self-examination that inevitably leads into a cul-de-sac, trying to make herself admit that what she felt mostly now was free. She insisted sometimes, as a test, that her grief was for herself and thus compounded her shamefulness. She kept at this until it seemed that she felt guiltiest over not feeling guilty. Believing this for a while gave her a whole new basis for despair. Norma trod gingerly, avoiding foods Burl liked, favorite arias, his part of the newsroom. She was careful to check the index for the obituaries, to avoid tripping across them by accident. She lost weight. At night she wore a sleep mask and earplugs, using a large floor fan to blanket random sounds with roaring white noise. She mounted large sheets of cardboard in the bedroom windows and, thus interred, could exist undisturbed by the world's neurotic heavings. She slept soundly and long, a sleep that made her want more sleep and left her yawning after just a bit of food or a few hours' work.

She looked up and blinked. It was so quiet over coffee, reading the paper in the milky light which was the only kind that reached into the place. Reflected off white brick and pale stone, it came in like fluorescence. If you weren't used to it, it was depressing. Norma liked this light. It reminded her of blustery days in Grand Rapids, her girlhood home, days that didn't have any morning, particularly, just a silvery northern afternoon the color of skim milk in a cup, then nightfall practically following you back from school. Such days made you glad to be home.

It was odd, that first time with Abe. They went to an evanescent French film whose quirky charm faded even as the credits rolled off into the celluloid firmament. Norma loved it, but Abe appeared dazed when the lights came up, lost.

"Shall we get something to eat?" she asked.

"I'm not very hungry. I don't eat much, actually."

At the restaurant he sipped sweetened hot water from a latte cup wrapped in his worn-looking hands. She couldn't even eat the salad she'd ordered, watching him watching her. It soured her mood, made her feel she was with Oliver Twist, only the opposite: he didn't ask for more, in fact wouldn't take any in the first place.

"Really, this one's on me, order something," she urged the next time, as the waiter stood by expectantly.

"No, thanks, just the water." Abe practiced smiling indulgently, wearily, projecting a cosmopolite's tolerance he hoped would be reflected back. "It's a modest vice of mine. I'm still a good tipper."

"My God, you're just like him. He wouldn't eat either. We'd go to the movies and he wouldn't have any popcorn. It drove me nuts, and it was my own fault."

"Burl? Nonsense, you helped him lose weight. Best thing he ever did. That was his biggest problem, Norma. Besides, I'm not Burl."

"I know," she said, but her appetite was gone.

Lying awake in the darkness with Abraham wrapped around her, she absently tugged with her lips at the hair on his arms as she tried to recall who or what memory these bony limbs recalled. He felt familiar to her. She had to be careful not to pull so hard that she woke him, and when things got too damp and warm she blew cool air to dry them off. Blowing, she realized that it was her father whose arms around her had long ago pressed down this way, hard and soft at the same time. She had liked to play with the hair on his arms too, until it became a rain forest and she dispatched a typhoon, blowing to make the skin cool again. Abe's hairs against her lips felt like stitches, which was in keeping with her thoughts. She pictured needles entering his tortured flesh and searching painfully for a vein, scalpels drawn like magic markers across an expanse of skin, a trail of red the color of nail polish following wherever they went. She remembered her brother wandering the hospital like a ghost, tethered to an intravenous unit. Goodness was often beyond the power of the human imagination, but misery and mayhem could be conjured too easily.

Since the advent of Abraham, Norma had resumed eating. As had become his habit, he rose before her and cooked a hearty breakfast, a rustic pan-fry of red potatoes, onions, rosemary, sausage, and eggs, which he served so lovingly and which tasted so warm and good that Norma couldn't resist, despite her resolve to be more careful about her weight. Abe drank his standard breakfast drink, a mysterious mixture of protein powder, vitamins, fruit juice, and who knew what else.

She had by now overcome her long-standing inability to eat while sitting with a man who wasn't himself eating too.

"Good God, what a backward idea." Abraham had been appalled. "Like Scarlett O'Hara stuffing herself with biscuits before the big barbecue so's not to seem a pig in public. Besides, feeding you gives me such enormous pleasure. When you eat, it's as if I do."

How could she deny him? And he was a marvelous cook. When she had learned, after their first couple of nights together, that he had no place to stay, she'd had him move in until he could decide whether to remain in New York, and then both of them conveniently forgot that the arrangement was supposed to be temporary. Norma soon found herself coming home to elaborately planned multicourse dinners served as if in a restaurant open for a single customer, except no waiter ever kissed her temple when placing an entree before her, or massaged her tired shoulders as an appetizer. Without asking, he threw away her bathroom scale.

His cooking got better and better. With time on his hands, Abraham became a culinary Phillip Nolan, Edward Everett Hale's man without a country, devoting himself obsessively to learning about the land that forever barred him. He ransacked libraries for recipes, watched cooking shows on television, ordered crown roasts and spring lamb and wild turkeys in advance from the local butcher shop, its prices so outrageous they could barely be held, in their boxy red lettering, by the little cards stuck in front of its displays. In a sense, he was forced to learn. Disguising one's cooking is almost as difficult as disguising one's handwriting, and though he could pass off one or two of Burl's favorites as recipes they had shared over the years, it was clear that his whole style had to change. Or rather, that he couldn't just reassume Burl's. With effort, his style became more subtle, more deliberate, even more formal. He went through gallons of cream mastering frustrating sauces, pouring try after try into Alexander's dish, figuring there could be no higher standard than that of a spoiled housecat, and learned the true sense of a whole collection of fattening French words he'd only known before by taste, or in passing: beurre blanc, for instance, or bechamel, or his old-time favorite, creme brûlée. Alexander ate quite a lot around Abe; fed on creamy dishes often souped up for his benefit with anchovies, the cat gradually swelled until he looked like a furry football with legs, and perhaps from some natural pride or vanity never known to interfere with the appetite of dogs began to steel himself against the temptations of the supper dish with an abstemious sip or two of water, as if in substitution, and a pained but determined walk away.

Convinced finally that Alexander's disdain for his creamy works was more a matter of principle than cuisine, Alter tested his output—the same dish, sometimes, three or four times a day, until perfected—on a man he'd spotted a few times in the park and pegged as homeless but still clinging to appearances.

Each time they had seen each other, there was a flicker of recognition. Abe sized him up: he was remarkable for his erect carriage, his old-world style, the dark blue necktie with the cerulean shirt, the raglan overcoat worn bravely soiled, and the jade-green beret with the strange pin stuck in it like the emblem of a foreign military. In the army of the homeless, Abe thought, here was a member of the special forces.

Yet when Abe finally started a conversation, he quickly learned that Snipes—for that was his name—wasn't in the strictest sense homeless. He lived in a rooming house—were there really such things left?—somewhere around Morningside Heights, and he was an entrepreneur. "Buying and selling," he explained. Rubber stamps, mimeograph supplies, men's hats, women's girdles, heavy cups and saucers for the kind of eatery that was dying out in New York. He seemed to trade only in the obsolete, the obscure. "It's been better," he admitted. "I do some other business, it brings in something."

But Snipes knew about food; he'd been "in the restaurant game," was the most Abe could get out of him. Grimacing and wagging his head, he would struggle to convey to this poor tyro what was amiss with the soufflé placed before him. Spooning huge gobs into his mouth, he held up a hand to forestall any pressure for a premature response. Abe sat in parody of anxious anticipation, waiting to know the verdict.

"The eggs," Snipes said, frowning, eating, wary. "The freshness of the eggs. The grande cuisine requires better ingredients than this. You can't do it scooping up stuff at the Waldbaum's."

It was a subtle process. Snipes was still unsure how such good fortune had managed to befall him, so he was unwilling to condemn the food outright lest he jeopardize his new prosperity. Effusive praise might lead similarly to unemployment; a success doesn't need a taster. So the response must be mixed, but he must be sure not to deliver it too soon, lest the pretext for eating every last bite should vanish. Snipes wasn't homeless, but he was hungry.

Abe was hungry too, of course, but mainly for somebody to feed and talk to. Stuffing Snipes was a way to nourish a former self, as if the wheel of karma were a lazy Susan that could be turned back laden with food.

The first time Norma met him, Snipes kissed her hand. Later she claimed to have been charmed, although no meeting with Snipes was ever unambiguous. Where the floor was covered with wooden tiles, he lamented the expense these days of genuine hardwood, and with much feigned wistfulness described Norma's decor as youthful.

With Snipes generous about eating but stinting with praise, Abe was beginning to achieve a certain proficiency when one day he found himself wandering through Macy's, drawn to its housewares department, where a familiar-sounding voice caught his attention. It came from the center of a crowd off to the side, attending some sort of demonstration, and when he wandered over he realized it was his old friend Frederic. He was pushing a line of pans.

Frederic hated these things, Abe knew, but a certain style of living had to be maintained, and he also felt obligated—the Frenchman's burden?—to bring decent cooking to the masses. It drove him absolutely to despair to imagine that all over America, people were eating frozen greenbeans smothered in Campbell's cream of mushroom soup and topped with canned fried onion rings.

"—and so we sauté the onions lightly, you see how easy?"

Frederic seemed to know his lines well. Abe hung back at first, unnoticed or unrecognized, his stomach churning with fright, yet he knew that if Norma was fooled Frederic surely would be too. Abe worked his way to the front of the gathering, where Frederic occasionally looked right at him.

"Meanwhile, we have our veal over here, our mushrooms porcini, our sherry, our cream ready to go, everything *mis en place*, as we say . . . "

No sign at all. Finally Abe brazenly volunteered to be shown how to handle a zesting knife; his hand shook as he raised it. And he was chosen, perhaps because a certain level of humorous ineptitude is assumed in any man chosen at random. His heart pounded as Frederic took his hand to adjust his technique.

"Just relax you hand now. Nervous, eh?"

When he returned to his place, amid a smattering of applause, it was as if he had never existed. A little robotically, Frederic resumed his patter.

Abe felt awful, his loneliness underscored by his friend's failure to recognize him and his own failure to reveal himself. Would he live his whole life this way, he wondered? At home he shut himself up in Norma's cramped, windowless kitchen, which at least opened across the countertop to the living room, so that the entire apartment was suffused with fragrances from the stove. He baked cakes and bread, fixed imaginative lunches, and spent whole days preparing a single meal for her, chewing and spitting as he cooked.

For still he ate practically nothing. Lean and stringy, sandy gray hair curling around the backs of his ears, a wreath of beard surrounding his face, he hadn't altogether lost the air he wore when he wandered the streets in Salt Lake City. Just as Burl had been fastidious about his appearance, so Abraham was careless in his. Most details, in fact, seemed slippery, as if his mind had been greased like a pan, and Norma was frustrated by his distractedness.

"Abe?" She'd pass a hand before his face when he seemed lost in himself. "I think you'd forget your own name if I didn't say it every so often."

He only sighed and forced a little smile. He had the dazed air of someone recently in a terrifying car crash. He looked—and felt—as if there was something he couldn't quite understand; he was a bad dancer unable to pick up life's rhythms. Maybe this is what passing so close to death does to you, she thought. All those monks who went around with memento mori were just playing a game. Too much of death pollutes a life.

Two lives: she began to think of him terminally and to act accordingly. She saw them in Italy together, Abe enduring the hardship of travel so they could share his dying wish, Abe sipping wine as he watched her eat the extraordinary food, Abe sticklike, wasted by malignancy, even his skin shades of gray. Her fantasies were tainted.

"Norma, please! I'm not going to keel over and die this instant," he would declare impatiently as she fussed over whether he was warm enough, or had had enough rest. "I've been cancer free for years. All my life, really. Trust me."

He was beginning to regret the tale he'd concocted to cover his scars. All her flushed anxiety over his health made him nervous. Norma tried to treat every day as if it were their last, but to Abe this only meant a wooden and exhausting spontaneity that was difficult to distinguish from obligation. Dragged to movies, theater, and miscellaneous romantic outings involving boats and skyline views, he was impressed not with the indomitability of the human spirit but rather by the paltriness of the levees we erect against the murky and indifferent river of life. It was scary.

Abe's reluctance to travel didn't bother Norma, who was herself a homebody and was comforted by the stability his uninterrupted presence seemed to imply. Theoretically, they both loved the beach, but Abe wouldn't disrobe in public, and Norma lately felt pale and fat, like a giant cheese. She wasn't so anxious to disrobe in public either. Besides, the traffic was always terrible. When all was said and done it was easier to stay home. Manhattan was pleasantly depopulated for much of the summer, and its tonier neighborhoods, free of rotting garbage and cooled by the nostalgic-smelling rivers, offered a vision of city life after the neutron bomb, awnings intact, citizens erased.

When they grew bored with the East Side, they wandered the city more widely, just as Burl had done in the grip of his fast so long ago. On the Lower East Side, its squat brick projects set at sporty angles in plazas of tired grass, the city felt hotter, the very buildings seeming to pant through their open casements, cheap curtains fluttering like tongues dangling in the heat. Norma and Burl watched Dominicans play peppery softball in the waterside parks, and whenever they passed a cart Abe insisted on buying something for Norma so he could have a taste, or sniff the smell. Norma grew in this way to appreciate the salty, rubbery foods of the streets, just as she was beginning to learn from Abe to appreciate eating itself, a pleasure, like most, she had tended to slight in the not-so-distant past. From a wizened Puerto Rican they bought the only thing on these expeditions Abe could eat: snowy coconut ices in pleated white paper cups. Creamy and cold, the ices seemed to Abe luscious, the cup softening as the sweet contents melted in the heat until, toward the very end, you had to squeeze in order to coax the last slushy licks from their wet container.

Finally one humid Saturday they took the narrow Lexington line downtown, emerged in the breezy plaza near New York's unprepossessing City Hall, and clambered clammily across the Brooklyn Bridge, surrounded by the city as if by a wraparound movie screen, the walkway a cocoon of road noise. Buffed a little raw by sun and wind, they found a taxi and took it out to Burl's old building. It was something they'd planned to do for a while.

The building sat swathed in heat, its bricks soaking up the sun until the place was like a giant kiln. The lobby was relatively cool now, but that would change as evening fell. The smells—of old glue, stale oil, and Pine Sol—were enough for an instant at least to make Abe vanish. Standing on the marble floor, the place devoid of furniture, he was Burl.

His parents had paid the rent all this time, even after the funeral, as if maintaining the teddy bears and cartoon bedspread in the room of a lost child. It was only now, months later, that they could bring themselves to address the matter of settling the dead man's affairs. Increasingly, what he had done to his mother and father weighed upon him. I took their child, he accused himself.

I killed their baby. Men who commit such crimes aren't safe in prisons.

He looked around the lobby in a kind of awe.

"Which way?" he said, just as he had been reminding himself to do.

Norma led him up the stairs. It was so familiar; the little tiles on the landings, the smooth banisters, the tiny moldings on the front face of the steps. Norma let them in with her keys, fumbling with the elaborate locks featured on all New York apartments.

"Try the other way," Abe suggested. "Here, let me."

Inside, a kind of order had been imposed. Where Burl had left a shambles, there was now the strangely unlived-in neatness he recognized as Stu and Betty's trademark, except in this case the place genuinely was unlived in. It was awful to think of them bending over, cleaning up his mess.

"So this is where Burl lived," Abe said, a note of genuine wonder in his voice.

"This is it," Norma sighed.

Walking along the near wall, he saw that the books had been reshelved in size order. The newspapers were gone, and atop his desk there was only the typewriter he had left there.

"He was always so neat," Norma said as he looked around. She stood still.

"Burl? I hadn't really thought of him that way."

The kitchen was immaculate too. The refrigerator door opened easily, without any of the heft or clinking that contents impart. The doors and shelves were absolutely empty, except for a damp-looking orange box of baking soda. His life here seemed so long ago; the thought crossed Abe's mind that Burl must be living somewhere else. There was hardly a trace of him in this place. As a child, Burl had longed to stand outside himself and watch, to see himself as others might. Was this now what it was like to witness the aftermath of your own death? You could only see the gap you left in the outlines of whatever lived on. You became like the hole in the middle of a doughnut, tasteless and ephemeral.

"Betty said to take anything we wanted. I thought maybe the typewriter."

It was a squat, characterless old manual, with no *Front Page* overtones. Abe tapped a key a couple of times; the spring action made him smile, and in his mind he could see the clogged, inky elite typeface on a yellow sheet of copy paper illuminated by carats and elision marks, inserts floating above and below the lines until it looked like sheet music, as if the poem really sang.

Abe heard sneakered footfalls moving gravely through the apartment. He and Norma were like the only couple in some forlorn museum. It would be less creepy if the place really were haunted.

"So where are his writings?" Abe asked.

"What?"

Norma walked toward him. They were both trying to be matter-of-fact.

"His writings."

"Um, on the shelves, no? Here—"

"His works in progress, I mean. He told me he was working on an epic poem, a novel, a play."

"Oh. I assume Stu and Betty have those."

The desk drawers were stuffed with them: manuscript pages, smudged and dusty index cards, the works. Abe was fascinated. Much of it he couldn't even recall; who was Burl Bennett, who had written such things?

"Maybe we should get somebody to look at this stuff. This epic, anyway. It might be publishable, even unfinished. Or we could finish it."

"Abe, Burl was no poet. He never got anywhere with that and never would have."

"Have you read much of it?"

"Some. Enough."

He remembered stuffing an envelope full of verses into her mailbox at the office. She had praised it, encouraged him to finish. People are so nice.

"Can we take it, then? Would his family mind?"

"They don't want anything. I think they were pretty devastated." Then, as an afterthought: "There was no will, apparently, but there aren't any real assets, either."

"No savings or anything?"

"Our friend was a sweet man of enormous appetites, and he spent accordingly." Norma fingered a painted wooden ball she had brought back for Burl years ago from a trip to Venice. It sat on a metal ring at the corner of his desk. "The police say he drained what little cash there was while he was out West."

The afternoon light inside the apartment, the late kind that came when the lamps were just switched on, had always so pleased Burl with its cozy warmth and intimations of safety and dinner, but to Abe, sitting at the dead man's desk, it seemed now indistinguishable from gloom. Carefully, even tenderly, he moved through the apartment, fingering things, opening cabinets, moving a lamp or table here and there out of some fastidious impulse to correct. It was like an exhibit; he half expected the bedrooms to be roped off. He sat in the green throne, the wingback armchair from which Burl had conducted so much of his life, and was astonished. He sank deeply, like a child in a grownup living room. Even the bed threatened to swallow him, its mattress beaten practically to a sack of stuffing atop a board that instantly made itself felt through the punished bedding. All the places to lie or sit were like species of man-eating plant, oiled and concave flytraps that lured humans and closed up around them.

"He was huge," Norma said as Abe struggled to rise from the sofa. "I used to hate it when he sat on anything in my place. I used to make him sit with me on the carpet."

Abe wanted to stay. The place seemed so private and snug, so broken in. The depressions in all the chairs made it feel quietly haunted, as if each of those places were occupied by a ghost. Above the largest one in the sofa there was a mark on the wall, left by Burl's head. For an instant it seemed he would be less lonely here than at Norma's, and he thought of asking if he could sublet.

"How 'bout this?" Norma said from the other room. "You've been complaining about my spatula."

She held it up like a rat by its tail. The pots and pans, the oven mitt callused by grease and heat, the loose-limbed whisk and beat-up bottle brush, and especially the nondescript plates arrayed silently in the cupboard, all these things made Abe feel powerfully like Burl. Lit by a circular fluorescent tube attached to the ceiling, the kitchen inspired in him a reverence verging on pantheism. He imagined the sugar bowl and the spoons, the cups and saucers, the toaster and blender, all the sloe-eyed residents of this former forest of food conferring worriedly about where the Big Man might have gone, one scratching his nonexistent chin, another arms akimbo, all their hands gloved, all their eyebrows floating high and light the way Burl's would have done in antici- pation of a meal. When these denizens of Burl's kitchen heard the key in the lock they must have leaped with excitement, falling all over themselves to get back into position just in time as the door opened. They were orphans now, every one, in the cartoon Burl's life had become.

As he took up the cherished spatula, brandishing it not like a scepter but cradling it instead with reverence, it all came back, the whole life he had lived and then ended, the person he was and wasn't, the great weight he always carried.

"Um, yes," he said, clearing his throat. "Let's take the spatula."

This item at least must be liberated. It would make cooking feel so much less strange at Norma's. And not only the spatula; his good knife, his sharpener, the corkscrew he liked that relied on brute force rather than cleverness (was he any longer strong enough to use it?), his own grater and so forth. Soon he was piling these things into a bag—did Norma wonder how he knew precisely where they were?—along with a couple of cookbooks (excuses to prepare some of Burl's old favorites), white peppercorns, bay leaves, and anything else that struck him too forcefully with the power of possession.

"I have a grater," Norma reminded.

"That's okay," Abe said, packing it anyway and reaching for the plastic baster with the bubble on the end, which he liked because it seemed like the eyedropper Cyclops might have used when Odysseus got done with him. "Just a few things."

He took another bag back into the living room and began to fill it with Burl's manuscripts, but then changed his mind and put them all back. What was the point, after all? The author was dead, and Abe had no desire to be his literary executor. Let sleeping dogs lie, he thought.

LIKE BURL BEFORE HIM, Abe lacked any instinct for stewardship and had no interest in putting the unpublished Bennett papers in order so that they might molder uniformly once interred on somebody's shelf. Burl's projects didn't interest him either; Joseph Smith, for example, left Abe cold. But he did feel welling up within him two strongly parallel desires: the urge to write and the need to make sense of Burl's life, to figure it out somehow, give it the flesh of sense for which adipose and epithelium were no substitute. Given these twin desires, it was only natural that he should decide to write a book about the Bennett case. Necessity added a third motivation: he had to find something to do that would bring in some money.

He marveled at how in this, as in so much else, it was better to have known Burl Bennett than to be him. Burl's agent, for example, was warmly receptive. "I think it's a fantastic idea, and I'm delighted you called upon me," Larry said over the phone. "God knows somebody's got to get to the bottom of this whole business. Terrible. I cried when I heard."

"Yes. Burl always spoke highly of you too."

"Tell me, Mr. Alter, have you done much writing before?"

"Oh sure, lots, I can send you some stuff. But the beauty of this thing is that I knew the man intimately. Burl's story has everything—the mob, mystery, the struggle to lose weight."

"It's perfect, it's a natural. Just the kind of project I can sell these days. Geez, you sound like you know something about this business. Your friend had gotten a little carried away with esoterica. It isn't always easy representing a writer like that."

"Larry, believe me, I'm with you. No villanelles from Abe Alter. What you'll need more than anything is a proposal. Just do me one favor. Not a word about this to anybody. I want to do some checking before certain things become foreclosed, if you understand what I mean."

"Absolutely, mum's the word. I'll wait to hear from you."

"Also, can you sell a cookbook? I have one of those in mind too."

"We can talk about that," Larry assured him. "But let's do one thing at a time. Let's see what happens with Burl."

Let us see indeed, thought Abe. Deep down he didn't believe he would ever write the book, but it was a handy pretext for trying to learn the truth, and it gave him an added sense of purpose beyond cooking meals he could not eat. Reporting on the life of Burl Bennett was the sort of thing he could do well, and it felt good to undertake such a task. It had been a long time since he had done anything at all, short of clinging to life.

Norma, who agreed to help once Abe promised that the finished work wouldn't embarrass her, took him downtown to *The Tribune*. It was eerie, walking past the place Burl used to sit and seeing there somebody he didn't know, with pictures of her children and dogs over the desk, a box of her own Kleenex in the corner, the chair and keyboard table all at different heights.

"That's Hanks in the corner, he wrote a lot of the stories. He's on the phone, you can talk to him later." Norma led him along, showed him around, introduced him here and there, and then took him into the library, where he set about reading the coverage of the Gemignani affair in Burl's absence. Predictably, *The Tribune* had dug into his background, his connections, his place on the map of organized crime in New York. Abe was startled to see a short profile of Burl in which he was presented as a moody, enigmatic figure with a financial interest in a shadowy restaurant frequented by mobsters. The Gardenia's murders, the disappearance of the only witness, and the press coverage that followed had generated a furor while Burl was wandering the streets of Salt Lake City. One of the consequences had been a police department internal affairs investigation of how things were handled, but this had resulted only in a report critical of the department's procedures for protecting witnesses and a request for more money to do a better job in the future. Meanwhile, the case against Gemignani had collapsed. He was still going to work every day in the family's import-export business.

It was interesting about Gemignani, Burl observed. He didn't ride the subway or wait in line at movie theaters, but otherwise he seemed to lead the life of a bourgeois, without the entourage of bodyguards one might have expected in such a person. Abe made a mental note to check further into this later. Who knew, perhaps it was even possible to meet him.

Abe's research on the Bennett book had to be squeezed in during the time each day when he wasn't in the kitchen, which is where he was most often. Armed with Burl's old equipment, he had resumed cooking with relish, so to speak, and was fascinated to see that his works had begun turning as if alchemically into more of Norma, to whom he presented these single entrees— he could only cook for one, of course, but these were Burl-sized portions—so lovingly and seductively, so beseechingly as well, that she could do nothing but eat them with praise on her lips. And so she grew. Abe remained light and spare, his skin thrown loosely over his bones, yet he was a bodybuilder now—a body-builder working on someone else's body. In doing so he developed the jealous pride of a sculptor, really the selfish, anal sort of fasci-nation any sentient being has for his own works, or his own chil-dren. Norma's body, he saw, did not grow in a linear fashion, or hold to any one weight over any given period of time. Rather, it moved in a range, swelling and ebbing like some inland sea pulled by the moon. What Abe was doing, he saw, was moving the range.

"Look at me," Norma wailed, backing up to fit all of herself within the slender mirror behind the bedroom door. "My clothes are all tight, my bottom is spreading—I'm starting to feel like one of those precious French geese who suffer food abuse for someone else's pleasure."

Abe would murmur patronizing reassurances, at the same time kneading her shoulders and kissing her neck that they both might revel in her fecundity. Often they ended up making love, roughly and fast, the way Burl used to cook. Her increasing amplitude was thrilling to Abe, perhaps even to both of them. She must have sensed his growing passion and the change in his lovemaking, which had been as comfortably modest, as faint, even, as her own, whereas now they were creating something new together. He loved the way her curves gained definition, her skin seemed to improve, her coloring redden, her breasts stand out as if laden with sustenance. The richness of all this seemed inexhaustible.

Abe also found a wicked fascination in watching Norma eat. The more she consumed, the more fastidiously she consumed it.

She cut her meat with exaggerated delicacy, switched hands, and delivered her fork to her mouth with exquisite deliberation. After one or two bites she would put down her utensils to dab tenderly at her lips. It seemed to take forever for her to get through a meal. Abe guessed all this was because she was afraid.

He suspected himself of malice but didn't worry about it. Like many people who have been through a lot, Abe excused himself. Who knew what tomorrow might bring, or whether there would even be a tomorrow? Even his identity felt tentative, and it made him more comfortable that Norma's might be set to evolving as well.

Already she looked very different. As her size increased, she had to get different clothes. She adopted billowing garments that hung like drapes in modest earthtones, with scarves, and began spending more time on her skin. In the bathroom, her robe off her shoulders, she coated herself with lemon and olive oil, which only made things worse. If Abe saw or even smelled her doing this he made love to her on the spot, licking her shoulders and neck clean and then making her come with his mouth until his whole face was salty. He bought her some better olive oil too, a thick and fruity green that he dribbled on her breasts and spread with his tongue.

"God, I love you," he said with some feeling. "You're the only thing I can eat."

As she held him, his hair damp and fragrant, the two of them smelling indistinguishably of olive oil, she gnawed at her lower lip. It was clear from the way he acted that she had never seemed more desirable to him, yet by now she was quite large, large enough that she no longer had the courage to weigh herself. People at work noticed; she made references to it, and they failed to offer the reassuring contradictions she was hoping for. Absently, she felt along the rubbery seam beneath his left arm.

Abe could see that more than her body had changed. She rustled audibly when she walked now, smoothed herself when she stood still, and seemed to take on exaggerated femininity. She asked Abraham to lift things he knew she was strong enough to handle by herself. She wore more makeup, and she crossed her ankles when she sat. She began speaking with great care. The way her back swelled and her shoulders hunched with fat, as if to swallow her neck, and even the way she entered a room, instinctively adjusting herself, reminded him of Burl. Norma was like some long-lost twin.

One night, after work, she wouldn't eat his dinner.

"But it's veal rollatine, stuffed with Stilton and walnuts. I've got calluses from pounding cutlets."

"Abe, listen to me—"

"Just taste it, will you?"

"No, *listen* to me. Listen! I have to go on a diet."

"Drama tomorrow," he said. "Pomerol tonight."

"Abe—"

"You have to eat *something*."

"Stop it!" Norma began to cry. "Do you hear me? This has got to stop, I can't stand it anymore!"

"But diets don't work, you should know that by now. What do you want to lose weight for anyway?"

"To get my body back! Abe, I'm turning into somebody else!"

"Nonsense—"

"I am!" Norma was frantic at his incomprehension. "It's not just the way I look, it's the way I feel, the way I act, it's incredible!" She swallowed hard. "Abe, you just can't imagine what's it's like to feel like a different person all of sudden. It changes the whole world, you know? The whole world. You feel reality differently, the colors, the texture changes when you don't feel like yourself—"

"It tastes different."

"—and the world treats you differently. I feel patronized all the time, dull-witted, leadfooted, *slow*, not just in other people's eyes but even my own, and it's driving me out of my mind. So no veal birds! No Pomerol! Just the salad, and no dressing, on anything."

"And what am I gonna do with all this food?"

"Feed it to your friend Snipes."

"He finds this recipe a little vulgar, actually."

"Well, he's right. It's all vulgar, and I'm through with it. Just don't feed it to Alexander. He's going on a diet too."

Later she put their $35 bottle of olive oil back in the kitchen and came to bed in a flannel nightie. The following night she came home with a bagful of the dispiriting accoutrements of her new aspirations: carrots, rice cakes, and a portion scale. To Abe's growing sorrow, her approach was rigidly disciplined. No fats or oils; she ate only vegetables, and she began to lose weight.

Their sex life dwindled to nothing; Norma's body didn't shrink that fast, but the knowledge that it was going unreplenished had a bad effect on Abe. He became detumescent knowing that someday soon she would share that state.

"I don't know what to do with myself if I can't cook for you. My days are empty."

They were at dinner, although it wouldn't seem so in any other household, since neither was eating.

"I'm starving," Abe said. "I experience physical hunger for the first time in your presence. I used to feed you, you'd eat my dinner, and then I'd eat you. My food chain's been broken."

"That's just the trouble. I've been eating for two, and I look it."

"Most women would be glad to have someone preparing wonderful meals for them, taking care of the house, *encouraging* them to overcome their unhealthy obsession with weight." Abe tried acting hurt. "I see this is the thanks I get."

"Oh, please. Spare me the wounded-spouse parody."

"Your body image is so distorted, do you realize that?"

"Abe, I've put on 37 pounds since you moved in here, and I was eight pounds overweight at the time."

"You're weighing yourself, is that it?"

"Yes, I'm weighing myself. Who told you you could get rid of the scale?"

"It only reinforces the tyranny that society exercises over women through their bodies."

"You said losing weight was the best thing that ever happened to Burl. Why not me?"

"I'm not so sure anymore. He paid a high price."

"What's that supposed to mean? You think it's my fault, don't you? I want to lose a few pounds, regain control of my body, and you blame me for killing him!"

Abe slowly shrugged. He knew this was bad, but even when you see an accident coming, you can't always swerve in time.

"You miserable man. Who in the hell are you? I want you out of here tomorrow. First thing in the morning. Leave your key with the doorman."

A period of seething followed: door slamming, silence, rage. Abe wasn't sure what to do. He knew an act of self-abasement was in order, tried to apologize, but found himself rebuffed. Norma's face was ruddy and stained with tears when she threw his pillow and pajamas onto the living room sofa. In dejectedly making his sleeping arrangements for the night, Abe moved a little table and saw once again the wine stain left like blood when passion had flared briefly between Burl and Norma. He lay down in his pajamas, finding the sofa uncomfortably soft. How quickly we become spoiled; he had slept in so much worse, it was difficult to believe. He could still smell the cardboard, and behind it the gassy odor of his old vent. It made him sad to recall that on that vent Burl had imagined only bliss with this woman, in his innocence never dreaming that all the drab and banal abrasions that have scarred every other relationship would scar his own, were he ever to have one. He saw then that he truly wasn't Burl. Abe, for example, was a grudge holder, even on behalf of someone who was no longer living. Burl would never have behaved this way, Abe was sure. Marx said something about function subsuming personality; it was shocking to think that shape might do the same, maybe even more shocking that he hadn't had these thoughts by now himself. What had he been thinking all this time? Of course Norma was right. It was horrifying to turn into someone else; was he not living proof? The worst thing is, you don't even know what you'll find in yourself anymore. He fell asleep wondering whether he could stand life on the streets of New York.

It didn't come to that. Abe and Norma reconciled, gradually, and if he didn't resign himself to her stringent diet, he certainly became more patient about it. He made salads a specialty and began serving arugula, sorrel, nasturtiums, and grasses, using soy sauce, various citrus squeezings, rice vinegar, and sesame oil by the eyedropperful to add flavoring.

"Elegant but austere," Snipes said, munching on raw greens with goatlike disinterest. "Good taste, but no flavor." Abe didn't see him much after that. He began to feel that Snipes was avoiding him.

Norma didn't seem much happier, even though she was getting what she seemed to want.

"You really are losing," Abe said, sipping his latest breakfast favorite, hot lemonade. It was a Saturday morning; they had passed another moderately cordial night. A strange but necessary correctness had crept into their relations.

"Yes, people are noticing."

"Do you feel any different?"

"I feel that I'm regaining myself. It's such a relief."

"For me too."

"Abe, you know in a way I feel I'm regaining you too. When I wasn't sure who I was, I couldn't be sure somehow who you were either. Isn't that strange? Now I feel sure I know who you are again."

"Who am I?"

"Stop." And she hugged him. "I know exactly who you are."

Norma's progress wasn't steady. Abe carefully skinned and steamed vegetables, tossed them with controlled portions of plain pasta, choreographed colors for maximum eye appeal, and yet she sometimes failed to lose weight for days. Worse, at times she actually gained.

He couldn't always tell by looking, and she didn't always report the scale's verdict, but her mood gave the secret away. When the news was bad she was edgy, taut. She didn't want to talk, and she drank his carefully prepared coffee standing up, leaving for work early.

"Look, sometimes the body does what it wants to do," Abraham counseled. "It's not your fault. Patience."

But she seemed to blame herself, and eventually Abe drew the right conclusion: she was eating somewhere else.

For the weight conscious, the streets of New York are a minefield, every block boobytrapped with hotdogs, shish-kebab, knishes, pretzels, ice cream, and all kinds of stir-fry. Norma found herself increasingly unable to negotiate these obstacles without eating something. She was always hungry, and she felt certain she had never fully appreciated food. Why was it that she had never before noticed the smell of onions cooking on a curbside hibachi coated with sausage fat? How had she failed to worship the tang of sauerkraut on a salty-sweet frankfurter? Even the napkin was delicious, infused by the food you'd held with it, soothingly soft, tinged with mustard and sauerkraut juice when you wiped your lips. Norma set out for work each day filled with resolve, but the primitive satisfactions available for the taking all around her beckoned like sirens with their irresistible appeal to the senses, and before long she was standing near a preferred hotdog stand, ordering just one more. Sometimes afterward she wept with grief, but also at the depth of pleasure that flavor could provide, and at discovering that she was this way. She thought this was how it must feel to have some forbidden sex and discover that you love it more than anything you have ever done. The clandestineness was parallel too. She felt sure people knew, yet was certain this was only her own shame and paranoia. How could they? She was entirely furtive about eating now, the secrecy only adding to the satisfaction of it, and she couldn't believe they inferred anything in particular from the grease stains that sometimes marked her blouse, or the ketchup or mustard that added an abstract touch to her makeup until she remembered to go into the bathroom and get cleaned up.

Work was okay, but Norma did it more in the way of biding time before she could reasonably allow herself to eat again. It was something to do between meals. She ate carrot and celery sticks at first, from a plastic bag with a locking top, foods she had always enjoyed and always munched at work but which now tasted like chilled packing material marinated in brackish water. She swallowed them only to get them out of her mouth.

How she had misjudged the world until now! What a puritan she had been, scorning so much that was delicious. Around this time, for example, Norma rediscovered the paper's cafeteria, the humid tang of which had always revolted her before. One night she went up promising herself a salad and instead fell in love. She was seduced by the veal parmigiana: ground patties breaded and covered with melted cheese, swimming in a thick tomato sauce that left a delicious heartburn lingering in the esophagus long after it was eaten. She became a regular. They had turkey tetrazzini, roast beef, barbecued ribs, Mexican night (the man who made the burritos always stuffed hers extra full), and a full range of pies. The milk squirted sweet and freezing from a big stainless-steel machine with a kind of udder hanging down. It was heaven.

The strange thing about the joys of eating, Norma found, was how fleeting they were. They lasted while you had your fork in your hand, after which, disarmed, you were overtaken by guilt, shame, and, sometimes, pure cold fear. It made her think of Alcoholics Anonymous, with its emphasis on a higher power. Hunger surely was one. Like everything that might be sacred, eating was also more than a little profane. She felt unclean when she finished a meal, queasy not from eating so fast, although she noticed in herself a tendency to wolf food nowadays, or from eating so much, but on some moral ground. It was as if she had experimented with being a kept woman and then found herself liking it.

Abe, a kept man, was pleased to see that following a precipitous decline, Norma's weight stabilized, after which she gradually reinflated to not much less than her former size. During this time she virtually stopped eating at home. Around the apartment she became just as abstemious as he was, drinking lots of water and borrowing some of his vitamins but keeping her foraging habits largely private.

Weekends were a problem, since Abe was hard to shake. Sunday morning, over the crossword, Norma would start to feel it gnawing at her just as she gnawed on her pencil eraser.

"God I'm hungry."

"Can I fix you something? Fruit salad maybe? With some cassis?"

"I don't *want* any fruit. I want a bacon cheeseburger. I want salt, Abe. I want fat."

"Those desires are atavisms, I find, and they arise in everybody sooner or later. They're vestiges of our lives as hunter-gatherers. Of some former life, like the wolf in every dog. That's why we all love barbecue so much, with the skin crisp and black—"

"Stop."

"—and the meat smoky and wet—"

"Stop!"

"This stuff is hard-wired, Norma. Natural selection saw to it. We needed those preferences, for fats and sweets, for example, because food wasn't always available. People who really loved that stuff survived and reproduced. Our tastes, our cardiovascular systems, and our food supply have been out of synch ever since. As a cavedweller, Burl would have had a marked evolutionary advantage: the ability to store energy better than almost anyone else."

"So we're victims of plenty."

"Of civilization. Of our own success. Cultivation made butter and cheese and steaks available all the time, and modern economies enable us to afford them."

"What a mockery. So now I'm dying for a cheeseburger."

"We're all dying for cheeseburgers, or rather from them. Our preferences, once a survival mechanism that enabled us to distinguish, say, good ripe fruit from poison berries, are killing us now. Our preference for sweets persists even when it's easily satisfied from a vending machine."

Norma looked away guiltily.

"We're maladapted," Abe said with a shrug. "We can't change fast enough. But evolution is ruthless. Look at our late friend Burl. Gone, childless, his genes buried with him."

"A little Calvinistic this morning, aren't we, sweetheart? You're saying we're doomed by our taste for guilty pleasures."

"Well, a high-fat diet, consumed by people who like fatty foods, is correlated to heart disease and cancer."

"And so we're condemned to a lifetime of denial?"

"Or the denial of our lifetime. Sit around, eat bad stuff, die young. Unless you have cheeseburger-proof genes."

"Abe, this is too depressing. I can't imagine living my whole life this way. But now that I think of it, that's how I've *been* living my whole life. Along with most of the women I know, I've been hungry for years."

Abe had worked his body around on the sofa and was massaging one of Norma's feet, looking for just the right spot to press with his thumb.

"Maybe the Zen masters had it all wrong." There it was. Norma opened her mouth as if to moan. "Maybe desire turns out not to be the root of all evil after all. Maybe desire is indispensable. Besides, all that hard-wiring can help us there. Think of how good sex feels, and why." He kissed the inside of her ankle and let his lips linger on the bone. Imagine the marrow! "And tell me a better way to taste fat," he said, kissing again, holding tight at her reaction to the loaded word. "Or salt." He enjoyed the little pinpricks on his tongue as he ran it up her leg, and she giggled.

"Tickles," she said.

"You too. You need a shave."

"Look who's talking." She pulled him to her by his thick beard, like someone pulling at a mask. "Look who's talking."

They made love for the first time in weeks, in the friendly way of couples who have been together a long time and been through a lot, and soon after that Norma resumed eating a little more than salads at home, allowing Abe to prepare safe pasta dishes and the like. As she grew, Abe's desire again grew with her, and she responded to the change in him passionately. She loved being wanted in this way. Both of them liked the way she seemed

to envelop him, too. But this appetitive genie couldn't be forced
to spend any time back in the bottle. Norma tried everything, and
for a while everything worked: high-protein diets, carbohydrate
diets, self-help books, even meditation. There were notes on the
refrigerator and special shakes for which she kept a portable
blender at work. The pounds fell away, and the pounds came
back. She felt elastic, a balloon into which someone exhaled and
inhaled, exhaled and inhaled. Each time, when a round of huffing
and puffing was over, she was heavier.

Abe was no help, of course. Gradually, not even altogether
consciously, he was increasing the caloric punch of the low-fat
meals he prepared for Norma. In part this was because of his own
cravings. He often ate a spoonful of whatever he prepared for her,
and he craved fat just as much as anyone else. He craved too the
memories each buttery spoonful brought back, of the time when
he was the person he had always wanted to be but didn't even
know it, of the days when Burl had a place in the city's chain of
being and in the phonebooks of dozens of people. A bit of egg reminded him powerfully of snug winter mornings in his neighborhood coffee shop, hidden behind the steamy plate-glass window,
hunched happily over his greasy fried eggs and bacon, the yolks
lethally runny, the bacon just before crisp. A garlicky greenbean
brought him back to Chinatown, and the tang of the air in his favorite restaurants, which in turn brought him back to the cafete-
rias of his boyhood, which brought him further back still, to the
watery canned greenbeans he was always being urged to eat,
mushy gray-green things but familiarly briny and quite edible with
enough butter. Who needs madeleines, Abe told himself. Or tea.

Besides, Norma clearly liked this richer food better. And Abe
liked Norma fat. He admitted this to himself and considered
whence this impulse might arise. With his customary lack of self-
awareness (a failing that hadn't been Burl's), he ruled out revenge;

he loved her, and he'd tried to help her lose weight. He did acknowledge that he might be guilty of selfishness, in that he found
her growing opulence so gripping. The heavy sound of her footfalls,
the balls of her bare feet leaving little marks on the carpet, these inflamed his love like music. Her great feminine amplitude, which
filled his arms so perfectly, made him wonder why anyone would
want any less. Other women seemed desiccated by comparison.

For Norma, her transformation was a very different experience. It made her understand that *in extremis* all of us are controlled by our appetites, and that these in turn can be controlled
by others. She grew wary of Abraham for this reason. One day
when they were reading in the living room, Norma fidgeted un-
happily until she announced that she could no longer bear having sex.

"I'm disgusted with myself," she said. "I'm revolted."

"But you're so incredibly beautiful."

Her book landed painfully against his ear.

"I can't listen to this, Abe. You can't have me anymore, you
just can't, not until I get myself back. You're a hog, you've had me
ever since you moved in here, you used me as a kind of stomach.
You're responsible for this."

That was when she started fasting, which changed everything.
To her surprise, Norma found the experience leavening, even intoxicating. She ascribed this mainly to the lightheadedness—and
lightness of body—she felt without any food in her stomach or
her system, but of course it was also the intoxication of power
that she felt. Her new pattern was to begin the day with a glass of
orange juice and then glide imperviously past the temptations of
the street vendors en route to work. She drank orange juice for
lunch and again in the evening, about a quart in all daily.

Her weight began to fall. Soon she could see hints of her old
self in the mirror, the way people used to say they saw her father

in her eyes, her mother in her mouth. Fast days piled one upon another, and Norma's weight plummeted. She felt light. Her waking hours seemed feverish, religious.

"I wonder if this is how it was for Burl," she asked Abe. "Did he say anything? About the time he fasted."

"Not much."

"He certainly told you it was because of me."

"He fasted many times," Abe said noncommittally. "He was always trying to give up eating, lose weight."

Time slowed for Norma. Robbed of her customary bodily distractions, she could almost see it. At home on a weekend, it became fascinating to her once again to contemplate the end of a thread up close, just as fascinating as it had been when she was a child and could spend what seemed hours lost in admiration of the dust motes floating in a shaft of summer light.

Then, as now, she could lose herself in the simple sensation of rubbing the nubby fabric of the sofa, stroking a cushion back and forth again and again as she held it wrapped in her arms. It was all a question of patience, and she felt now that she had all the time in the world. She could see the attraction of fasting for the truly pious: it was a way for even the weakest to exercise great strength, just by doing nothing. The hunger strike as a form of protest no longer seemed merely obstinate or idealistic. Now it looked instead like the ultimate triumph of the individual over unacceptable circumstances. She would simply refuse to take in the world.

"It gets harder," Abe said.

"It gets easier. I could go on this way forever. I'd never eat again, if I could avoid it."

"Believe me, it gets harder. Your body won't go along."

"How would you know?"

"Remember Burl after a while? Weak? Irritable? Dizzy? As I recall, he collapsed finally. It wasn't for want of will."

"He did talk to you about that."

"It wasn't for want of motivation."

"What did he tell you?"

Abe fell into a calculated silence.

"Please don't, Abe. I don't want to see that martyred look any-more. What happened to Burl didn't happen to you. You're not entitled."

"I don't know what you're talking about."

"You're so transparent."

"There are worse things in a man."

It began to seem a hunger strike to both of them now. With no one to feed, Abe began cooking again with renewed enthusi-asm, on a level he had never tried before and only for its own sake, pouring his increasingly accomplished works into the trash when, as was often the case, he couldn't find Snipes. He ran through dozens of eggs, a sea of cream, enough puff pastry, it sometimes seemed, to repave Manhattan. There was curry and co-riander, peanut butter and potstickers, tripe and truffles. The apartment grew fragrant and steamy, the rugs, drapes, and uphol-stery suffused with layer upon aromatic layer. It drove Norma to distraction.

"It's for my new project. A cookbook."

"You just happened to decide to write a cookbook."

"I've been planning this for years."

"And you thought this might be the right time. When I'm not eating."

"Neither of us is eating. What difference does it make?"

"The difference is that I don't want to be around all this rich food. It makes me sick. Aren't there any vegetable dishes? What happened to your book about Burl? People don't buy cookbooks full of buttery concoctions anymore anyway."

"They would if they could."

Abe was calling it *Die Smiling*. With wanton disregard for what he viewed, perhaps through Burl's eyes, as society's neurotic obsession with cholesterol, sodium, fiber, and the like, it was to feature a series of frankly lethal recipes organized around chapters on Holidays, Entertaining, Seduction, and so forth, with sumptuous illustrations. The first recipe in the Dessert section called for eight pounds of Godiva chocolates, melted. Abe thought it was the kind of book he would love to receive as a present. Not eating such foods—not eating *any* foods—had killed Burl, after all. Abe grew excited about the project and began gathering episodes of historical gormandizing to serve as colorful marginalia—like everything else in the book, the margins would be generous. More important, he began experimenting in the kitchen with the recipes he hoped to include.

Thus was Norma forced to dwell with her enemy, food, in all its most dangerous forms. Yet she was not seduced, for her enemy did not come in camouflage. On the contrary, the very richness of the stuff, its naked succulence, made it repugnant to her. A bowl of fruit on the dining table might have made her swoon, but the fat, humid smell of Abe's latest kitchen venture made her want to gag. The wolf gave himself away by his scent.

But he managed again to reach her dreams. She still liked to sleep with Abraham wrapped around her like an animal skin, except that she had given up taking his arm hairs in her lips. Instead, in her sleep, she gnawed at his forearm. It had begun as an aggressive form of kissing, but gradually she stopped using her lips as a buffer, literally baring her teeth to worry his arm just as a dog worries a bone. It never seemed to wake him, although sometimes it hurt enough that he would pull his arm away with a grunt. In the morning he was puzzled by soreness and bruising, until finally, upon waking after a particularly aggressive night of chewing by Norma, he sniffed the bruises; his skin smelled of saliva, the way he'd remembered smelling as a child after playing with the neighbor's dog. Understanding hunger, he made no attempt to interfere, cherishing these stigmata as justly his.

At least somebody was eating. Life seemed so barren with nobody consuming anything. Abe began to long once again for solid food and felt anew the larger hunger Burl had felt when wandering the streets of Salt Lake City. He walked the park, looking for Snipes, but there was no sign.

Abe and Norma went on this way for weeks, both of them so hungry they finally turned to one another. Like so many couples who come to know that they will soon part, their everyday dealings became suffused with nostalgia. They had something new and tender in common now. They were hungry, and so they tried to consume one another, licking, biting, sucking, and sniffing with the fervor of rescued castaways brought before a banquet. The primary flavor experience was salt; Norma's diligence and growing expertise was rewarded with a fountain of salty flavor, an acquired taste, to be sure, but one she had acquired long ago with Burl— amazing the way they all taste alike, she thought—and on some days the only flavor (and the only calories) she consumed. Abraham too enjoyed the salty flavor of Norma's sexuality, and afterward the scent of it spread all over his face, reminding him each time he inhaled of what had gone before.

But to feast on living flesh is an ineffective way to take nourishment, except as a means of whetting the appetite, which may be why Norma one day brought home a small brown bag wrapped in an air of mystery. Abraham was suspicious of it right away and so followed her into the bedroom, where he arrived just in time to catch her kicking it under the bed, which he pretended not to have seen her do. He assumed she was eating again, clandestinely, and the whole cycle repeating itself this way was too much. He sat down at the end of the bed and thought of his mother and

father, of whom Norma's soccer-style sideways motion powerfully
reminded him because of the way it reprised Burl's angry, kicking
concealment of his low-calorie brown-bag lunch under the bed.
He sat there and said nothing, merely looking down at his stocking feet until Norma came up from behind.

"I'm sorry, it's a present. I didn't want you to see. But maybe
this is a good time to give it to you."

She began undressing him, tugging at his clothes, fussing at
his buttons, yanking his belt to undo the buckle. Abraham wasn't
in the mood. He was feeling too sorry about everything, too
guilty and hopeless and on the verge of blurting everything in an
attempt to begin to make amends. But Norma's mouth was already
on his neck.

"God, I'm so hungry," she whispered, and suddenly he was
too, and then the lights were out and he felt the absence of her
touch for a few moments, followed by some lotion or oil on the
side of his neck; he could feel the plastic applicator. But then he
felt her tongue in the same place, and felt her moaning almost
through his skin as she licked this off. She kissed him so he could
taste it also, and when she placed her tongue on his the sweetness
of it exploded in his mouth. Now he understood. The present was
a plastic honeybear, which she used to squeeze a few more drops
of amber sweetness onto him, this time on his nipples.

And so Abraham was partly right; Norma had resumed eating,
but in a way not very different from the way he had. She didn't
eat so much as she experienced flavor. But who can be content
with just one or two flavors? She wouldn't hear of participating in
the tastings that Abe sometimes engaged in, cooking doll-sized
portions of pasta Bolognese. On the other hand, she would continue to eat her lover, and so brought home other tastes. These
were simple at first, and sweet; from honey she moved on to
maple syrup, and then raspberry preserves. Taking a page from

Abe's own unfinished cookbook, she melted some chocolates and, still warm from the stove, drizzled them on his chest and stomach and private parts. This she loved so well that when she finished Abraham was licked entirely clean; she didn't mind the scars, they were just more texture under her tongue, but when she rose up from her work so that he might reciprocate, he could see even in the dim light in which she preferred to dine that her face and ears and shoulders were smudged with brown like the face of a child in the aftermath of a chocolate ice cream cone.

She tried rubbing him with cilantro one time, which was fragrant but not so satisfying for the one doing most of the eating, and another time she massaged him with homemade vinaigrette, which tends to separate when rubbed into the skin. Olive oil infused with garlic is something else again, although the odor for the rest of the night was too much for both of them. On still another night, using a basting brush, she covered Abraham with marinara sauce, spreading it thinly but evenly across his chest and stomach. Then, straddling him, she produced a grater and a block of hard Romano.

"I always loved pizza," said Norma as she strained to grate the cheese, which fell on him like snow. "I never got enough of it when I was eating."

Guacamole worked well, too, as did babaganouzh, rich with paprika and sesame oil. They both liked the texture of amaretto Reddi-Wip when she squirted it on him, but in deference to Abraham's refined sensibilities, she agreed not to use it anymore. Instead, using the whisk he had inherited from Burl's kitchen, Norma whipped huge stainless steel bowls of cream laced with Grand Marnier until her arm hurt.

Abe sometimes ate too when they made love, when he got a chance. But Norma's hunger was the greater, and it was for the most part she who dined on Abraham, to his growing impatience and distaste. He didn't want to seem selfish, but it was becoming tiresome sleeping in a bed of oils, creams, and other glop. Even after she licked him clean he felt the need for a shower, but Norma was offended if he rose in order to take one, and so he dried himself as well as he could on the sheets, whose stains by now seemed indelible, and waited until morning. He felt his skin becoming chapped in places that hadn't known such irritation since before Burl lost weight. He needed sleep.

And water. It was hard for him to make it through the night without drinking something. His stomach was too small for him to consume great quantities even of liquids, and so he sipped most of the day. But in the wee hours—was it all the stuff they were eating in bed?—he needed more fluids.

It was not always a happy thing for Abraham to wake up in Norma's apartment. Nothing about it felt his, and on this particular night the feeling was especially lonely. Even with the window slightly open to the chill October night, the room was badly overheated and he woke up feeling sweaty and oppressed, almost as if in a fever. Norma wasn't beside him; she must be in the bathroom. But no light escaped from there. Perhaps she had risen feeling as bad as he had. Her absence made the room and the darkness seem even more dispiriting and, parched, Abraham rose to get some water, wondering if he should look for her.

What he heard when he opened the bedroom door brought him suddenly and fully awake. The noise was loud and, in the dark, a little chilling. It was like an animal eating—not like any sound Alexander might make, canine rather than feline, wolfish even, ravenous.

Abraham moved toward the sound delicately, feeling his way along the wall, taking care with his footsteps not to compete with the thing that drew him. He walked toward the kitchen, drawn by the noise and a dim gray light like the stirrings of an unwashed, unwelcome dawn. He was already close enough for the chomping and slurping, rattling and tinkling, resting and rooting, to be sickening.

He turned the corner to find Norma sitting cross-legged and dark before the open refrigerator, bathed in its light like a Hindu goddess surrounded by the riches of the fat land she has blessed. Her face and hair were smeared with food, her mouth so full she could barely close it, and all around her were the cartons and dishes that had held her treasure: bread, cream, and milk; a brick of butter bearing teeth marks; cheese, crackers, mayonnaise; pickles, paté, an open box of Purina Cat Chow. Her jaw worked steadily. In her hand she flourished what, judging from the Mrs. Paul's box in her lap, must have been a fish stick, and on her face, when she saw Abraham, was not the slightest sign of recognition as, glassy eyed, she chewed.

"BURL? YOU'RE SAYING——you're actually Burl Bennett?"

They sat in the living room, in enough autumn sun not to need any lights. They'd both slept a little. Abe had put Norma to bed and, having decided to reveal himself, slept soundly alongside her like a fugitive at peace with the idea of surrender. They hadn't talked, Norma had cried a little and asked him to help her, which Abraham had promised to do. Afterward he had had the foresight to clean up the mess before retiring for the night so that they wouldn't be confronted by its wreckage in the light of morning.

"You'd message me all lowercase. I pretended to drink carpet cleaner right here on this floor. Look at my eyes."

Norma stared into them. Shock and revulsion spread quickly across her face.

"Burl is dead." She drew her legs up under her on the sofa, pulling her robe down over them. "Who are you? Are you crazy?"

Her lip quivered. Abe felt slatternly in his pajamas and wished he had thought to get dressed. He made his own skin crawl.

"I had stomach reduction surgery. It forces me to live on liquids. It accommodates my digestive capacity to my metabolism."

"You're sick. This is some kind of sick joke."

"The scars are from cosmetic surgery after I got thin, to eliminate all that excess flesh. I never had cancer."

"You sick man," Norma wept. "You sick, sick man."

"I wanted to be someone else. I needed to get all that weight off my back. And I was scared. They were trying to kill me, I thought. Maybe I was paranoid. Maybe I am a sick man."

"You're completely insane. Who *are* you?"

"Burl. I'm Burl Bennett. It's a fantasy I've always had, of starting afresh. Circumstances made it convenient. It was chance, really. Each step seemed rational when I took it."

"The sight of you is just repugnant. You evil, hateful man."

"I understand how you must feel." He sounded like an idiot to himself. "I'm trying to be honest with you. I love you very much."

"What are you talking about? You despicable fraud. You fooled me, you stole my love under false pretenses."

"I'm sorry, Norma. Wasn't I the man you wanted? Didn't I at last conquer my weight?"

"I can't be around you. Look what you've done to your family. Abe? Burl? What do I call you? You've tortured your mother. Can you imagine what her life has been like?"

"Yes. I feel guilty about that, because I suspect some part of me did it on purpose. I'll try somehow to make amends. I'll tell everyone. Soon."

"Abe, Burl, do whatever you want, just get out of my life. This is too much."

"I need your help, Norma."

"After all you've put me through, how can you even suggest such a thing?"

"You asked me last night. Remember? For my help. And I promised to give it."

"You're the whole reason I needed help."

"But that was before the truth was known."

"It was while you were lying, in other words."

"Can you blame me? You never wanted Burl. You seemed to accept Abe."

"You attacked me with food. You tried to kill me—not with a knife or a club, but you tried to replace my old identity with a new one. It was like *Invasion of the Body Snatchers* around here."

"It wasn't conscious. It can't go on, that's why I decided to tell you."

"I'm not sure I can ever look at you—whoever you are—in the same way again."

"Good."

"And the stories you told me! The things you knew about Burl. How could I be so stupid? Oh, God, how could you do all this?"

"I could claim that I was eating so much in those days that it literally altered my mood, affected my grasp of reality. And there was fear too. But there are no excuses. I just put one foot in front of the other. You'd be amazed at what you're capable of."

"I'm already amazed. But it's awful that you didn't feel you could reveal yourself to me at the outset, or call on me for help."

"You're right. I'm calling on you now."

"You have to tell Betty."

"I will, soon enough. I have some things to sort out first."

"I feel for her, Burl. Shall I call you Burl? I liked that name."

"Yes."

"I think back to what you've told me, about growing up with your mother. Seems like our relationship is kind of a rerun, wouldn't you say? Except she never made you thin."

"And I never made her fat."

"On top of everything else," said Norma, wiping her tears. "Incest."

Shields's phone was so old it was pink. It was a pushbutton model, but it had a row of old-fashioned-looking acrylic buttons across the bottom; the red one was hold. The phone was dirty too, which he disliked intensely. He would have to clean it; no one else would. He hated being on hold. He studied the phone at such times, became too aware of it, of all the time he had spent with his left arm, elbow on the desk, holding the receiver propped to his ear.

"This is Dr. Stringer."

The guy at the motel had recollected the name. Shields had been calling people back—years of experience had taught him how often it paid to do so—and bingo, the man had remembered Dr. Stringer, whose intercession had helped persuade the guy to take Burl back. For Shields, at whom Burl's supposed death continued to gnaw, this was a way around the hospital's uncooperative administration. He couldn't resist. He'd been through a great deal over Burl; he understood the dangers of knowledge in so public a case—would he then have to lie?—but still he was compelled forward.

"Dead? Oh God, no! God, I was so afraid of that, of pneumonia or exposure or even murder. He was living on the streets, and I just knew something awful would happen to him."

"On the streets?"

"He had trouble adjusting, he wouldn't participate in our counseling sessions, and he had no money, although we might have helped him with that, maybe found him a job and some kind of temporary shelter."

"Dr. Stringer, you're a surgeon. What did you treat him for?"

"I'm a bariatric surgeon. Didn't you know? Mr. Bennett had weight reduction surgery."

"I don't understand. Did you cut off his fat?"

"I performed a banded vertical gastroplasty. It's a surgical procedure in which we partition the stomach so that only a small pouch remains available to food."

"No kidding. You make it so he can't eat."

"We make it very difficult to eat very much. Patients usually live on liquids and small amounts of solid food. With determination, some do manage to eat their way out of it, gradually reversing the procedure."

"And you did this on Burl."

"I do them on a lot of people. They mostly work, and his worked too, at least physically. We only do them on people who are morbidly obese, meaning they're so fat it's life threatening. And we thought we saved his life. He came in here straight from being pried loose from a doorway in some motel. I understand the fire department had to use a buzz saw. Oh God, tell me he's not dead."

"I wish I could," Shields said.

"Oh Lord, that's just awful. And it went so well, you know, he was like a new man. We cut his weight in half, got his blood pressure under control. He was breathing, he was mobile. He grew a beard and looked altogether like a different person. You wouldn't have recognized him."

"No," said Shields. "I wouldn't."

In a small office on the edge of the garment district, Abraham Alter reached up and took a press release out of his in basket. He read it carefully, as if fearing a hoax:

FLINT, MICH., March 21/PRNewswire/—Global Dryer
Corporation, the industry leader for over thirty years in
warm-air hand dryers for public washrooms, responded
today to a study purporting to show that dryers are not as
sanitary as paper towels.

Norma's binge had shaken Abe and Norma out of their elaborate folie à deux. Abe had had to move, of course, and found a
small place in Inwood, way up toward the Bronx. He'd found work
as well, and a modest life other than inflating the woman he
loved. Although they remained bound to each other, Norma gradually became reacquainted with herself and her accustomed metabolism. She shrank, and although she sometimes missed the euphoria that foods had induced before, she was grateful for the
composure that came of eating normally, with no outer goad or
inner compulsion to drive her intake. Even her swollen cat began
to subside. Abe was happy about all this, understood why it was
necessary, and even enjoyed the luxury of his own place indoors.
He tried to concentrate on the matter at hand:

> "We have a hard time believing in the credibility of a
> study that was underwritten by a paper towel manufac-
> turing association in Great Britain," said Rudy Chauder,
> chairman and chief executive of Global Dryer Corpora-
> tion in Flint, Mich. "This report contradicts nearly a
> decade of independent scientific and medical research
> into hand drying and sanitation."

The building was old, so old the windows still opened. Abe
peered through the grimy glass across 39th Street to the structure
opposite, a masonry beehive of workers ironing, sewing, pushing
papers, talking into telephones. If he leaned over he could see
down into the street below, clogged with trucks and the dark-
skinned workers who made the district hum. It brought a lump to

his throat. He loved the city so much, it made him want to fly. He could just pry that filth- and paint-encrusted window open (Burl surely would have had the strength) and leap out into the metropolis, hurling himself onto its bosom for eternity, his broken body pressed up against the pebbly sidewalk.

> One study, conducted in 1991 at the University of Ottawa and presented to the Centers for Disease Control in Atlanta, states: "Electric air dryers may be superior to the other two drying methods (paper, cloth) in the elimination of bacteria as well as viruses after hygienic hand washing."

Abe blinked. *May be superior.* That might be just the opening, if he was to make any use of this. He thought for a minute, turned back to his computer, and started writing.

"The debate over disposables versus reusables sometimes seems as old as laundry itself. The fact, though, is that it really doesn't go back more than a generation or two. When they were first introduced, after the trauma of war, disposables were all the rage." Abe tried to imagine those times, Stu and Betty just kids, practically, Burl not yet conceived of. "They were in keeping with the spirit of the age, which was obsessed with modernity and hygiene, and by ignoring the environmental consequences, they reflected the naive faith the nation then had in a world without limits and open to the American destiny."

He looked up at the clock: 11:40. From the next room he could hear the muffled strains of melodrama from the TV sets they had going most of the day. Even through the walls it sounded false. It was where they kept track of things for another of the Piker Publications, *Soap Opera Gazette.* Accustomed to noisy surroundings, Abe tuned it out and resumed writing.

"We now know better, of course. Disposables turned out to be misnamed; progress was not what it seemed. It's evident by now that you can't throw anything away. Our trash, our history, is always with us. The towels and diapers and surgical supplies we used once and tossed are still around. 'Throw it away' has no meaning."

Abe squinted at his screen, yanking on the magazine he had mounted L-shaped on the corner of his dirty monitor to keep the glare at bay. He turned up the contrast as far as it would go and took a long pull on one of the protein shakes he sipped most of the day.

"We've read all the claims," he wrote. "We know about the contention that reusables supposedly consume more total resources than disposables. We've seen the supposedly biodegradable plastics, which never degrade, and the 'safe' materials that somehow, someday, leach harmfully out of landfills into groundwater."

Careful now. Never strident.

"Laundry veterans have been through all this before. Polyester was supposed to revolutionize the industry. Now it's a standing joke, a cuss word clothing designers daren't use on their own product labels.

"Fortunately, hospital and other institutional administrators are starting to realize the same thing about disposables: they're okay for some things, but better not shut down the laundry just yet."

He hit the save key and stretched. Not a bad morning. Hadn't even been necessary to get into the hand-dryer controversy. All he had left for the day was a little editing, mainly putting together "50 Years Ago in *The American Launderer*," which was always fun. State legislatures requiring clean linens in hostelries, references to laundresses, high-falutin' prose with remarkably formal grammar. The war had complicated things enormously; all those uniforms, resources suddenly so scarce. In Switzerland, patriotic women set up war laundries for people who couldn't get soap. He might even get around to handling this week's guest column, which had come in with the headline, "Laundry—Love It or Leave It."

He had one more piece to write himself, but that could wait till tomorrow, when he would once again become Milt Laver, pounding the laundry beat. Everyone in the industry seemed to think this was a real person. Laver got long letters from readers meditating on tying equipment, or urging that he investigate the supplies racket (commercial bribery was rampant in cleansers, and ever had been). Some people even phoned for Laver, and after a while Abe decided to oblige. When the call was for Milt, he lifted the receiver and said simply, "Laver."

Later, as Abe was leaving, Phil Soto, the editor, winked.

"Very nice work on that editorial, Abe, but you know the old man isn't gonna like that business about polyester. It's still around, you know. Kinda negative, don't you think?"

Crusaders, they were. It was moving, just to be a part of it.

"You know me, Phil. Always gotta push the envelope."

At lunch he took a walk, which he usually did when the weather was nice. It was easier than having to explain why he never seemed to eat anything, and it was a chance to feel better about what he was doing for a living by communing wordlessly with thousands of others who spent their days doing things equally bizarre.

Abe got the job with Norma's help. She had interceded with Soto, an alcoholic former *Tribune* copyeditor, but Abe's trumped-up resume also played a role. It claimed he'd been an editor at various far-off places, years ago, before going into institutional laundry management.

"*The American Launderer* is really the premier journal of its kind," Soto had said in reviewing his application. He had worn a pair of Ray-Bans during their interview, and sat behind an old mahogany desk covered with papers that looked as if they hadn't been touched since first coming to rest there. "Bible of the industry. It's a small universe you're writing for, but you'll have a major, major impact."

After a few weeks—Abe's rise was meteoric; he was already inspiring jealousy in his colleagues—he had begun to fret, and to his great surprise, he discovered that he was angry. It was the new life he had somehow attained. Had this been somebody's plan? That he should traverse the country, become thin, shed his identity, live on the streets, win love, and later lose it, all simply to become a star at some pathetic trade magazine? To make a name for himself—literally—in laundry?

He bought a secondhand personal computer and began writing again, screenplays this time. He wanted something more naked than his customary fare, a way of storytelling almost independent of language, so that meter and rhyme didn't matter, but a form in which violence had a prominent place. He thought of writing a movie about Joseph Smith. He was tired.

But still he walked at lunch. He tried to imagine the lives of the people he passed on the street, which he thought he could do in general terms from their attire, their gender, their physiognomy. It was only obituaries again, snapshots of the dead. You couldn't rely on appearances or the outlines of a few facts. Look at these people. They have children and affairs and jobs and hobbies. They get sick, they worry, they suffer. They carry their passions in their heads, next to the programming they need to get through the days: the way to work, the English language, where they put the keys. He wanted to stop and ask them: How? What is the way to this variegated feast? Where is it held, what is the etiquette, what made him unfit for it? He thought of Simeon Stylites, driven by God knew what to spend his life on a small platform atop a pillar, and of Lydwina, who prayed to become less beautiful and was rewarded with festering wounds that never healed. The lives of the saints were really chronicles of the inability to engage with life, stories of social perversion whose moral implications, from the perspective of an era without a concept like sin, were murky. Their piety is our mental illness. They had the nerve to believe steadfastly concerning things that are invisible.

Abe and Norma were still close, and she loaned him the money to get set up in his new apartment.

"I'll keep your secret, Burl. Abe. I better call you Abe, right? Just so I don't slip in public. But not for long. You can't just go on this way, living another man's life."

"Why not?"

"I can't live that way, and neither can you. Otherwise you wouldn't have told me. I'll leave the timing to you. But there are a lot of people who want Burl back."

ABE'S JOB WASN'T SO demanding that he couldn't
also pursue his ostensible book, which was supposed to be about
Burl but which seemed drawn again and again to the figure of
Gemignani, who burned in his mind like a bulb for a moth.

Abe was rusty, not having done this sort of work since long
before he stopped being Burl, but it wasn't extraordinarily difficult
to do a superficial job. He first read everything he could find
about his subject, much of it obtained by using his computer to
log into remote databases, God knew where, in the middle of the
night. An interesting case. Gemignani was almost a socialite; his
name was associated with a number of high-profile New York
charities, including a couple of toney little museums, a fancy East
Side hospital, and the public library, where he rubbed elbows with
some of the city's grandest and richest. Noticing that Gemignani
had been divorced long ago, Abe made a trip downtown and had
the file pulled from the archive, inscribing himself, on the necessary form, as his journalistic alter ego, Milt Laver. The divorce papers included less information about Gemignani's finances than he

might have expected, but still there was some, including the names of several Gemignani business enterprises—he was big in real estate, evidently—and his social security number, which helped pinpoint place of birth. Massachusetts, strangely enough. There weren't too many other lawsuits, and none was of particular interest. No criminal record. A dizzying array of real estate transactions, mostly well disguised by names such as 1537 West 48th St. Partners. Abe made a mental note to go through all these later, looking for interesting names. Gemignani had a clean driving record and was thin: six foot one, 180 pounds, according to his license. And he didn't own any cars. Abe assumed they were all leased or owned by one or more of his businesses and quickly found them registered to the import-export concern: a Volvo wagon and a small black BMW. There must also be a limousine, he guessed, but leased. The voter rolls showed him a registered Republican, although his name didn't turn up in any state or federal election reports. Candidates probably couldn't afford the taint, and he could get the money to them any number of other ways. The divorce papers had also mentioned a vacation home in Sag Harbor, which Gemignani had been allowed to keep. Looking at the listing of assets, Abe was sure that a good many had been left out. He also got the marriage certificate and the daughter's birth certificate, the high school yearbook ("scholar of the dollar," they called him at St. Peter's in Long Beach), and, from a compliant registrar's office, the information that Gemignani had graduated cum laude.

He began finding excuses to go past the apartment building— off Lexington Avenue—in which Gemignani lived. It was a fine old brick structure with granite facing on the first floor, the shiny brass stanchions holding up the awning obviously polished frequently by the staff, which included a round-the-clock doorman. It rankled. Abe felt the guy was living the life Burl was somehow entitled to but had been deprived of. He began increasingly to blame Gemignani, and to want to lay eyes on him.

He called the export-import business during the night and was pleased to have his instincts confirmed: there was a phone machine that announced the hours of operation, 8 A.M. to 5 P.M. And there was a coffee shop diagonally across Lexington that had a couple of tables with a view of the front door of Gemignani's apartment house. Mornings before work Abe sat drinking coffee, letting his french toast, pancakes, whatever he'd had to order just to sit there in peace, get cold. He brushed off the waiter's questions and always left a generous tip.

On the third morning, at 7:30, a navy Lincoln pulled up in front of Gemignani's building and sat there idling. The driver read a tabloid laid against the steering wheel and sipped from a styrofoam cup.

In a few minutes Gemignani emerged, with his daughter. The startling thing was that he was bald, much balder than he'd seemed in Shields's photo that night so long ago. And he wore glasses. When he and his little girl got into the car the driver folded his newspaper and handed it across the backseat, put aside his coffee, and drove away.

During the week, at least, this ritual seemed to go off like clockwork, except when Gemignani was traveling or otherwise not going to the office. On those days Abe saw the daughter and the wife leave together on foot, heading north on Lexington and west on 79th Street, mother's hand lightly on daughter's shoulder, the two of them in good coats and fine fettle.

When Phil Soto took a three-week vacation from *The Launderer*, Abe begged and pleaded until Soto, who lived in White Plains, agreed to lend him his oldest car. "Just do me a favor," said Soto. "Don't park it on the street overnight, okay?"

It had been years since Abe had driven in New York. It felt funny, with so much space between himself and the wheel; he couldn't get the seat the way he wanted it, couldn't get his arms comfortable.

The day was unseasonably cold. A light freezing rain had left a glaze upon the city and continued this morning to fall intermittently so that he struggled on and off with the windshield wipers and turned on the headlights when he eventually managed to find them. Abe felt the cold miserably and slid the heat switch all the way over to high. How did people survive in this climate, stripped down to muscle and bone this way? It was the opposite, of course, in summer; one needed two bodies, the way one needed winter and summer wardrobes to cope with the weather.

He felt a little foolish driving all the way out on the Long Island Expressway and then the Southern State Parkway, like a spy or one of those mad stalkers obsessed with some starlet. It was a long way, stop and go at times, with perhaps too much time to think, and in his search for distraction he fiddled restlessly with the buttons on the radio. The weather seemed to get worse as he moved east, the skies at times pouring down sheets of water that eradicated visibility—was this why cataract had two meanings?— but he kept driving until finally he found the town and then the house, set way back from the road. When he peered through the bare trees and past the leaf-covered lawn, the place was visibly occupied. It was a fine old Colonial, white with black shutters and smoke curling from the chimney. The place inflamed Burl's envy. He imagined hot tea, needlepoint, the cozy warmth of a fireplace. He drove past twice in a deepening funk, the second time noting the limousine next to the garage. Not the Volvo, he observed. The limo.

Had Gemignani done this because of the nastiness of the drive? Or because he wasn't altogether comfortable being unprotected?

Abe wondered if the man was really so much a part of something larger than himself that he never went anywhere alone.

On his lunchtime walks and after work too, Abe made a point of going past Gemignani's office, on 6th Avenue, or sipping a milkshake in the ground-floor coffee shop, until finally one day, just hanging around outside, he spotted his man—alone. Traffic was all jammed up, and Gemignani waded out into the sea of yellow and disappeared into a taxi. Without thinking, Abe did likewise, and was thrilled to tell the Russian behind the wheel, "Follow that cab."

They didn't go far, just up a block, left to 7th and then down to 19th Street, to a nondescript little apartment house of white brick set back perhaps two feet from the row of handsome brownstones it interrupted. "Slow down, but don't stop," Abe told the cabby, and then got out around the corner. He walked back to a position on the corner and waited outside a restaurant, now and then looking ostentatiously at his watch. After about 10 minutes he decided his quarry would be a while, and so he went inside and ordered some coffee at the bar. He sat for half an hour and then went back outside, pretending once again to be waiting for someone but keeping an eye on the row of buildings from which he expected Gemignani to emerge. Abe wondered if he was always cold because he never ate. Cars passed. Finally a black Oldsmobile with a livery sign in the window came slowly up the street and stopped in front of the little white brick building. Not too much later, Gemignani came out and got into the car, which drove toward Abe. He turned his back and went into the restaurant, where he had some more coffee. After a few more minutes he emerged, jittery and freezing, to fling his hand up for a cab, exhilarated at the prospect that Gemignani had a mistress, and that he went to see her by himself.

There were eight units in the building, Abe learned on a subsequent walk-by, and later, at the public library, he saw in the reverse directory that there were eight names and numbers listed for the building, which was a piece of good fortune meaning that none of the residents had an unlisted phone. Five of the names belonged to men and one was a woman's. Two others used only first initials; they were obviously women as well. Abe guessed it was one of them.

Just to be safe, though, he ran motor vehicle checks on all three. One was 53. Another was five feet four inches tall and 152 pounds. But the third was 29 years old, five feet six inches tall, and 122 pounds. She was Carla Davidson.

Abe began spending some time during lunch and after work on the corner outside Davidson's apartment, which is a cold and boring thing to do unless you are on a quest. Abe didn't mind the time; he began to let other things drop, to cut corners on his job. He saw less of Norma. He spent a week of lunch hours and early evenings on 19th Street before he caught Gemignani again, this time for 90 minutes on a Tuesday instead of lunch. No wonder the guy seemed so fit. When Abe saw the dark sedan pull over and wait, he walked quickly toward it and noted the name of the car service from a sign in the rear window. Later that day he made a phone call.

"Hello, Ms. Davidson. Our records indicate you recently used our car service, and I was just calling to see if you were happy with the service you received."

"Oh. Yes, sure."

"Was the car on time?"

"Yes."

"Was the driver neat and courteous?"

"Um, it was for someone else, actually."

She sounds nice, Abe thought, having confirmed that he had the right person. Another one wasting her bounty on the dead.

Shields didn't believe in ghosts, but he had the feeling Burl was around. It was hard to say why; it was just a sense he had, and even if he hadn't any such sense, he didn't feel ready to close things out without touching all the bases once more. So he called people simply asking if they had heard from Burl at any point since his disappearance, just so he could complete the file. Strictly routine, he said. The problem was that people didn't take "strictly routine" seriously enough. Several, including Norma Ruifelen, to whom Burl had been close, didn't bother to answer the messages he'd left on their phone machines.

Theoretically, Shields knew, the place to get to the bottom of all this was in Salt Lake City, in its streets and restaurants and, sorry as it was to consider, its Skid Row. But he had the feeling Burl was around, so he went to the trouble of photocopying the entire guestbook from Burl's funeral. Then he spent some time with someone from the paper and with Burl's mother, checking off everyone they knew. Shields noted which ones he thought worth talking to and then made a list of the nine that no one could identify. Since all but one had signed in with name and address, it wasn't difficult for Shields to find almost anyone in the book. When he did, unfortunately, they were of no particular use. He wondered if it was even worth the trouble to find the lone privacy freak, a guy by the name of Abraham Alter. Shields had the same superstition that any professional inquirer has about such things: that the stone you don't turn will surely be the one hiding the key.

Abe got into the habit of rising early and stopping on his way downtown for his one-sided rendezvous at the coffee shop on the corner of Lexington, the one with the view of Gemignani's apartment building. He watched Gemignani come out every day, and then, in the eerie light of the city's towering streetlamps, waited downtown for him at one end or another of his lover's block. At home, he'd stare into the bathroom mirror, frightened. He was conscious that he wasn't writing a book anymore. When Gemignani didn't come out in the morning, he assumed a business trip and stayed away from 19th Street. Carla Davidson received her visitor about twice a week, it seemed, sometimes more, sometimes less.

One day Abe had a rendezvous at the coffee shop with Snipes, who still wore the same soiled raglan overcoat and beret.

"Just coffee," he said, the picture of disdain.

"Five-dollar minimum at the tables," the waitress said.

"Bacon and eggs," Snipes said with a sigh. "The bacon crisp but not burnt, the eggs softly scrambled, the potatoes and rye toast well done."

When she was gone, he pushed a thick brown paper bag across the table. They sat at a booth on a bright, precociously wintry morning, early enough that the restaurant wasn't crowded. When, Abe wondered, did they ever do any business? But there was a lot of takeout in the morning, coffee mostly. With a sideways glance, Abe unfolded the top of the bag and peered inside. Then he rolled it back up and put the bag beside him on the vinyl seat, covering a small slit through which the dirty white stuffing showed.

"What you wanted?" Snipes asked.

"Yes," Abe said, pushing an envelope across the table. Snipes took it and slipped it urbanely into his breast pocket.

"Aren't you going to count it?" Abe asked.

"Isn't it all there? And if it isn't, what am I gonna do about it?" Snipes laughed and leaned forward. "You're the one sitting there with the gun."

One evening, when the car came up the street, Abe was waiting on the steps of the brownstone next door. When the driver honked, Abe quickly approached.

"Hey, you here for Joey?"

"I dunno, the call is from a girl named Davidson."

"Carla, right, that's Joey's girlfriend. Do me a favor, here's fifty bucks, lemme give him a ride, we got a little surprise party planned. That's my car right there."

The driver fussed with agonizing slowness over his clipboard and paperwork until finally, dubiously, hoping someone would come out and make things all right, he drove off. Abe took a deep breath and returned to the steps of the neighboring brownstone, scanning the oncoming cars as if expecting someone. There was still room in his diminished stomach for butterflies next to the bitterness.

Finally Gemignani emerged. He wore a black raincoat, not the kind worn by insurance adjusters but the fashionable kind, unbuttoned, and he frowned as he tried to process the missing car.

"Was that your car?" Abe asked.

"Was it here? Yes."

"He'll be right back. He said he had to make an emergency phone call."

"Phone call? Oh, man."

"I'm glad I was still here to give you the message," Abe said, coming down the steps. As he approached, a kind of protective mask—against garrulous New Yorkers? human decency? hit men?—spread across Gemignani's face. He looked at his watch and turned his back to pace a couple of steps, putting some distance between himself and the stranger. When he turned around, Abe said, "Mr. Gemignani, we've never formally met, but we need to have a talk. If you try to run, I'll kill you. I have nothing to lose. Please get in the car, passenger side."

Gemignani, astonished, hesitated, and Abe quickly pressed the gun against his jugular. A couple passed on the other side of the street. "I don't care who sees," Abe said, striving for just the right note of manic intensity. "I won't kill you unless I have to, so please cooperate. It won't take long."

Both men knew this was a lie. Abe opened front and back doors and watched Gemignani carefully get into the front seat. "Slide over behind the wheel," Abe said, getting into the back. "Drive. Have an accident and you're a dead man. My life means nothing."

Abe was struck by how stale his own speech was, even as he spoke words that seemed to him as true as any he'd ever uttered. "Up to 8th," he commanded. He thought of movies, bad TV. Our whole vocabulary of violent coercion comes ready made from the media.

They drove toward the Lincoln Tunnel. Abe could see that Gemignani was looking for a way out, a cop to flag, something. What an insight it had been, doing away with toll takers on the outbound side. Almost everyone who crossed the Hudson had to cross back again, and so they collected a round-trip toll in New Jersey. That meant no westbound attendant. But there was a cop standing casually between lanes leading to the tunnel's mouth.

"Don't think I wouldn't kill you right here," Abe said, pushing the pistol up against the soft spot at the base of Gemignani's skull.

"What is this? Aren't you gonna tell me who sent you?"

"Burl Bennett sent me."

"Burl Bennett is dead," Gemignani said, glancing nervously in the rearview mirror. "Is this some kinda Halloween prank?"

Abe hadn't noticed it was Halloween. Tomorrow was Burl's birthday.

"Do you believe in life after death, Joey? Are you religious?"

"I'm agnostic." Gemignani looked back warily. "But no, I don't believe in reincarnation."

"Or the Resurrection?"

"Look, what's your name? What should I call you?"

"Gabriel."

"Ok, Gabe, you got the gun, tell me, what's it all about?"

"It's about how Burleigh Bennett died."

"From what I read, that was pneumonia. Out west somewhere."

"Interesting you followed that case."

"Why not? I've been to Gardenia's—that's the restaurant he owned—and our families knew each other."

"Really?" Abe was interested to see how elaborately Gemignani would lie.

"Sure. See, you got this all wrong, Gabe. You don't know the background."

For some reason traffic was light, and they soon emerged from the tunnel.

"Stay on the helix, then out Route 3."

"Hey, c'mon, where you taking me here?"

"The background. Let's hear the background."

"You're gonna kill me, aren't you? Oh Jesus." Gemignani slapped the wheel in frustration. "What do you want from me?"

"Just keep talking. Make like Scheherezade."

"Well," Gemignani sighed. "My father knew his father. They were friends. They did some business together."

"That's very interesting. So you're telling me if I take you over to see Stu Bennett he'll give you a big hug and kiss."

"Oh, no, not him. See, I know Burl better than you did. You don't even know about that whole business."

Abe was quiet for an instant. Gemignani drove slowly, prolonging the journey, until at Abe's direction they left the highway and headed out a deserted roadway flanked by low-rise industrial buildings.

"I'm not sure anybody knew Burl at all," Abe said evenly. "Why don't you tell me about him."

Gemignani glanced back in the mirror to see how seriously this was meant.

"It's like I said, my father knew his father. But his father wasn't named Stu. His father was Gene. Gino Gardenia."

Abe's mind raced with possibilities.

"What are you talking about?" he demanded. "What the fuck do you know about Gardenia?"

"Hey hey, he was a sweetheart. Just that he was a sweetheart. That's all. A nice guy, a soft touch."

"Then why the fuck was he mixed up with a family like yours?"

"Because it was a family not so different from his own, really. Because he was in business. And we were in business."

"And you're saying Gene Gardenia was Burl's father."

"Only he didn't know. The son, I mean. Gino knew. Not too many other people knew."

"You're a liar."

"Ask around. You'll find out."

"How do you know?"

"I told you. My father knew Burl's father."

"And you killed your father's friend's son."

"Wait a minute, I never killed anybody. I don't know where you get your information from, but it's common knowledge Burl Bennett died of pneumonia in Arizona or Utah or somewhere."

At Abe's direction, they left the highway and drove out into the Jersey meadowlands, wending silently through the emptiness. Heart pounding, Abe adjusted the weapon in his sweaty palm.

"Pull over," he said.

"C'mon now, do you know what you're dealing with here?" Gemignani was angry. "Do you know what the fuck happens if you kill someone like me?"

"Stop the car."

"C'mon," Gemignani said. "It's a mistake. You're making a huge mistake."

Abe could see that Gemignani was torn between ingratiating himself and taking some kind of desperate action. He pressed the gun to the back of Gemignani's skull once again.

"You're probably not gonna die tonight," Abe said quietly. "Just pull over."

Warily, Gemignani complied.

"Out of the car."

"There's nothing here, Gabe. You bring me all the way out here and then you're not gonna kill me?"

"Not if you play your cards right."

"What do you want from me?" Gemignani asked. "I don't even know who you are."

They stood at the edge of an empty field, in the lee of a thick piling that supported an elevated roadway. Cars rushed past out of sight, overhead.

"I'm Burl Bennett, Joey."

Gemignani nodded.

"I thought so. I suspected you were alive."

"You know everything."

"Information is important to me. It's the basis of everything."

"How did you know?"

"It's my business to know, even when people don't want me to. You had surgery. You became thin."

"And do you know what's going to happen here tonight?"

"Yes."

"What?"

"Burl will stop pretending to be someone else, thanks to what he's learned here."

"I thought you didn't believe in life after death. You killed Burl. The man in his place is more interested in revenge."

"You killed Burl. I brought him back to life."

"You? You were responsible for the deaths he saw."

"I wasn't. Others were responsible for that. I'm a businessman. I'm in business. I only did what I had to do."

"You carried out a campaign of intimidation against him. You blew up his car."

"I was testing him. I was testing his faith."

"In what?"

"In himself."

"And he was found wanting."

"No. He's right here. He passed with flying colors."

"But I'm a different person. I have a gun."

"You said you were Burl Bennett."

"Things change."

It was dark, and quiet except for the muffled sound of traffic passing invisibly through a tunnel of light overhead.

"This isn't you, Burl. You're like your father. Kill me and Burl dies with me."

They stood across from each other. Abe now held the gun with his arms extended, remembering the times with Stu on the firing range when he had learned to shoot paper men in lethal places, how to stand, the cups on his ears against the noise. He thought of Gemignani like a sack of potatoes by the side of the road, like a piece of old luggage, like a collection of rags with a head attached, and he imagined the funeral, the weeping family, and then thought once again of his own sad funeral as he tried to figure out whether to take another life, and whose.

HE DROVE FAST, consciously making a getaway, the car bouncing on undulating portions of the dugout roadway leading back to the helix and the tunnel. He felt wrung out but alert, sad that he had taken a life but pleased that he had left Gemignani in a New Jersey landfill, perhaps among some of his former colleagues who had come to sorrier or more sudden ends. Joey would walk a while to the main road and eventually catch a ride. The life Burl had taken was Alter's.

It was late by the time he got back to the city. He drove east from the tunnel, across Manhattan and down the F.D.R. Drive. He took the Brooklyn Bridge, which always made that humming sound as you traveled on the metal roadbed, and wended his way to Smith Street, where he parked the car and walked gingerly, in his heavy, steady style, toward his destination. The evening was cool, quiet. The place would soon close for the night, he knew, but he didn't plan to eat, and this was usually a good time to catch Louie Naumann for a quiet talk.

When Burl arrived, he hesitated for many long seconds, working up his nerve. He stared at the beaten wooden door and scrutinized the details of its aggressive antiquing. He and his uncle had gone at it with a chain and a six-pack, having a party making it look old. The times they had had.

Entering the restaurant, Burl felt as if he held what was left of his stomach in his hands. He walked forward with small, uncertain steps, as if afraid he might spill something, and asked for Lou in a voice that struck him as timid. But Lou emerged smiling and sent for coffee.

"Any friend of Burlie's, Mr. Alter. Will you have some dessert? We got some beautiful chocolate mascarpone cake, it's on me. Used to be his favorite."

When they were settled, the visitor groped for a way to begin. "I wanted to talk to you about Burl. To see if you could tell me anything more about him, about his life before he left New York."

Lou sighed heavily and rubbed his forehead. "Abe, you know, I keep some Calvados in back. Have some with me, will ya? I'd feel better; I think he'd feel better."

Relaxed by the alcohol, they chatted warmly about Burl, remembering foibles and laughing a little.

"I miss him," said Lou. "I really do."

"Me too. I miss him terribly."

"You were close, the two of you."

"Yes, although we lived far apart."

"Funny he never brought you around to the restaurant, you being such good friends and all."

"Oh, I don't eat much. And I hardly ever came to New York."

"Poor Burlie. You know, you sound a little like him. Not your voice so much as your manner. Refined. It's nice to hear it."

Burl sipped his aperitif, its fragrance and bite bringing things back in a rush.

"I wanted to ask you something, Mr. Alter—"

"Abe—"

"Abe, listen, Abe, I always wondered. I mean, I'm an open-minded guy. He was my nephew, you know? I just wanted him to be happy."

"What?"

"I wondered—if he ever had any girls. I never seen him with any."

Burl was unsure how to respond.

"Except for Norma from the paper, I mean. You know her? I know they were close, but I also know usually when they went out he came over here afterward, for a midnight snack, kind of. Meaning a couple entrees at least." Lou snorted fondly. "Did he ever mention anybody else to you? I mean girls or guys. It wouldn't matter to me. He just should have had somebody."

"He mentioned women. He mentioned infatuations that he had, women that he wanted."

Lou looked at him for a split second too long, and Burl was frightened but then touched, and he turned to his glass to cover up the feeling. It made him almost ill to sit there and not speak the truth.

"Poor Burlie," said Lou. "Geez."

"How are his folks taking it?"

Lou shook his head.

"He was their only child. His mother is devastated. I suspect his father is too, although he won't speak to me."

"Does he blame you for any of this?"

"He's always blamed me, for everything. He did the best he could, but he always blamed me."

Lou poured more Calvados into both glasses and took a large gulp. Burl tried to drink faster as well, but he wasn't used to it and marveled at his own former capacities.

"He doesn't know how lucky he is," Lou continued, taking some more liquor in his mouth and holding it there momentarily before swallowing. "See, to know things is a burden."

"I can imagine."

"Maybe you can. You look like you can, come to think." Lou sighed and drank.

"I knew some things about Burl he didn't even know about himself."

"Like what's that?"

"Like about his father."

"What? What about his father?"

"Like who his father was."

Lou shrugged lightly, looked down, and took a drink.

"It's sad about my nephew. He never had the burden of knowing about himself, but then again, he died in ignorance. Which is sad. I thought sometimes he was entitled, just like sometimes I think his stepfather is entitled. Unless he already knows."

Burl sat very still. His face showed no expression.

"Sometimes I think he knew all along," Lou added sotto voce, sipping coffee. "The man drinks, but he's not stupid."

Burl said nothing.

"How much do you know about it?"

"Not much," Burl said. "Just Gardenia."

"And how did you find out?"

"Research. I was going to write a book."

"Have you told anybody?"

"About Burl's paternity? No."

"You really do sound like him."

"I know." Burl downed the rest of his brandy. "So tell me about it."

"Are you gonna put all this in a book?"

"No."

"What's the difference, what do you wanna know all this for?" Lou drank and looked away. "It's ancient history."

"I think he always wondered why he was fat. It was one of the defining circumstances of his life. I think it's why all this happened."

"It's a whole story. I've never told anybody except my wife, and she hasn't told anybody. Least as far as I know."

"It's a secret."

"It's a secret."

"Tell me."

"It's such a long time ago now, what's the point?"

"Maybe you should have told him, though."

"Not my place. But I wish someone had."

"Who? Nobody knew."

"Somebody knew. You found out. It was up to her, that's the way I always felt. But she was adamant. Well, she did what she thought was best for her family."

"Tell me. It's like telling him, but indirectly. Use me."

"It's my fault, see. And then I thought good had come of it. I still think so, a lot, except the way it ended. And it ended in sickness, which could happen to anybody. He died of pneumonia, I understand. It was just that he died so far away from his family. It was like he went away to die. It was almost willful."

Both men drank more brandy.

"That's why I thought AIDS." Lou looked questioningly at his visitor. "The way he went off, and pneumonia in a guy so young."

Burl said nothing.

"Who knows?" Lou sighed. "Who the hell knows? But it started with me, that much we do know. I got her working here, while I was off scrounging gigs on the drums." Lou looked up. "G'night Angie. G'night Theresa. See you tomorrow. Oh, that's right, Thursday then. Be safe."

Lou poured some more brandy. They had made a serious dent in the Calvados by now.

"Who? You got who working here?"

"My sister. His mother, Betty. Friend of mine was a waiter, and we needed money. He asked me to come down; they had mostly men working Italian restaurants in those days, just like today, but Gardenia's old man, he was running the place then, he had an eye for the ladies, see, and Betty was young and good looking. And I wanted to play drums."

"Burl said something about knowing his grandfather only from pictures."

"He came through the war just fine, all through the South Pacific on a battle cruiser, and then gets himself hit by a cab on Lexington Avenue. Forty-five years old. Can you imagine?"

"Lasted longer than Burl."

"That's right," Lou said, gulping brandy. "That's exactly right."

"So there was no money."

"No money. No insurance. Nothing. I think I was 16, 17, too stupid to stay in school, too lazy to work. I lived for music in those days, sneaking into clubs. I'd steal the new stuff. Records were smaller then, see, and I was a punk. But I got some gigs. I went out to the Poconos now and then."

"So there was no money."

"So when my friend told me about the waiting job I sent my sister instead. So she got the job."

"And Gene's father had an eye for the ladies."

Lou took out a cigarette and lit up with an old-fashioned lighter, the kind that isn't disposable.

"When I came here, see, Betty and Stu were already married. They met right here, when Stu and Gene got back from the service. Gene had girlfriends, he had a job uptown, and he didn't come around here much except to eat. It was his father's place then, it was like there wasn't room for both of them. But when the father died, he took over, and then he was here every day."

Lou took a long drag.

"I didn't pick up on it right away, that something was going on. It took me almost a year. I musta been blind. But they were real careful; Betty was married. She'd always been something.

"When I found out, I was furious, of course. Insane. My only thought was, this fucking prick is taking advantage of my sister. I wanted to bury a bread knife in his chest." Lou puffed his cigarette again. "They both insisted it wasn't that way, but I still don't believe it. That useless prick, always with the big smile. Only you gotta understand my sister. She was very independent, even in those days, early on I mean."

Lou cleared his throat and took some brandy.

"'I'm a big girl, mind your own business.' That's what she told me. But I didn't find out about Burl until later. The kid was three, four years old by then, and you could see an awful lot of his father in him. I put two and two together. And I think she had to tell somebody anyway; it was driving her nuts. By the time I found out, I was close to Gene. We were friends."

Lou swirled his drink and downed it with a small cough.

"I couldn't stay here, see, and look at this guy who knocked up my sister. I went in and told him I wasn't gonna work for him, I couldn't do it. I was ranting and raving, carrying on. Then he showed me the papers for the trust."

"The trust?"

"For the restaurant. He put it into an irrevocable trust in Burl's name. I even went to see a lawyer about this, guy I know uptown, made sure it was kosher. What the hell, it was probably good for his taxes too, Gene was no dummy, but still. Turns out my nephew owned this place when he was in kindergarten."

"Do you think I could have a little more brandy?"

"Listen, you sure you don't want some food? It's not too late, I can have them make you something."

"Just the Calvados, thanks."

"You're not like my nephew that way. That guy could eat. Okay, how 'bout some fresh coffee. Frankie," he called loudly. "Freshen us up over here."

Burl swallowed some more brandy. It seemed easier now to keep up with Lou.

"The point is, it wasn't just Gene taking advantage, like I thought. I mean, it was, but something more complicated was going on too. He'd made provision. I guess he actually felt responsible, maybe he knew he wouldn't be having any more kids, or they could fend for themselves, whatever." Lou took Burl's forearm conspiratorially. "The family always had money anyway. They had real estate, they made a fortune on Long Island." Lou gave a dismissive wave. "This restaurant wasn't that big a thing for them, by that time."

"I don't understand. She continued to work here, right?"

"For quite a while," Lou nodded.

"It wasn't still the money."

"Not by that time. No no no."

"If she didn't need the money, why did she stay on here?"

"Abe, lemme explain something to you. When Gene had his heart attack, God rest his soul, he was here, we had a doctor eating at that table right over there, and the hospital is just a few blocks. So he didn't die right away, see. But he knew he wasn't going to make it. After we got there I sat with him for a while, just the two of us, and he asked me to look after Betty. And to look after Burlie. And he said, 'Make sure that asshole Stu comes out all right too, I'm counting on both of you now.'"

"Was this all out of guilt?"

"They loved each other. Get it? Gene and Betty loved each other. Even after a few years, when Betty was so angry at him, I don't think you can get so embittered about somebody unless you love them. I think her anger was because he wouldn't make a life with her."

Burl looked at the older man, his face a question mark.

"You wanna know what kept them apart, right? Did Burlie ever tell you the story of how he got this restaurant? As far as he knew it, anyway."

"About his father saving Gene's life."

"In Korea, that's right. Well, I got a lot of problems with Gene, which we won't go into right now, he wasn't a saint, but he understood his debt to Stu Bennett and never turned his back on that obligation—except, of course, to carry on with my sister for years, and to give her a child. But she was loyal to her husband too. It's hard to explain now, when people get divorced, do what they wanna do. It was different then.

"Hey, are you okay? I wish you'd eaten something with all that liquor. Do you drink much? And here I'm talking your ear off. I really shouldn't have gotten into all this, it was selfish. I fell down, see. By the time he died, Gene and I were very close. I respected the man, nutty as he was sometimes. I love my sister and I loved my nephew. But I didn't hold up my end. I didn't hold up my end."

"You did what you could," Burl said. "You can't blame yourself for pneumonia."

"He was a sweet guy, Burlie. He had a lot of his old man in him."

"What was he like? The old man."

"Gene was all right. Knowing everything I know, I mean when I got the full picture, I gained a lot of respect for Gene. He had kind of a sad life. I think he really loved my sister. He married very late and not very happily. Dolores was her name; she also passed away quite a while ago. A nice woman, too. But Gene wasn't happy, and he started eating. He was always on the heavy side, but they got a lot of that out of him in the service, thanks God, otherwise who knows how far Stu'd have carried him, huh? Anyway, as he got older he turned in on himself a little and just started eating. I mean, he could pack it away. I used to have to laugh sometimes; first Gene used to eat up the profits, then Burlie came in and did the same thing. Anyway, Gene ate and ate until eventually he got good and fat. I think he sorta ate himself to death."

Burl held up his glass and peered into it. Like father, like son, he thought, downing the rest in a gulp.

———————

The next morning, after a sleepless night, he called in sick. "Abe Alter is dying," he told Soto, sounding raspy and afflicted. Then he phoned Norma and asked if she was free after work.

"Of course, your birthday," she remembered. "What do you want to do?"

"I want to have an outing."

"At night? In this weather?"

"It's warmer today, and I know just the place. I'll pick you up at 10. I've got a car."

He spent the afternoon among food, sniffing, mainly. He thrust his nostrils into bunches of fresh beets, where he smelled the sour earth, and browsed in a fish store, where he inhaled the sea. He wanted to unwrap the cheeses, uncork the wines, cover himself in applesauce, run amok amid the iron rawness of all that red meat. And he bought, exercising all the restraint he could muster but still quickly filling the trunk with the fruits of his wandering.

In the Village he drove around in the traffic until he found, on Bleeker, Love & Death, the novelty food store he'd remembered from the old days. They made cakes in the shape of a vulva and, of course, life-sized penis-shaped chocolates, but he was more interested in the other half of the business, the one with the post-Halloween sale. He got handfuls of hard-candy skulls, day-old bread in the shape of femur and tibia, gingerbread corpses laid out in gingerbread coffins. On the way home he bought flowers.

"So where are we going?" Norma asked when he arrived later that night.

"New Jersey."

"So I needn't dress up?"

"Just dress warm. It's kind of a revival meeting."

"The candles you wanted are in the cupboard over the sink," Norma called, heading off to the bedroom to change. "Take as many as you want. And I left the portable cassette player there on the counter, do you see it?"

When the car was loaded, they drove. The night was clear and unseasonably warm, and through the unnaturally clean windshield the streetlamps shone bright as beacons, fanning in all directions one after another down every city street.

"This is great, you get two birthdays. Maybe later I can give you your present."

Even at this hour there was traffic. Cars crept through the Lincoln Tunnel impatiently, in fits and starts, stopping occasionally to stew in their own fumes until finally Burl's little rental car seemed to stagger out of the tunnel to begin a long, determined climb of the giant helix-shaped roadway away from it. Recalling his flight in this direction—how long ago was it now?—made Burl's chest tighten.

His arms tingled as he drove. He'd spent the morning pounding away at his computer keyboard, writing the letters he hoped would help him clean up the mess of his life. He'd written first to the Brooklyn district attorney's office, explaining without too much detail that he was alive and well. He'd written to Engel, catching up on the news and promising to repay him. He'd written to Mickey Mituoulu, asking if he would represent Burl in determining whether Wanda—O Wanda!—had borne him a child, and if so securing some kind of involvement for him as father. He'd written Larry, his agent, proposing a book about his adventures, the ending still undetermined. Then he'd written his Uncle Lou, apologizing for what he'd done and explaining that for now he didn't plan to share what he knew about his paternity. Finally, with some pain, he'd written to tell Stu and Betty that their son wasn't dead. This one he hadn't sent. This he would handle in person.

Burl and Norma left the highway soon after it straightened and drove north on a fast but undivided roadway, the cars rushing past offering the stirring whizzing sensation that Burl had enjoyed when he'd experienced it behind the wheel so long ago. The road turned into the main street of some older communities, and as he slowed he began to notice that they still bore the signs of Halloween. The houses had jack-o'-lanterns on their well-lit porches, and when he passed a school the windows still had paper skeletons and witches in them and black and orange crepe paper draped behind, all of it visible in the silvery moonlight.

"Candy corn?" Norma held out a bag sheepishly. "Left over from last night. I love this stuff, but the kids in my building weren't impressed."

"Jaded," said Burl, reaching for a piece. He let it stay in his mouth and melt slowly, its sickly sweetness a powerful echo of excesses past. Being born November 1 had made for macabre birthday parties when he was a child.

"I've been out this way," said Norma. "I think. It's hard to tell at night. I can't place it."

Burl said nothing. They were just about where they were going anyway, and in a matter of seconds he turned off the road and drove through the gates of the cemetery. They drove slowly, cruising stately along the winding roads that separated the subdivisions of the deceased into high-rise and low-rise neighborhoods, mausoleums and graves, rich and modest of means. It was approaching midnight by the time they located Burl's cenotaph, and the night was cooler.

"Taken to a grander banquet than even this life," Burl read with a flashlight. Set flat into the ground atop the place where he might have been buried, the tablet was shiny and, he assumed, black. Burl had never seen it before.

"Where did the inscription come from?"

"I wrote it," Norma said.

"It's nice," Burl smiled. "Thank you." Then he walked back to the car to get the rest of their things. He laid a plastic cover, of the kind painters use on furniture, over the flat stone memorial, and on that unrolled a thin Japanese futon, which he covered with a cotton blanket. Norma arranged the flowers all around and tried lighting the candles, but it was too windy. "I was afraid of that," Burl said, fetching from the trunk some votive candles, set deep in glasses, which he'd had the foresight to buy.

In this flickering light they spread about the long tablet the broad repast Burl had prepared: cold meats, stuffed grape leaves, smoked fish, oily black and fat green olives, cold asparagus salad, chicken and pasta in pesto, oak-leaf lettuce in a mustard vinaigrette, a vanilla-tasting chardonnay and some pomegranate eau de vie to accompany a dessert of fudge brownies. As a kind of garnish, these things were interspersed with the bone-shaped bread, the gingerbread corpse, the candy skulls. When he and Norma were seated, Burl filled their wineglasses.

"About all this food," Norma said, looking worried. "I hope we're not going down that road again."

"These are some of the dead man's favorites," he said. "Have you ever been to Mexico? On what we call All Souls, which will start"—he looked at his watch—"any minute now, they have Dia de los Muertos, the Day of the Dead, when they commune with their departed loved ones by visiting them at the cemetery. They bring food, play music, camp out. It's something for the whole family. I think it makes death less frightening and the dead less distant. It's a way of bringing back those who've gone."

"Well, at least I haven't had dinner."

"Me either. Since he died, I just haven't been able to eat."

"Can you really do that forever?"

"Well, I thought so, but now I'm not so sure," Burl said, reaching over for a thin slice of cool, moist ham. "I'll have to start slow, though."

And with that he took a small bite, savoring the salty taste in his mouth.

"Do you think all this food will bring Burl back to life?"

"I do," he said, nibbling an asparagus and then swallowing uncertainly.

"I hope so," Norma said, rising to her knees and pulling him to her. "I've missed him."

"Me too," he said, just as she covered his mouth with hers.

Carefully, carefully among the dishes, she leaned back, pulling him toward her, until she lay upon the tablet, still kissing, and he settled lightly upon her, wrapped in her arms and legs and accepting her sweet tongue in his mouth like the sacrament in some long-awaited communion, grateful for it, grateful after all his sins.

Harvest American Writing

Diana Abu-Jaber
Arabian Jazz

Daniel Akst
St. Burl's Obituary

Tina McElroy Ansa
Baby of the Family
Ugly Ways

Carolyn Chute
The Beans of Egypt, Maine
Letourneau's Used Auto Parts
Merry Men

Harriet Doerr
Consider This, Señora

Laurie Foos
Ex Utero

Barry Gifford
Baby Cat Face

Donald Harington
Butterfly Weed
The Choiring of the Trees
Ekaterina

David Haynes
Somebody Else's Mama

Randall Kenan
Let the Dead Bury Their Dead

Julius Lester
And All Our Wounds Forgiven

Sara Lewis
But I Love You Anyway
Heart Conditions
Trying to Smile and Other Stories

Dan McCall
Messenger Bird

Lawrence Naumoff
The Night of the Weeping Women
Rootie Kazootie
Silk Hope, NC
Taller Women: A Cautionary Tale

Karen Osborn
Patchwork

Mary Lee Settle
Choices

Jim Shepard
Kiss of the Wolf

Brooke Stevens
The Circus of the Earth and the Air

Oxford Stroud
Marbles

Sandra Tyler
Blue Glass

Lois-Ann Yamanaka
Wild Meat and the Bully Burgers